SPECTRAL

AJ CERNA
SPECTRAL

MAGIA BOOKS

EPISODE GUIDE

SPECTRAL | EPISODE 1

SPECTRAL | EPISODE 2

SPECTRAL | EPISODE 3

SPECTRAL | EPISODE 4

TRIGGER WARNINGS

Spectral is a story that takes our characters from the gritty, semi-futuristic city of Los Angeles into the minds and pasts of the deceased. This includes scenes that may be troubling to some, such as sexual assault, addiction, murder, suicidal ideation, shootings, and violence. If you are sensitive to any of these elements, please take note.

HOW TO READ SPECTRAL

Please note that *Spectral* is a serialized novel comprised of twelve episodes clocking in at around forty-to-fifty pages each. Each episode consists of a "cold open" and four parts.

Episodes are *not* meant to fully stand alone (though some are "monster of the week" in nature), but rather build to a complete story.

New episodes were originally released weekly in April of 2024 through May 2024.

I hope you're amused by my weird little experiment and enjoy this as you would an amazing arc of an anime or manga series!

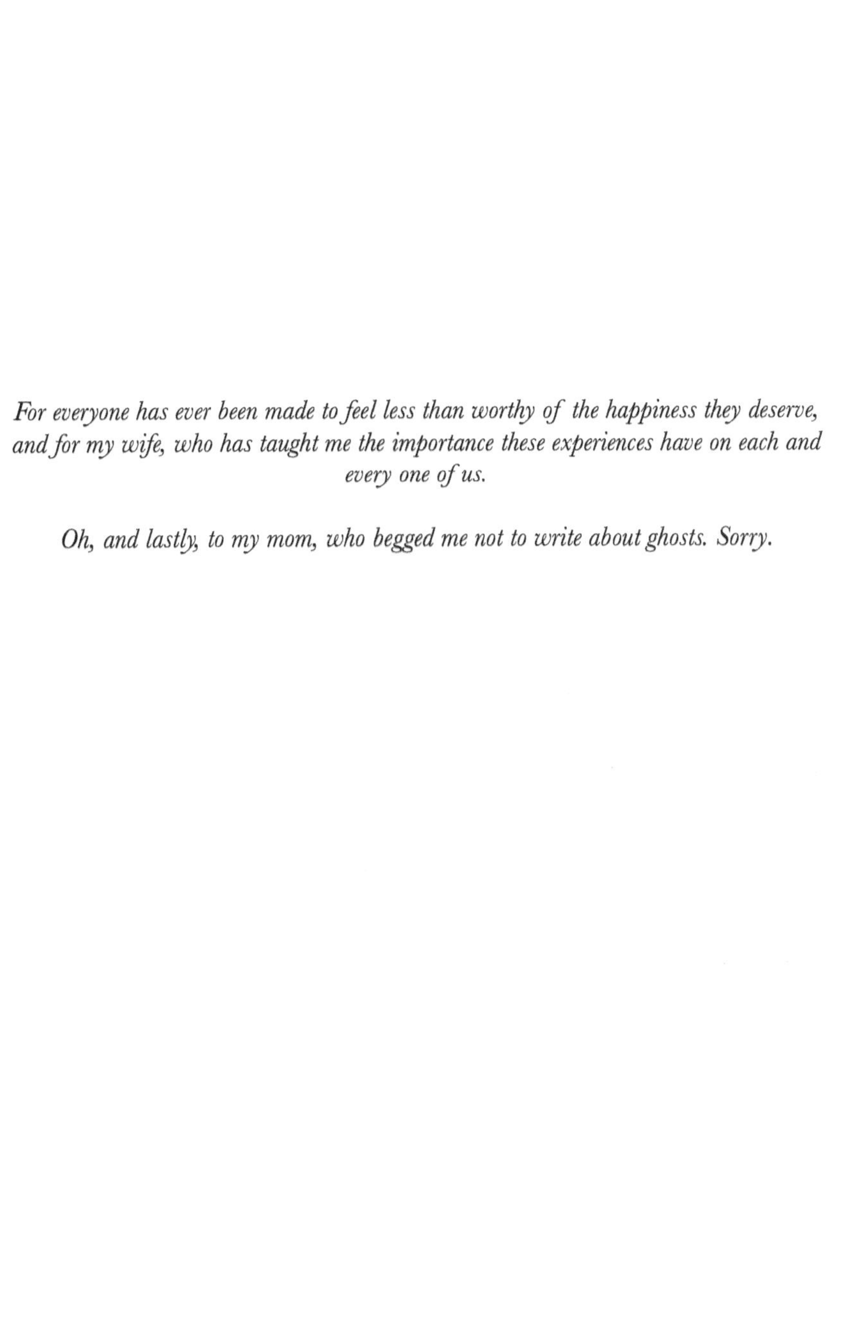

For everyone has ever been made to feel less than worthy of the happiness they deserve, and for my wife, who has taught me the importance these experiences have on each and every one of us.

Oh, and lastly, to my mom, who begged me not to write about ghosts. Sorry.

"I'm sorry. Please don't lock me away.
Not again."

SPECTRAL | EPISODE 1

A HOUSE...

I WAKE TO A LOUD ROAR. An all-too-familiar heat berates my face.

If I keep my eyes closed, I can pretend it doesn't feel like my eyelids are about to melt off.

Yeah, right, stupid. As if keeping them closed will stop me from burning alive. With a groan, I force them open.

Yep. My entire room is on fire. Again.

But I'm not scared. Burning to a crisp at seventeen somehow seems… merciful. Most people would be terrified. Me? I'm only frustrated.

As the flames lap at the surrounding walls, my frustration turns into indignation.

I thought I was past this. That this was the start of my new life. That things would be different.

I grab my pillow and smash it into my face, expelling a muffled, blood-curdling scream.

"Okay!" I cry out from under the memory foam cushion. "You win! I get it. Ha-ha-ha. Can you stop already? Just *leave me alone!*"

The roaring of the flames sounds like laughter. Like the chorus of a thousand demons cackling all while flipping me off. This image in my head is somehow worse than my room being razed to the ground.

I let out another scream into my pillow for good measure, but I know it doesn't matter. There's no one to scream at anymore. I've already done enough screaming. I've screamed at myself. I've screamed at every one of my parents—foster, adopted, or biological. I've screamed at God Himself.

None of it's done me any good. Months pass without incident, but no matter what, *it* finds me.

If only I knew what "it" is. For the longest time I called it the Ghost, but even I knew that made me sound crazy. So instead, I now call it the Entity.

That makes me sound less insane, right? *Right?*

A bead of sweat slides down my neck and drips onto the coarse, scratchy sheets. I sigh as the flames eat up the gaudy curtains and ascend the walls of my sparsely decorated room. Lily told me to make it my own, but I knew something like this would happen. So why bother? The most personality in it comes from the stock floral curtains that I'm confident have been there since the early sixties.

I cross my arms and stare at the ceiling, justified in my defiance—never mind that I look more like a five-year-old throwing a tantrum.

No. I'm not moving this time. It's their *turn.* Whatever wants to claim me can have me. My seventeen years of existence brought with it countless near misses, and I'm *tired.* Tired of caring. Tired of trying. Tired of not knowing the true source of all the pain. If I do nothing but sit here, maybe the Entity will make itself known. Either that, or the truth will reveal itself in the afterlife—if such a thing exists.

Or what if it's worse? What if an afterlife exists, and I'm as clueless there as I am here?

I only hope my adopted parents—a jolt of panic threatens to sit me up on the spot. *Where are they?*

There's no way they're sleeping through this raging hellscape. I'd bet good money they've already run off, leaving me to be chargrilled alive like an underfed chicken. And when asked by the firefighters why they left their adopted kid inside, they'd be like, "Oh, we thought she'd be out here already." Or maybe something closer to, "Well, she's not really our child. She comes from a troubled background so…"

This is all their fault.

How naïve could they be? They mean well, but they should've known better than to go for the almost grown, high-risk foster kid with a well-documented penchant for arson.

A quaint house in a suburban Burbank neighborhood is an expensive price for their stupid mistake.

But they aren't the only morons. I should've known better, too.

My arms still crossed, I tighten my lips and grit my teeth. Whatever has beef with me can just have me.

So determined am I to confront this faceless Entity that when the firefighters break through my window, I scream at them to get out—to leave me in the encircling blaze. My yells don't faze them. They probably can't hear me through the roar of the flames, but I still put up a fight. Even as they hoist my light one-hundred-and-five-pound frame, I struggle, punching one of them in the face before they overpower me.

No doubt they only see me as a mentally unstable girl. And who's to say that's a wrong assessment? Even *I'm* not convinced it's wrong.

After struggling to free myself from the firefighter's annoyingly powerful arms, I finally give in. Whether it's the emotional trauma, the smoke, or plain exhaustion, I can't tell. I let him shove me out onto a ladder sprouting from the top of a fire engine. As I descend, feeling the grooves of each rung dig into my feet with every step, I look up, seeing thick black smoke spill from my bedroom window.

I can sense the opportunity to confront the Entity slipping away. It's not coming. Not with so many people around. Never with so many people around. Only when I'm alone.

Another fireman tries to help me off the ladder, and I smack his hand away. I feel helpless enough without having to be coddled.

When my bare feet settle onto the rocky asphalt, I spare a glance at the once-picturesque two-story home that's served as my residence for the past six months. It's the longest I've spent anywhere since I was ten. It's also my last chance at a normal life. And now it's gone.

"You couldn't resist, could you?" I say, my eyes focused on the bedroom window. A lump forms in my throat as sadness and fear replace my frustration.

I hate this part—when my brain catches up and puts the entire thing into perspective. I try to stop it, but am overwhelmed as my breath quickens and the hyperventilation sets in.

I wrap one arm around myself and force deep, slow breaths, crouching down close to the pavement until I'm curled up into a ball. With my free hand, I flick a skin tag that rests on the left side of my neck. Back and forth. Back and forth.

Suddenly, the illusion I call the Entity doesn't seem so real anymore. Suddenly, I know the truth. No matter what lies I tell myself, I know who's to blame. This fire, like all the chaos in my life before it, is my doing.

I cover my ears, as though it'll drown out the sound of licking flames and eliminate the deep shame setting in.

"Why am I like this?"

SPECTRAL

EPISODE 1
ENTITY

ONE

I'M SO EMBARRASSED. So ashamed.

I can almost see myself, as if I'm standing outside my own body. I look like a child, settled on the ground, knees to my chest, arms wrapped around my legs. Why not rock back and forth like a stereotypical nutcase while I'm at it? No. Not today.

Willing my legs to stand, I…remain seated, my legs not so much as flexing. Great. Limb failure. That's a fun one.

But it's okay. I've gone through this before. Like my therapists say: focus on my breath.

In. Out. In. Out.

Seconds pass in what feels like hours. Finally, sensation returns to my hands. And my feet…? Yup, there they are. Hi. I stand up and my surroundings come back into focus. I'm beside a bright red fire engine. Probably closer than I should be. Wow, it's huge. How much would it hurt to get hit by one of these bastards barreling down the street? They don't get enough credit for how huge they are.

As I focus on the smooth polymer body of the fifteen-foot-tall engine next to me, voices begin to fade in.

Oh, shit. I'd forgotten there's a bunch of people around. Crowds butt up against the caution tape on either side of the street, excited chatter filling the midnight air. Oversized men in firefighter uniforms brush past me.

That's right. A fire. My house. No. My parents' house. Adopted parents'. The stress around the whole situation threatens to rise up again, but I shove that feeling the hell back down again.

"Are you okay?" says a brusque voice next to me.

I turn to face a man clad in mustard yellow who wraps a blanket around my shoulders. Did I just have a complete mental breakdown in front of a total stranger? Had he been there the whole time? "Yeah, I'm fine," I say, probably (definitely) too quickly. Avoiding eye contact, I scan the street to get my bearings.

Fire. House. Parents. No. Adopted parents, dammit! Where are they?

I find them on the other side of the street, leaning up against a neighbor's car. Damien's arm is around Lily, the look on his face of a textbook, perpetual comforter. It's somehow his best, yet most annoying, feature that I've grown to loathe as much as rely on. And Lily…her normally stoic expression has transformed into that of a weeping gargoyle, sobs wailing out at controlled intervals.

I don't know why this surprises me. Losing your house is enough to break anyone, but I'd always seen Lily as unflappable, borderline sociopathic. Like she could lose her whole family without batting an eyelid. I promise, that's a good thing.

So, to see her bent over, gargoyle-faced and all, it's hard for me to not feel shame. Shame over something I can only assume I was responsible for. Though, I guess that's a problem in and of itself. Most people know if they've burned down houses.

I want to comfort her. To tell her I'm sorry. Instead, I turn away to face the heat of the weakening flames. Whatever the firefighters are doing must be working.

At least this house didn't burn down. Not completely anyway. I don't have the faintest idea of how long it's going to take, but I doubt it'll take as long as the last fire. Every cloud has a silver lining, right?

Hot sweat runs down my neck and back, and a warm breeze reminds me that all I have on is a ratty undershirt and pair of kiwi-printed pajama shorts. No socks, no shoes. If I'd died today, at least I'd have died in comfort.

"Are you okay?" a voice says behind me. I bristle at the question, but seeing that it's Damien, I respond.

"Fine." It comes off as harsh, but I hate that question.

"Are you sure?" His face is his standard annoying mix of comfort and concern.

"Isn't this your house that's burning?"

Damien's face drops. "Oh, shit. For real?" He backs away from the burning house as though seeing it for the first time.

I snort against my will. "How can you even joke right now?"

"Oh, I didn't realize there was established protocol for how someone reacts to their home burning down. Maybe this is how I mourn."

"But what about..." I motion to Lily, whose ashen face still sits in wailing disbelief.

"That's probably the right reaction, but she'll be okay."

This guy is unbelievable. "That's it? No third degree? Aren't you at least a little...?"

"What? Suspicious?" His voice is nonchalant.

"Yeah!" I practically yell. "Are you too stupid to have read my file?"

"Did you start the fire?" Damien's tone is neutral—friendly, even—without a hint of accusation behind it.

"I...no." I don't think so. I bite my lip and swallow nervously. This is where most people turn on me. My record speaks for itself, and not to brag, but I make a pretty badass scapegoat.

"Well," Damien says. "That settles it."

"Settles what?"

"The mystery of the burning house. Well, maybe not settled, but we know who didn't do it."

"Are you stupid?"

"Do you want me to blame you?"

"Well...I...no...?"

Damien smiles his idiot dad smile. "Let's call it an act of God, then. You don't live in California without being insured up the ass for a fire. We'll let those people take care of it."

I smile. I think it's a smile. At least it's as close to one as humanly possible, given the circumstances. Lily's expression brings back the knot in my stomach. Damien may be stupidly optimistic, but I can already see suspicion eroding the caring veneer of my adopted mother.

Our eyes connect for the briefest of moments. It's barely perceptible, but I catch the look. Enough of a look for me to infer one important detail: Lily blames me.

I'm shaken from my self-pity by the sound of police sirens. The quick one-two *whomp-whomp!* is all that's needed for my body to tense up. Fight-or-flight mode activates, and the blanket around my shoulders tumbles to the asphalt.

"Red light, Kiddo," Damien's voice has an unexpected calming effect on me. "You don't have to run anymore."

I take a few deep breaths and nod. This was a house fire. The police showing up isn't surprising.

And then I catch sight of the vehicle itself.

Son of a...

Of course, it has to be Detective Chu. I try not to think too much about the fact that I recognize a specific cop's license plate number. That's completely normal.

"Remember," Damien says, "you did nothing wrong."

"Tell that to *him*."

A pair of obnoxious, shiny black shoes hit the pavement at the same time. He gets out of his car so damned weird that I've committed it to memory. Out pops Detective Chu's smug, golden boy face. Why? Why is he here every time something goes wrong in my life?

If I were a superhero, he'd be my arch nemesis. If I were a supervillain, he'd still be my arch nemesis.

Seeing his jet black hair, pleated khakis and too-polished-for-what-he-does shoes, I want to run. The question of "fight or flight" has fully resolved into flight. He hasn't seen me yet, so if I take off now, I could make it without being caught. I've done it before and have been successful on some occasions.

I bounce on the balls of my bare feet, testing to see how much it'll hurt to bolt down the road in the opposite direction without so much as a thin layer of rubber protecting them. Even within the small two-foot radius I'm standing in, there are a few jagged pebbles that jut into my soles. It wouldn't be a comfortable run.

"Why am I not surprised to see you here?" Detective Chu says, smugness oozing from every syllable. He walks up to me, nodding to Damien. "Mr. Green."

This isn't the first time he's met Damien. As my adoption case was going through, he was all too eager to volunteer the "inherent risks" someone like me posed to an upstanding couple like the Greens. He took time out of his work day to actively try and ruin my life.

"Detective, do you mind?" Damien's tone shifts, his face darkening with a rare display of annoyance. "We're going through something here."

"And I'm sorry to see that," he says, in a not-so-unsympathetic tone. "But that's why I'm here."

"Oh. So, who started it?" Damien asks, giving Chu a smart aleck tone. I feel an instant pang in my stomach, something like betrayal. While I'd never worry about him giving me up to the likes of Chu, it's clear he doesn't fully trust that it wasn't me. So much for "case closed."

"I'll give you two guesses as to who a prime suspect on my list is," Chu says.

"She didn't do it," Damien says, his voice more certain than before.

"How would you know that?"

"She told me."

"You know what would happen if we believed the word of every suspect?"

"So we're going with that logic now?" Damien says. "Not evidence?"

"I'll go with you," I say. The words are out before I can stop them.

Both men look at me.

"You'll what?" Detective Chu said.

"I'll go with you," I say, confidence solidifying with each successive word. "That's what you want, right? To question me?"

"No, Luna," Damien said. "You don't have to. Contrary to what some cops think, you can't just bring anyone in for questioning."

"Considering her history and her proximity to the crime," Detective Chu says, "I most certainly can. We aren't living in pre-Civil War times anymore. If there's an obvious suspect, no matter what rights you think she has, we have every right to question her in the interest of public safety under the Security Accords of 2048."

Of course he quotes some line from some public record thing. Loser.

"She's just a minor."

Detective Chu's face twitches. It's a thorn in his side that I still can't be tried as an adult. "We're bringing her in for questioning. You know where to find her. You can pick her up after."

"SIX MONTHS," Detective Chu says as he enters the small, dimly lit room. The floor is a particularly depressing shade of beige linoleum, and the walls and ceiling are painted a somehow flamboyant white with some choice black scuff marks spread all over. I'm sure it's meant to make me already feel like I'm in prison, and you know what? It works every time.

I shift my weight on the hard metal chair, but no matter how much I try, I can't get comfortable. It's one of their tactics. I'm pretty confident they have these chairs specially made to make suspects more likely to talk. They can use whatever cruelty they want. I have nothing to hide.

I think.

"What?" I ask.

"Six months," Detective Chu repeats. "That's how long until I can try you as an adult."

"You have to know how creepy that makes you sound."

He shoots me a "knock it off" look, but I can tell the comment made him uncomfortable. "Enough with the jokes, Ms. Guerrera."

"I didn't realize I was joking, *Detective Chu.*"

"Am I crazy here? I thought you came in voluntarily."

I hold back another biting remark. He's right. I did come here voluntarily. But I'm so used to our antagonistic back-and-forth that it's become second nature.

When I say nothing more, he smiles and points to a camera at the top corner of the room. "'This is being filmed for the record. For the safety of our Republic, you are under a moral and legal obligation to answer all questions to the best of your ability, even at the risk of self-incrimination.'"

"Wow, you make it sound *so appealing*."

"Do you understand?"

I give him a deadpan look and nod.

"I need a verbal confirmation."

"In other words, talk, or you'll lock me up and throw away the key?"

"Need I remind you that you came here voluntarily?"

"Yes, I understand," I say. "Old habits."

"Thank you." He sounds like a babysitter who finally got a kid to eat a bite of broccoli.

I try to bring the very best out of our men in blue.

With a heavy sigh, Detective Chu takes a seat across from me. "Okay, then. Let's get started with the basics. Why'd you do it?"

I roll my eyes. "Can we start with something more cliché, please?"

"You're legally obligated to answer my questions, cliché or not."

"Fine, then." I turn to the camera. "I *didn't* do it." *At least I don't think I did.* Considering I don't really know, they can't hold it against me in a legal sense, right?

"You're sure?"

"Y…yes?"

"A question?"

"Calm down. I just didn't expect that question. Yes. Yes, I'm sure."

"Let's rewind." Detective Chu pulls a netscreen mini-tablet from his jacket pocket, unfolding it with a click. I bet he practiced that, because even I have to admit it looks pretty cool when it snaps open like that. "At age six, you pull a knife on a playmate of yours."

"They use the word playmate in the lawsuit, but that bitch was a bully."

"So you pulled the knife on her?"

I glare at him. He knows this whole story, and yet he insists on revisiting it every time we sit down. "I don't remember pulling a knife on her. She was unharmed, and the lawsuit dropped. Anyway, you wanna skip all that and get straight to the other arson cases?"

"We'll get there," he says, not raising his eyes from his tablet. He's like a kid in a school presentation. He has this whole interrogation planned a certain way, and there's no room for deviation. "After your mom passed, your father turned to muze, isn't that right?"

My back straightens. "What?"

"Muze, the narcotic sold mainly on the streets of Skid Row."

"No, I know what muze is. The other part," I say. I can feel my breath quickening already. "My mom's not dead. She walked out on us five years ago."

Detective Chu tilts his head, eyes narrowed. Genuine confusion. He looks back at his netscreen, then back up at me. We'd done this dance several times before. Each time he takes me through my "timeline of malfeasances," as he calls them. The first is always a knife to my elementary school bully. Then he pushes on to my mom leaving, Dad's drug use, and my secondary career as a delinquent. So why was today different?

"She *walked out on us*," I repeat, "*and never came back.*"

I've never seen Detective Chu uncomfortable before. He crosses his right leg over his left, and then, apparently deciding it's too uncomfortable, he crosses his left over his right.

"My mom passed," I repeated. "Why would you say that?"

"I'm sorry you had to find out like this."

"Find out what?"

"We called your father," he says as though each syllable could break me. "Given your age, we go to next of kin, and allow them to decide how to—"

"What the hell happened?" I try to slow down my breath, but can already feel that method failing.

There's a knock against the two-way mirror.

Detective Chu stands up.

"Don't mess with me, Chu," I say. "Just tell me what's going on."

His gaze shifts from the mirror to me. "We found her body in a car submerged in the Salton Sea."

"What?"

"It's inconclusive," he says.

"But you've conclusively found out she's dead?"

No response.

"When?"

Another knock on the glass.

"The pollution from the lake made it difficult to get an exact time frame, but she passed around the time she went missing."

Another knock.

He holds up his index finger to the mirror. "Hang on. She has the right to know. It's her, but there's no way of knowing how she died. She...her body decayed too much."

It had taken several years, but I'd somehow come to terms with Mom's disappearance. Dad had been a mess from day one, so she'd pretty much raised me alone. One day, she couldn't take it anymore, so she left. It's a tried-and-true, stereotypical sob story. Hardly original. Still, a part of me was happy. Happy that at least one of us could run off and live their life. Happy for her…*happiness.*

My chest heaves. Oh, God, here comes the hyperventilation.

In. Out. In. Out. *Inoutinoutinout!*

Oh, no. It's happening too fast now. I try to slow it down, but whenever I try to focus on slowing my breath, I see her face, dead and slowly pickling in the water.

Detective Chu says something. Probably an unhelpful, "Are you okay?"

No, Detective Chu. I want nothing more than to tear at my skin, but I settle for a solid jab, digging my nails into my face without dragging. My vision flickers, and though I let out a scream, I can't even hear my own voice.

I close my eyes and punch at my temples with both hands. It's irrational, childish, self-destructive. Everything my therapists told me not to do, but it's beyond my control at this point. Even the warbling of Detective Chu's voice has disappeared entirely, instead replaced by a cacophony of… memories?

My eyes flash open, and instead of an interrogation room, I'm in a wide-open space the size of a football stadium. The floor is lined with what looks like charcoal scribbles on a cement floor.

On all sides float giant jumbotron-style netscreens.

And then a feeling passes through me like an ocean wave. One I haven't felt for a decade. My mind hones in on Alyssa Crane, the little girl who bullied me, making fun of the unsightly skin tag on my neck that's been there since I was born, though I don't quite remember what she says.

That feeling dissipates. Suddenly, I'm reliving the first time Dad beat me—or at least the first time I remember. The details are murky, but the feeling of anguish is all too real. I'm like a seven-year-old kid again, helpless even as Mom watches on in horror.

Then it's the night Mom left. *No.* The night she was killed.

The pang of insecurity as I move from home to home, never quite fitting in. The confusion that flames brought to my second foster home.

Each memory plays out on all sides of me in this stadium of misery, pelting me like arrows.

As I collapse to the hard ground, I look down at my hands, realizing with abject horror that this is no illusion.

It's no hallucination. This is happening for real.

TWO

I SMACK at the sides of my cheeks, as though trying to swat mosquitoes off a bit *too* aggressively. But the strange view remains the same—an indescribably trippy landscape that looks like it's straight out of a dream.

My heart rate starts to escalate for the second time in less than a minute. This whole up-and-down can*not* be good for my long-term health. My anxiety gives way to depression, and an unexpected weight sets in, though it's a weight I recognize, the weight of uncertainty that came following Mom's disappearance—or her death, I guess.

Somehow, I know what I'm feeling is a direct response to that specific memory. And just as quickly as it arrives, the feeling is gone. Like a ghost passing through my body or a cold air pocket.

"Stop," I yell, though to who I have no idea. I cry out again, filling the stadium-sized void with my screams. I cry out at the memories that surround and encapsulate me like a parade of netscreens, piercing my very existence. The highs of my greatest successes pass, followed by the lows of my worst moments. Emotionally exhausted, I cry out again. "Stop, stop, stop, *stop!*"

But the emotional roller coaster continues. I keep on yelling, hitting my face with each "stop" in the hope that the real world comes back into view and that these feelings go away.

They don't.

Years pass in an instant, and after I relive every important moment in my short existence, the charcoal-scribbled cement floor below me gives. I collapse into a free-fall, my stomach pushing its way up into my throat as my body slams into something soft and...crunchy?

My emotions level out. It may be the single most relieving thing to have happened to me in my life. I push off the ground with the heels of my hands, one of them breaking into something mushy. And then the scents catch up.

The smell of over-ripe banana, moldy bread, and general refuse fills my nostrils, and one of my hands is caked in a dark yellow fruity sludge.

God, this is not my day.

A brief scan of my surroundings doesn't do much. I'm in a generic-looking five-foot-wide alley, both buildings on either side made of slate gray cement. Not exactly helpful downtown, where practically everything had been destroyed and rebuilt into its most utilitarian form in the years during and since the Second Civil War.

I wipe my hand clean on the wall, leaving the banana sludge residue in a dark yellow smear.

"Freeze!" a voice calls out from behind me.

I raise my hands and slowly turn to face a cop who must be in her early twenties. Her enthusiastic scream makes it all clear. It's like she wants me to do something wrong. But my thoughts only linger on her for the briefest of moments. I notice her vehicle just outside the alley, lights flashing a neon red and blue, illuminating the dark and filthy alley.

"Where am I?" I ask.

"What do you mean?"

A spike of irritation. I don't have the mental capacity to explain whatever's going on right now. "Detective Chu," I say. "He's probably looking for me. Where am I?"

"A few blocks from LAPD Central Station."

I was close. Dangerously close. Probably no more than half a mile from where I'd disappeared.

"I'm Luna Guerrera," I say, hands still up. "I think—"

"Ma'am, keep your hands up!" The ridiculous, overzealous nature of your standard young cop returns. "We've been looking for you."

"Yeah, that's what I just sai—"

"On the ground now!" Her shoulders tense and she grips her gun tighter. She looks around the alley, even above me. Had she seen me fall from out of thin air? But her gaze settles back on me, her intensity returning.

I follow her orders, slowly getting to my knees and to my stomach, working to avoid the bags of garbage lining the area.

She's on me, *fast*.

Before I can even attempt to resist, my arms are pinned behind my back, and a pair of sharp metal cuffs bite into my wrists. With a hard yank, she pulls me up—lifting me with a depressing effortlessness.

God, I hate being small.

"What's going on?" a man, who I assume is her partner, says from the driver's seat of his vehicle.

"It's the fugitive," she says as she opens the back door.

"Wait, you mean *the* fugitive? The five seconds ago vanishing act fugitive?"

"I'm not a fugitive," I say, resigned, understanding how fugitive-like I probably look to any outside perspective. "I can explain." *I think.*

"You can save it for when we get back," the woman says as she tucks my head into the back of the police car.

I allow myself to be seated. There's no point in resisting. The woman's shoulders ease up as she shuts the door behind me. I spare a glance at the badge, which reads "Officer Gaines."

Once she hops into the passenger seat, her partner punches an address into the GPS, and the vehicle begins its excursion through the L.A. streets. In spite of the bumpy infrastructure of the surrounding urban jungle, it's a ride I'd call comfortable, were it not for the less-than-friendly company.

"Officers, report in," I hear Detective Chu's voice ring out from the front seat. "I need an update—" *Click.* The radio shuts off.

"So, how'd you do it?" she says.

"Do what?"

"It's not every day that someone gets accused of being a magician," her partner says. "Even as a joke."

"Witch was thrown around, too," Gaines says.

"Like it's the goddamn sixteen hundreds. But this ain't the Salem Witch Trials, and we're about as far from Salem as you can get."

"Um...okay." I don't know how to react to this odd line of questioning. That I'm not a witch? That I'm not a magician? That I escaped through a portal to another world? All these thoughts run through my head so quickly that I almost don't notice us rolling under the 110, *away* from Central Station. *Almost.*

I swallow, hoping they don't notice my body tense.

"So, how'd you do it?" Officer Gaines asks again.

"Do what?" I repeat.

"It's like I'm talking to a wall here." She turns around and looks at me. "You're going to have to tell us how you did it, or we're gonna have a problem."

This conversation's taken a left turn. "I don't know."

She sighs. "Bullshit."

"Where are you taking me?" I ask.

"Huh?" It's her turn to play dumb.

"You turned off the radio," I say. "We're not going to the station. Where are you taking me?"

She looks me in the eyes, her expression turning from a fake innocent one to cold and deadpan. "I'll answer yours if you answer mine."

"I already answered yours," I insist. "I. Don't. Know."

My heart races as the two cops exchange a look. I've heard about cops doing this before from Gabe and the others. They take their suspects to undisclosed locations and pry more information out of them. If they're lucky, any information we give can result in a nice little bonus.

My friend Hank told me it's something they did to him, and that they beat him nearly to death in the process. But as much as I love Hank, I can only trust thirty-five percent of what he says. I'm hoping Hank had just imagined the whole thing, but as Officer Gaines and her partner look back at me, I know what's going through their heads.

But what do they want from me?

"Where are you taking me?" I demand.

Gaines turns around and taps on the radio. An oldies song I don't know the name of whispers from the back speakers.

"Where are you taking me?" This time, I'm yelling.

With a couple more taps, the speakers overpower my screams, the bass reverberating inside my chest, feeling like it's squeezing my heart. With one final tap from her console, the windows and the barrier between me turn black, transforming the backseat into a soundproof chamber.

I continue to scream, even though I know they can't hear me. My jaw clenches as the music continues to assault my eardrums and insides. The police's frequent use of weaponizing audio was well known, but I didn't realize how painful it would be. I thought it was an exaggeration.

With a graceless groan, I roll around in the backseat, tucking in my legs and stretching out my arms. The cuffs narrowly graze past the soles of my shoes, and with an exhale, I pull my cuffed hands in front of me.

I pull at the door handle to find it locked—no surprise there—but I had to at least try. I slide over to the other door and do the same. Also locked.

"Let me out!" I yell continuously, kicking the back of their seats with all my might. Maybe I can annoy them into shutting off the music?

Several minutes pass, and the panic starts to swell up inside me. Between the reverberations of the music and the rising temperature, it's as though someone is trying to slowly smother me to death, each breath warming the air and sending me closer to unconsciousness. I find myself licking salty sweat from around my lips, my shirt even more drenched.

With closed eyes, I throw the weight of my body into one more kick to the back of her seat.

My legs stretch out completely and I feel myself fall. A pocket of cold air hits me like an ocean breeze, and I collapse onto the hard floor. Any relief I have is squashed the moment I open my eyes. In front of me is another stadium-sized chamber. No, the *same* stadium-sized chamber with the same countless netscreens of memories that populate it.

Sure. I guess this is my life now. Out of the frying pan, into the flames, or however that saying goes.

Like last time, I'm overcome with a crushing sense of depression, but unlike last time, I feel just the slightest bit more in control. Don't ask what I mean. I don't get it myself. Before, I could barely stand each time an explosion of emotion hit me. Now, I find myself taking it in stride— meaning I'm only slightly on the verge of a complete mental breakdown.

At the very least, this slightly less painful experience allows me the opportunity to take in my surroundings.

It's the same as before: a large open space, the ground made up of charcoal scribbles, as though some high art snob had his way with an entire football field. I stare up at one of the many netscreens surrounding me on all sides.

The first time I was here, I was crippled by fear and confusion. While I'm no less confused, I'm not nearly as scared as I was at first. It's like going through sleep paralysis for the fifteenth time. You know what to expect, and that you're not going to die. As if in response to my emotions, this void landscape stalls in front of me, and the air stills.

I sigh, twisting my wrists in their cuffs and loosening a knot of anxiety in the process. This place isn't so bad when you're not being pelted by painful memories. Like a dark, silent oasis, one that contains an entire library of memories for me to...peruse through, I guess?

I pass a netscreen showing a particularly painful one—the one Detective Chu is so fond of bringing up. It's a memory that's shaped my future, but I only have the vaguest of inklings of it. Simple emotions, really. A feeling of shame followed by fear.

I stare at the screen in front of me. A six-year-old cherubic face smiles back at me, mouthing indecipherable words. I reach out and touch the image. My fingers tingle as they pierce through, and as if by magic, I feel like crying.

"HEY, WHAT'S THAT?" the girl asks.

I'm in the memory now. Jesus, I'm actually *in* the memory.

I reach toward a skin tag on my neck. *I* don't actually reach out, but the body that I'm in does. "What's what?" I also don't say that, but my past self does.

"That." Okay, I'll admit she sounded roughly six times more aggressive in my recollection of the memory than she does now. It's amazing how different certain events feel with a bit of distance and perspective.

Young me feels at the tag on my neck. I've been told my whole life that it would eventually go away, but even now, I catch myself flicking it back and forth when nervous or anxious.

"Mommy told me it's a mole."

"That's not a mole, stupid," the girl says. Okay, never mind, this girl's a devious bitch. "These are moles." She stupidly points out the freckles on her face. I want to yell out how dumb she looks, but only young me is in control of this memory, and I doubt young me was much smarter.

"Those are freckles, dummy," young me says. Yes! Both old and young me are on the same page. Plus, even at this tender age, I proved to be as bitchy as the next person when pushed.

Little me (and old me) don't see the hit coming. I'd like to say I take it like a champ, but I hit the ground hard and my vision goes black.

I WAIT FOR MORE, but nothing else happens as I'm catapulted out of the vision. My tailbone practically splits as I smack onto the rough pavement. It's clearly been a while since the city's done its due diligence on the sidewalk here.

A pained exhale escapes my chest, and I pray that nothing's broken. But I know there's little time to mourn the shattering of my tailbone. The last time I was spit out of that void, I landed in front of an overzealous dirty cop.

As carefully as I can, I take in my surroundings. Red and yellow neon lights paint the front of a ramen shop. Did it throw me all the way to Little Tokyo this time? It's not a great distance, but it's far enough away that I doubt I'll run into anyone of consequence. A glance in either direction confirms my theory. In true L.A. fashion, the night crowd walks all over me, taking enough care to avoid stepping on any limbs, but grazing me as they do, as if trying to make a statement as to how inconvenient my presence is.

As I lay here, my mind returns to what I saw in the void. Why had that memory stopped there?

While I don't remember the moment she attacked me well, I think I remember what happened next.

As soon as I stood back up, I pulled that girl's hair and yanked her to the ground, like a badass. It was one of the few fights I've ever truly won—before I became so grossly undersized.

After that, she never bothered me again. Dad always said the world was a terrible place. If I never stood up for myself, no one else would.

That was the first day he was truly proud of me. Maybe even the last time.

My mood sours. Dad. What had he known about Mom?

Whomp-whomp!

The telltale flashing red-and-blue lights bring me back to reality, and I sit up, panic rising in my stomach.

"Get the hell up, urch!" a cop yells out from his megaphone.

I want to yell back and tell him he's the urch, but I choke down the deeply witty comment, hoping to the high heavens that they don't notice my handcuffs as I tuck my hands between my thighs. I breathe a sigh of relief as the car sidles along silently down the road, likely to scold someone else from their resting place.

That's how things are done here. The police make their rounds, herding all undesirables to one place, checking their itineraries to make sure they're allowed outside the barrier.

It's lucky that the cops who just passed by seem more interested in others than in me.

I slowly rise to my feet.

I can't go back to the police station. You don't break out of an interrogation room, escape the custody of a pair of dirty cops, and live to tell the tale. And I can't go back to Damien and Lily until this whole mess is resolved.

With a deep breath, I take off at a jog. There's only one place I can run to now. The only place the cops won't be able to take me in. And it's the place where every officer would be funneling me, anyway.

Home.

THREE

I TEAR my way down the Los Angeles streets. They haven't changed the slightest bit in the six months since I left them. Even this early in the morning, there are countless bars, restaurants, and lounges open, some with customers spilling out, sloppy from the night's adventures. Bright lights descend on me from all sides, reflecting off of the wet pavement and the thick grime that coats the uneven tar pavement. I take in the acrid scent, and my nose wrinkles. My stomach drops at the familiar and unpleasant sensation that forms. There's a comfort to it, but that doesn't make me like it any more.

"Excuse me," a robotic voice says, and an android brushes past me, its feet brushing the sidewalk as it does so, simultaneously scraping off some of the grime and sucking it up into its innards. I don't know why they even bother trying to keep this place clean.

The models that frequent this part of the city tend to be decades old, so putting them to work is nothing but an exercise in futility, especially the closer I get to Skid Row.

As I approach Third Street, I can sense the change coming. Vagabonds line the sidewalks, holstering both guns and swords to their sides like it's the Wild West. Though neon lights still illuminate the surrounding area, the number of open businesses has thinned, and the number of cleaning androids thinned even further.

And then I see the ten-foot-tall concrete barriers come into view that mark the border into Skid Row. Each year, they push it out a little farther to fit the growing population, and each year, the LAPD funnels more and more of us into this more unsavory district.

Dad always complained about this. He complained about a lot of things, but the injustices in L.A. were some of the few things he was passionate about.

Following the Second Civil War, one of the "amends" that the Rebels made was to allow more subsidized housing.

"The reality is that neither the U.S. nor the Rebels gave a shit about us," Dad said. "They wanted to look like they cared, but this was just another way to push us aside."

The result was an expansion of many city districts with large populations.

For its part, Skid Row expanded from fifty blocks to hundreds of blocks, encapsulating around eighty percent of the area surrounded by the familiar parade of freeways that envelop us.

"And practically overnight," Dad continued, his hand mimicking an explosion, "the homeless population rose from around 5,000 to 90,000. It's been rising year over year ever since."

And for the majority of my life, it's a population I've been a part of. If nothing else, it's free. But it's never been a home I've been eager to return to.

"Don't be too grateful," he'd say. "They don't do it out of the goodness of their hearts. It's just the small price the government pays. It's easier for them to pretend we don't exist."

He talked a lot of game, but as far as I know, he's spent his entire life within the confines of those concrete barriers—not that he had a choice.

Yes, it was free, but *we* aren't. Sitting atop the barriers are machine gun turrets manned by androids. I can only enter through one of the fifteen gates, and in order to leave, I need an itinerary. That can be a job interview, an errand, or a new residence. The last one doesn't happen very often.

"Please, show some identification," the rubber-skinned sentry android says, holding out his hand. The rubber is practically falling, revealing his metallic skeleton underneath. He's seen better days, but I have little doubt he could still snap my neck without a second thought.

I pull out my netscreen and let him scan my ID app. With a satisfying ding, the concrete gate begins sliding open, scraping against what's likely a pile of garbage resting on the other side.

"Please proceed," he says, but I'm already walking through, head held high as the stench starts to hit me.

I keep my pace at a slow walk. It's rarely a good idea to run through Skid Row. You'll attract the attention of the wrong people. Either they'll think you have something valuable and chase you down, or, like predators, they'll see you as prey and chase you down, anyway. I consider my current clothing choice—just a tee-shirt and pair of kiwi-print pajama shorts. Not the most ideal attire when making your way through the seediest part of the city. But it's not like I haven't made this pilgrimage a thousand times before.

Whenever a foster home didn't work out, it was a place I returned to, and before that, the majority of my life was restricted to two square miles within the district, often making runs for Dad. So, you can say I'm familiar with the area.

Even as someone with little exposure to the outside world, I can tell how awful it is here. A parade of tents covers the streets, with some residents cooking their meals over barrels of fire.

Mice and the occasional opossum weave in and out of the trash that litters the road. My nose wrinkles at the now unfamiliar smell of refuse, each inhale a poisonous breath. This is home.

My slow and deliberate walk through the streets is a welcome return to what came before. The act of keeping my eyes and ears open for attacks is a comfortable anxiety. It's not fun. It's not nice. But it's something I understand.

Several blocks later, I find myself outside the Main Stay apartment— my home. Well, at least one of the one-room units is mine. Ours. My family's.

The main entrance to the apartment is deceiving. It looks like it belongs to an old-school movie theater, with a marquee that could have, in some other time, displayed the showtimes of some of the great classic films. These days, it sits blank, with no promise of escape. For as long as I've known, that "main entrance" has been boarded up. It's a place that once had grand ambition, but, like everything else, had fallen into disarray with time, beaten down by the cruel reality.

As I make my way to the real entrance—a small metal door to the left —a high-pitched whistle catches my attention.

"Hey, Girl, whatcha doin' walkin' around dressed like that? You gonna send us all the wrong idea. Or hell, maybe you sendin' me the right one."

I recognize the voice and turn to see a group of three leaning against a rusty chain-link fence across the street.

"Gabe," I say, locking eyes with the ringleader of the group.

The nineteen-year-old face splits into a grill-laden smile. "Oh, shit! Luna! Girl, what're you doin' makin' me think you're out here lookin' for a good time?" He breaks out into a laugh and high-fives one of his cronies, as if he'd just made one of the funniest jokes known to humankind.

I cross my arms over my chest. "Very funny, jackass." I'd had run-ins with Gabe and his crew countless times in the past. I hated him, he hated me, but he'd also never miss an opportunity to make a pass.

Growing up as small as I am, you learn to talk your way out of most fights as opposed to, you know, actually fighting them. I don't like it, but staying on Gabe's good side has always been in my best interest. Not only do they keep things somewhat civil in these surrounding blocks, but they're also responsible for keeping Dad's fix in line.

"Hey, yo, Luna," Gabe continues. "You back here because you missed me or what?"

"I don't think I've fallen that low just yet, but when I do, you'll be the first one I call."

He reacts with a smile.

It's a delicate balance I walk with Gabe. I insult him just enough for him to get the point, but not so much that he gets genuinely insulted.

My eye catches a glint on his arm. Wait…

"You see somethin' you like?" Gabe removes the black glove from his right hand to reveal a chrome appendage, each finger moving so quickly that they almost look like spider legs. He punctuates the movement by flipping me off with his metallic hand, the grinding of each gear and bearing almost inaudible. "They knew I couldn't stay at the bottom forever."

In Gabe's world, the amputation of a limb was a rite of passage, meaning he was ready to take on more deadly runs.

I don't linger too much on his arm. The last thing I want is to make him think I'm intimidated. So I rest my eyes on the boy next to him.

"And when did you graduate from the Little Leagues, Marco?" Last I saw, the kid was running around doing bum errands.

"Last month," Marco says, sheepish.

"And what's with the cuffs?" Gabe asks.

"Don't get any ideas," I say, my voice deadpan.

"Too late," Gabe says with a chuckle. His goons laugh and give him another high-five. He's careful not to use his metal hand, and I can't help but wonder how many times he made that mistake already.

Boys.

Ignoring them, I turn to face the front of the Main Stay. Sitting out front, I see Hank performing his usual anxious pacing. To the uninitiated, he looks like a pigeon. I mean, not literally, but his head bobs with each step as he circles the sidewalk in front of the boarded-up main entrance. It's just him working out his constant anxious energy. He's harmless.

When he sees me, he gives me an awkward and jerky wave.

"Luna! You're back! It was your longest streak yet!"

"Oh, is that right?"

"A hundred and seventy-five days today. Well, technically a hundred and seventy-four until around nine a.m. this morning."

"You're counting?"

"I got anything better to do?" He gestures to the blank sidewalk around him.

I let out a genuine laugh. Hank is one of the few good things about this place. Even through the bad times, he's here for support.

"How's Dad?"

Hank shrugs. "You know how he is. He never leaves unless he's looking for his fix."

I frown. He shouldn't be leaving at all, let alone when looking for a fresh supply of muze. I look back to where Gabe and his crew were standing, but find that they've already wandered off down the block.

"When did you last see him?"

"Two and a half days ago, I dunno."

I know I can take his word to heart. No one remembers days like this guy.

"Hey," Hank says. "If you're going to be sticking around, thought I should tell you. There's this guy rolling up and down Main with a crow on his shoulder. With a top hat!"

"The man or the crow?"

"What do you think?" he says, as though it's the most obvious thing in the world. I guess he has a point.

"Anyway," Hank continues. "He says he's some kinda hero. I don't like him. He doesn't belong here."

Unfortunately, his factually accurate comments about numbers of days are mixed with questionable and paranoid ones about people he's seen walking around. I've learned to filter out the good from the bad.

"Yeah," I say, "none of us really belong here, do we?"

Hank only grunts in response and continues his mad pacing back and forth.

I take the caged door to the left of the main entrance, entering the lobby. A dim light flickers overhead. It's bright enough for me to see where I'm going, but only just, as if embarrassed by its own sorry state.

To the building's credit, the lobby floor is made of marble, but it hasn't been cleaned in years. I've only seen an effort made once in my tenure. Scorch marks litter the entirety of the floor in five to six-foot intervals, not to mention actual litter. Cereal boxes, toilet paper, lighters, ashtrays, shoebox lids, newspaper scraps, and foam cups filled with ash pile up two feet high on each side of the hall, creating a narrow path leading up the stairs and onto elevators.

A handful of tenants sit in a corner of the lobby, smoking something I know isn't a joint. Somehow, it feels like the place has even less ambition than usual.

I'm relieved to find that no one is asleep in the elevator. On occasion, I'd find someone passed out after a trip, and I'd be too nervous to ride with them. The only other option is to climb the perilous stairwell, which has a greater chance of being blocked by a body or two. Plus, with our unit being on the tenth floor, lots of time and space to be attacked.

These things cross my mind every waking moment of my existence. Again, it's awful anxiety, but it's an anxiety I've grown used to in my near two decades of life.

As I ascend in the rickety lift, I'm struck by a feeling of helplessness. I may not live here now, but no matter what, I always make my way back. Is this my future? Forever heading back to the Main Stay? Is this my life's equilibrium?

An awful thought crosses my mind. That if Dad were dead, I'd have no reason to come back. No reason to keep falling back to this low point. I'd almost prefer that, though I'd never say the thought aloud.

When I finally make it to Unit 1017, I hold my breath and twist the doorknob. The door is light and hollow. It'd hardly be able to hold anyone back if they wanted to break in. But, all the same, I feel a pang of annoyance when the knob turns the entire way. As usual, Dad hadn't even bothered to lock the door.

I can't tell you how many times our apartment was broken into because of him. Though, I guess "broken into" isn't quite the right phrasing, given his carelessness. Most of the time, there wasn't much to steal, but I do remember an early argument between my parents when Mom's silicon wedding band was nicked.

On more than one occasion, Dad's aversion to locked doors led to us stumbling in on some randoms using our room as a hangout spot. In at least once instance, we walked in on a couple doing a bit more than that.

The moment I step foot into Dad's apartment, I'm struck by a sour and overwhelming stench. Somewhere in the kitchenette, I'll bet he's left out some food that's gone rotten. The other scent mixed in with it is likely from the air vent, where another rat probably died.

An initial glance to my right confirms my thoughts. Sitting out on the counter are not one, but two sandwiches. Dad's always been forgetful. He has a tendency to make food, forget about it, get hungry again, make more food, and forget about it again. These sandwiches have likely been sitting there for a solid week. And who knows if he's eaten anything since making them?

"Dad?" I say, entering the kitchenette. I open the fridge. All that's in there is moldy bread and an unopened carton of oat milk. The contents within are warm. As I close the fridge, I notice the seal doesn't shut completely. Based on the moldy bread, it's not like he's been using it much, anyway. "Dad?" I repeat.

Though I'm uneasy about what state I'll find him in, I at least want him to know I'm here before I see him, hence my taking my dear sweet time in the kitchenette.

I call out his name one last time before heading into the main bedroom, which doubles as the main living space. There's really only enough room for a queen-sized bed. I'd spent the majority of my life laying on the ground at its foot, kind of like a dog, but I never mentioned that to Mom or Dad. I worried it might hurt their feelings.

I find Dad sprawled out on an unmade bed, a loose tee-shirt draped over his thin frame, and the top of his baggy jeans unbuttoned.

Yup, this is what home is, all right.

"Dad," I say in a whisper. I know it won't wake him up, but it seems rude to yell him awake. I grab his shoulder, noticing just how loose and wrinkled his skin is, and give him a light shake. "Max."

His eyes flicker for a few seconds. He's definitely on his meds. I guess that's a good thing. I worried that, with me gone, his supply would run dry, or he'd screw things up with Gabe and find a way to cheat himself out of his fix. He's done it before. It's never good, and always ends up with him seeking out the cheaper, more dangerous alternatives. Not on my watch.

"Estrella?" Dad whispers, his voice barely more than a soft croak.

I sigh.

"Nope," I say. "Terrible guess."

"Oh," he says, realization returning to his glazed eyes. "You know, didn't I tell you—"

"A thousand times," I say. "It's fine."

It'd heard that story enough to last ten lifetimes. I've been on this planet for seventeen years. I think that entitles me to my own name, but I fight the urge to correct him.

"I'm back," I say, forcing a smile.

Several long seconds pass. The glaze over his eyes slowly clears and his pupils focus on me. "No. Luna." He shakes his head softly, realizing for the first time who I am—never mind the fact that he's already just talked to me. "You're not supposed to be back. You're supposed to be..."

"Hank said you've been going out."

Dad's concern slowly wrinkles into a chuckle. "You can't expect me to stay cooped up here forever, can you?"

"It's not that you were out, Dad," I say. "It's why."

"What, you don't trust your papa to make his own life decisions?"

"Don't call yourself Papa," I say. "I've never called you that. And no, I don't trust you to make your own decisions."

Dad doesn't argue. He just gives the slightest of shrugs.

I groan. "Well, anyway." I cast my eyes onto the dresser. "I have a favor. Don't ask questions."

"Uh-huh?" His voice is still slightly vacant, but I can tell he's present.

"Do you have your stunner here?"

The smallest half-grin crosses his face. "It's in the top drawer, sweetie."

"Don't call me sweetie. You never call me sweetie." I retrieve the roughly four-inch long and half-an-inch in diameter cylinder from the top drawer. With a begrudging reluctance, I hand it over to Dad, who, to his credit, avoids looking too smug about the situation.

"Okay, so this is going to feel weird," he says. "Like a shock."

I nod. "Got it."

He presses the end of the cylinder to the center of my cuffs and double-taps the opposite end. With a loud zap, I feel a current of electricity run through my body and out my fingertips. For the briefest moment, I feel like I'm about to collapse, but as my knees give out, my muscles re-engage as though being restarted.

The cuffs hiss and snap open. I breathe a sigh of relief and toss them to the floor. They hit a pile of clothes with a muted *thunk*.

"Thanks," I say. "Do you still have my clothes here?"

"You know I never touch your drawer," he says, pointing to the bottom left of the dresser. I don't know whether to be depressed or grateful by that fact.

I grab a pair of tech cargos, a workout tank and vest, and retreat into the bathroom. After a quick wash of my face, I throw on the change of clothes, relieved to be free of my nightwear.

When I get back into the living room, I see Dad hasn't moved. The stunner still sits in his hand, the vacant expression on his face returned.

"So," I say, getting his attention. He blinks, returning from whatever world he was in. "How's your supply?" I scan the room. Apart from its textbook filth, I see a beat-up and peeling faux-leather box sitting open, thirteen vials resting in their spots. The color is a light red, slightly off from the dark red of his standard muze. The heat rises in my face immediately. "What's this?"

"Hmm?" His tone is vacant, the perfect match to his face. I know he has no idea what I'm talking about, but that doesn't stop the anger from swelling.

"This?" I motion to the leather box. His "first aid kit" as he calls it. I know he's not looking. He's blasted out of his mind and still trying to get his bearings. "What did I tell you about experimenting?"

His eyes finally settle on his first aid kit. His expression doesn't change.

"You know this wasn't the deal," I say. "The deal we set up with..." I have to stop. If I keep talking, I know I'll yell. Dad's on a fixed income. Before I'd left, I'd perfectly calculated his expenses. Between his food, bills, and fix, he could survive (just barely, but he could survive). Plus, the strain of muze I'd set him up with was the perfect dose. It kept him alive, kept him moving, and kept his tolerance down if used properly. I'd known there was a danger of him going through his supply too soon, but had hoped his lack of spending money would keep him from making any foolish choices. I guess I was the idiot here.

"They raised their prices," he says, his voice still vacant, but it's coherent, so there was that at least.

"What do you mean?"

"Gabe. His boss raised the prices. I couldn't afford what I usually got. But it's okay. This is cheaper. Almost as goo—"

I don't let him finish. I rush through the front door and slam it shut behind me. I'm down the elevator and back in front of the building marquee in what feels like seconds, a far cry from the slow march in.

I scan the dark, neon-laden cityscape and head in the direction Gabe and his crew walked down earlier. I have no idea if I can actually find them. Between their nightly route and aimless wandering, it—

Gabe's idiot laugh echoes from around the corner. I'd recognize it anywhere. That stupid, condescending laugh.

He doesn't even see me coming as I shove him as hard as I can into a cement wall behind him. He doesn't hit it as hard as I want, but being as small as I am, I'm used to that. I only hope he can feel my anger.

"Yo, what the hell's your problem?" he yells.

"We had a deal, you prick," I yell right back.

He holds up his gloved metal hand to keep his goons from pulling me off him. He makes a show of it, almost as if he wants to highlight that he's doing me a favor, but I know it's really just to protect his fragile ego. To squash any doubt that he could take on a five-foot-nothing girl.

"You're right, we had a deal," Gabe says. "Six months ago. Ask your pops. We've delivered on time twice a month without fail to that shit palace of yours. But things don't stay the same forever. Costs have gone up, and we had to make tough decisions."

"Like raising prices without warning?"

"We *gave* him fair warnin'," Gabe says, his finger in my face. "And we can't roll over for every sob story in Skid Row, especially when we can sell the inferior product at better margins."

I grit my teeth. This is more brazen than normal, even for Gabe, but it confirms my worst fears. They know Dad's a customer for life. It could be the lowest grade shit in existence, but so long as it did the job, he'd take it. Why waste the good stuff on such an undiscerning customer like him when they can just feed him what amounted to table scraps? He'd probably OD before long anyway. May as well wring him dry while they still could.

"Don't act like you're some victim," Gabe says. "Your pops wanted it. When he realized how much more he could get for the same price, he practically rolled over and begged for it."

I can feel a mistake forming in my fist, but I can't stop myself. It flies toward Gabe's oversized nose and makes contact. A strong crack courses through my arm, followed by a feeling of elation.

Oh, yeah. This is satisfying. It's like years and years of pent-up strife are unleashed in an instant. But even as that emotion arises, it passes.

His head smacks into the wall behind him and he slides to the ground.

As I've said before, I'm not the strongest person in the world, but even someone like me can get a lucky hit in once in a while. It turns out this was that lucky hit. And just like that, I know I've crossed a line.

Gabe and I never got along. Not once. But we put up with each other. I put up with his snide comments, and he tolerated my mouth and my attitude.

But as soon as he gets up, we're going to be living in a world where his goons and a bunch of strangers saw him get decked by some pint-sized girl. He'd have to do something about that.

Once he gets up, he'll do everything in his power to ensure I suffered for what I'd just done. And I have no idea what he considers as a fair trade for that. So, I do the only thing I can think of in the moment. The only thing I could rely on in my brief existence.

I run. Because my life now depends on it.

FOUR

IT'S STILL DARK OUT. The embers of dawn have yet to fully make themselves known over the hills to the east, but the energy is already worlds different from what it was even just under an hour ago.

Before, I had walked through an uneasy silence, as though passing through a dragon's lair. But now, chatter permeates the expanse of tents that layer the streets. And it comes at the absolute worst time. Rather than darting straight between the tents that serve as housing, I have to weave around as tenants exit their homes for their morning rituals, which often consists of finding the source of their next fix or meal.

I thank God for how small I am as I squeeze between a man and a woman, apologizing as I do, not just for disrupting their morning, but because I know Gabe is likely to be much less polite as he knocks them down in his pursuit.

I turn a corner, and run straight into a hot dog cart, a metal handle ramming into my ribs, hard, knocking it back a few feet. If it had actually been in use, I'd've been burned or knocked straight on my ass. As it is, it's clear this cart hasn't been in use for business for at least seventeen decades, with its exterior caked in dirt and inexplicable crust. It's probably found a second life as someone's wardrobe.

Feeling guilty as I do it, I give the cart a kick toward the corner from where I came, hoping it'll make the experience that much more painful for Gabe.

Not waiting to see the result, I keep on running. The plus side is that I know this place as well as anyone. The downside is that so does Gabe.

I cut into a nearby alley. Under normal circumstances, heading through a dark, sparsely populated area in the already dangerous Skid Row isn't something I'd do, but I'll do anything to lose my tail right now.

I hop between several (hopefully) sleeping bodies, and as I approach the center, I see a fire escape ladder hanging down several feet up. With a smirk and an outward breath, I jump against the wall, stretching my arms upward to catch the opposite side so that I hover a few feet above the ground. I'm barely tall enough to make this work, but I handle the meager hand I'm dealt and bring my other foot over, straddling between both walls. Using the bricks as footholds, I pushed myself up, and up, and up, and up, until I can reach the ladder hanging from the fourth floor fire escape.

I grab on to the bottom rung and feel it out with my fingers. Bits of rust jab into the creases of my knuckles, and I start to pull myself up, praying it can carry my slight body weight.

My hopes are dashed as the ladder slides down with a sickening scrape, peppering me with copper-colored flakes, forcing me to close my eyes.

Clang!

The rung I hang on to tears into my hands as the whole ladder comes to a stop. I grit my teeth and pull myself up, my feet cycling in the air before they catch on to the brick wall behind me. Pushing up with my feet, I grab on to the second rung, then third, and finally I'm able to bring my feet up onto the bottom rung.

In my peripheral vision, I catch sight of Marco entering the alley. He curses at me as I make it onto the landing and pull up the ladder. Unable to help myself, I flip him off.

"Looks like you're still in the Little Leagues, Marco!"

He doesn't even try to climb up the wall, instead pulling a handgun from his belt.

Crap.

Sparks fly around me as bullets scrape on the metal grating on all sides.

I dive into an open window and onto a thankfully unoccupied bed. Unfortunately, the rest of the room isn't unoccupied, and I lock eyes with a kid who can't be older than ten. His eyes are wide and his body stiff. He'd likely been woken up by the gunshots. If I were his age, I would've screamed by now. Instead, he scoots up to the wall, wrapping his blankets around him, as if that's going to protect him from anything.

I hold up a finger to my lips. "Stay low."

The boy nods and crab walks onto the ground, where he lays flat on his belly, blankets over him, still acting like that would do much of anything against a stray bullet.

I close the window behind me and lock it. "Are your parents home?"

He shakes his head.

Good. That means there's no one else here. "Stay hidden, and if anyone asks where I am, tell them you saw me and that I went through that door. Got it?"

He nods.

I want to escape, but not at the expense of some kid's life.

Without another thought, I leave the room, pass through the kitchen, and out the apartment's front door.

I turn right into the hallway, not entirely sure where it leads, but I have a bit of time before anyone catches up with me.

"Luna, Luna, Luna," I hear Gabe's taunting voice before I see him. I turn around to see his gross, stubbly face. Thankfully, the building is in disrepair, and the poor lighting spares me the finer details.

I glance back, and, just my luck, it turns out I'd turned into a dead end.

I face Gabe, taking in his smug and infuriating expression.

"You may have been gone for half a year, but you still have the same bag of tricks."

"Please," I say, leaning into a condescending tone. I can't help myself. "It was three on one. What's sadder is that it took you so long to finally trap me."

"You really have to learn to control that mouth of yours, you know that, Girl?"

My skin crawls at the comment. I hate it when people tell me what I can and cannot do, and I hate it even more when they cap it off with the word "Girl." But I'm too scared to come up with some smart-ass retort.

The reality is I'm trapped, and Gabe has had it out for me forever. And now I've given him an excuse. Never jeopardize someone's reputation.

I want to run, but my back's already to a corner, with the only exit leading to a locked janitor's closet. I try my best not to feel like a trapped mouse, even as I know my options are limited. With a smirk, Gabe lunges.

I dodge the first swing, seeing an opening under his arm, which I take without hesitation. Air is pressed out of my windpipe as his arm wraps around my neck. I struggle to shove my chin between his arm and my throat, but he easily overpowers me with a yank back. He brings his free arm down onto my chest with a relentless slam. My sternum rings, and somehow, even more air is catapulted from my lungs. I struggle to regain my breath, anything to give myself some much-needed oxygen, but before I can so much as cough, he shoves my face up against the wall, his metal hand pressing on the back of my head and his joints digging into my scalp.

His breath is ragged. In it I hear exhaustion, sure, but beneath it is something darker. More carnal.

Whatever this is goes beyond pure assertion of power, beyond simple revenge. This is an act of dominance. I'd seen this before. Felt this before. There's only one way this is going to end.

Before I can stop them, tears well up and run freely down my right cheek, pooling up against the wall. I struggle to move. To fight back. To do anything. But my arms are twisted and pressed against my back.

"Let go!" I scream.

A harder press against the side of my head is his only response. He's beyond words. Animalistic.

I don't see a way out. No one around to help. No one around to stop what's about to happen. But I'll be damned if I go down without a fight.

The sound of an unbuckling belt is all too prominent in my ears. I kick back the heel of my foot and make contact with flesh. It's only his leg, but the blow throws him off, loosening his grip on the side of my head. But it's short-lived. Any progress I've made is lost when he runs my cheek along the wall of the hallway, and onto the short, scratchy carpet.

I continue to struggle and flail, but it's too late. His hands feel up my waist, and I let out a feral scream.

The lights in the hallway flicker, and a second later, darken altogether.

And then, silence. It had been silent before, but it's a different kind of silence, like walking from a small room into the open air. I know right away what's happening.

Like in every other situation over the past few hours, a part of me willed this into existence. Had wished for an escape. And this is as close as I could get.

Gabe's hand eases off my head. "What the...?"

On cue, a feeling of extreme euphoria followed by a one of mammoth depression hits me in a one-two punch. Compared to how it had felt the previous two times, it's much less impactful, but still present. Someone's taken the dial and turned it from eleven to six. But there is still an oppressive force at work, like a set of invisible walls pressing in on all sides.

The only thing keeping me from falling into the usual cycle of reliving my memories is the distracting image of Gabe. Pants unbuckled and partway down his legs. He stumbles back as he stares at the spectacle around him. At the huge netscreens that circle us like vultures, moving images of my past on full display.

Is he actually getting a glimpse of my memories, or are each of those screens displaying something different? Maybe something else from his own past?

Regardless, it's hard not to at least smile at the look on his face. Eyes wide, mouth agape, pants around his ankles. I may be getting a bit too much pleasure out of seeing this guy freak out.

"You doin' okay there, creep?" I say, my voice level.

Gabe doesn't answer, his body trembling with each breath.

"Hey, Gabe, I'm talking to you."

As if hearing me for the first time, he glances my way. Somehow, his eyes grow even wider, and he crab walks back, tripping over his pants. Even amid the circumstances, it's funny to watch.

"B-behind you!"

I'm not prepared for what I see. An object the size of an elephant bounds toward me. Except, it's not just an object, nor is it technically bounding, but floating with a shaking intensity. Lord help me, but what's coming at me is a giant head. The face glows blue, its features wispy, almost as though they've come straight out of an ancient Japanese painting.

It's hard to see through the bright florescence, but the features of the face are feminine; its eyebrows are arched, its nose squash and wide, and the shape of a rose is etched on its forehead. I can't put my finger on it, but I almost recognize it. When would I have seen a giant floating head?

Despite its otherworldly beauty, the face is clearly angry. Its mouth opens and screams wildly. The entire void shakes in response, the scream reverberating in my chest, feeling like it can stop my heart at any moment.

I want to run, but the face is wide and getting closer by the millisecond. Even if I try, there's no way for me to avoid it. Instead, I put my hands out in front of me and brace for impact.

An instant later, a horrifying coldness washes through me, like my body's been frostbitten from the inside out. A cold so cold it burns. Those painful memories that I've been reliving with a dampened intensity are now dialed up to twenty.

It only lasts a brief moment. Perhaps less than a second, and then eases up, followed by the most overwhelming relief I've ever felt. Like my body could collapse onto the ground into a literal puddle.

My solace is broken by Gabe's guttural scream. The face that had blown through me envelops his entire body. His cries grow increasingly manic by the second, threatening to tear his throat. His mouth hangs wide open, and he floats straight up in the air. I can see the sound waves emanating from his mouth as much as I can hear them. His eyes bug out, and his body falls to the ground, contorting in unnatural ways.

The screaming continues for way too long. It's a miracle that he doesn't spit up blood for all the work his vocal cords are doing. Gabe may be a monster, but it's hard for me to see him like this. I want to help him. But where would I start?

And Gabe's close. An inch from death, and getting closer. I don't know how, but I can feel the life draining from his body. A sick satisfaction fills my insides. Who's to say this guy deserves anything less than death? After what he'd just done, a slow and torturous end is pretty damned fitting.

"Stop," I find myself saying, though I don't know why. "Stop," I repeat. It feels useless. Who am I kidding? It *is* useless. Gabe is literally having his life sucked from him by some otherworldly being, and all I can do is say stop?

"Stop it!" I yell out a third time, this one at a respectable decibel level. I expect nothing to happen. What *could* happen?

Unable to stop myself, I run over and grab Gabe by the shoulders. "I said stop it!"

The previously elephant-sized face emerges from his mouth, its gaze piercing, impatient, angry.

The whole void rumbles beneath my feet, and not just the ground, but one of the floating netscreens surrounding us shakes as well, exploding as a figure bursts through at superhuman speed. Wait, not one. Two. No, three figures.

Shards of...glass(?) from the netscreen litter the ground, sticking into it like a set of knives into a loaf of bread.

Despite their speed, the figures land with impossible grace, slowing to a near-stop before settling onto the ground.

The figure at the front is a girl, likely not much older than me. Her blonde hair is up in a ponytail, and covering her chest is what appears to be some kind of armor. Armor? What was this, medieval times?

Just behind and to her left is a man who has to be in his mid to late twenties, despite the fact that his stubble shows an inability to grow a real beard. He wears an all-black outfit that resembles the tactical gear someone in the Marines would sport. To the girl's left is a boy, definitely younger than the man, but older than the girl. His outfit consists of a black trench coat that is somehow armored, accented with neon orange and blue.

But this trio saves the best for last, because without warning, the blonde girl at the center reaches off to the side, and pulls, as if from nowhere, a katana longer than her entire body.

"You sure this time, Seb," she says.

"This is it," he says, his voice deeper than I expect it to be.

"You're sure?"

"I can't help it if it was jumping all over the city."

"City? Ha! Sure it was," she says in a fake mocking tone.

The kid grunts, as though he were caught telling a lie—or at the very least, an exaggeration. "Fine, it wasn't hopping exactly, but it was faint until just a minute ago."

"There you go, Seb!" The girl's voice is cheery, dare I say bubbly. "See? The truth will set you free!"

"Kids, focus," the lone adult in the vicinity says, clearly fed up with the banter. "We've made it into the Mirage"—the way he says that last word, it sounds like it's important—"but our job's not done yet."

"Right," the boy says. "On it, Teach."

"And don't call me that on a mission. It makes you sound like a child."

The boy—Seb—raises his hands, palms out, as though he's performing reiki on the empty space in front of him.

"Who..." I say before I realize I'm speaking. I can't exactly wait around, and while the space we're in is open, there aren't many places to hide. I'm surprised they haven't seen me yet. "Who are you?"

"Oh, wow!" the teacher in the group says with a smirk. "There's someone trapped here. No, wait, *two* someones. Look alive! Learning experience, team. What do we do in the case of extra hostages?"

"Hang on a second, Teach," the boy says, his face wrinkling in confusion as his hands settle in my direction. He exchanges glances with the blonde girl. "Not a hostage."

"Ummm...can someone please tell me what's going on?" I say.

The blonde girl groans and smacks her forehead with her free hand in a melodramatic fashion. "I'm sorry to be the one to say it, but I'm kind of here to kill you."

To Be Continued...

SPECTRAL | EPISODE 2

A LITTLE GIRL'S BIRTHDAY PARTY...

SOMETHING HAS ALWAYS BEEN off about me. Back when Alyssa Crane made fun of me and the skin tag on my neck, we got into a fight. It was only later that I was told that I grabbed the knife from her parents' kitchen and pointed it at her.

I don't remember that moment.

In the years since then, flashes of random clarity of pulling that knife from a wood block in the kitchen have surfaced on occasion. But after so many years of being told what had happened, I consider these glimpses as nothing more than false memories.

And then there was a time when some boy was being an asshole to me at school. I don't recall what he said, just how it made me feel: small and worthless—something I'm used to now. But back then, it was a new and hurtful feeling. We got into a fight, and the next thing I know, I'm expelled, with everyone saying I'd beat the living crap out of the kid. Go me?

As with the knife memory, I've only had flashes of this event cross my brain at annoying times. The same goes for my two—now three—arson incidences, one of which saw me allegedly burning down the house of my foster parents, Mr. and Mrs. Segal. To this day, I don't understand why I'd ever do that. I'm still haunted by it.

But the pattern is clear. No matter how hard I try, I always screw it up in the end.

"But why?" you may ask.

Believe me, I've tried to find out. I did my best to convince my therapist on multiple occasions to consider I may have Dissociative Identity

Disorder—DID or multiple personalities. All I knew was what I'd seen in movies or on the netscreens: that traumatic events can bring out alternate personalities.

That butthead refused to diagnose me. Actually, he flat-out refused to even *entertain* the idea for the entire session, saying it was so rare that it was all but impossible.

So, without any idea of what's wrong with me, I've turned to my own explanations. The Entity, I call it, mostly to myself.

I try my best to forget my mistakes, but the Entity is always there to remind me. If there is conflict in my life, the Entity will somehow make it worse.

But giving it a name doesn't change anything. I've spent my life trying to ignore it. To forget that it exists. The past twelve hours have made that impossible. My adopted parents' house has been burned, I've escaped police custody twice in a row, and on three separate occasions, I've now entered a strange otherworldly realm, a realm made up purely of my memories.

I call it the void, and it's about as nightmarish as you can imagine.

All of this is made ten times worse when you're confronted by the strangest of things: some crazy blonde with a giant anime sword saying, "I'm kind of here to kill you."

It's safe to say this isn't a problem I can ignore for much longer. Whatever this is needs to be dealt with, like right the hell now.

SPECTRAL

EPISODE 2

COMPANION

ONE

"WAIT, YOU'RE WHAT?" I say, barely registering the words just uttered. Most people don't really go around declaring their desire to kill.

"You're doing it again, Vero," the scruffy-looking twenty-something—apparently their teacher—says.

"Oh, sorry!" the girl's, Vero's, tone is intensely apologetic, as though she didn't just express a desire to murder. "We. *We're* here to kill you. I know. I have to stop making this about me all the time."

"Nope, that wasn't it," the teacher says. "But whatever."

"You're what?" I don't know why I ask her to repeat it. She's already said it multiple times. I'm not used to people being so freakin' brazen.

"Don't make me say it again," she responds. "I already feel bad enough saying it twice."

"You having fun chatting up the Spectre?" the teacher says. "Do I need to step in?"

"Is it just me, or does she feel a lot less Spectre-y than normal?"

"Just kill the damned Ghost."

"Sorry, you know I get all caught up in the moment." She runs at me without another moment's hesitation. One second she's twenty feet away, the next she's right on top of me. How on earth did she move so fast?

The metallic armor that she wears digs into my chest as she butts her shoulder into me. An intense pain I've never felt before explodes, like I'm being hit with a bat covered in glass shards.

And then I'm tossed backward, flying—that's right, *flying*—through the air before another explosion of pain hits my back, followed by an unexpected bout of anxiety accompanied by a memory. Had I been catapulted through one of those massive memory screens again?

But the moment dissolves as I drop to the ground, landing on my feet. Suddenly, all I can feel is the immense pain in my chest. I look down, looking for any signs of blood. I find none.

"Ow!" I yell out. "Dude, you slammed me right in my boob!"

"Yeah, I'm sorry! I swear I wasn't aiming for that," the girl says, jumping back a solid fifty feet. Wait, fifty feet?

"Ugh," the teacher says, sounding like a convenience store clerk who'd just seen an annoying customer enter. "How many times do I have to tell you? *Lead* with the weapon. You had it out and everything! I don't know why you kids always try to go fisticuffs at the start. One slice and we'd be done already."

"Something's off about this one, Teach," she says. "I wanted to test and see—"

"Just do the thing!"

"Right!" Vero says. "Doing the thing." She jumps straight at me, her comically large sword cocked back.

Oh, no, no, no!

I somehow sidestep out of the way just as this terrifying bitch slices into the wall like it's a giant stick of butter.

"What is happening?" I say, though I have no idea to who.

"You need some help there, Vero?" The teacher's voice manages to be both impatient and nonchalant at the same time.

"No, no!" Vero emerges from the wall, breath heavy. "I got this. I swear I got this."

"The still-standing Spectre in front of us says otherwise."

"Wait, wait!" I stretch my hands out in front of me. "The still-standing what?"

"I underestimated her. But don't worry, I *got* this, Teach!" No one is listening to me, and Vero takes another big leap in my direction, which I somehow manage to dodge.

The teacher of the group whistles. "She's a quick one! Faster than you."

"And here I was, thinking she might *not* be a Spectre," Vero says.

How did that just happen? From what I can tell, this chick has to be moving near the freakin' speed of sound. I should be cut into several pieces now, not dodging her. And yet, I somehow find myself doing just that. She slices vertically; I step to the side. She slices horizontally; I hit the ground or jump. She comes at an angle; I jump back an inexplicable dozens of feet, narrowly missing the very tip of the sword. It's not easy. I'm clumsy, desperate, and ungraceful, but dammit, I'm still alive.

As I jump back again, I hit an invisible wall within the void. "I don't know who you think I am, but I swear I'm not that person or thing you seem to hate."

Vero swings and misses as I dive to the right and into a tumble.

"You're starting to piss me off!" I say with a groan.

"The least you can do is let me hit you so I can gauge a level," she says with an extra swing.

"So you can what?" I say.

"Less talking, more fighting," the teacher calls out like a spectator in a street fight.

"Sorry!"

This comment slows this Vero girl down just the slightest bit. Not much, but enough to give me a window to attack. This medieval-looking armor may be pretty beefy up top, but her lower half looks like normal black pants, with armored boots rising just past her knees. I'd like to say I'm not one to take advantage of little weaknesses like this, but that'd be a barefaced lie. I've punched and kicked more sets of balls in my life than I can count. And while this girl may not have a set of balls for me to punch...

I jump ahead and aim my punch at the only spot I can think of. It connects square in the groin, and my hit is rewarded with a scream.

"Looks like the no-level Spectre is giving you a run for your money, Vero," the voice of the teacher calls out. "And this one fights dirty. Need backup? You look like you could use backup."

The girl ignores her teacher, instead tapping at her wrist.

"Vero?"

"Not yet," she says, groaning, breathless. "There's seriously something weird—"

"Seb?" the teacher says.

"You got it, Teach!"

"I told you two not to call me Teach out here."

"Right, you got it, Jace!"

"Don't use my first name either!"

The other kid with Reiki hands flicks his wrists, and before I can even blink, he's dual wielding a set of automatic pistols.

Like, what? Pistols? Where in the hell had those come from?

I jump to the side, narrowly avoiding a stream of bullets. Two things cross my mind—one, how are those pistols shooting *streams* of bullets? Two, how am I able to see the streams, let alone dodge them? It looks as though they're cutting through water, leaving a tunnel of air behind them. Is everyone able to see like this, or has my vision somehow been enhanced along with my speed?

Whatever. I'm using these new superpowers to my advantage and taking this guy out. Both he and that Vero girl are fast, but I guess I'm faster? I run circles around the gun-wielding nut, just staying ahead of the bullets as I narrow in on him in a spiral. Almost there. Just a little closer.

And...

Oh, no. Out of the corner of my eye, I see Vero headed my way, giant-ass katana cocked and ready for blood. That's not fair. I can barely fight one of these guys, let alone both at once. I flinch as she closes the gap between us and brings the blade down on my head.

Clang!

No, that's not the sound of my head, but for the briefest of moments, I'm dumb enough to think it is. Maybe this void has made my head as thick as granite and as loud as steel?

When my eyes open, I see another sword. This one is at least as long as the human-length katana, but much wider—about as wide as I am. The grip alone has to be two feet long, and the hilt a stylish and jagged mess, cascading outward like a misshapen star. At the center of the hilt is an orb the size of my head embedded, glowing an alluring sky blue.

The blade's shaft is jagged and threatening, the serrations enough to scare most enemies into submission on sight alone.

Oh, and did I mention that it's floating in the air, somehow preventing the katana from cutting into my beautiful skull? I jump back, away from the death blades and watch as my new best friend clatters to the marble floor—when had the floor turned to marble? I look across at my opponent. She's also frozen in place, obviously as bewildered as me about the rogue assailant.

After a quick shake of her head, she slashes her blade to the side, readying for another attack.

"Hold it!" A translucent shield materializes on the teacher's left arm, and he jumps between the sword and Vero.

"I told you," Vero says. "There's something off about her. I made physical contact and I still couldn't get a read on her actual level."

"Wait, shit," the kid with the Reiki hands—and let's not forget the pistols—says. One pistol is gone, and a hand outstretched in my direction. "It's not her."

"What do you mean, it's not her?" The teacher says, tensing up. "Then what have we been fighting? A Spirit?"

"Working on it!"

"Where's the Spectre?"

"Working on it!" Seb calls back, the other pistol vaporizing into thin air as he holds up the other hand, scanning the surrounding area with both arms outstretched.

"Okay," the teacher's attention falls back on to me. "You have five seconds to talk." A scimitar materializes in his right hand.

"I have no idea what you're talking about," I say. "You're the ones who attacked me!"

"Five."

"You've got the wrong girl!"

"Are you working with Hanajima?" Vero asks.

The teacher smiles. "That must be it."

"Who?"

"Hiro Hanajima," he says. "Walks around with his Spectral Companion in a bird. Don't play dumb. What other unsanctioned Mediums are out here?"

"You're all saying things like I'm supposed to know what you're talking about!"

"Four."

"Ah, shit," I'm fed up and exhausted. Just what in the hell do these people want from me? "I swear, I'm not who you think I am."

As if on cue, the giant friendly sword pops up into the air, and darts in my direction, hilt over tip, as though ready to slice through me. I want to dodge, but my instincts have other plans. Instead, I throw my hand in front of me, palm outstretched.

The grip lands in my hand, and my fingers wrap around it. I don't know how, but I've avoided getting sliced in half with what is apparently my sword.

Another thing to tick in the "bad" column is the fact that any hope I had of convincing these three morons that I'm not their enemy has evaporated into thin air.

The teacher stops counting, his face transitioning from confusion to anger, both in my direction. I'm not sure I like that.

Actually, I know for a fact I don't like it.

He nods his head, and in an instant, his whole attire changes. No longer just wearing an all-black special ops gear, he's covered in a layer of armored plates, though unlike the other two, this covers most of his body. Like everything else in his gear, it is a shade of black, and looks to be made of carbon fiber material.

But I don't have to admire his new getup, as he wordlessly runs in my direction, both shield and scimitar drawn. "Make sure the two of you stay clear," he calls out to his students. "This one could be dangerous."

Awww! Dangerous? Me? I've been called that before, but never regarding any physical threat I pose in one-on-one combat. My flattery has to wait, because the guy is already on me. Despite having this enormous sword at my disposal, I have no godly idea how to use it, nor any desire to slice anyone in half with it. I do the only thing I can do, and dodge to the side as his scimitar comes down.

"Come on, wimp!" a voice calls out—a female voice at that. "If you're gonna use me, use me."

The teacher recovers and swings at me again. His scimitar connects with my oversized sword with a loud clang.

"Oh, yeah, that's better!" the voice says. "Now chop his head clean off."

"What?"

"Or impale him through the gut. I'm not picky."

As my sword crosses with the man, I glimpse the orb on the hilt. Hovering over it is a face—the same face that had pushed its way into Gabe's body. Only now, the face isn't elephant-sized. "Well?" it says.

I'm embarrassed to say it, but I drop the sword. Sorry, but talking heads on swords isn't normal for me, even when the sword is the only thing protecting me from certain death.

"Fine, you don't want to do it?" the sword says. "Then I will."

The giant broadsword then makes a clean cut toward the teacher, who blocks the blow with his own weapon. How did I end up rooting for the guy who wants to kill me? Whoever this sword is, I can sense its malevolence.

Panic runs through me as I see the teacher struggle to keep up with the floating blade. He won't be able to keep this up for long. It's only a matter of time before he's cut down.

If only there was something I could do. If only I could save him. And then the very ground of the void wraps around the man's legs, and I flinch as the blade cuts through his neck. Or at least, that's what should have happened. Instead, he falls straight through the ground, disappearing altogether.

"Teach!" the other two cry out. The blade wastes no time, making a beeline in their direction next. They may have just spent the last few minutes trying to kill me, but they don't seem terrible. Not like the sword does. The ground around the two students erodes, and like their teacher, they fall into nothingness.

I hear a frustrated groan. It somehow echoes throughout the entire void and in my head all at once.

The blade floats over to me—as blades do—face even more present, expanded to a human-sized head. "Why? Why'd ya do that?"

"I...I don't know," I respond, still baffled that I'm talking to a floating humanoid head. I say humanoid because while it does somewhat resemble a person's face, there's something otherworldly and alien about it. The face groans in unveiled frustration, sounding almost like a child who didn't get what she wanted.

And then, I'm falling again. This sensation I recognize. It's the same feeling I've experienced twice over the past several hours, and like a cat, I work to set my feet downward. It works, and my feet settle onto the carpeted floor of the apartment hallway we'd been spirited away from.

Less gracefully, Gabe's body crashes next to me, creating a hole in the aging drywall.

I look up, seeing the rip in the void close, the mysterious spectral face looking back on me as it does. I notice an odd look in her expression: a look of resentment.

As our eyes lock, one thing becomes clear to me. This is it. This is the thing I'd spent my entire life fearing. I sense it in the emotion that rises inside me as I peer into its soul. Like a window to an unfriendly but somehow welcome place. A feeling not unlike visiting home after several months.

I want to cry back out at the face. To ask it why, and not just why, but how? But the rip closes, and with it, my connection to the being. But as has been proven twice over, this is a door I could open again. Maybe not at will, but through some other means. Duress.

My attention settles back on Gabe, who writhes in a puddle of his own vomit, still groaning from the shock and the trauma.

I don't help him to his feet, and I don't ask if he's okay.

"Gabe!" a cry calls from across the hallway. Marco had just rounded the corner, no doubt shocked at the odd spectacle that was the five-foot-nothing Luna having just smashed his boss through the drywall of a shitty apartment building.

The other goon is close behind, and before I can even speak, both have handguns locked on me.

I want to run to the side and close in on them in the blink of an eye, like I'd done back in the void, but even I know that whatever abilities those were are gone here in the real world. The same spryness I'd experienced there feels as though it's been closed off along with the giant ghostly face.

Still, I can't find it in me to recoil. Being killed by people as common as them doesn't seem threatening to me in this moment. Instead, I stare back at them, eyes unblinking, unafraid. I stand between them and Gabe. I know they won't shoot.

"You'll honor the agreement we made six months back," I say. "You'll sell my dad the same cocktail as before, undiluted, unaltered, and at the original agreed upon price."

"Give me a break, Luna," Marco says. "We can't promise that."

"Yes, we can." Gabe's voice is weak but clear behind me.

I turn to see him struggling to stand, his metal hand clutching his left shoulder. His chest heaves with soft, steady breaths, and the side of his mouth is caked with remnants of vomit.

"But, Gabe—"

"Did you hear what I said, Marco? I said we can."

"What about—"

"I'm sorry," Gabe said, nostrils flaring. "Did you just question me?"

"No, I—"

"It sounds a hell of a lot like you're questionin' me."

"It's just—"

Like a feral cat, Gabe is on Marco. His metal hand connects with the goon's nose, emitting a sickening sound of metal on flesh. But Gabe doesn't stop there. He mounts the bigger goon and unloads blow after blow on his face, each successive hit opening up a different part of his face. An entire lifetime of unfettered anger is released onto one poor soul in a brief thirty-second moment.

When he is done, Gabe is breathing heavier than before, exhausted, still weak, but satisfied, the knuckles of his metallic hand protruding through his glove, chunks of flesh hanging off the sharp joints.

Marco's face is completely caved in, ground into a mushy pulp. The other remaining goon stares on, eyes wide and confused. Does he shoot Gabe, shoot me, or fall in line? His weapon falls to his side as he chooses the latter of the three options.

And then I realize why Gabe had done it. After what had just happened, he needed to do something to protect his reputation.

He turns back to face me, flecks of blood splattered across his face. There's an animalistic nature to his expression, but buried beneath, I can sense traces of fear.

He won't look me in the eyes. He won't lay a finger on me.

Whether it's because I saved him in the void or because he's afraid, I don't know, but it's one less problem for me to worry about.

Without another word, Gabe and his remaining lackey walk down the hallway through the door to the stairwell.

I watch in silent shock as the blood bubbles forming around Marco's nose slow and his chest stops rising. There's no ambulance where we live, no law enforcement, and no goodwill of anyone to help save him.

On this day, Marco will be just another casualty of the cruel existence we live in. A casualty who will go unnoticed until his remains start to smell and bother the tenants.

If history has taught me anything, around this time next week, a fed up group of neighbors will carry his body to the border of Skid Row and toss it to one of the android sentries. They'll pick it up and, after ensuring there isn't a pulse, they'll carry it over to the more civilized side of the gate, where standard trash days and rule of law apply.

I don't cry, but I do mourn the kid. He's a reminder of what I don't want to become. Another statistic in the city.

TWO

I WALK the streets of Skid Row in a daze. It's still not quite light out, but sunrise is rapidly approaching. My mind is stuck on the image of Marco's dead body in that apartment complex—on the too-long moments it took to carry him into the stairwell, just so the boy in Apartment 4C didn't have to see it. He doesn't deserve that. No one deserves that.

Step. The image of Gabe beating Marco down, metallic fist red and dripping. *Step.* His bloodied and battered face, struggling to breathe through the swelling and the blood. *Step.* His chest rising a final time before stilling altogether.

I only just knew the guy, but no one joins Gabe's gang just to stick around Skid Row. I'm sure he had dreams of getting an itinerary to leave its confines. Just like me. And the last interaction I had with him was me flipping him off, taunting him like a child. I cross my arms, hugging myself tight as I walk. Who knew I'd live to regret something so trivial?

I hardly notice a catcall from a nearby tent. My usual instinct to flip off the whistler is suppressed by that regret. No one here knows what just happened. I don't think anyone would care if I told them.

This is life in Skid Row. You can be healthy and full of ambition one second, and gone the next, no one being the wiser, and no one caring. It was like a glimpse into my future.

I could be dead tomorrow, and no one, least of all my dad, would notice. Would care. What's the point of struggling if this was the inevitable outcome?

I almost don't care to solve the mystery of the dangerous face. Instead, I want to melt into the grime-ridden sidewalk, away from this world.

Still, my feet move on their own. Back to the Main Stay. Back to my home and the only family I have.

I reach into my pocket and pull out my netscreen. There are thirty missed calls. Six of them are from a number I don't recognize. Probably Detective Chu or the police calling to ask if I wanna come back in for questioning? Yeah, right. Not anymore.

The remaining calls are from Damien. A flicker of excitement emerges from within me, only to be batted down by reality. He's a nice enough guy, but I already know where this is headed. From the instant he and Lily signed those docs, I knew I'd walk these streets again. I don't even want to listen to the—geez, seven?—voicemails. That's too many voicemails, Damien. And, ew, they aren't even voicemails, they're *vizmails*. I knew he was old, but no one uses those anymore.

I take in my surroundings. Few people are out, and they aren't paying me any mind. I flick a bud from my netscreen and place it in my ear. When I tap play, a bust of Damien hovers over the mini tablet—or rather a section of his body from his chest to the bridge of his nose. God, he's so old.

"Hi, Luna," he says. "Just checking in to see how you're doing. I'm not getting any answers here at the station other than that you're on the run again. I don't know what to think."

"'This isn't going to work out,'" I say under my breath. It was a tried-and-true line I'd heard many times in the past.

"I just hope you're okay. Lily and I both want to know you're okay. You don't have to tell us where you are or why you did what you did, but just let us know you're okay. Love ya, Kid."

The partial bust disappears, and I skip to the next one, which features a slightly more lined up image, with most of his face now hovering over my netscreen.

"Me again. Can't get a hold of the detective, but if I'm going to believe the buzz and chatter around the station here, it sounds like you broke out of the building with a battering ram or some impossibility? I dunno. I'd like to think I spent a good amount of time with you, and I hope you don't mind me saying, but I have doubts you could lift a donut, let alone a battering ram. Mark me suspicious here. Just wanna let you know *not* to come back to the station. Not until we figure this out and talk to our lawyer. Can't wait to see you again. Stay safe."

I skip to the next one. Each message is more of the same. A bit of an update on what's happening with the police, a warning, and a well wish, all in various forms of visual disarray. I don't know how someone can so horrifically not keep themselves in frame over the course of a thirty-second vizmail.

I skip to the last one, which features Damien smiling. "Enough of the silent act. Let us know you're safe. You know what? I'm coming to visit. See you soon."

Wait. Coming to visit? What did he mean coming to visit? As if on cue, I realize I've just turned onto Main Street, and can see the prominent marquee that hangs at the base of the complex. And below it, the figure of an out-of-place Damien. He stands, hands shoved in his pockets, unsure of what to do while loitering at the heart of America's dumping zone. Should he act casual or on high alert? He wasn't succeeding at either.

"God, I hope you didn't park nearby," I say as I approach.

His body tenses up upon first hearing my voice, but his shoulders slacken the second he sees me approaching. A bright smile lights up his face. How can he smile like that after all that's happened?

"Uh, actually, I parked around Little Tokyo."

"You walked a mile through all this just to get here?"

"And I've only been threatened sixteen times." Damien laughs, but it's coated with a nervous edge. I'm surprised he's made it this far with his shoes still on his feet.

"Still a fifty-fifty chance your tires'll be gone when you get back."

His nervous laugh extends an extra few seconds, but when I don't join, his laugh fades. "Oh, okay, then."

"How'd you get an itinerary?"

"I hope this doesn't come across as insensitive, but the gates are meant to keep people in, not out."

"Huh," I say. That thought never crossed my mind.

"He's here again!" a cry from behind Damien yells out. "The man with the crow and the top hat!"

"The man with the what?" Damien asks.

"He's harmless," I say. I lean in closer to Damien. "And a little paranoid."

"You ain't a damn hero!" Hank yells to no one in particular.

"Right," Damien says.

"It's okay, Hank," I say to the homeless man. "It's just Damien." I talk to him as if he's supposed to know who Damien is. I hope my tone will at least comfort him.

It seems to do the trick, as Hank nods and sits down on the sidewalk, his back against the boarded-up main entrance to the building.

"How'd you find me?" I say, instantly regretting the question, as I already know the answer.

"You know, this was the address on file for your father," Damien says.

"And it's no secret that you have a tendency to find your way back here in between homes."

If there's anything in this world I hate, it's being predictable. Predictability means you're easy to manipulate, and therefore, a target. I know this, and yet, even *I* can't fight my instinct to return to square one whenever my world falls apart.

"I guess I'm gonna have to find somewhere else to go the next time I burn my life to the ground."

"Please don't," Damien says. "Please don't burn things to the ground anymore—uh, if that's even something you ever did." He added that last part frantically. "But also, don't go somewhere else. I know I'll feel better at least knowing where you'll end up, even when things turn bad."

"What's your deal?" I can't help but say. "Who in their right mind acts like you? Who in their right mind adopts someone at age seventeen? What's going on? I've read stories, you know. About sickos who take in minors so they can take advantage of them and marry them the next year."

"Luna!"

I don't know why I said that. Being a girl in the adoption system, you learn to be careful. But there's a difference between being careful and outright saying what I'd just said. "Sorry. It's…why adopt me now? I'm so old. In six months, I'm legally on my own."

"Lily and I," Damien says, "know you've been on your own for years now already. Most of your life."

The comment stings a bit, I have to admit. It's true, but feels different coming from someone else.

"And that's all the more reason we wanted to take you in," he continues. "You've been given a bad hand. You've had to make do with very little. The first time most people feel that is when they're legal adults."

"So?"

"So we want to be there for you—beyond your last year of adolescence. We want to be around for you for the rest of our lives. We can't change the past, but at the very least, we can help make your future easier."

"Ew," I say before I can stop myself. I can't help it. He'd just had his house burned down, his adopted daughter on the run for the crime, and he's still here, talking this sappy bullshit.

"Yeah, it sounds cheesy," he says.

"How's Lily?" I ask.

"Still freaking out. Can you blame her?"

"You're not freaking out."

"Oh, don't let this exterior fool you, Luna. I am a massive ball of anxiety right now," Damien admits. "I think it's some unwritten rule that if one person in a couple is a complete mess, the other has to make up for it being the most levelheaded human in existence. I guess I'm up. But she's not mad at you. Freaking out, ashamed, but not mad.

"Ashamed?" I say. "Why?"

"She blames herself. Thinks we weren't there for you."

"So she does think I burned it down," I say. I don't know why, but that simple fact hurts more than I want to give it credit for.

"Don't hold it against her. She just wants you to be happy. Comfortable and happy."

"Trust me. I want nothing more than to be comfortable and happy, too. Contrary to what old people say, our generation doesn't go around actively trying to make life more difficult for ourselves."

"I know." Damien's tone is soft. Soothing. "Look, I want you to come back home."

"I am home," I say, a little too forcefully. "And besides, your home's been burned to the ground, hasn't it?"

"Only partially, and you know what I mean," Damien says. "And yes, no matter what happens, nothing will change the fact that your home will forever be here at the Main Stay."

"This place is a shithole," I say.

Damien sighs, exhausted.

Why is it so hard for me to have a genuine conversation?

"I just want to help," he says. "Can you at least tell me about your disappearing act at the station? No one's said anything to me. I heard some commotion, and the next thing I knew, you were gone. So, what happened?"

I bite my lip. It would be hard enough to have this conversation as it is, but it's much harder given the circumstances.

"Hey," he says. "I'm not gonna rat on you. Besides, they don't have any jurisdiction here, remember?"

How do you tell someone that you've been teleporting through some inexplicable void that features your most horrifying memories playing in a loop?

"I can't explain."

"Rumors are spreading that you fought your way out of the station."

"Of course they are. Do I sound cool in those rumors?"

"Very cool. And it's incredibly embarrassing for the LAPD to have been beaten down by some teenage girl, but even the police haven't disputed those initial rumored reports." He pauses, waiting for me to say something. Anything.

"I can't explain what happened at the station," I say.

"What do you mean you can't explain? Did you or did you not fight your way out?"

"Of course I didn't! Have you seen me?"

"Then what happened?"

I want to say that the actual explanation would make me look crazy. That somehow the truth would make him think less of me than if I had just pummeled my way through the brick walls of the station.

Instead, I say, "I need you to trust me."

Damien stares back at me, a neutral expression on his face.

"I... have some stuff to figure out. Not sure if you caught that side of me. It's a constant. And it's exhausting. Kinda like me."

"How can I help?"

"You can't."

Damien swallows, a nervous tic I've noticed in my short time living with him. "Fine. Just don't go radio silent on us. Check-ins at least once every twenty-four hours. Got it?"

"You got it." I smile despite myself.

"And if you're caught by the police, you have my netscreen number. We're staying at Lily's parents' home in Beverly Hills Beach. And can you do me a favor?"

"Sure?"

"Let me know when you figure things out. I don't want to run into you on the street, only to find out you've solved whatever problem this is without letting your family know."

I smile. "You got it." For once in my life, I mean it. "I promise I'll call you."

"And even if you just need help. Lily and I can give you a hand. We won't snitch. Promise."

"Fine. Even if I need help. Just promise me one thing. Don't leave me anymore vizmails. It's embarrassing, and not just for you. And don't say snitch again. You also said rat earlier. Don't say rat either."

Damien laughs and turns to leave, only to stop and look back at me. "I never thought I'd be on the other side. Growing up, I wasn't the greatest kid—not that you're a bad daughter!"

I smile at his fluster.

"But it's weird knowing this is how they probably felt all those nights that I didn't come home. You just feel so...helpless. Lily and I took you in so we can help you, and with everything that's going on, all we can do is..."

"Trust me?"

He shrugs. "I'll need to put my money where my mouth is on that one. Good luck, Kiddo. And check your account. I put some spare cash in there. If you need more, just say the word." With a last wave, he makes his way up Main Street.

I blink away a rogue tear that had threatened to give me away. I like Damien, but even I don't want him to know this is the most wanted anyone has ever made me feel. Not twenty minutes ago, I was ready to close the book on any ambition for a normal life.

Against all odds, I now find myself...wanting to go back to that life with the moron and his just-as-dumb wife. To live in that house with a family that, for some reason, actually wants me.

I sigh. In order to do that, I need to figure out whatever this crap is—this Entity that's been following me; these voids that keep sucking me up and spitting me out.

I need to get to the bottom of this mystery and reclaim my life.

And, for once, I feel like it's possible.

THREE

"WHAT DID YOU DO?" Dad asks as I enter our apartment.

"Huh?"

"What did you do?" he repeats.

I narrow my eyes, unsure what in the godly hell he can be talking about.

"Nothing?" I say it as a question. I'm not sure if it's a lie just yet.

"Nothing?" He holds up a leather bag. This one doesn't share the textbook crust and peeling of his old one. "I get a brand-new supply and you tell me it's nothing?"

"Oh, right," I say. "I had a word with Gabe. He apologizes and says he shouldn't have switched up your muze cocktail. You're welcome."

Dad's face forms an unreadable expression. Somewhere in there is relief, but it's clouded by something else.

"What?" I say, knowing I won't like what I hear.

"It's just that...this cocktail means I can't take more hits."

I sigh. "You know the other stuff would kill you, right?"

"This stuff'll kill me, anyway."

"Well, forgive me for wanting to see you live a little longer!"

Dad growls in annoyance, but says nothing. He can be a real baby sometimes.

"Hey," he says, his tone shifting into soft territory. "What happened to you?"

"What do you mean?"

He motions to my face. For the first time, I remember that beatdown from Gabe. He had smacked my face into the wall and onto the ground. I touch it for the first time, feeling a tender scrape on my cheekbone.

In retrospect, I'm surprised Damien hadn't mentioned it, but with everything else going on, he probably didn't want to come across as overbearing.

"It's nothing," I say.

"How stupid do you think I am?"

"I don't know. What time of day is it? How long has it been since your last hit?"

"Jesus, Estrella."

"It's Luna! If you're gonna fawn over me, at least get my name right!"

"Fine. Luna. No matter what your name is, I want to make sure you're okay."

"Are you kidding? I have a name. I've had it my whole life. Could you just get it right once?"

"Don't change the subject."

"We're on the subject of my name."

"We're talking about that scrape on your face."

"You don't get to worry about me if you can't even get my name right!"

"I'm allowed to worry about my daughter." For once, the slightest bit of passion bleeds into his tone.

I glare at him for several seconds before turning away. "Do me a favor and try not to OD while I'm gone. No crawling back to Gabe for another cocktail. You don't have the money." In fact, I should pay Gabe a visit and tell him not to do anything Dad says. He'd listen to me, too.

"And where are you going?"

"Out." The truth is, I don't know. After talking with Damien, I'd gotten all fired up about confronting this Entity and putting an end to my lifelong troubles, but the reality is I don't know the first thing about where to go next. All I know is I won't be making any progress wasting any time with Dad.

"I'm sorry," he says.

I turn to face him. He never apologizes.

"I'm sorry you have to deal with me."

I stare back at him. He sits cross-legged on the bed, pants still loose and unbuttoned at the top, slipping down his slight frame. His eyes are cast toward the floor.

"And," he continues, "I'm sorry that I keep getting your name wrong."

"You'd think seventeen years of life would allow me my own name."

"It's just that..."

"Yeah, I know. You and mom argued over what to name me. Sorry I didn't end up with your pick. Most people get over it. But don't worry, Dad. Once I figure this whole thing out, I'll be out of your life. It turns out I have someone who wants me. And get this, they remember my name."

"Don't take it like that, sweetheart."

"Do *not* call me sweetheart!" My voice cracks as I yell, and it may be the single most embarrassing moment of my life. "You don't get to call me that. You don't get to call me sweetie, either, and I'll never call you Papa. We're past that ever being a possibility."

"You do *not* speak to your father that way!" Somehow, his voice booms. Despite his scant figure and sunken cheeks, he commands a formidable figure. "I don't care how mad you are at me, but you don't speak to me in that way. I raised you better than that."

"You didn't raise me at all. Mom did. And after that? Try every foster home in L.A. County. You couldn't take care of a goldfish, you muzed-out deadbeat!"

I see his hand before it lands, but can't avoid it. It connects with my right cheek, right where my scrape sits.

The tears fill my eyes before I can stop them, though not from any pain from his weak hit. I knew this was where the conversation was headed. I often goad my dad into these moments to get him riled up. To get him to act like a dad for once. Hitting me is about the only thing he's ever done that's been remotely paternal. And while I'd egged him on to this moment, his slap against my cheek isn't as cathartic as I'd expected. It hurts more than I want it to. Not physically—my dad's as weak as they come—but it's as though his single acts of paternal instincts have lost all power.

He stands, panting after one underpowered slap aimed against a smaller figure. I've never respected him in my life, but I don't think I've ever seen him look so pathetic. Suddenly, I'm angry over something he's done ten times over. A simple thought: who hits their daughter?

And an even more shocking realization. That I deserve better than this.

He's no father of mine.

How had it taken me so long to realize that?

"Fine," I say. Usually, I'd argue—tell him I'll say whatever I want. But he's not worth the breath. I pull a keycard from the drawer and sync its code with my netscreen before shoving the card back into the mess of underwear. "Lock the fucking door."

I shut it behind me.

THE CRISP MORNING air gives way to its first semblance of heat when I step out of the apartment building.

Now what do I do? I can't come crawling back to that place again. At least not so soon. I throw open my netscreen. Damien said he put some money in my account. I wonder if it's enough to…

My eyes widen at the figure now sitting in my bank account. That's a lot of zeroes. Too many zeroes. It has to be a mistake.

I knew he was well off, but why would he give me so much? I could live for the next year by myself with that money. Is that his plan? Is this just another way for him to get rid of me?

I shake the thought from my brain. No. He and Lily both adopted me for a reason. I deserve more than what I have. I deserve more.

"That crazy fool's back again!" Hank's scream brings me back to reality.

"The crow man?" I say, half-listening.

"I keep tellin' him he ain't no hero!"

"What does that even…" And then it hits me. My mind flashes back to the fight I had in the void. No, those weirdoes called it a Mirage.

"Are you working with Hanajima?"

"Hiro Hanajima," the teacher had said. *"Walks around with his Spectral Companion in a bird. Don't play dumb."*

It couldn't be that easy, could it?

I keep my eyes pointed forward. "Where is he, Hank?"

"Huh?"

"The crow top hat man. Hiro."

"Why's this guy claiming to be some hero?" Hank says, as if offended by this claim.

"Focus, Hank. Where is he?"

Hank sits back against the wall, as if exasperated by the idea of the mysterious man.

"Where is he, Hank?" I say, my voice barely above a whisper.

He looks back up at me, his eyes almost pleading. "You believe me?"

I blink in response. Normally, no. More than half of what the man says is utter nonsense. But after everything I've been through, I'm not so sure. Maybe I've been the crazy one. "I do," I answer.

He points down the road toward Seventh Street. "He's around the corner. Thinks just because there's a wall in the way I can't see that damn crow." His finger points up on an overhang where a large black crow stands.

Hang on…is that crow wearing a top hat? I didn't realize it was the *crow* who wore the top hat.

"Stop pointing," I say.

"Girl, no one gives a shit what I do," he says just as the crow in the top hat takes flight, rounding the corner.

"Son of a…" I take chase down the street, passing several tents and turning the corner. I expect the bird to have disappeared, but I see it land on the shoulder of a man standing outside an alley. The brief glimpse I catch of his face shows Asian features, and scrappy stubble peppers his chin. He catches my eyes for the briefest of moments and hobbles—yes, hobbles—down it. Hobbling I can deal with.

I increase my speed and turn into the alley, almost too fast to notice the cane being swung at my face. I duck, feeling the wind graze my hair. I slide to the ground and whip around. My shoes grip the pavement and I launch myself at the wispy figure of a man in front of me.

"Oh, shit!" he cries out before I crash into him. He goes down without a struggle. In fact, his body is so slight, it's as though he's actively assisting me in tackling himself to the ground. Suddenly, I'm worried his bones will shatter as soon as they slam into the cement.

Thankfully, the man isn't made of porcelain. Yes, he does hit the ground, but he doesn't shatter. Instead, he struggles, trying to shake me off, but to no avail. Even at his taller height, he doesn't have the strength. Would it even have hurt if he'd hit me with that cane of his?

"What're you doing?" he says, a soft indistinguishable accent coats his question.

"What're *you* doing?" I say, flipping him over and twisting his arms behind his back. If he's resisting, I can't tell.

"Caw! Caw!" The crow swoops down, missing my head as I dodge to the side.

"Don't make me hit a bird in a top hat, 'cause I will!"

"Kuro, it's fine," the man calls up to the bird.

Kuro the crow settles on a lamp above us and squawks in my direction.

"Why're you following me?" I say.

"I'm sorry, but who tackled who here?"

"I'm not the one with the creepy spy bird. Hang on, is he wearing a tie, too?"

Yup, the crow's wearing a white tie with a single black stripe in the middle, cutting the tie horizontally. How had it taken me so long to notice this thing?

"So," the man says, "the government's now using kids to take down their marks. Is that it? It's bad enough you're fighting Spectres."

"What?" I say. "Government?" Against all logic, I press him harder against the ground.

Kuro squawks.

"What're you talking about? What's the government got to do with this?"

"Don't play stupid with me, Kid," he says with a scoff. "I saw you in there with them."

"Where with who?"

The man chuckles. "You're kidding."

"Oh, my God. Do you wanna go around in circles again or just tell me what you're talking about?"

"I saw them enter the traveling Mirage with you," he says. "Or is that just one big coincidence? Are you just a new recruit, or is it something else?"

My mouth opens and closes, but no sound comes out.

"You have no idea, do you? Did those clowns teach you nothing?"

"Those clowns tried to kill me."

For the first time since tackling him, the man's look shifts from pure confusion to a knowing smirk. "Oh, this is good. That explains it. You're a *target*."

I don't understand most what he's saying, but I can tell that the last part is one hundred percent true. I only nod.

"That explains it. Let me up."

I press him harder into the ground. The crow squawks from above. "Hey, not so fast! You still haven't explained why you're following me."

"I wasn't following you. I was following your Mirage signal. It's what us Mediums do. We find Mirages, enter them, take out the Spectres that cause them, and make the world a safer place. But as of early this morning, I started feeling one that was hopping all over the place. In some Burbank neighborhood, near downtown, in the middle of Skid Row."

"What, are you saying I'm a Spectre now? That's what the others thought." I say. "Sorry to spoil it for you, Bud, but I met the Spectre in that Mirage, and it ain't me."

"It may not be you, but it is *linked* to you." He pauses for several long seconds, as if waiting for some reaction. When I give him nothing, he continues. "Can you please let me up?"

"If you try to run again, I'll break your legs."

"Jesus, Girl!"

"And don't call me Girl."

"All right," he says, "And I won't run."

I climb off of him, and he lets out a deep sigh. He stands and wipes off his loose tee-shirt and cargo shorts. He climbs to his feet, which I find are standing in a pair of wooden clogs. What country is this? What *century* is this?

"So, what's your deal?" I say. "Are you one of them?"

"One of those government dogs? No. I run a decidedly more selfish enterprise. Though you may consider this the luckiest day of your life."

"I doubt that."

"Let me guess. You've been a victim of random occurrences for as long as you can remember? Things you can't explain? Things that endanger your life and the lives of those around you?"

I stare into his eyes. The stuff he's saying is outrageous, but I don't get the sense that he's lying to me.

His smirk deepens. "And you're faced with a problem. A spiritual entity that shadows your every step. You don't have a clue when or how it will strike, but when it does, it leaves chaos in your wake. OooOOoo!" He holds out his hand and shakes it, as though imitating a ghost.

I suppress the urge to react—the urge to cry out in agreement or just cry altogether. "How do I know you're not lying?"

The man throws his hands up in exasperation. "If I was looking to rip you off, I've just made the absolute worst pitch imaginable. Who in their right mind would believe me?"

"You're in L.A., Man. This was a city built on crazy."

"Enough deflecting," he says. "I can see that look in your eyes. You're tormented and afraid. You don't have the foggiest what to do with your life. You want to get rid of this Spectre? Well, I can help you do just that."

FOUR

I BLINK in disbelief at the strange man in front of me. How much muze had he consumed that he'd think I'd just fall in step with whatever plan he had for me?

"I'm sorry, but who did you say you are again?"

He greets me with a smile. "I'd be skeptical, too, if I were you."

"You think? It's not every day that someone comes along and says, 'Hey, you know that incredibly specific problem you've been having? Well, I'm coming out of the blue when you need me most and offering an unlikely solution to your problem.' Yeah, sorry, but there's no way I'm that lucky."

"Luck's the last word I'd use," he says. "You've already had a run-in with the government dogs. That means they've noticed you. When you first opened your Mirage, you sent out a beacon to a world you never knew existed. In an instant, you became a target of the Department of Spectral Defense."

"The what?"

"It's a government entity that was created fifteen years ago. It's a long story, and even they don't understand everything."

"No, but I'm sure they understand more than me," I say, letting the comment linger in the air. "That means I want more information," I say when he doesn't get the hint.

"How far back do you want me to go?"

"How far back do you need to go for me to understand?"

The man sighs and leans on his cane. He may as well be sitting for as much weight as he's placing on it. "In the years that followed the Second Civil War—"

"Oh, shit, you're going way back," I spout out.

He blinks in annoyance and clears his throat. Point taken, Diva. "Following the Second Civil War, there was an uptick in malicious activity in certain areas all over the world, including the U.S. After a few key incidents, they only had one conclusion: that Ghosts were real, and we had to fight them off."

"Or what?"

"Have you seen what a Spectre can do to an unsuspecting victim?"

Gabe's demented face flashes in front of my eyes—his body contorting as the Spectre seemed to eat him from the inside out. "Yeah…" My voice is soft.

"Many missing persons cases can be attributed to them being swallowed up by a Mirage and eaten alive, their soul being used to keep the Ghost—or Spectre, as they're called—alive and rampant."

"And these Mirages?"

"I don't know how else to explain it other than to call it a pocket universe. It's where the Spectre and its familiars—or Spirits—reside, often reliving its most traumatic experiences. It builds up its fear, anger, and resentment—whatever emotion that led to their being trapped in our plane of existence. Eventually, it spills out into the real world, capturing unsuspecting victims."

"What does this have to do with me?"

"It has to do with you insofar that you have the potential for a Spectral Companion. There is something linking you to this Spectre, and it has the potential to form an even stronger Bond with you."

My mind has already wandered off into space. I don't know what this guy's saying anymore, or why I'm even listening. So all I can ask is, "Why?"

The man shrugs. "I don't have the slightest idea how you've spent your life. I don't know who you've slighted, who you've impacted, who you've *killed*, but whoever this Spectre is is linked to you. That makes you both dangerous and useful."

"You said you can solve my problem. What did you mean?"

He smiles. "Do you want to find out? You've already proven you can fold me like a lawn chair, so I can only do this if you agree to it."

"Agree to what?"

"I can help you understand who this Spectre is, and I can help you get rid of it forever."

"Cut the crap and the snake oil salesman routine," I say. "What're you asking?"

"I'm asking if you'll venture back into the Mirage with me. Once you solidify the link between you and your Spectre, we can find a way to free you from its clutches."

"And what does that mean?"

"You will make that Spectre your Companion. You will make it stronger. And when it's strong enough, I will help you free her, eliminating her from your life forever."

"But how…"

"Do you really want to ask a million questions now?"

"Yes, I do."

"You'll understand much better once you have her under your control. How about this? We can finalize this whole thing after this first part is taken care of."

Every ounce of my being tells me to run. It's too easy, too convenient, too lucky. But then he said the magic words: that he can help me get rid of it forever. He gets rid of it, and I head back home with Lily and Damien, far, far away from the Main Stay and even farther away from the prying eyes of Detective Chu.

"So, what do you say?" he starts. "Do we have a deal…uh…sorry, what's your name?"

"Luna Guerrera," I say before I can stop myself.

"Hiro Hanajima," he says. "Well?" He holds out his hand.

With an uneasy breath, I take his thin, bony hand and shake.

"Squawk!" The crow cries and descends on me before I can stop it. I recoil, pulling back at our handshake, but not quickly enough to escape its beak, which snaps at the top of my head, ripping a few strands of hair free.

I swipe at the bird, only to catch air. "What's the big idea?"

"Sorry, but I figured that would be the most effective way to open up your Mirage."

"Why would it…?" I look around and notice we're no longer in that narrow alley in Skid Row. The openness of the Mirage is almost overwhelming, but at this point, familiar. Colors dance around us in a kaleidoscope of light. Were it not for the impending sense of doom that came with this place, I'd almost consider it beautiful…in an avant-garde art show kind of way.

"Huh," Hiro says.

"Huh, what?"

His eyes land on one of the countless screens surrounding us. "These memories look unquestionably linked to you."

"I thought you said that was normal."

He laughs. "Oh, no. Nothing about what's happening can be classified as normal. I've only known a handful of others in my lifetime who have anything close to this. But your link is even stronger than most. In most cases, the memories linked to the Mirage are that of the Spectre, not of the Medium."

"Can you still help me?"

Hiro waves his hand in front of him. "Relax. I always keep my word. Now, the only thing that's missing is—"

Any further conversation is interrupted by a howl. I've heard this howl enough to know what's coming next. A giant translucent face smashes through one of the screens and heads for us.

"Ah, speak of the devil," he says, planting his feet in the ground. "Kuro?"

The crow that had just snagged a strand of hair from my scalp lets out a loud caw and takes to the air.

"Sorry, Kuro," the man says. "No meal for today."

The crow lets out another caw, which I take as one of disappointment.

"No, I'm not feeling great, but I can take on this Zero-Level Spectre."

With a few flaps of his wings, Kuro flashes a bright crimson before turning into a pair of batons that the mysterious stranger snatches out of the air. Upon closer inspection, they aren't your standard set of clubs, but sport sharp, glowing edges.

Perhaps noticing the confusion on my face, the man says. "Kuro here is my Spectral Companion. Unlike government Mediums, our abilities originate from a Spectre that's linked to us."

"I still don't know what any of that means."

He holds up one finger and sprints full-on at the Entity making a beeline toward us. "Hang tight."

Spinning one of his bladed batons, he darts forward, swinging his weapon and running it straight *through* the Spectre. At first I think his attack is ineffective, but then the Spectre floats to the charcoal-ridden ground, letting out a high-pitched scream.

"What I mean," he continues, already out of breath, "is that you share a special connection with this Spectre, just as I share one with Kuro here."

"What kind of special connection?"

His shoulders slump. "You mean you don't know who this person is? It's not some loved one haunting you? That's how people like you and I are created. And it gives us an edge. Allows us abilities your standard government dog Mediums could only dream of. Instead, they store the Essences of their Spectres after they've been killed and use them to grant inhuman strength within Mirages."

"You're still talking like I know what any of that means," I say, staring at the giant floating head that somehow writhes on the ground. I drag my eyes over its features. As threatening as she looks, she had saved me in the past from the others…the dirty cops who tortured me, the government Mediums who'd tried to kill me. And then there's Detective Chu…I squint at her face, noticing some familiar features.

"Mom?"

The man smiles. "Ah, so we are getting somewhere. A loving mother, is it? Well, I wouldn't waste too much time trying to connect with her. At least not now. Most Spectres are—forgive the pun—ghosts of their formal selves, driven by grudges, hate, love, or other unfinished business. They run on pure emotional instinct. I'd compare her to a violent mama bear. She won't give you the time of day, but the second you're in danger, her instincts will drive her to do unspeakable things."

My mind flashes back to that initial fight with those Mediums. In my moment of need, she transformed into a blade that helped me fight them off. Then again, she did get upset when I refused to kill them.

"Okay," I say. "So, what do we do now?"

He tosses me a metallic armband, and I snatch it out of the air.

"What's this?" I look it over, noticing a gem rising out of one end.

"That is called a Syncer. It's like what the government Mediums use, but with some necessary modifications. Snap that cuff on your non-dominant wrist. This is how we tame your wild beast of a mother."

"Your word choice is terrible." I snap the cuff around my left wrist. "Now what?"

"Now, the real battle begins." The man hobbles back over to the Spectre, whose daze has slowly started to subside. He gives it a few quick hits with his bladed batons, sending the giant face screaming and reeling back.

"Under most circumstances, the goal is to kill the Spectres, ensuring they don't create another Mirage and lure an unsuspecting victim ever again. It also frees their Spirits. But when it comes to you, you're given an extra advantage. Like Kuro with me, this Spectre will be your new partner. But in order to do this, you must earn her trust. I don't know what your relationship was with your mother, but this is key to you making her your partner."

He motions to the giant face, which hovers sideways on the ground, nearly lifeless. "She's weakened, so now is your chance."

"To do what?"

"To walk up to her and lay your hand on her. As you've noticed, this entire Mirage acts as a hall of memories for the deceased. In connecting with her physically, you can cement an emotional Bond between the two of you. This Bond connects you for the rest of your—or its—life."

I stare down at the creature laying in front of me. This is what Mom had become? How?

"Better do it before she gets up. If you take too long, I can't guarantee she won't snap at you. I may know what I'm doing here, but I'm not at my prime. Even your Spectre of a mother's taken a lot out of me." He punctuates that last part with a series of deep breaths.

Somehow, I don't think she'll snap at me. She may be little more than a feral animal with a malicious vibe, but she did protect me last time. Then again, she's also apparently responsible for every difficult moment in my life since her death. Maybe she *would* snap at me.

I walk up to the writhing head and do what the strange man tells me to, and regret it instantly. It's as though I've entered the Mirage for the first time all over again. So far, this has been the least painful experience I've had in this hall of memories. I assumed I'd just gotten used to it, and somehow grown immune to the pain of each moment I've had to relive. But these memories are floating back to me once again with renewed vigor. Now, I don't just feel what I felt at that moment. No, I feel something more.

"Well?" I can hear Hiro's echoing voice in the midst of me reliving all of my memories all at once.

"Well, what?" I say back, somehow finding room to feel annoyed despite the sheer number of emotions running through me.

"What do you feel?"

"Apart from confusion, anger, fear, indignance, helplessness, and pure hate?"

"Yes, yes, apart from all that. Don't act like you don't know what I mean."

I groan. "Did I mention annoyance?"

"You know what I mean," he says.

That's what is so annoying. I know exactly what he means. While I'm feeling countless emotions from countless moments all at once, there is one that stands out. One emotional through-line that separates itself from the rest.

"Protectiveness?" I think that's the emotion. The closest things I can think of are the feelings I get when seeing a stray cat or dog. Oh, or my dad, I guess, but somehow less so with him than the strays. The emotion doesn't quite match up with what I'm feeling, but I guess everyone feels emotions differently.

"Got it," he says. "Hang on to that emotion. Try to match it. This Spectre has a connection with you, and matching its emotion will strengthen that connection until it clicks into place."

"Sorry, how do I match an emotion?" I lose that protective feeling and in its place is another annoyed one. As if feeling it, the head writhes and cries out.

"Just…" Hiro scratches at his neck, his face contorting into a thoughtful expression. "What are you protective of?"

That's the thing. I don't know. I don't know if I've ever been protective of anything in my life. Not really. Even with my dad, the protection is more of an obligation than anything else.

I let out a frustrated growl.

"Whoa, there it is!" Hiro says. "Whatever you're doing, it's working!"

I feel no difference. "Are you sure?"

"Yes, just don't stop!"

Don't stop what? I latch on to whatever that feeling is. A sort of angry sadness mixed in with protectiveness. It's a pathetic cocktail of emotions, but as I lean into it, a ribbon of golden…electricity?…connects us. "What's happening?"

"Right now, we're dealing with a Zero-Level Spectre. It has a tenuous connection to its past, but not much. It's like taming a wild stallion. Match its emotion and make it bend to your will."

"Is that how you tame a stallion?"

"Why would I know how to tame a stallion? Don't lose your connection!"

I focus in on the emotion, and after a few seconds, I feel our connection strengthen. It's as though I'm being pulled by a magnetic force. "What's happening?"

"Don't stop! And when you get closer, *punch* the Spectre!"

"What?"

"She'll serve as your weapon, but for now, you need to fight her. Dominate her physically."

"Why are you making this weird?"

"Do it! Treat her like your dog."

"Can you stop?"

"Don't lose focus!"

I refocus my emotions and do my best not to think about the fact that he just told me to treat my mom like a freakin' dog. I draw closer and closer to the Spectre, and I ball my hand into a fist.

The giant head turns to face me, its eyes piercing. While I can feel its vulnerable and strangely human emotion, none of that is apparent in its face. I wind up, and as I unleash my punch, her face disappears. My hit collides into thin air, causing me to lose balance and fall to the floor.

Around me, the Mirage starts to erode, like the grains of sand after meeting water. We pop out back onto the street as if nothing had just happened.

"I thought I needed to punch her."

"No," Hiro says with a laugh. "I just wanted to see what would happen. When taking out other Spectres that *aren't* your Companion—which will be every other Spectre going forward—you will have to fight them. Since you and this one are linked, it's more about the emotion and the physical proximity."

"Very funny."

"Look at your Syncer."

I do, and in the cuff, see the gem, which now flickers with a blue fluorescence.

"Congratulations, Kid. You've just captured your Spectral Companion."

To Be Continued...

LUNA

SPECTRAL | EPISODE 3

THE VERDUGO HILLS...

ISABEL LETS OUT A SLOPPY EXHALE, half-sounding like a drunken horse. She doesn't remember how much she's had, but she's far beyond the cozy confines of sobriety. It fits her mood well enough.

The surrounding dirt path is sparingly lit. The bright lights that paint the Burbank landscape are nowhere to be seen, with only the faintest moonlight peeking out from above the trees behind. Against her better judgment, she'd made a hike up a local trail, branching off to a cemetery only known by the local health nuts.

The vegetation-ridden trail wouldn't make the trek much more difficult for your average hiker, but it's enough to make a drunken nighttime stroll just a little more difficult.

Isabel's face sours as she finally sees Alan Arroyo's headstone. She doesn't even want to be there. She'd gone out of her way—made a *point*—not to be there, and yet here she was. Why bother skipping the celebration if she was going to show up later? Only weirdos—junkies or health freaks—populate these hills so late. What had she been thinking?

She takes another sip from her flask and chuckles after bringing it back down. Right. She hadn't been thinking at all. She'd been going off of pure instinct, and that pure instinct led her where her sober self refused to go. Hard to believe it's been three whole years since Alan's death. Three years since—

Snap!

Her flask tumbles onto the grass, and Isabel is caught between finding the source of the sound and saving what precious spiced rum she can from the spongy dirt beneath the blades. She fails at both. The flask is all but empty by the time she picks it up, and she still can't place the sound by the time she stands back up.

It could be a mountain lion. They've become rarer in recent years, but are occasionally spotted, though Isabel hadn't heard of any attacks. Being the first victim of a mountain lion attack in decades would be just her luck.

Another snap stands the hair on the back of her neck on end.

"Who's there?" She presses the button on her headlamp and it brightens to reveal a limping figure in the middle distance.

Oh, hell no. She turns to flee, but her foot catches on an uneven clump of dirt on the ground and she takes a hard fall. She doesn't feel much thanks to the alcohol, but she at least has the presence of mind to wonder if she'll need to check herself out when she gets home, once the effects wear off.

She scrambles on the ground, her feet somehow not able to gain purchase on the grass as she slips and takes another tumble, this one mercifully much lighter. Her face heats up in anger. Why had she let herself drink so much? Even worse, why had she decided to hike out to the middle of nowhere?

"Izzy?" a voice calls out to her from the darkness.

Panic fades to relief as the voice helps put everything into place. The voice. The limp. It all makes sense now.

"Colin?"

She lets out another equine-like sigh of relief as Colin's limping stride grows more recognizable. She'd recognize it anywhere.

He'd suffered an injury in high school. Ever since, he's walked around with a limp, refusing a cane or any aid that would make him look weak. Isabel always thought that was stupid. In ten years, he'd have to get surgery on his leg again, and for all he knew, it'd have to come off altogether.

"Izzy, is that you?" Colin says.

Isabel lays back down on the ground, propping herself up on her elbows. "Yeah, it's me." She feels like the biggest idiot in the world. In horror movies, you always scream at the girl who trips in her high heels when the killer approaches. If Colin had indeed been such a killer, she would have been no better than your typical slasher movie victim. So embarrassing.

"I'd ask what you're doing out here, but...you know." He drops a bouquet of flowers and extends a hand to Isabel and she grabs it. Despite his limp, he has no problem helping her back to her feet.

He's always been super strong, even after his injury.

"Why didn't you come today?" he asks.

Isabel scrunches her face. It's not quite a frown, but it seems to do the job.

Colin backs up, his hands up in the air. "I'm just curious. We all were. We missed you."

"I just couldn't...be there today. I hate what those meetups have become."

"What's that?"

"Hangouts, where we all drink and laugh and reminisce. Like he didn't die. Like he didn't matter."

"Izzy, the whole reason we meet is because he *does* matter."

Colin's right. She knows it. But Alan's death changed everything. It ripped them all apart. Made them all feel like strangers. As a result, March thirty-first is the only day any of them speak to each other. They meet up at the Indian restaurant in downtown Burbank with too-spicy food before making the trek to his grave, usually after multiple drinks in town and at least one in-hand.

"I know," Isabel says. "I just couldn't deal this year. When I visit Alan, I just wanna be sad. And I can't be sad with Huy making jokes every five seconds, or with Ash bringing up the same two stories as if we've never heard them before." And the truth is, if she cries, she refuses to do it in front of other people, no matter how much they say they welcome it.

"You know, Alan—"

"'Wouldn't have wanted us to be sad?'" she interrupts. "Is that what you were about to tell me? I don't think any of us bothered to ask him that before he died."

Colin breathes out between tight lips. Isabel's seen that stressed look on his face before, and can't stop the pride from swelling inside her. At least someone else is along for the ride with her in this shitty mood.

"I get how you feel."

"No, Colin. No, you don't. I don't care what you and everyone else say. You don't k*now* how I feel."

"Then help me understand."

Isabel shakes her head. "Why are you even here?"

"You've always known how to dodge questions."

"I'm sure you were there with the others today. Why are you here now?"

Another exhausted and stressed sigh. "For starters," he bends down and picks up the dropped bouquet. "I forgot to bring these. You know how embarrassing it is to show up with nothing to give him? I didn't hear the end of it, Izzy."

Isabel laughs despite herself.

"And second," he continues, "I knew you'd be here at some point tonight. We all did. Didn't know when, but we knew it. No matter how tough you are, I didn't want you to be alone." His voice softens as he limps closer to her, close enough that she can smell the beer on his breath. He'd always preferred ale to hard liquor. The exact opposite of her. "I know how tough you can be on yourself. But no matter what you think, it's not your fault."

Isabel bites her lip, the emotions overwhelming.

"Izzy," he says. "It's not. Your. F—"

She cuts off the last word with a kiss, pressing her face hard against his. The last thing she needed was to be told again and again that Alan's death wasn't her fault. Colin tries to pull away, but Isabel brings him back in, not wanting the moment to end.

Several long seconds pass before she lets him breathe.

"Why'd you do that?" Colin says.

"Haven't you always wanted to?"

He doesn't answer, his face an implacable block of stone.

"Okay, I'm alone on that one," Isabel says with a laugh, this one truly devoid of humor.

"I just...Alan..."

"Is dead," Isabel says. "And I thought you said it wasn't my fault."

"His death not being your fault has nothing to do with..."

He pauses a bit too long. "Nothing to do with what?"

He's not even listening. Instead, he's looking past her, jaw dropped and eyes wide. "Colin, what's wrong with you?"

"Are you not seeing this?"

"Seeing what?" For the first time, Isabel realizes something is off about the lighting. Namely, that there was any lighting at all. Almost blinding, now that she notices. How hadn't she noticed it right away? A lurch in her stomach serves as a reminder of her inebriated state, and she vomits right on the spot, coating the grass in curry and rum. At least, it should have been grass. Instead, the ground is now made up of hardwood flooring.

Isabel wants to ask what's happening, but instead she unleashes another wave of vomit, some of it splashing back onto her blouse. After one last retch, she stands back up and wipes the tears from her eyes that had pooled up from the exertion.

"You okay?" Colin says, his voice anxious, distant.

"Where are we?" she asks. It's silent, as if they've descended into a soundproof room.

"It looks like...a theater?"

Isabel looks around. He's right. The two of them stand at the center of the stage. Blinding lights shine on them from above, and she makes out multiple tiers of seating in the auditorium. She's relieved that they're empty. The last thing she wants is to throw up in front of a literal audience. "Do you recognize it?"

"It's our school theater."

"Why are we in our high school theater?"

Before he can answer with an inevitable "I don't know," the entire room shakes. It's not an earthquake, which Isabel has felt her fair share of. It feels more like the result of stomping. She's watched a lot of old Godzilla movies and has spent way too much time thinking about what a true stomping rumble would feel like if it ever occurred. In her head, it feels a lot like what she's feeling now.

A rhythmic *booom...booom...booom...*

"What the hell is that?" Colin whispers, his comment barely audible.

And then music blares. Not obnoxious, unsophisticated music either, but classy Beethoven-like shit that even someone as uncultured as Isabel recognizes. Never mind that it's only because of Alan that she'd ever recognize anything like that.

Are they in some elaborate concert? And then, as if in answer to the unasked question, a figure—no, several figures—catch her eye. They look like ballet dancers. The kind from the movies. She's seen nothing like them in real life before, but she guesses they exist somewhere. They wear pink tutus and spandex, along with bright neon blue shoes.

But that's where anything normal about these ballerinas ends. Their faces are scribbled out, as though the women were drawn on scraps of paper before some murderous child scratched them out with charcoal. And then they turn, revealing a literal paper-thin physique, inexplicably standing upright and dancing on stage.

Tap-tap-flick. Tap-tap-flick—like the sounds of a page turning in a book, their moves well-rehearsed, graceful. Isabel and Colin stand still, as if their presence would be revealed if they moved, even though they're at the center of an illuminated stage.

The dancers continue to weave in and out. In and out. *Tap-tap-flick. Tap-tap-flick.* One of their feet catches on the vomit pooled in the middle of the slick wooden floor. Isabel expects the dancer to slip. Instead, her foot scrunches like a soggy receipt. The liquid bile spreads up her calf, knee, hip, and before long, it envelopes the entire ballerina, crumpling her in on herself. Another ballerina catches on the crumpled one, and before long, there's a line of soggy paper ballerinas, their graceful turns fidgeting, fizzling, and sinking with the rumble of each Godzilla step, which grows closer with each passing second.

In the back of the auditorium, the double-doors explode off their hinges and a figure stomps in. She can't tell for sure, but as a monster stoops under the threshold, she realizes it must be ten feet tall.

That's too many feet tall.

"We should get out of here," she says, taking a few steps back, only to slip on her own vomit and crash onto the floor.

"Get up, Izzy!" Colin says, and she feels him tugging at her arm.

She climbs to her feet, but as she flees, the once distant figure is on them in an instant, a wide-eyed smile on his face. He jumps and as he clings on to Isabel, a coldness rushes through her. A familiar sensation. One full of guilt and fear.

Colin screams, louder than she's ever heard anyone scream in her life, and her vision blurs into a bright light.

SPECTRAL

EPISODE 3
MUCH ADO

ONE

MY EYES flicker open as I wake. My body tenses up immediately and my fists clench on instinct. There's nothing new about this. I've always been on the anxious side. It was only within the past month that I felt safe enough not to wake with a start every morning.

I don't find myself on the ground in Unit 1017 at the Main Stay as I expect. I'm in a plain, white room. The comforter on top of me is just as obscenely white—not in a fancy way, but in a way that screams "I didn't know what to buy so I bought this." Between the comforter and the walls, it's like someone who didn't understand the concept of clashing colors did all the shopping. The scratchiness of the comforter is further evidence that it wasn't purchased with use in mind. I can also tell that it's probably never been used.

I blink stupidly as my eyes scan the room. Apart from the bed, there's nothing to show any personality or semblance of living. There's no dresser, no mirror, no furniture of any kind. Even my netscreen sits on the floor next to the bed. It's charging, so I must have taken the time to sync it up with the outlet. The reality of where I am floods back to me, and then I look at my bare wrist. No fancy device. No Syncer.

What happened to the Spectre?

Actively thinking about that sentence, I realize how stupid it sounds. Spectre? Really? As in being haunted by a Spectre? As in *capturing* a Spectre? But the memory feels as real as any I've had in the past. Even the most vivid and dark ones. It doesn't have the same nebulous feel that dreams do, where I lose one thread after another with each passing second.

I was exhausted after my run-in with that Spectre. Between the fire, the sound torture in the backseat of the cop car, multiple Mirage jumps, and a final fight with the spirit of my mom, I was dead tired. And that strange man, Hiro, offered to let me stay at his place. Had I really accepted the invitation of some weird stranger just like that?

I cover my face with my hands. How tired was I to make such a stupid mistake? But what was the alternative? Run back to Dad? No, thanks. And I can't go back to Damien and Lily yet. That's not even taking the police into account. What I do remember is that this place is a *huge*, one-story penthouse. Hiro offered me my own room from the get-go, making it clear that no funny business was on the table.

I reach under my pillow and pull out the butcher knife I'd snagged from his kitchen. I don't know if it would do much against a Medium warrior like Hiro, but I was taking no chances.

Pulling back the covers, I notice the black stains my feet leave on the pitch-white sheets. I need a shower.

I tiptoe my way through the massive loft, not to stay quiet, but to reduce the number of stains I leave all over the off-white tile flooring. Clearly, I paid no mind last night, because I can see my footprints from the elevator door to the kitchen bar, and back to the bedroom. Hopefully, he doesn't notice. Or that he doesn't care.

Sitting on the kitchen bar counter is my missing Syncer holding the Spectre gem. It glows soft, but persistent, growing brighter and darker every few seconds, like a creature breathing.

I open a set of blinds in the living room, and bright, warm sunlight spills in. It's the middle of the day, so I hadn't slept that long, and a nearby clock confirms it's only three-sixteen.

"Caw! Caw!" I hear next to Hiro's home netscreen, noticing for the first time that something sits covered in a sheet. I shut the blinds. Does Hiro leave his Spectre in a birdcage? Talk about dehumanizing.

"Sorry," I whisper, not knowing if he (she?) would understand me. Ignoring its caws, I return to the cuff and snap it onto to my left wrist. I can feel the difference instantly. Like my very being has expanded to fill another. It's empowering and scary at the same time. How safe is this?

I place my finger on the gem, and it's warm to the touch. When I let it go, a translucent screen fills my view.

Spectre: Level Zero

I tap the gem again and the screen disappears. "Okay, how do I..." I double-tap the gem. Nothing happens. "Come out!" I yell, partly embarrassed as I do. When nothing comes out, I become *completely* embarrassed, and a little happy no one was around to hear me doing that.

"Caw!"

Well, almost nobody.

I try rubbing the gem like a genie lamp, and despite what movies have told me, that doesn't work. All I've ever wanted is to have a genie to call my own, but apparently that's too much to ask. I'll just stick with my mountain of anxiety and ghost mother who's determined to wreak havoc on my life, thank you very much.

I thumb the gem, holding it down like it's a fingerprint scanner, something I've grown very familiar with in my years of going in and out of the foster care system. My hard work is rewarded by a high-pitched scream as the Spectre streams out, looking a hell of a lot like a freakin' genie, though I wish she wasn't so loud.

After the initial scream, the giant face, which stands (floats?) a solid seven feet tall, stares back at me. It's not nearly as aggressive as it was before, but I still sense an animosity. What had I done to upset Mom so much?

I stare at her features. The eyebrows and round face do look similar to mine, but I can't say they look like Mom's. And forget about the emblem on her forehead. What determines the look a Spectre takes on?

As we look into each other's eyes, the animosity I initially felt fades. A warmth radiates from her, and that animosity transitions to something like understanding mixed in with gratefulness and relief. For the record, I have no idea how I'm interpreting emotions of a non-human being, but I guess we're all learning new things these days, so you'll have to take my word for it.

She just floats there, eyes focused on me, like an untrusting pet. Wow, did I just compare my mom to an animal now, too?

"Hi," I say.

"What do you want?" she says.

I'd almost forgotten she can talk. She was pretty talkative the first time she saved me from the government Mediums, but we hadn't had much time to hold a conversation the second time around.

"I'm...I just..." I have no idea where to start.

"Hungry," she says, ignoring my non-response.

"Oh?" I say, looking around the kitchen. "I'll just...what do you eat?"

"More."

"More what? I assume you don't eat sandwiches and pancakes."

"More."

Suddenly, I understand. More. More Spirits. More Spectres. More food. And then I feel it, too. Her pangs of hunger.

"It's a special Bond, isn't it?" I hear from behind Mom.

Her head whips around and she gasps softly, shocked by the unexpected presence.

Leaning against the wall next to the birdcage stands Hiro. He wears a pink fluffy robe and pair of bright green slippers. "The relationship between Medium and Spectre is unique. Mediums without a Spectral Companion can't understand."

"You've used that term a lot. Spectral Companion. What is it really?"

"It's what she is to you and what Kuro is to me. A Spectre with a personal relationship with the Medium. Most people don't have one. Most people *can't* have one, because it requires a preestablished relationship with the Spectre. It allows the Medium to connect emotionally. Without it, you would never have been able to catch her as you did. You would've had to free her."

"Free her?"

"Send her to the afterlife."

"So, kill her."

He shrugs. "It's what most other Mediums do. It's what every Medium from the Department of Spectral Defense does. Like I said, what you have is...special."

As Hiro takes a couple more steps forward, Mom floats back toward me before retreating back into her gem, as though his very presence frightens her.

"I don't know about special," I say. "There isn't much I recognize from my mom in her. Besides, it's this thing that's caused me so much trouble. After everything she's done...taking control of my body, starting fires, I don't know if I can trust her."

"Such is the connection between Spectral Companion and Medium. But you have the right idea. In spite of what I said before, she's no pet. She is a malicious Spirit, one that needs to be freed like the others."

"You mean killed."

"I mean freed. Best not to get too attached. She'll need to be freed if you want her out of your life."

"And why do you want her?"

Hiro's eyes settle on mine. He doesn't want to share. "I've been around for a long time. I've freed a lot of Spectres, and whenever you do that, they leave behind a part of themselves. They're called Essences. Our Spectral Companions consume them, and they give them strength. In turn, they give us strength. But when you live as long me, there are diminishing returns on each Essence consumed. I can't even fight Level One Spectres these days, and yet the Level Zero Spectres do next to nothing to sate Kuro's appetite. If he doesn't eat soon, he'll...be freed, for a lack of a better term. And I've lived so long that the only reason I'm alive is due to whatever strength he gives me."

"So if he dies, you die."

Hiro nods, and suddenly, his proposition makes sense.

"So, you want me to use Mom, to build her strength, and free her once she's strong enough to satisfy your Spectre's hunger?"

Hiro sighs. He can tell how bad that sounds. "That's correct. Once she hits Level Two, I think her Essence will be of sufficient power to at least get me up and running. I'll be able to hunt Spectres again myself and continue living. And once she's gone, you'll be free to live your life, free from constraint."

I collapse onto the couch, not even caring how dirty my feet are. "And if she's freed, will I die?"

Hiro shakes his head. "You're not as old as me. You live on your own physical strengths. When she's freed, it'll almost be as though nothing's happened. So, now that the dust has settled, and you've had time to consider, here is my proposition. I will help you level up your Spectre, and when ready, we will free her. Kuro will consume her Essence, and we will go our separate ways. Deal?"

This feels wrong. Almost cruel. To sacrifice my mom for my own selfish reasons. But why can't I be selfish? She's already dead. And she's the one who left me. Left me and Dad to fend for ourselves. And if this is my only course to happiness, wouldn't she want me to take it?

I find myself nodding. "Once she reaches Level Two," I say, "we'll free her, and give her Essence for Kuro to consume."

Hiro smiles, and I can sense the smallest shift in his posture—as though a weight has been lifted.

"Do you know," I say, "why she's done all these things?"

"What things?" Hiro makes his way to the far counter in his kitchen, tampering with a big metal machine. "Espresso?"

"The—no, I'm fine—the Spectre. Until earlier today, I would have thought I was being possessed by a demon. The moment I have my life together, she takes over my body and makes me do things."

Steam hisses from the espresso machine with a loud pop. "What things?"

"Makes me start fires. Pick fights—or find violent ways to end them."

"Well," Hiro responds, "it's hard to say. No two Spectres are alike. They're similar to people in that regard. But at her level, there isn't a lot to go off of. She can speak, but she likely won't have complete memories until she consumes more Essences. Until then, she'll have the barest recollection of faces, people, places, or events. They take actions purely on instinct.

This is amplified the closer link they have to a living human. Were you close with your mother?"

"I don't know," I say, maybe all too honestly. "How close are mothers and daughters supposed to be? I mean, she was my mom, but the further away we get from her death, the more I feel like I just saw her as an escape from Dad." I swallow. I'm not used to this kind of discussion. "You mentioned that she would gain more memories as she gets more Essences."

"That's correct," he says. "As she becomes more 'complete' as a Spectre, she'll grow closer and closer to her living personality."

The thought of bringing back my mom only to feed her Essence to Kuro is enough to churn my stomach, but I push down the feeling.

Hiro turns back to the espresso machine. "These are all thoughts you may want to address in the weeks to come. You may have heard this old adage, and while it sounds like an old wives' tale, I found it to be true. Ghosts and Spectres are driven by unfinished business. The reason they are still in this plane of existence is because there is something left undone in their lives. This is amplified once they make a connection with a living being, and often drives their impulsive behavior. You'll need to be aware of this as you interact with your Spectre, and when the time comes, it'll make her passing on that much more effective. Hopefully, by the end, whatever unfinished business she has will be put to rest." The machine behind him grinds and hisses as a dark liquid empties into his tiny ceramic mug. "And speaking of which, it's about time for us to get started."

"Started how?" I say, standing from the couch. I know he said he's going to help me "level up" my Spectre, but I hadn't the foggiest idea where we'd even start.

Hiro sips from his mug. "Oh, yeah. That's good." He glances off into the distance and sighs contentedly. Then after a few seconds, he blinks as he returns to the present. "You and I have a distinct advantage apart from other Mediums. Because of our connection with a Spectral Companion, we can sense the presences of Ghosts, Poltergeists, Spectres, and Mirages nearby. The only downside is that they aren't always present, and they don't happen as frequently as one would think. More often than not, they present themselves in waves. Think back to your situation. Your Spectre wasn't *always* around, was she?

I shake my head. "No. She seemed to pop up at random times."

"Exactly. So, what we have to do is find strange events happening nearby. Did someone go missing? Was there an unexplained fire?" he nods his head toward me at that last part. "Or is it something else? Chances are a Spectre could be behind it." He takes another sip of his drink. "I mean, or not. These things can be pretty hit or miss."

Hiro walks over to the couch and plops down, taking another sip of his drink and laying back. "So you have a lot of work to do. Try to search within the Los Angeles area—I try to stay away from anything longer than a day trip."

"What?"

"Sorry, did I say something confusing?"

"I don't even know where to start."

Hiro groans. "Okay, fine. Use the word 'disappearance' or 'missing' in a netscreen search or something. Think about what you read in the feeds whenever people go missing. Pretend you're a detective and you're the star of your own net series or something."

"I've never read any reports about people going missing."

He stretches out and closes his eyes. "Well, now's your chance to learn. Some of these can be real misses, though. Not every Ethereal Entity is a Spectre, so I wouldn't search for hauntings or anything. Ghosts scare people, Poltergeists tend to just break shit and hurt people, but for our purposes, only Spectres or above are what we want. They're the ones who create Mirages. They're the ones who will give you what you need to level your Spectre up. That's all we care about here. If you can't level up your Spectre, I won't be able to level up *my* Spectre when it's time for Kuro to chow down."

"Chow down?"

"Sorry, I mean consume your mom's Essence."

"Are you hearing yourself?"

"Just do your research, okay? And…wake me up if you find anything worth a drive." The man is practically asleep by the time he finishes that final sentence, leaving me by myself.

I growl in annoyance. I know he can't hear me, but it's cathartic just to let it out. He's left me to do all the work like some crappy intern. But with nothing else to do, I grab a seat on a stool at the kitchen bar and plop my netscreen on top of it. With a few swipes, a translucent screen floats above it, and I pound away at the blue laser keyboard spread out on the counter.

Ironically, while cops can no longer track netscreens as a means of tracking down suspects, they *can* gain access to all searches from an IP address. Not that there's anything super telling in what I'm searching, but I can't help but wonder what they'll think of me digging into recent disappearances. There's no way they're not tracking me. What conclusions will that golden boy Chu draw from it?

I start by digging into a topic I haven't had time to research. Mom's death.

My heart sinks when the first result pops up. It's not new news, but a report on what Detective Chu had told me in the interrogation room—an update on the years-old disappearance of Kim-Ly Guerrera, my mom. Just as he said, she was recently found when they fished her vehicle out from the Salton Sea. The cause of death is unknown, and due to the corrosive nature of the Salton Sea, there was no way for them to tell how she was killed. By the time they found her, all that was left was a skeleton and her clothing, and even most of that had been eaten away.

I glance down at the gem in my Syncer, and then back over to Hiro, who snores softly on the couch. Pressing my thumb down on the gem for the second time, Mom pops out with a screech. Neither Hiro nor his Spectre make a single sound. They adapt quickly.

I snap my fingers, gaining the floating head's attention and point at the screen. "What happened to you?" And can this floating-headed Spectre can read?

"What?" she says, her Spectral brows furrowing.

"What happened to you after you plunged into the Salton Sea? Or before? Do you know what the Salton Sea is?" I grab the translucent screen and toss it in her direction. It floats a few inches from her face.

If what Hiro says is true, I'm wasting my time, but I have to at least try, right?

Mom stares at the screen for several seconds, staying silent as she does so before turning around to take in the rest of the apartment. Whatever was there wasn't of much interest to her.

"Hungry," she says.

"I'm working on it."

"Work faster." For a Ghost with amnesia, she conjures up a lot of sass.

I pull the screen back in front of me, my attention returning my search. Maybe once I capture more Spectres and she becomes more aware, she can provide more insight to the mystery of her death. For now, I just need to focus on finding more Spectres to take in.

Most of my progress throughout the afternoon leads to dead ends. There's one promising disappearance of a boy earlier this week in Irvine that turns out to be a boring murder, and another where the missing woman is found safe and sound following a psychotic break.

A few hours pass without much to show for it, but then I stumble upon one potential lead. I say potential because I still have no idea what the crap I'm looking for here.

"Hey," I say, turning around for the first time in hours. The giant head stares back at me, sitting quietly on the marble floor, her chin and lower back part of the head just chilling. I can't tell if the floor is holding her up or if she's hovering.

"Hey," I repeat, this time stretching out my leg and kicking the back of the sofa.

Hiro's head pops up, the hair on the back of his head a ruffled mess. "You found one?"

"You tell me."

Within the next half-hour—after I wash the Skid Row filth from my body—we're in his car and making our way north. It had taken me hours to find the barest core of the story, but Hiro somehow managed to ring up one of the key witnesses presented in the article. It's some guy named Colin, who claims to have been present when a girl was taken. The story he told was outrageous, and had only been picked up by some equally outrageous website poking fun at local nuts. I'd almost dismissed it outright, but the parallels were too close to ignore.

After finding parking in a nearby garage, Hiro leads me to a casual Asian fusion restaurant. It's the kind of place parents take their kids after a movie or while shopping—their menu offerings anything but authentic. After ordering an aggressively mild-looking take on the sundubu-jjigae, we take our seats, keeping an eye out for what Hiro says will probably be a shifty-eyed, underslept man of around eighteen or twenty.

"So, what's our backstory?" I ask.

"Our what?"

"Are we pretending to be journalists?"

Hiro snorts. "No. I told him I heard about his situation and wanted to hear more. Nine times out of ten, these people just want someone to talk to. You saw how that article framed him. Made him look like a lunatic. He has no one else to talk to but us."

"We're not even claiming to be writing anything up? Letting the truth out? Anything?"

"It's not about that right now," he says. "Maybe he wants some answers or to spread some truth, but most people who meet with me just want someone to talk to. They want someone who won't judge them."

"So he agreed to meet a complete stranger just to talk?"

"I think you underestimate how desperate these situations could leave people."

He's got a point. Earlier this morning, I'd been exactly this person. Scared, confused, angry. I likely would have listened to anyone, too. I wouldn't have responded to a random phone call, but that could be the difference between being a boy versus a girl.

"Ah, I think we've found our guy."

Coming in through the glass doors is a young man with short hair and a hoodie. His eyes are pink, with bags underneath to complement them. One hand is shoved into his pocket.

Hiro gives the man a wave, and after catching the gesture, the man hobbles straight to us, head down. Hiro isn't wrong. This is definitely our guy. Hiro offers to pay for the guy's over-priced sushi. I assumed he'd be more of the stingy sort, but the world is full of surprises.

Hiro leads with small talk, somehow avoiding template questions like, "How's life?" or "How about that hundred-and-thirty-seventh day in a row of blistering sun?" in the process. He speaks with a surprising amount of empathy and deftness. Before I know it, the conversation has transitioned seamlessly to the man's high school life.

"Is that how you met Isabel?" he asks.

I expect the scared man to blanch at the question, maybe even to get mad at the sudden transition to the topic at hand, but instead, he nods. With enthusiasm, even.

"That's right," he responds. "Our entire group of friends was in a high school production of *Much Ado About Nothing*. You know anything about Shakespeare?"

I shake my head, but am surprised to see Hiro nod in affirmation. "That play's one of my favorites."

"I played Don Pedro, she played Hero, and our friend...well, her boyfriend, played Claudio. And throughout the story, you know Claudio is trying to get with Hero, right? And, in one scene, he thinks his friend Don Pedro has taken her for himself?"

Is that what these plays are all about? People just sleeping around? How is this relevant?

"Well," Colin continues, "in this case, he was right."

"Huh?" I say, probably too loudly. Probably too annoyed that he was speaking in a language I didn't understand.

"Isabel and I hooked up while she was dating him—his name's Alan, by the way. He was the one who was playing Claudio."

I still don't understand why he insists on linking everyone to their Shakespeare names. "So, she cheated on him with you," I say before I can stop myself. See how quickly I get the same point across?

A single look from Hiro is all it takes for me to realize I'd stepped out of line with my question. I stare at a loose grain of rice on the table in front of me. It hadn't been an accusatory question. Colin had told his story in such a roundabout way that I wanted to make sure I understood.

"Yeah, that's right," Colin says, his voice resigned, holding no malice.

"What happened next?" Hiro says after a few silent moments.

"This wasn't a spur-of-the-moment thing," Colin says, getting defensive. "Ask anyone who knows me, and they'll tell you I'm not the kind of guy to just thrum any chick I come across—sorry," he adds with a glance in my direction, as if it makes his comment any less awkward. "I really liked—*like*—Izzy. She was going to break things off with him. And when she told him..."

He doesn't finish the sentence, but his point is clear.

"Nothing was ever the same after that," he says. "Forget about Izzy and me being together, but our entire friend group just split up. There weren't any angry conversations, no extra drama; we just drifted apart. It affected all of us, but it affected Izzy most of all."

"And what about you?"

Colin shrugs. "Izzy is a better person than me. She took it personally. Blamed herself for his death. Even though none of us hang out anymore, we come together once a year to remember him, but I could tell she was never 'there,' you know? This year, she skipped out altogether. Too guilty. Me? I don't blame myself. Maybe I should, but Izzy and I had something. I'm sad Alan's dead, but I'm also sad how it affected things between me and her."

"So, what happened?"

"Oh, right," he says, as if realizing for the first time why we were there to begin with. "When she didn't show up, I stuck around at our meeting place north of Burbank."

"What do you mean north? You mean among the eight-million-dollar houses?"

"In the Verdugo Hills. There's this old abandoned cemetery that Alan's family used. Old money or something, I dunno. I had a feeling she'd show up later, so when the others left, I stayed behind. When she did, we talked for a bit. And then..."

The pause stretched on for more than thirty seconds before Hiro cut in. "And then...?"

"It was like a dream. So strange, I can't remember much. A different world. Our high school theater."

"Wait," I ask, "was it your high school theater or a different world?"

"Both? It was surreal. I really did think it was a dream at first. That maybe I'd imagined the whole thing. But then I found her netscreen sitting next to me back in the cemetery. I don't know what happened, but whatever it is took Izzy away from me."

Colin's eyes go dark and wide, his irises opening up to an inhuman size. "And I think...I worry it's coming for me next."

"Coming for you?"

He nods. "I don't know if this sounds insane. Okay, yeah, I do. It sounds insane. But it was like...I got the sense that Alan was the one who took her. Like it was one big elaborate revenge for what we did. Does that sound insane?"

"Yeah," Hiro says, his face and voice both patronizing. "It kinda does."

AN HOUR LATER, Hiro and I traipse past the thick vegetation that surrounds a trail. I'm grateful that the sun's started to set, making the hike that much cooler than it would have been, but the idea of hiking back with nothing but a set of headlamps makes me uneasy. I can walk through one of the most dangerous parts of the country with little issue, but put me in the dark semi-wilderness, and my imagination runs free.

"What was that about?" I ask.

"What?"

"What was up with what you said to that guy?" I say, realizing that no matter how much I'd been rolling the thought over in my head over the past forty-five minutes, I'd given Hiro zero context surrounding my comment. "You were being an asshole. After everything he said, you called him crazy."

"No, I didn't."

"You may as well have."

"The less people know about all this, the better," he says.

"So you *were* trying to make him feel crazy?"

"Spectres already consume enough humans a year as it is. We don't need for him to get curious and wander into a Mirage on his own. Unless we need him to, of course, which we very well may."

"Huh?" I say. My mind reflects back to Gabe and how "useful" he had been back when he'd stumbled into Mom's Mirage. "Why would we need him?"

Hiro stops and turns to face me, and his light shines directly into my eyes before he turns it away. "Have you learned nothing? Think about it. What was it that helped you capture your own Spectre?"

"I thought I was supposed to fight and kill this one," I say. "Wouldn't Mom just turn into a sword?"

"Sure, a gigantic sword helps, but that's nothing without vulnerability."

I replay the entire sequence out in my head. I had synced emotions with Mom, and that put her in a weakened state, making her vulnerable, easy to catch. "So the solution is to link a memory the Spectre has with a specific emotion."

"Bingo," he says, turning back around. "You're smarter than you look."

I furrow my brows. "How do we know what emotion will work?"

"Going into a Mirage for us Mediums is a traumatic experience. We not only experience memories, but we experience them as though we are them. The most impactful memories rise to the surface, giving us hints as to how to bring about a certain emotion."

I nod, though I know he can't see me. It all makes sense. This trip to the cemetery isn't a one-and-done deal. These Spectre-seeking escapades likely take at least two trips. One for recon, and another to execute. Literally.

"Right?" I say after sharing Hiro my thoughts.

"That is correct. You're certainly a far cry smarter than the government dogs they have hunting these bastards."

I want to ask more about the government's involvement, but before I speak, we spot a short, black gate ahead lining a hill. There's nothing to this small plot of land. It can't be much bigger than half an acre in size. Only a handful of headstones sit at its center.

"Name?"

"Uh...Luna Guerrera?"

"Not you, stupid. The name of the deceased."

"Oh. Alan Arroyo."

He scans the few stones that populate the lot before settling on one farthest away from the entrance. "And here we are. Alan Arroyo." He rolls his "Rs" in a patronizing fashion. "Well, I think you're up, Luna Guerrera." He rolls his "Rs" in the same patronizing fashion.

I nod, pushing back a cheeky remark. Without him even specifying, I know exactly what he's talking about. It's time for me to work my magic.

It's time for me to open the Mirage.

TWO

I HOLD my hands out in front of me, palms facing outward, and wait for something to hit me. I don't know what I'm waiting for, but I'm confident I'll know when it does.

"What the hell are you doing?" Hiro says, breaking me from my concentration.

"I'm trying to feel for the Mirage," I say with confidence, though the very fact that he's asking what I'm doing is enough to destroy what little confidence I have. "I'm doing it wrong and looking like a total idiot, huh?"

"Yeah."

"It's what the other guy was doing."

"What guy?"

"One of the government Mediums who tried to kill me. He did this when looking for Mom inside her Mirage."

"It works a bit differently with them."

I drop my hands. "So, about them trying to kill me…"

"It sounds like they thought you were a Spectre, and they were trying to free you."

"They said kill."

"I can't be blamed for their lapse in verbal judgment."

"And when Mom showed up, they started calling me something else. A Spirit. What's that mean?"

Hiro sighs. "Now's a good time to break down how these Ethereal Entities are divided up. The lowest of the low are called Spirits. They have no will of their own and simply act at the behest of a Spectre. Think of them as the will of the Spectre incarnate. They usually stay within Mirages, but sometimes trickle into our world.

"Ghosts are the next level up. They're the ones you likely hear stories about. They wander about in the real world. Sometimes they create cold spots and give off malevolent or warm feelings. They may even resemble the deceased.

"Next up is Poltergeist. These are typically driven by their anger. I mean, every Ghost and Spectre has anger, but the Poltergeist thrives on that energy and can interact in the real world.

"Finally, we have Spectres. These are Poltergeists on steroids. But the big difference is that they don't come into our world. After creating their Mirages, they tend to wait, stewing in their own hate and anger for years at a time, only poking in to abduct folks unlucky enough to wander by their lair. They're like spiders, sitting in their web, waiting for a snack to drop in."

I wrinkle my nose at the analogy, reflecting on everything being shared with me. "They thought I was a Spirit, then? Just an entity meant to represent the Spectre?"

"A minion of your Spectre, yes," Hiro says with a nod.

"Hmm," I say. "So, you hate the government Mediums."

"Hate is a strong word," he says. "So, yes. Hate would be accurate."

"Why?"

Hiro looks down at his Syncer as though looking for the time. "To them, the world of Spectres is one to be bottled up and exploited."

"So, how's what you do any different? You both kill or 'free' Spectres, right? You both consume their Essences to power you."

Hiro gives me a deadpan look, as if insulted that I would even question his motives. "It's not what they do, but what they use it for."

"And what do they use it for?"

"What the government always does. They finds ways to exploit something and use it as political leverage. If they knew what you really were, who knows how they would have used you?"

I blink. "And what am I?"

"You're like me. The government Mediums don't have Spectral Companions of their own, instead relying on the Essences of Spectres to bolster their physical abilities *without* an Ethereal link. The two of us are special. We have abilities they can only dream of."

I look down at my own hands, clenching them and unclenching. "But I don't feel any different in the real world. It's only in the Mirage that I felt...faster."

"That's just how it works. The only abilities that carry over into the real world are linked to longevity. If you keep your Spectre fed, you can ensure yourself an unnaturally long life. Like me."

"Great."

"The Department…they don't know all this yet. I've been around for over a hundred and fifty years, and they're just figuring it out. Even still, they're finding ways to take advantage of it.

"And speaking of advantage," he continues. "You and I have one massive one. Our own Spectres have a connection to us through a shared trauma."

"Some advantage."

"The ability to free Spectres and utilize their skills is innate in our DNA. The government dogs need to train harder and utilize tech in order to come remotely close to our level. They don't look for weaknesses. When they fight, it's only a numbers game. A higher level is the only factor between victory and failure. Our connection through trauma allows us to cut into a Spectre with greater ease, even if they are at a higher level than us.

"And that's not all. These government agents are divided up by specific skills. For example, they break up their teams into groups of three. One Medium to track Spectres, one to act as the Attacker, and one to act as the Defender. But you and I aren't limited to one of the three."

I wait for him to continue, but I think he's finally finished. "Are you done?" I ask. "I don't even know if you answered my question. Did I even ask a question?"

"Long story short, yes, you looked like an idiot holding your hands out. That's the form of a government Medium with no innate skills. You only need to stretch out your awareness. Take deep breaths."

I start to relax and feel my eyelids droop.

"No, no, don't close your eyes," Hiro snaps. "If you close your eyes, you won't be able to see the portal opening."

I open them back up and glance around. As my consciousness wanders, I feel it pulling, though what "it" is I can't tell. It's a slight tugging, and my head tilts almost involuntarily to the right. About twenty feet away, I see a pin in the air. Or, more like a pin*prick*. As though the air has the tiniest of holes punched into it.

"I think I found it."

"Great, now make your way over to it."

I obey, though as I approach, the pinprick doesn't seem to get any bigger. I stop right in front of it, at my eye level.

"Now, stick your finger in there."

I give him a disgusted look.

"Oh, your generation, I swear!" Hiro throws his hand up in exasperation. "If you want to open it, you're going to have to put part of yourself within the Mirage. It'll just take a second, and from there, you can expand it outward."

"I don't know what that means," I say.

"It means that as soon as a piece of you is through on the other side, push your entire being into that part of your body and push back. Almost like you're crawling out of the covers in bed in the morning."

I give him another odd look, but he just stares back at me with a serious expression. With another deep breath, I stick out my index finger and stick it into the pinprick. If I hadn't seen it, I wouldn't have noticed my pointer finger existing in a random pocket universe.

I work to push my consciousness away from my head into my index finger. Somehow, it works. As though riding a train through my body, I arrive at my fingertip. With an extra push, the air around me changes instantly. I open my eyes to find an auditorium.

"Well done, Luna," Hiro says with a clap.

But the applause of an audience of hundreds cuts off his own. At least, I imagine it's hundreds. With the light shining in our eyes, I can only guess, but the floating heads above the seats indicate that no matter the size, it's no average group of theatergoers.

"Here we go," Hiro continues. "It was one thing to be reliving your own traumatic moments, but how do you think it'll feel delving into someone else's life?" Hiro takes in the surroundings. "So, each Spectre grows and expands at a different rate. You'll become more adept over time, and based on how well formed the scene is, I imagine he's been around for several months, at least."

"Huh," I say. I don't know why, but I still can't believe we found this place. "So, the lead worked. We found the perfect target for Mom to absorb?"

"That's right," Hiro says, "but we can't get ahead of ourselves. Each Spectre is like a puzzle—one that you need to solve. I may be experienced, but due to my Spectral Atrophy, I can't do you much good in a fight."

"Is that what your condition is called?"

"That's what *I* call it, yes. Each Essence packs less of a punch than it used to. That's why you're here."

"Is this the part where you remind me about our deal?" I say, sensing his growing apprehension. "Don't worry. Whatever this whole Medium thing is, I don't want it." My mind focuses on the rock that had settled in my gut the moment Mom became my Spectral Companion. It made me sick, anxious, envious, and a mixture of other emotions that weigh me down with every thought. The sooner I get rid of this, the sooner I can move on to the next stage of my life.

The lights pointing at us from the second tier of the auditorium shut off, and another set above us come on. Music emanates from the front of the stage. I squint to see what looks like figures crafted out of newsprint playing string, woodwind, and percussion instruments in the orchestra pit below the stage.

A pair of similar figures make their way to the stage, one wearing old-fashioned military attire, and the other a poofy dress. Both sport exaggerated silhouettes. They join hands at the center of the stage, and I step back to avoid bumping into the literal paper-thin humans.

"Silence is the perfectest herald of joy," the male figure says in a smitten tone. "I were but little happy if I can say how much, Lady, as you are mine, I am yours."

My nose wrinkles at the public display of affection, and as I do, the male figure transforms in front of my eyes into a very real figure. An actual human figure. A boy, no older than seventeen. My age. Maybe even younger. The female figure changes with him, turning into a girl.

I blink, recognizing her. She's the girl from the article.

"I give away myself for you," the boy continues, "and dote upon the exchange."

That entire line is complete nonsense. I look around the theater. Its previously artificial aesthetic has changed. No longer does it feel like a child's diorama, but an actual building. The paper figures in the stands are rounded out into normal humans. Kids, mostly. High school kids.

This feels a lot like how it felt before in my Mom's Mirage whenever I relived some key moment.

I think I've just transitioned into a memory. And with it, my emotions connect, becoming one with the person whose memory I'm pulling from. My eyes turn to Isabel, the female figure in front of Alan. I swallow as a strange feeling overcomes me. One of unbridled love toward her. Practically overflowing and untamed. It's an unexpected feeling, but one I recognize as not my own. This is what Alan feels toward her.

The memory transforms with a wisp and a spiral, and the two roll around a cramped and sweaty bed, clothing askew, breath heavy, and the air humid with passion, an eruption impending.

Another wisp and a spiral, and time passes in an instant. Isabel's hand is in Alan's, surrounded by a group of friends. Among them is Colin, eyes locked on Isabel. Alan notices.

Helplessness.

I explode back to the artificial version of the stage. Another paper figure dominates the center, one that represents Alan. A birdcage lowers from the ceiling, slowly enveloping Alan as he yells out, cries out, and shakes the bars. I can't hear him, but his intent is clear. He's terrified, though of what?

A wisp and a twirl, and Alan sits on a park bench, the L.A. sun beating down on him as he hunches over his netscreen. His mind is thick, clouded, and panicked. Isabel is at his side, but her presence only makes him feel worse.

Insecurity. Rejection.

Why is this happening to me? I hear ringing in my ears, and I can tell immediately it's an emotion from Alan.

Just when I think something clicks inside my head, a roar interrupts the flashback, and it disappears into a puff of smoke. A pounding reverberates throughout the theater, and a ten-foot man-beast explodes out into the open from the front entrance.

"Jesus Christ!" I yell out.

"Yeah," Hiro says. "Did I mention sometimes these Spectres can skew toward the terrifying?"

"Why's he so big? Why's he so freakin' scary?"

The beast bounds toward us like a gorilla fists, landing on the ground in a four-footed gallop.

"I think it's safe to say that this is the Spectre of the Mirage," Hiro says.

I nod and think back to his instruction. I pull up my Syncer and double tap it.

Spectre: Level N/A

"Um, Hiro?"

"One last thing—sorry, I swear I told you this," he says, "but you need to make physical contact with the Spectre before you can gauge its level."

"Shit," I say.

"Don't worry. I can tell you can take him. But that's not important. What's important are his memories. What did his memories reveal?"

"Wait, you weren't there with me?"

"What do you think I've been doing? I've been fighting off some of his Spirits so you can gain your needed intel to take him out."

"Oh, got it."

The beast makes an inhuman leap from the aisles, over the orchestra pit, headed straight toward me.

"Shit!" I flinch, and the world explodes into a bright light as the world around me rumbles. Sparks fly and I peek open my eyes to see Mom's sword floating in front of me.

Her face pops out from the gem. She doesn't speak, but I can read her emotions. Somehow, "What're you gonna do? Fight already!" comes across in a single expression. With what I imagine is a sour look, I latch on to the hilt and grab the blade, pulling it back, and using its momentum to swing around and take a swipe at the terrifying Spectre in front of me.

The hit connects, blade meeting resistance, and a shriek follows.

"Gotcha!" I yell, against my better judgment. Though when I look up, I see the Spectre staring back at me as though it hadn't suffered a paper cut, let alone an attack from my blade. "What the hell?"

"You thought it would be that easy?" Hiro says

"All I had to do was touch the other Spectre."

"That's because *that* Spectre has a connection with you. This one couldn't give two shits about who you are or what you want from him. It's times like this that pulling up stats is helpful. And, hey, good news! You have access to his details now."

With a flick of my fingers, I pull them up.

Spectre: Level Zero
Type: Defender

"Okay, it says it's a Level Zero Defender," I say. "That's good, right? That means I can take him physically."

"Probably," Hiro says, "but it all becomes a hell of a lot easier if you sync with his emotions. But since he's a Defender, I bet his Attack is terrible."

Just then, the big smiley asshole launches another gorilla attack on me, but I block easily.

"Ha!" I scream. This is literally a fight between two monumental weaklings, though to the uninitiated, I'm sure it looks pretty badass. As Hiro had told me, I don't stand much of a chance of hurting him with my attacks. At least not at my level.

I dodge another blow from the creature. What had I learned from those memories? That he felt stuck and insecure? As though he wasn't in control of his own life? How can I capture that in a bottle?

Another dodge and the monster crashes through the wall of the auditorium, which reveals a black abyss of nothingness. Immediately, everything around us gets sucked into the hole. The auditorium fills with flat paper figures floating into the wall like a sideways twister.

"Hiro," I say. "We need to go!"

"Why?"

"I think we need that other guy!" I try my best to yell under the reverse gale that fills the room, but I can't tell if it's making it through to him.

But Hiro smiles all the same. "Very good! You're learning well. Sense another hole in the Mirage and do what you did to get in, but reverse it."

"Reverse...?" I start to argue, but resist the urge. He's had half-assed and nonsensical explanations in the past, but they almost always work out. So I give it a shot. What was it, like pulling back the covers of my bed in the morning? So I reverse it, grasping at the air around me and mentally pushing it over my head. I fall, and with a light thud, land in the soft grass of the cemetery.

Hiro lands next to me, a wide smile on his face. "So, what did you discover?"

THREE

"I'M SORRY, WHAT?" Colin says. "You're saying that *thing* is Alan?"

"What's left of him," Hiro says. "He's what we call a Spectre. Think of him as a Ghost with unfinished business. His resentment and lingering emotions created that world you saw. A Mirage. That Mirage has captured your friend. Is any of this sinking in?"

The man stares back at us with a blank expression.

We're in the same Asian fusion restaurant in downtown Burbank that we'd met earlier that day. This time, I ordered the pho.

I'd been paranoid that the man wouldn't respond, but true to Hiro's prediction, he came without question. All he needed to do was utter the magic words: "We can save her."

"But can we?" I asked before Colin had shown up, plunging a strip of raw meat into the hot soup.

Hiro shrugged. "You said you saw her, right?"

"I saw a version of her in the memory," I said, recalling the series of moments I'd seen while in the Mirage. Alan had been young, but Isabel looked exactly as she had in the photos. According to Hiro, that wasn't normal. The memories should be frozen in time. The only way a Spectre could replicate a person like that would be to utilize the real person they swallowed, using them as a reference point.

She could still be alive, he assured me.

I repeat the farfetched line to the poor soul in front of me: that we may have a way to save her. That it's not too late. He needs little convincing. On one hand, it's no surprise he's hanging on to the hope of a loved one, but I thought it would take a lot of effort to convince him what we saw was real. Though, as Hiro pointed out, Colin had already lived through the impossible. He knows what happened wasn't fake and is willing to accept anything.

"Plus," Hiro told me. "What was it that you said? That this guy and the missing person were in love? Love can make all of us do stupid things."

This includes convincing Colin to venture out into the darkness of the night. He leaps at the chance to reclaim his lost love, and the soup in my stomach curdles. Am I making a promise I can't keep?

Colin has made the trek several times before, he tells us, so while he does have a bum leg, it won't be a problem. The trip takes three times as long as the first, though it at least gives us time to answer some of the bigger questions.

"When we get there, you'll bring me into this...Mirage, you're calling it?"

I can't get past the fact that Hiro answers in the affirmative so openly. "You got it. Just like last time, the world will change around you, and we won't be in any place to guarantee your safety."

"But it's real, even though it's called a Mirage?"

"It's real enough," Hiro says. "It's not a figment of your imagination, if that's what you mean."

Colin smiles. I know that feeling. The discovery that you're not crazy. The realization that the doubt you placed in yourself was *mis*placed.

"So, why me?" he asks.

"Wanna take that, Luna?"

"Oh." That catches me off guard. I didn't realize there'd be a quiz. "To free her, I need to...uh...match emotions with him. His primary emotion, I think, revolves around you. Your affair with Isabel brought out feelings of insecurity and rejection. It was as though he realized he had no control over his life."

"Those are likely the last feelings he had before he kicked the bucket," Hiro says, casting subtlety to the wind.

"And you need me why?"

I glance at Hiro, who nods. "We need to get him to relive that moment. If we do, it'll make him more vulnerable to my attacks."

"You're going to *kill* him again?"

"He's already dead," I say, only half-convinced myself. "We're...*freeing* him." I don't even buy the explanation, but Colin nods softly as he hobbles down the dirt path.

"Okay."

"He's probably going to be angry with you," I say to Colin.

"No probably about it," Hiro says. "He'll be furious."

The man nods. "It's nothing less than I deserve."

In one short sentence, his actions come into focus. As altruistic as he seems, they're all self-serving. It's not about righting wrongs with Alan. It's not about coming completely clean. No, it's about clearing his own guilty conscience. If offered the chance, even in the face of seeming impossibility, who wouldn't take that? I think to my last interaction with Mom. If I'd known it would be my last time seeing her, what would I have done differently? And what would I give to have a chance to fix it?

As we climb up the small hill leading into the cemetery, I nod.

"You ready?" I ask.

Colin takes a deep breath and shrugs. "No?" He laughs. "What am I even doing here? This is crazy, right? I must have a screw loose to be out here with two strangers, looking to piss off an old friend."

"I'll take that as a yes?"

"It's as good as we're gonna get."

I look at Hiro, who nods.

I find the pinprick in the air again and pull back the imaginary covers.

In the blink of an eye, we're back within the confines of the papier mâché auditorium. Paper cutouts of ballerinas surround us. It's almost as though they were expecting us and had incorporated us into their routine.

Colin swallows hard and sniffs, though he doesn't shake. Dude's braver than I thought he would be. I was sure he'd at least be shaking, maybe even stumbling over his cane.

The ballerinas weave in and out between us in a slalom pattern, soft voices whispering all the while.

"Break a leg."

"Break a leg."

"Break a leg."

"Break a leg."

"Break a leg."

"We get it," I say. "The guy liked theater."

"He liked anything that included a stage," Colin says. "Any opportunity to express himself. No matter what happened, if he hadn't died, I'm sure he would have found a way to make a living off it." His voice elicited true admiration. If I didn't know any better, I would have thought Colin had a crush on Alan, not Isabel. Then again, who's to say it wasn't both?

"Break a leg."

"Break a leg."

"Break a leg."

"Break a leg."

"Okay, I've had enough," Hiro says. With a swipe of his hand, a jet of air cuts through the paper ballerinas, slicing them in half before they dispersed into a gray dust. An eerie silence follows, punctuated by Hiro's heavy breaths. Had that been worth the effort? The silence doesn't last long. Out of the orchestra pit, *"Greensleeves"* starts playing. "Never a dull moment in here."

Slowly, the whole theater starts to rumble.

Stomp.

Stomp.

Stomp.

With each stomp, the theater shakes more, and the music grows louder.

And then backstage explodes. I turn to see the gorilla beast I've learned to be associated with Alan. What a strange form. He's like ten feet tall, muscles bulging, like a weightlifter, his golden hair long and loose, his tongue long and dangling, strands of drool practically touching the ground. Perhaps most prominent are his eyes. Wide, bloodshot, crazed and yet somehow emotionless at the same time.

I summon Mom and slice through a piece of drywall that threatens to slam into us.

The Spectre's eyes scan me over, a hint of familiarity in them, and then land on Colin. His eyes narrow.

The lights in the theater flicker and warp, bending and twisting as though made of rubber.

"Okay, now's your chance," Hiro says.

I reach out with my emotions, sensing the Spectre's own, and trying to match it before swinging my blade into his side. Just like last time, it connects and cuts through, but doesn't make as much of an impact.

"Don't forget, you can't just match your own emotion," Hiro says. "You have to sync with your own Spectral Companion."

"What?"

"Did I not tell you that?"

I have no idea, but there's no point in arguing now. Fighting a Spectre in a Mirage is exhausting. Tapping into your own emotions is hard enough, but finding a way to sync it with two other separate entities is a whole different level of difficulty.

Okay, Luna, think. Vulnerability. That's an easy enough emotion for me to line up with. I spend ninety percent of my life feeling vulnerable in one way or another, no matter how much I try to hide it. I exude that emotion into my blade, but am met with resistance.

"Come on, Mom!" I yell. "Think of a time you were insecure!"

"Don't tell me what to do," is the sword's sassy response.

"What happened to the bloodlust you had in our first fight?" I ask.

"It's not that easy, you know," Hiro says.

"Oh, I *know*!" I yell back, dodging another attack from the Alan Spectre. "Any help would be great. I think I got this guy's dominant emotion, but it doesn't do any good if Mom doesn't cooperate."

"You can't just speak to her like she's a person. She's not fully sentient yet. On an emotional level, she's closer to a dog."

"Did you just call my mom a dog again?"

"Did he just call me a dog?" my sword hisses.

"The point is you have to emit a certain emotion. Emit that energy."

"What do you think I'm doing?"

"Well, you're not doing it well enough."

"Thanks for the words of encouragement, dick!" I say as one of the Spectre's hits actually connects with me. My world blacks out for a split second as another bludgeoning attack hits me from behind. As the papier mâché dust clears, I realize that second bludgeon was actually me slamming into the wall of the theater. I catch my breath, my Syncer beeping. I tap it with a weary hand.

DANGER! Defense down 50%!

"Defense down 50%?" I say.

"It means you can likely take another hit or two head on. After that, you'll be vulnerable. Your Spectre currently acts as a shield."

"So it'll be like getting hit as a normal human?"

"Not quite, but it'll be a lot easier for you to die."

"Oh, that's comforting!"

"Just try to dodge."

"You think?" I pry myself from the wall and leap down to the ground just as the gorilla man slams into the dent in the papier mâché drywall.

"Hey, am I supposed to be doing anything else?" Colin yells out, ignored and alone at the center of the stage, save for the respawned dancing ballerinas yelling out "Break a leg" every half-second.

"Let me deal with my thing first," I say with a weary groan. "We'll get back to you in a second."

"Now, remember to capture that emotion—"

"And try to push it out to my Spectre. Yeah, I get it. It's not my fault if it's not working." I sync my mind with a vulnerable memory and feel my wrist vibrate.

Spectral Companion Sync: 100%

"That's it," Hiro says. "That means you and your Spectral Companion are in sync."

I leap up and slash at Alan's back. The blade connects once again, but still doesn't seem to have a lot of effect. With him stuck in the wall, it's an opportunity to regain my composure.

He twists around within the dent, facing me.

I'm synced with one Spectre. Now, the other. Come on, *think*. Remember what it was like fighting against Mom. How I felt most of her emotions when I actually touched her. What if I did the same to a Spectre that wasn't mine?

I slam my blade under the monster's chin and press my tiny hand against his gigantic forehead.

"Help!" the monster cries out to me. First in his gorilla voice, and then in another one. A more feminine voice. "Help," he cries out again. For the briefest of moments, I see someone else within its body, almost as though they're encased in him.

Isabel. *Is she actually alive?*

And then I'm knocked back, with the monster returning in full force.

"She's in there," I say to Colin, who's still back on the stage, clearly not knowing what he's supposed to be doing in this superhuman fight. "I actually think we can still save her."

"How?" he says.

I think back to the core of all this. The key emotion that keeps Alan on this plane of existence. We'd brought Colin with us because we thought it would trigger his insecurity. His helplessness. While the man's appearance seemed to trigger something, I'm not sure it's done what we wanted it to do.

"Hang on," I say, taking another leap and a slash at the Spectre. The beast dodges me, but is caught off guard when I barrel into him shoulder-first. I stop on impact—not much a five-foot-nothing someone can do against a ten-foot barrel of muscle. But it accomplishes what I want. I'm flooded with a series of memories. I try to pinpoint his key emotion again.

Yes, *there's* the insecurity I'd felt before, along with the rejection. There's no mistaking it. But as I delve further, I notice something else.

I flash back to the same series of memories I'd seen earlier. Him meeting Isabel, their lustful and passionate love affair. But no, it's not love that I'm feeling in those early moments. It's hardly even infatuation. It's lust. Pure lust.

The two are in bed, thin sheets draped over their bodies. Isabel curls her fingers around Alan's. He reciprocates, mind still high, an approaching calm.

"So, you'll stay?" Isabel says.

That emotion spikes once again. Insecurity. Wait, why insecurity now?

Alan shakes his head.

The Spectre knocks me back and I slam into a row of velvet seats, though at the speed I'm traveling, everything feels like hard metal or wood.

DANGER! Defense at 25%!

A notification pops up in my Syncer.

"You said he wanted to leave L.A., right?" I call out to Colin.

"Huh?"

"Where did Alan want to go after high school?"

"New York."

"Of course he did," I whisper to myself. That insecurity isn't an insecurity that comes with knowing your girlfriend cheated. It's the kind that comes when you feel trapped. When you feel like you're not good enough.

My mind races back to everything involving home. My deadbeat dad. My nonexistent friends. My inability to escape, no matter how many opportunities I get. I push the emotion outward, and something clicks into place.

Spectre Sync: 100%

"Well, that was easier, wasn't it, Mom?" I say to my blade.

I can somehow feel her put on a mischievous smile. She's ready for blood.

I take another leap toward Alan, and when my blade connects this time, it cuts right through. I land on the opposite side and turn around.

The Spectre screams out as the top half of his body falls to the hardwood floor. But these are Ethereal Entities, so his body still writhes around as though still connected. I hear a gasp from behind, and turn to see the bottom half of the Spectre. A head sprouts from his chest.

"Izzy?" Colin says, hobbling down a set of stairs.

"No, wait!" I cry out, but the top half of the body, using his arms as legs, crawls over to the half-crippled man. I dart over there as fast as I can, slamming my palm into Alan's chest as he makes contact with Colin.

We zip from this non-reality into another memory.

"Say something," I hear Isabel's ragged whispers. The two are sitting in a park. "Say something!"

"I think... I think the two of you will be happy together," Alan says with a smile. Against all odds, it's genuine. A relief floods through him. Unmitigated happiness.

"You're kidding," she says. "That's it?"

"I can't stay here."

"You didn't even get into school."

"I know," he says, that wavering insecurity returning. "But I have to try. Who am I if I can't even try?"

"You're just going to leave me?"

"I'm sorry, but did I miss something? You cheated on me with Colin."

"I made a mistake, you idiot!"

"Maybe it wasn't a mistake."

Another wisp and we disappear and reappear onto a rooftop. On its edge stands Isabel, and a panic rips through Alan.

"Izzy, don't do it!"

"Why not? You're leaving me!"

"I'm not leaving you."

"Yes, you are."

"I'm…you're not being fair."

Alan approaches cautiously, his emotions torn between fear, hatred, and again, insecurity.

"If you leave, then I leave." She hovers one of her feet over the edge.

"I'll stay!" he says. His hands are up, palms out, as though he's calming a wild horse.

"You will?" Isabel's breath softens. "You'll stay?"

"If you promise not to jump, I'll stay." He makes his way to her side and holds her hand, this time grabbing on tight, pulling her in close.

"I didn't want to cheat on you, you know," she says.

Alan smiles awkwardly. "It's okay."

"I just thought that you would care. But you don't, do you?"

"That's not true."

It is.

"Then why are you leaving? I'll never be good enough to keep you. To keep you for myself, or to keep you here."

At this moment, I can feel Alan's emotions, and Isabel isn't wrong. That he doesn't love her, and needs to leave. But he can't say that.

A pained expression passes over Isabel, and with an angry effort, she pushes him over the edge.

With a bone-crunching squelch, I'm brought out of the memory into the papier mâché theater. I recoil from the memory and nearly wretch from the effort.

I look over at Colin, whose eyes are wide. He's witnessed the very same memory as me.

The girl's eyes flicker open from within the Spectre's body. She doesn't react to her surroundings, her mind likely still in a daze, though when her eyes settle on Colin, a soft smile emerges.

"Colin."

"How…" Colin's voice shakes. "How could you?"

FOUR

A ROAR BRINGS us all back to reality—well, some sort of reality. When you're surrounded by paper-thin dancers and a giant man-Ghost who's been cut in half, it's kinda hard to gauge what's real and what's not.

The roar comes from the mouth of the Spectre, whose top half had grabbed on to Colin and me to share with us the moment of his death. In a cascading landslide, it all falls into place. That feeling of insecurity wasn't a feeling of not being good enough. Despite not getting into the school of his dreams, he thought he was good enough. What worried him most was Isabel. He liked her, yes, but didn't see her as the love of his life.

I reflect back on the "performance" this Mirage had put on for me. On the image of the man trapped in the cage. The last prevalent emotion that kept him alive wasn't anger or fear or plain insecurity. It was that of a boy being trapped by life's circumstances. That, after all his work and determination, he'd be left to live a life here, just because some girl was too selfish to let him go.

The Spectre's upper body gives another roar and crawls over to his standing lower body.

"Colin, please!" Isabel cries out as Alan places his chest and head back onto his body, muffling her cries for help. And then he looks at me. His face, for the first time, looks strangely human.

"He's giving you a chance to leave," Hiro says, his voice distant as he strides closer. "Now that you know the truth, he wants you to make a decision."

"He's innocent," I say.

"Well, we always knew that."

"Not just innocent," I say. "He's a victim of murder."

"It appears so."

"So, what should I do?"

"I think you know what you have to do," Hiro says. "Remember, if you leave a Spectre to languish, it will only grow angrier. It will consume everything around it until there's nothing left. It will spill out into the cemetery, absorb more hikers, lead to more deaths. Is that what you want?"

"But he just wants justice," Colin says.

"And to be free," I say.

"So, get him justice. Free him." Despite his words, there's no warmth in his voice. Hiro doesn't care for this man. All he cares about is getting in his Spectre count so he can continue living his life.

But that doesn't make him wrong. If we bring the girl back to the real world, she can face justice. If we take him out here, he will be truly free for the first time, and won't be sentenced to an eternity reliving his worst memories.

And me? The sooner I get the Spectre count for Hiro, the sooner I can get rid of this burden and escape from my own trapped existence.

It takes no effort to conjure up this emotion, and it syncs up with Mom almost instantly.

The Spectre, seeing me grip the hilt of my blade all the tighter, growls at me, as if understanding what I'm about to do.

I leap toward him, and a piece of me breaks as I see the look on his face. Confusion and defeat. My blade cuts through him in what I know is a critical hit. When I come through the other side of the attack, I see him struggling, angry. He lets out a loud roar and swipes at me, his last defiant emotions trying to take me down with him.

"Don't struggle," I whisper. "You don't want to be stuck like this forever." I attack again and slice through one of his arms. He cries out again, sounding like a pained elephant in the savannah. "I promise, this is the best way for you to be truly free."

Memories flood me. Emotions. Passion for his art, love for his friends and family, and an unclaimed ambition. This was his life.

He continues to cry out. He's a sad dog about to be put down for reasons he doesn't understand. After a few more slashes, the Spectre's body opens up again, and Isabel spills out.

And still, the creature is alive, though just barely. I put my hand on his chest, sharing with him my own vulnerability. My own humanity.

He doesn't speak, but in his catatonic state, I can almost feel a request.

"Go...with...you....?"

I look up at him and see the request in his eyes. I have no idea. Can he?

"Now's your chance, Luna," Hiro says behind me. "He's vulnerable."

"Of course, he's vulnerable," I say. "Didn't you see what happened to him? He's upset. He's trapped."

"You've described every Spectre in existence."

"Not like him."

"Oh, God." I hear Hiro slap his forehead. "You're not doing him any favors by leaving him behind."

"What if I take him with me?"

"That's not how this works."

"And why not?"

"You can only level up your Spectre by letting it consume the Essence of another Spectre. You can only find its Essence by setting it free."

I look at the large Spectre in front of me. He's not even fighting back. There isn't a struggle left in his somehow tired-looking body. Is it possible for a Ghost to look tired?

"Hey," Hiro says. "Don't forget what you're doing for them."

"Killing them."

"Freeing him. He's already dead."

"Killing him again. Only this time, there's no coming back."

"You're setting him free. Setting *them* free. To let them continue in this existence is to let them continue to linger. To dwell. To suffer."

"And what about Mom? What about *your* Spectre?"

"Our Spectres are unique."

"So, that's it? We're unique, so rules don't apply?"

Hiro's face darkens. "You can't let him live."

I stare back at the heaving, sad creature in front of me. It's hard not to feel sorry for him. He was cheated out of life, and continues to suffer in death. Needlessly. Pointlessly.

"Oh, for the love of..." I can hear the tone in Hiro's voice shift. "These creatures...they lie, cheat, and will do anything they can to trick you."

"Maybe," I say. But I know the emotions are no lie. But I can't turn back now. I weigh my decision. The danger Alan poses to the outside world is too great.

I blink tears from my eyes as I launch off the papier mâché flooring, swinging my blade through Alan's gorilla neck. With a backward cut, I free the girl from the Spectre's innards and she spills onto the floor.

Then I tap into that key emotion. That feeling of being trapped. Flashes of my apartment at the Main Stay, Gabe and his goons, Dad; everything that's keeping me down and keeping me from moving on in life comes at me in a whirlwind. I slice through Alan again. He may be a

Spectre now, but at one point, he was just like me—a kid with dreams and no way out. Though, unlike me, his time is over. No longer is he able to put on the shows he so desperately wants. Never would he find companionship. In Spectre form, he was stuck in limbo, in a purgatory where he can relive that dream in some form. As my blade cuts through him one last time, I even rob him of that opportunity.

With a final scream, the Spectre erupts in a glow of light.

Everything around us shimmers with an eerie glow before dissolving. Paper ballerinas continue their dance as they dissolve in flames, and the self-portrait of Alan trapped in a birdcage hanging above the stage breaks apart with a crack.

The entire world decays, and in its place, the bright, hot, unforgiving night L.A. breeze cuts through me, and we are back in the small cemetery in the middle of nowhere.

"Is it over?" Colin's voice is weak and shaken. Not that anyone can blame him.

"It's over," Hiro says. "Well, the situation with the Spectre is over. I imagine the two of you have a lot to discuss." He motions to the girl, who rests almost peacefully in the soft grass.

Colin's lips tighten as he glares at the sleeping woman. "I just can't believe she'd do something like that. That she'd kill one of our best friends —her boyfriend." He turns to Hiro. "So what happens now?"

"You go on with your life."

"But what about her?"

"What about her?"

"You saw what she did, didn't you?"

"And?"

"So, what happens to her?"

"I'm sorry, but don't misunderstand our role here," Hiro says. "We're not private investigators, we're not cops, we're not law enforcement or government agents of any type. What happens next between you and her is up to you and her. For what it's worth, I doubt the judge will take the word of a now dead Spectre. You try to spin the tale of what you just saw and they'll chalk it up to a high particulate day illusion."

With that, Hiro picks something up off the grass and starts to walk away. "Let's go, Luna."

With a few anxious glances back, I follow him away from the cemetery. Colin leans heavily on his good leg, his weight somehow doubling. What happens when the woman wakes up? Where would their conversations lead? Would he turn her in to the LAPD? Would they believe him?

"That's none of our business," Hiro says, as though reading my thoughts.

"You sure about that?" I say. "If it wasn't for us, none of this would have happened.

"Correction," Hiro says. "If it wasn't for us, that girl would still be trapped inside the Spectre. Who knows how long it would be 'till she died. That Spectre would have wallowed in self-pity for days, weeks, months, years, or even longer, attacking more helpless hikers. All we did was free a Spirit and save an innocent life. Well, maybe not innocent. Even more important, that young man will finally get the closure he's been seeking, no matter how painful."

My head bobs up and down in what I guess can be considered a nod. Without us, that girl was as good as dead. This would be another unsolved missing persons case. Like Marco, another casualty of the lives we live.

"You did the right thing," Hiro says. "I know it's tempting to think that if we let them linger here they'll get another chance, but that only leads to more death and despair. It's not an easy job, but it does have its perks. You did good today. Stopped to think a bit longer than I would have, but I guess it's your first time, so I'll let it slide. And don't forget—never forget—the spoils."

"Spoils?"

Hiro rolls his eyes. "Did you forget about the whole point of doing this?" He holds up a black orb between his thumb and index finger. No, it's not completely black, more clear with a black cloudiness from within that somehow seeps outward. "This is the Essence of that Spectre. Every Ethereal Entity is made up of two main parts. We have its soul, and its Essence. In freeing the soul from this earthly plane, we also free it from its Essence."

"And where does its Essence come from?"

Hiro gave me a shrug, partially to answer the question, but also partially in a fashion that seems to say, "Who cares?"

"All I know is that an Essence is left behind when taking out a Spectre. If you take out a Ghost or Poltergeist, you won't be left with any spoils to speak of. I believe the Essence is still present, but has yet to take shape. Regardless, this is what you need to turn your mother into a more fully formed Spectre, one that will eventually satisfy my own." He tosses me the orb with an unexpected nonchalance, and I catch it with one hand.

The orb is heavy, like a smaller version of one of those Chinese meditation balls, only heavier. "What do I do now?" I ask.

"Feed it to your mom."

That's a specific bit of phrasing I never expected to hear, but my life stopped being normal a while ago. I hold down the gem on my Syncer and Mom emerges as we make our way down the (thankfully) empty trail. Her giant head looks around, as though confused by the purpose of her summon.

I hold the Essence up between my thumb and forefinger, assuming instinct will take over.

It does.

With little warning, her mouth envelopes my entire hand, like an overzealous dog taking a treat, except all I feel is a cool breeze as the entire head covers my arm, taking the large orb with it, leaving my body unscathed.

She vibrates with an exaggerated crunching. After several long seconds, my armband goes off. I pull up the main screen. Most everything there is the same.

"Um," I say. "No change?"

"Not yet," Hiro says. "It takes more than one Essence to level up."

"How many?"

"It all depends on how strong the Spectres are that you defeat." He pauses for a moment. "But you'll get there soon. Levels aside, I'm sure you feel the difference."

He's right. It's hard to pinpoint, but I'm standing up straighter than before.

And with the Essence's consumption, I find myself one step away from the life I have, and one step closer to claiming the life I've always deserved.

"Congratulations, Kid, but your journey has only just begun. One down, several to go," Hiro says.

Though, despite the many more Essences Mom needs to consume, and the depressing end to another Spectre's existence, I feel the slightest—just the slightest—bit optimistic.

To Be Continued...

SPECTRAL | EPISODE 4

A MOVIE THEATER...

AISHA CROSSES HER ARMS, eyes drifting sideways to her boyfriend, Trevor, who sits beside her in the dark theater. They may not be speaking, but she can feel the tension between them.

And the night had been going so well.

They'd eaten a tasty dinner at Shin-Sen-Gumi, laughing and sharing stories over a hot kettle of tea, like they used to when they first started dating. It was an amazing night. A perfect night. It was why Aisha felt comfortable enough to drop the big news. She hadn't planned on sharing it then. Maybe in a few weeks when the idea had sunken into her own brain—or maybe even in a few months when she finally started showing. There'd be no way for her to hide it then.

But, as it turned out, *tonight* was that magical night.

"Oh, wow, you're serious?" was the first thing he'd said.

Not the greatest endorsement for what would likely be the biggest event in their lives. He'd followed it up with halfhearted positivity. He put on a show about how great the news was, and how amazing life would be, but then went silent, stirring the remains of his ramen before rushing them out the door to the movie.

It was one he'd been looking forward to for weeks. Some revival road-show of an old horror movie from the '30s she could never remember the name of. But as they filed into their assigned seats, he didn't so much as utter a single word, pointing to a sign on their menu that demands silence as the picture played.

He couldn't shut up all damned day, and the second a baby was mentioned, he'd rushed them into the dark, as if eager for the excuse to stay silent, using the movie as a cover.

Aisha's hands clench into fists as she imagines violent and unspeakable acts on her boyfriend. No, not just her boyfriend anymore. Partner. Now life partner. She knows he can sense her gaze, and can almost feel a cold sweat trickling down his neck as he sits with his chin up, face focused on the gory murder scene playing out. He always does this—gets hyper focused when he's trying to pretend he doesn't notice her. It really pisses her off.

Normally, at these showings, he rests his hand on hers, tightening it before every jump scare so she can prepare, saving herself from a series of nightmares later that night. Not tonight. Tonight, he sits turned away from her, left leg folded over the right. This is the last place in the world he wants to be right now.

This was supposed to be fun and romantic. Instead, it's tense and awkward. And if she tries to start up a conversation, he'll make a big deal about being quiet in the theater for fear of being kicked out.

When the girl on screen turns around, the music blaring in sync, only to reveal a yawning cat, Trevor lets out a boisterous laugh, along with the rest of the audience. Is he seriously laughing right now? Acting like she didn't just drop that bombshell on him?

Aisha blinks, her mind rewinding back to the moment she'd told him about the news. Had he understood? Maybe she hadn't gotten her point across like she'd thought she had? Is it possible that he had no clue she was pregnant? She'd tried to be cheeky and cute with her reveal. What if it hadn't been clear? Was she reading into his attitude?

Another full-bellied laugh from Trevor and the rest of the audience. That has to be it. He just doesn't know. Aisha smiles to herself.

I'm such an idiot.

She reaches for Trevor's hand in the dark, but the instant skin touches skin, he slinks away, letting out another laugh along with the audience.

What the hell?

Aisha swears she catches him stealing a glance at her, and perhaps she imagines it, but she also notes a look of mild annoyance on his face. A spike of anger rises within her, and it takes all her willpower not to stand up and shout at him in the middle of the showing, but she lets the moment pass and takes a deep breath.

What would Pauline say? Whenever she's in a tough situation, Aisha tries to pretend to be her own therapist by predicting something her actual therapist would say.

"You just dropped a huge piece of news on him," Pauline would say.

"He should be happy," Aisha responds.

"*You're* happy," Pauline continues. "It *is* great news. But this isn't just good news. It's life-*altering* news."

"He should be happy," she repeats.

"And maybe he will be. But everyone processes news like this differently."

"Everyone processes news differently," Aisha whispers to herself in the theater, repeating the sage advice from an imaginary version of Pauline. With another breath, she settles into her leather seat, and somehow enjoys the remainder of the splatter-fest playing out on the big screen in front of her.

Before she knows it, the film is finished, the audience packing up and heading to the exits, mulling over that predictable, yet incredibly iconic stinger. Movies would go on to replicate that for the next several decades, so much so that it's become trite. At least that's what Trevor had told her several times before, each time as though it was the first time he's mentioned it.

God, I love him.

"Gotta pee," Trevor says, standing up.

It takes all of Aisha's willpower not to bring up the subject, but she lets it pass. There will be several minutes to discuss on the way home, and then there was home itself. He had no other one-bedroom apartment to escape to.

The two follow the crowd to the exits. After making their way down the long hallway, Trevor steps into the men's room, letting the door swing shut behind him without a word.

Aisha presses her back against the wall and slides down into a seated position on the ground. She resists the urge to rush in and bombard him with countless questions. That would only push him away and start this new chapter of their lives off on the wrong foot. Instead, she closes her eyes and breathes slowly.

A few minutes pass. Some men she recognizes from the theater make their way out, and the hallway goes empty.

A few more minutes pass.

Was he taking a shit or something?

No one enters or leaves the bathroom for several more minutes.

She flips out her netscreen and gestures a message.

You okay in there?

A few seconds after sending the text, she gets an error message. She stands. Wrinkling her brows, she taps at the air to send again, only to be rewarded with the same error message.

She's had her netscreen for an entire year and has never had a single error message. What was going on?

She swipes on a call, and it goes straight to voicemail. She glances to the left and right—no one around—and opens the door just wide enough for her head to poke through. "Trevor? You in there?"

Not so much as the sound of a dripping faucet.

This is stupid. She enters into the bathroom completely. A pair of marble sinks sit side by side, UV dryers to their right and left side, against their respective walls, illuminated by a set of theater lights behind them. Aisha turns left to see a set of three urinals on the right and a set of three stalls on the left. Keeping her feet light, she tilts her head to the side and lowers it to the floor, peeking underneath.

No feet stick out at the bottom of the stalls.

Perplexed, she opens the first stall. Empty. The second. Empty.

And the third?

She swallows, and with a soft hand, she presses at the stall door. It gives way to her touch with no resistance, revealing nothing but a clean toilet seat.

"Trevor?" she says, now feeling like a complete idiot, her heart rate increasing by the second. "Trevor?"

SPECTRAL

EPISODE 4
FURY

ONE

"UH-HUH," Hiro says, leaning against the counter in the kitchen of his oversized bachelor flat. He seems to have forgotten it's a video call, with the netscreen pointed from the waist up, and he's taken to scratching under his shirt as he carries on. "Look, we can buy you a coffee if it's about the cost."

The cost? We're not taking her out on some date, you idiot. It takes all my willpower not to push him out of the way.

"I've already told you," the woman on the other line says, "that I've given my statement and I don't have anything else to say to you people."

"But what if we could find—what was it—your fiancé?"

I see the woman practically pull at her braids from frustration. "Goodbye, sir."

"Is that a no?"

"That's a no, you parasite!" She slams her fist down, and once it connects with the desk, the line goes dead.

"What happened to people wanting to be heard?" I can't help but say. It's what Hiro had told me when we had zero issues meeting up with Colin, another recent victim of a Spectre. In retrospect, that *was* too easy of an explanation. I'd never bought the idea that people are inherently hungry to be heard.

Hiro lets out a deep breath, runs his fingers through his hair, and collapses onto one of the bar chairs placed at the kitchen island. After several long seconds, he snatches his netscreen, throws out the holographic keyboard and opens a browser.

"What're you doing?" I ask.

"Huh?"

"What. Are. You. Doing?"

"Stay in this business long enough," Hiro says, "and you learn not to let a few roadblocks keep you down. If you don't bounce back quick, your Spectre will starve."

"It's amazing how you still didn't answer my question," I say.

"I'm looking for a new lead."

"We have a lead."

"That one didn't work out. You saw the call."

"So you give up?"

"Can't spend too long on one case," Hiro says. "Always remember the sunk cost fallacy when it comes to businesses and Spectre hunting."

"Huh?"

Hiro sighs and finally turns to me. "I'm not one to press. If she won't give me anything to work with, there's nothing I can do."

"Don't take this the wrong way, but it's been a long time since you've slept with anyone, hasn't it?"

His eyes narrow, and he turns back to his netscreen. "That's none of your business."

"How many years?" I say.

"Luna."

"Five?"

"Luna."

"Ten?"

"Knock it off."

"More?!"

"When you're as old as me," Hiro says, "base carnal pleasures lose their luster."

"Gross."

"You brought it up."

"I'm not saying it to make fun of you," I say, "but that entire conversation lacked any bedside manner, you know? She didn't feel safe talking with you, and you didn't even *try*."

"She didn't want to talk to me."

"Exactly. She didn't want to talk to another man."

"Okay?"

"Do I even have to point out the obvious here?"

He spins back around on the barstool, one of his lanky legs up and propped on the seat, his forearm resting on his knee. He stares at me, eyes taking me in from head to toe. "What's the obvious?"

"I'm a girl!" I say.

"Yeah," he says, "but I don't know how I feel about letting a kid reach out on my behalf. It's manipulative and creepy."

"And how's that any different from what you've been doing already? Convincing me to throw myself into danger so you can eventually eat my mom."

"Uh…"

"All I'm saying is that we've lost out on two potential leads because *you* didn't feel comfortable 'exploiting women,' as you put it."

"You can't even vote yet."

"Just let me take the lead on this one. Please?"

"There are plenty of other Spectres out there," Hiro says. "Los Angeles has a population of almost ten million. It's overflowing with Spectral potential. There's a reason I've been able to live here for so long. It's just a matter of finding them. If we lose one or two, it's not the end of the world."

"It could be for that woman."

Hiro sighs.

"I'm hungry," a voice declares from behind me. I turn to see Mom's giant head, which rests on a dog bed at the corner of the room by Kuro's cage.

"How much time does she have until she starts to atrophy?" I ask. "She's been saying that for the past few days."

"I promise you that no matter how many Essences we feed her that she will always declare she is hungry. She has at least another couple of weeks before this affects her stats."

"My what?" the Spectral face says.

"And if we find nothing over the next few months? What happens then?"

Hiro motions to Kuro and to himself. "Over time, your Spectre will lose some of its strength. Any abilities or weaponry that have carried over to you will also start to fade away. Your Spectre will then lose sentience and the ability to speak. If you've been connected with your Spectre as long as I have, your own health closer reflects that of your Spectre."

"Oh, right. Your own health is linked to Kuro."

"That's right."

"What about mine and Mom's?"

Hiro laughs. "Yes, but not as intensely. I've had this Bond with Kuro for over a hundred and thirty years. This link gives one an unnaturally long life, meaning that as their life and abilities fade, real-life aging starts to take effect. You've only been Bonded with your mother for, what, a few days now? You have nothing to worry about. Yet."

I sigh, a feeling of relief washing over me.

"But," Hiro continues, "if we *weren't* able to find any Essences over the course of the next month or two, your mother would eventually dissipate into nothingness, her weakened leftover Essence dissolving along with her. If they 'die' without being freed, they leave nothing behind. No fear, no anger, no hatred. They take all these negative emotions with them to the next plane of existence."

"And what is the next plane of existence?"

"I don't ever want to find out." Hiro stands and limps over to Kuro's cage. "You should have seen him in his prime. Seen *us* in our prime."

Mom rolls over on the bed, looking a lot like a household pet. I know it won't be easy to let her go again, but that has to be better than the alternative. Committing to a Spectral Companion would be committing to a never-ending grind of research and fighting. If I were to spend all my time doing that, how would I even…

I look around the flat. "Where do you get your money?"

"Generational wealth."

"You came from a rich family?"

"No, but I've lived long enough to gain multiple generations of wealth."

"Oh. So, literally."

"I can live another two hundred years and not have to work another day of my life if I want to—barring Spectre hunts, of course."

"That much time, and you still never learned how to talk to women, huh?"

He raises his eyebrow. "Speaking with *women* has never been a priority."

I pick up my netscreen. "Well, maybe this is a chance to learn to expand your horizons a bit. Let me show you how it's done."

After a few seconds, he finally nods. "Okay, Kid. Surprise me."

I MADE sure the diner we meet at is crowded. My plan worked. The second I'd placed the call, it was clear the woman, Aisha, was more comfortable. I don't know if it was because I'm a girl or because I'm young, but after a white lie about being a private investigator—that part was not Hiro-approved—she agreed to meet. It's amazing how much more progress you make when you don't act like a heartless sociopath.

"And the police?" I ask, sitting across from the woman at a booth in the diner.

Her eyes are dark, bags resting under them, her braided hair fraying at the roots. "It's an open and shut case, they say. Once they realized I was pregnant, they said there wasn't a lot they could do. Labeled it as a 'voluntary disappearance.'"

I give a stiff nod and my lips draw into a line. I can't really blame the conclusion. It's lazy police work, sure, but it happens all the time. When you take on the responsibility of a kid, unless you have the help of a parent or grandparent, you're sentencing yourself to a living as a lower-class citizen for the next two decades. With abortion being illegal, the number of men just up and leaving after knocking up their girlfriends—or even wives—is a constant issue.

"You agree with them," Aisha says.

"What?"

"I can see the look on your face."

"No, no." I scramble for an excuse. "No, look. I'm just…taking in the information is all. Every bit helps."

"How old are you?"

"Nineteen," I lie, perhaps a bit too quickly. And maybe that was too young of a lie.

"Hmm." She eyes me up and down. I'm used to this part of any interaction. It's bad enough being young, but looking *younger* than I am is a never-ending hassle. "And you run a P.I. business?"

"It's family owned," I say with a nervous chuckle.

"Do you have a business card you can drop to me?"

I clear my throat. "I just…we work mostly on referrals, so don't need one."

"Okay, Veronica Mars."

"Who?"

"I'm already a sideshow on Talkly," Aisha says. "I refuse to be the victim of some hairbrained scam."

"It's not a scam, I promise. I won't even ask for payment." I realize it's a mistake as soon as I say it.

"Uh-huh."

She's right in step with me. At this point in the conversation, I should be ready with an excuse, but nothing comes to mind, so I sit there with my mouth hanging open as she stands up.

"All I want to know is what theater your boyfriend disappeared at." It's a simple question, but one that current journalists refuse to reveal in their pieces. That's commonplace nowadays, with no outlet wanting to be responsible for popularizing murder locations, turning them into violent meccas.

As if to spite me, Aisha picks up her mug and downs the rest of her drink. "Thanks for the coffee." A few moments later, she's out the door and down the street.

How had I let this happen? I grew up in one of the most dangerous areas in the United States and couldn't even stumble my way through this stupid lie. I lay my forehead down on the laminate counter. The cold, hard countertop flattens my reddened cheeks and nose.

I feel the weight of someone slide into the booth across from me.

"That went well." Hiro's voice is only modestly smug.

"Shut up."

"No, I mean it."

I drag my face up until my chin rests on the table. Hiro's gaunt face stares back at me and Kuro stands on his shoulder, looking equally puzzled by my pathetic posture.

"I don't think Kuro's allowed in here."

"It's fine."

"He's a crow, dude," I say. "Doesn't matter if it's a Spectre or not. They won't care if he has a tie and a top hat."

"I assure it's—"

"Excuse me, sir," one of the servers says, appearing out of nowhere. "You're going to have to put your…pet outside."

"Kuro," Hiro says.

With a squawk, the bird flies out the door as another patron walks in, practically knocking them over in the process. I can tell by the look on the server's face that she doesn't know whether or not to accept what just happened as normal.

"Sorry," I say with an apologetic shrug. "He's just weird. He won't do it again."

She rolls her eyes and walks off.

"What's up with you?" I say to Hiro. "Were you raised on another planet or something?"

"Kuro had to get her scent."

"Huh?"

"When I told you it went well, I meant it," Hiro says. "Kuro can track her location based on her Spectral scent. Or the scent of any Spectres she's been near. Once he's done his investigating, he can guide us to the location. You're welcome."

"I think you mean thank you," I correct him.

Hiro pushes the empty mug of coffee aside. "Why did you tell her you're a P.I.?"

"To get her to talk."

"You're lucky she didn't accept," he says. "You can't set expectations. The second you do that, it puts you on the line for results. *Their* results. I know you're a nice person, but you can't become a Medium for anyone but yourself."

"Don't you mean for you?"

"In *service* of your own self-interest. Don't act like you'd be doing this out of the goodness of your heart."

"Got it," I say with a nod. "I find Spectres, defeat them, Mom eats their Essences, and gets strong enough for you."

"And your life returns to its normal status. You'll forget about the world of Spectres and the daily fight for survival."

A sinking feeling forms in my stomach. This feeling has ebbed and flowed at pretty regular intervals since taking this deal with Hiro.

"Hey," he says. "This isn't the life your mom would have wanted for you, anyway."

That's presumptuous of him. But I nod again. It's not like I can ask her. My Spectre may be Mom's Spirit, but she hasn't regained any memories or personality traits that make her Mom. Those won't come until she takes in more Essences.

"What next?" Hiro asks.

"Why're you asking me?"

"You wanted to take the lead. I have some other things to take care of, but I trust you can figure out the next steps."

"Where are you going?"

Hiro only smiles at me, and I deflate.

"You don't believe her, do you?" I say.

"I believe she went out with her boyfriend and that she doesn't know where he is. Beyond that, so long as we have two of us, we may as well spread our resources."

He turns outside and points to Kuro, who rests on a lamppost, ignoring a few pedestrians taking his photo from the sidewalk. "Kuro's waiting for you right outside."

"IT'S no wonder you're two steps away from starving to death," I say as I stomp down the Los Angeles sidewalk.

Kuro's squawk is all I get in response.

"He eliminates half the cases out there because he doesn't know how to interact like a human. Now he sends a newbie like me to do his dirty work."

"Caw!"

"I know! How do you put up with him?"

"Caw!" he says.

I then look at Kuro's avian form as he glides ahead from lamppost to lamppost, waiting for me to catch up. "You used to talk, right?"

"Caw!"

"I mean, I know you said a couple of words before. But not much. Do you understand me now? Two caws for yes."

"Caw! Caw!"

"Is it because you need more Essences?"

"Caw! Caw!"

"Do you and other Spectres get less sentient if you don't?"

"Caw! Caw!"

I wrinkle my nose. Is he really responding, or am I just assuming? "Hey, Kuro, are we in Boston?"

No response.

"Are we in L.A.?"

"Caw! Caw!"

I nod. At least I know he understands, even if he can't speak.

We remain silent for the remaining ten city blocks. I'm about to ask how much longer it'll be when I see a large movie poster plastered on the outside wall of a building.

Derek Holiday's oversized face make up the majority of the poster, with several other character actors peppering the negative space around him. The movie is an action flick a couple of decades old, and as my eyes scan the marquee above, it's clear this isn't your standard first-run theater.

"This it?"

"Caw! Caw!"

"Thanks, Kuro. Are you going to—" without another squawk, the bird takes off. "Oh, I guess you're going now. Okay, sure. I can handle this myself." Then again, I'm not alone. I rest my hand on the gem that adorns my wrist. Mom's always here, even if she's not out of her little prison.

As soon as I enter the building, I'm hit with the overwhelming smell of popcorn, along with an unexpected sense of dread and nausea. I don't think the popcorn has to do with the other two things. This feels a lot like what I felt in the cemetery, only much worse. Thank God the theater is practically empty, otherwise I'd probably get called out for looking haggard and unwell, like a victim of the latest virus.

I scan the lobby, squinting for any sign of pinpricks that can lead to another Mirage, but can't seem to find any. She said he went into a bathroom, though. I'll start there.

Begrudgingly, I buy the cheapest ticket from the nearby machine and let the android staff guide me through the metal and carbon fiber detector.

There are only two men's bathrooms through the wide hallway of the theater. The first bathroom is a dead end. When I enter, that feeling of dread leaves almost completely. It returns the very instant I cross the threshold back into the hallway. Looking both ways for any other bystanders, I release Mom from her Spectral confines.

"What do you want?" she asks, sass as apparent as ever.

"You're hungry, aren't you?" I say. "Help me find your next meal."

She smiles and sniffs the air and ground like a bloodhound. "Food is everywhere…and nowhere."

"How profound," I say in my driest voice. "Focus on the everywhere."

The Spectre glares, as if to say, "Don't talk down to me."

I keep an eye out as we peruse the long hall, making sure no unsuspecting employee or theatergoer stumbles on the giant Spectre darkening the premises.

"A lot of Ethereal Spirits here," Mom says. I didn't realize she could even speak that intelligently.

"Oh?"

"Ethereal Spirits, but in lower form. Hundreds of them. No, thousands. Like a battlefield. Not worth eating yet, though."

We make it to the second men's bathroom. "But here…" she continues. "Here. Here."

"Thanks, Mom."

She smirks as I recall her to my wrist. In case there's someone else in the bathroom, I don't want the first thing they see to be a Spectre.

I walk in to see a man drying his hands at an air dryer. He stares at me as I lean up against the tiled wall by the exit.

"Um, the girl's bathroom is next door."

"I'm fine here," I say.

"Okay," he says with a shrug before shaking off his hands and exiting.

I've never understood the need for separate bathrooms, but at least in this case, it helps narrow down my search. As soon as I cross the threshold that separates the sinks from the toilets, a heavy weight assaults my insides. It's more intense than in the rest of the theater.

After checking the stalls for feet, I open them one at a time. As the second door swings open, I let out an anxious breath. Hovering above the toilet is a pinprick. I tilt my head to the side, noticing an extra ray of darkness spilling out from it.

"Okay," I whisper to myself. "Like pulling off bed covers."

Following Hiro's previous instruction, I stick my finger into the pinprick and dive into the Mirage. Bursting outward, the pinprick expands, and with each passing moment, the toilet stall disappears, in favor of a suburban landscape.

The air around me shifts and morphs. Gone is the echoey and damp atmosphere of the bathroom. In its place a natural warmth, as though I've just stepped out into the sun on a warm fall day. It's not too hot or cold, but somehow the very definition of what I would consider "ideal" temper-ature, if there even is such a thing.

I stand in the middle of a wide, perfectly paved road. On either side of me sit rows of old-fashioned houses. These aren't the apartment complexes most city-dwellers live in, but the type of suburban one I've only seen on the netscreens—even nicer than the one I called home in Burbank.

Most shockingly, though, is that the houses, streets, and even my own skin are painted in a stark monochrome.

TWO

I TAKE in my surroundings as I walk along the white picket fence separating the manicured lawn and flawless pavement. Not a single leaf from a tree is out of place, the slight breeze somehow feeling controlled, yet natural.

The houses are large, quaint things, cookie-cutter in nature, but I can't call them boring. Each one has a charm all its own, with one in particular sporting floral designs and unique shades of gray. And for some reason, it has a Christmas wreath decorating its front door. It's the kind of neighborhood I've dreamed about my entire life.

Don't get me wrong. I'm not an idiot. I never actually believed a neighborhood like this is, or ever was, possible, but the idea that you could walk safely without having to clutch your bag or tense your shoulders was an enviable and unachievable luxury I wasn't able to experience until recently.

Burbank may not resemble an idyllic Pleasantville, but I never once worried about getting mugged or assaulted when roaming around. It reminds me why I'm strolling these gray streets in the first place. I'm here so that someday, I can return to a home free and clear of any emotional or physical baggage that continues to haunt me.

I approach a narrow cross street, looking both ways as I step over to the next section of the grid-like block. The land itself is ridiculously flat, especially given that we're in L.A., where the idea of flat land is impossible north of Compton.

And then I see it: the house with the floral print etched on its exterior.

Not the same design or layout; it's the same exact house, all the way down to the inexplicable Christmas wreath that adorns its oak front door. I cast my gaze across the street to a larger home with a cherry blossom tree sitting in the middle of the yard. Standing directly in front of the tree is a woman in a dress and apron, face caked in plain makeup, waving at me, her eyes following as I pass the yard. Her smile is fake and horrifying, denting her foundation at the corners of her mouth and making her look more like a puppet than a human.

I ignore her. I'm curious what else I'll find in this strange Mirage. With a press of the gem on my wrist and a burst of blue light, which stands out in this monochrome world, I release Mom.

"Food?" Mom says as she floats alongside me.

"Hopefully soon," I say.

She groans in response.

I step off the curb and cross another street, paying closer attention to the surrounding homes. A few hundred steps in, and I see an identical floral-printed home to my left, and to my right…another eerie woman standing outside her cherry blossom-blessed home.

Wait, no. This neighborhood is the same two blocks copy and pasted over and over again.

"Spectre or Spirit?" I say to Mom, motioning to the woman across the street.

The floating head releases a contemplative groan. "Not food."

"Spirit, then." At least this woman is unlikely to try to kill me outright. In my very limited experience, these Spirits act more as distractions than enemies. Like NPCs in some video game. "You ready to pay someone a visit?"

"Do we get to kill her?" Mom asks.

"Maybe," I respond. "But not right away."

Another groan.

As I approach the front gate of the cherry blossom house, I greet the creepy woman's wave with one of my own.

"Oh, how delightful!" she says, breaking expression for the first time. "I did tell Mark that I'd hoped we'd be receiving guests this evening. Would you join us for dinner?" Her accent is odd. Like British with a California twist to it, if that makes any sense. Either way, it's overtly friendly, which makes me trust it even less.

I don't want to follow her, but there isn't a lot to do other than walk through the infinitely looping void. Everything about this Mirage is funneling me toward this one house. It may very well be leading me to my death, but I won't make much progress unless I discover and engage the Spectre.

"Sure," I say. "We'd love to have dinner. As long as my…friend is welcome." I motion to Mom, who hovers at my side. I hope Spectres don't seem weird to Mirage Spirits.

Again, the woman breaks out her unnatural smile. "The more the merrier! I'm Shelby Wheeler."

"Luna."

"Luna…"

"Um…Guerrera?"

"Oh, how sweet. And ethnic, too!"

"Okay."

Without another word, she guides us through the front door. The first thing that strikes me when we enter is the smell of metal and burned tortilla chips. It's like the walls themselves are made of it. And, speaking of the walls, the entire entryway is plastered in a bright damask wallpaper, interrupted by a wood aesthetic border that's been glued on every couple of feet. What decade is this look from?

"Have a seat," she says to us, motioning to a faux leather couch in the entry room. "Dinner should be ready in the next few minutes. I'm sure you can smell it. It's a pot roast."

"It…smells great." All I smell are metal and burned tortilla chips.

"Mark will be here soon. So we can just talk amongst ourselves until then." She sits down on the couch across from us, and as if a switch has just been flipped, her smile returns, her eyes still dead and staring ahead at me. Her body rocks back and forth, controlled and fast, as if caught in a time lapse.

In her silence, I take in my surroundings. There's a ficus to my right, a coffee table between us, and an analog clock above the threshold leading into what I assume is the kitchen. My eyes widen as I see the hands accelerating through the minutes in seconds. Within less than a minute, an hour has passed. The light shifts in the room as the sun inches across the sky outside, and all the while, Shelby sits there, smiling, silent.

I want to stand up and explore, but what action would this Spirit take to protect its Spectre?

"Um…is it time to eat yet?" I ask.

Shelby's rocking ramps down to real time, and the clock comes to a halt. "Oh, soon enough, my dear. But we mustn't be rude. Mark will be back from the office any minute, and he'll be heartbroken if we start without him." The corners of her mouth turn upwards yet again, and the rocking commences, the clock's acceleration following suit.

"Hey," Mom says. "I'm bored. When do we get to eat?"

I guess we are here for a meal, and we can't wait here forever. The last thing I want is to be gate-kept by an overzealous Spirit, but I'm not one to run into a scenario, guns blazing. You do that at home, and you're likely to get killed. I doubt the rules are much different in the Spectre hunting world.

I stand up slowly, my eyes focused on Shelby as I do. As soon as my knees lock, her eyes flicker and she stops her rocking.

"Oh, my dear," she says. "Please sit back down. Mark will be here very soon. Then we can eat."

"I have to use the bathroom," I lie.

She laughs. "No you don't. Don't be ridiculous."

"Would you like to take me on a tou—"

"SIT DOWN!" Her body stretches three feet taller, and her voice drops several octaves.

"Okay, screw this. Mom?" I hold out my hand.

"Finally!" Mom says, transforming from her giant head form into the intimidating blade. Her serrated edge glimmers in the overly bright lighting, a reminder of how dangerous she can be.

In one swift movement, I slice through Shelby's torso from right shoulder to left waist. She screams, high-pitched at first, slowly fading into the monster tone I'd heard only a moment before. Her body cuts in half like paper and then dissipates into thin air.

The clock slows down and halts. A stillness fills the room, as though the air has stopped flowing altogether. A few seconds later, it starts up again. No time like the present to do what I came here to do.

I push through the swinging door that leads into the kitchen. To my surprise, I see a slow cooker out on the counter, its lid steaming and warm, though no smell to accompany it. In the dining area, the table is set for three, along with a pitcher of lemonade and basket of bread. I guess the food wasn't a lie.

I don't dwell on the matter. I have work to do.

Okay, so, in the past, certain events or actions triggered memories. If I can find those triggers and see those memories, I can learn how to take out the Spectre.

I turn the house over like the freakin' LAPD, flipping over tables, pulling out drawers, and keeping my eyes out for any sign of a memory. Though as warm as this house tries to come across, it's devoid of any personality. There are no pictures, no paintings, no personal effects—nothing to reflect even the possibility of a repressed memory. Who is this Spectre, and what's their deal?

I check all the kitchen cupboards and make my way into the living room. There's only a couch, fireplace, and standing radio in sight, which I slice up with a few quick swipes. Nothing. No triggers, no memories.

"Come on, where're you hiding?" I say aloud, not sure if I'm talking to the Spectre or the hidden memories.

"Up the stairs," Mom says, the gem in the blade glowing with each syllable spoken.

"What's up the stairs?"

"I feel something. It's faint, but I think it might be tasty."

Ding-dong! The sound of a doorbell is followed by a frantic knocking. I dart to the entryway in an instant. A glance through the peephole reveals Shelby, apron and all, standing on the front step, smile still carved into the face of hers.

"Hellooo?" she hollers in that strange accent. "Anybody home?"

"She can't come in?" I ask my sword. "Isn't this her Mirage?"

I hear mom sniffing through the gem. "Still another Spirit."

"Shouldn't it be able to punch through the door?"

I hear banging behind me. I run back through to the living room and see not one, but a handful of Shelbys with their faces pressed against the sliding glass doors, knuckles rapping against the transparent screen.

"Okay, then," I say, ignoring the army of Shelbys and putting my superhuman speed to use. I tear up the carpet with each step up the stairs. One glance out a window on the second floor reveals a wave of aproned women, looking like an army of ants closing in on all sides. Glass shatters downstairs, wood splinters, and the sound of heavy high-heeled shoes on too-thick carpet bombard my senses.

"Where's the smell?" I scream to Mom.

"Left."

I follow her instructions and shut the paper-thin door behind me. It's not like it'll do me any good, but any space between me and those psychos is a good thing.

"Is it possible to get killed by a Spirit?"

"Why? Do you wanna find out?" Mom says.

"No, but if you don't tell me where to go, I might."

"The closet."

I don't even need to open it to know my Spectre is right. Like how I could detect the Mirage in the movie theater, I sense something particularly *heavy* in the closet. And then there's that smell of metal and burned tortilla chips, somehow growing stronger by the second.

The door to the hall implodes as I open the closet door and jump straight in. I don't even have time to second guess the fact that I jumped straight into a furnace.

Heat tears into my skin in an instant. It sears my insides, and I want to scream—do anything I can to make the pain stop. My skin simmers, and I can feel blood boiling underneath in a few short seconds. It's one of the worst feelings imaginable. I want to curse my mom's Ghost for her stupidity, but as quickly as begins, it ends. I realize the boiling of my skin and blood is an illusion. It feels almost how I imagine being electrocuted feels like. Just like with previous memories, this assaulting of my senses is a taste of the pain felt by a certain memory.

But which memory is it, and whose?

My eyes open, and a vision of color returns. The scene is strangely and unexpectedly comforting. I recognize the street and building, but everything is just the slightest bit cleaner. Except for the air. The air is thick with the smell of car exhaust.

In front of me is the Main Stay. I may be around its backside, but I'd recognize the shape of it anywhere, along with the dark alley that curves around the back. It's the same, but different. The surrounding architecture is mostly the same, but just a bit…off. *When* is this supposed to be? It's not the Main Stay in any period I've been alive. Dark shadows paint the area, though somehow less oppressively bleak as it is in the present day.

I'm drawn from my odd nostalgia by the sounds of screaming. Nine floors up, I see the head of a woman out the window. More screams between her and someone else. I think it's a man's voice but can't be certain.

And then she tumbles out, smacking onto a shutter sticking out from a fourth-floor window. The body plummets through a set of wires. Telephone wires? Electrical wires? I have no idea. But they snap off from the poles, doing nothing to slow the descent.

She smacks down onto the hard cement right in front of me. I hear a sickening crunch as her head collapses onto the pavement. Blood splatters onto me and into my open mouth.

The taste of metal—metal and burned tortilla chips—fill my senses and I retch. I somehow can tell the smell is a mix of blood and burned skin, but that's the least of my problems right now.

I'd just witnessed a suicide—not just any suicide.

One that took place right outside my home.

THREE

I SCREAM. Yes, it's only been a week or so since I witnessed my first death, but this is so unexpected that I can't help but react in a panic. I perform my one means of desperate escape that Hiro had taught—that mental motion of pulling the covers back over me.

The smell of exhaust in the air dissipates, and the humidity of the theater bathroom replaces it. Slowly, the taste of blood and burned skin vanishes along with it. My right foot soaks and twists as it plunges into the toilet. I have to catch myself on the stall wall to keep from tripping and face-planting on the door. I barely register how ridiculous I look as I take slow, deep breaths, one foot in the toilet, the other on the wet, tiled floor.

What had I just witnessed? I'm at a theater close to the Financial District. Why in the hell did I just see some woman jump from the Main Stay a couple miles to the east?

"What's wrong with you?" Mom says. I turn to see her normally large face floating at eye level with me. She'd reduced in size to fit in the stall. I don't know why, but it sends me over the edge. My stomach rumbles, and I frantically yank my foot out of the toilet, turn around, fall to my knees, retching up my coffee and croissant from earlier in the day. But even after my breakfast is gone, my shoulders continue to heave. Only after I vomit two rounds of bile, do I finally stop, though I can't seem to get the taste of metal from my mouth.

"I don't know," I say, answering Mom's question. Death is horrifying to watch at any time, but maybe seeing it in a Mirage amplifies its emotional impact?

I spit into the toilet, and rise from my knees, ignoring the sopping wet nature of the lower half of my pants. The toilet flushes as I pull open the stall door, almost loud enough to mask my surprised reaction at who I see staring back at me.

Leaning against one of the urinal partitions is the blonde girl who tried to kill me back in Mom's Mirage. Unlike the last time I saw her, she isn't wearing any armor. Instead, she sports a pair of bright leggings under a long skirt along with a long-sleeved shirt. Not what I'd call workout attire. At least she has the common sense to wear tennis shoes.

Dammit, I don't have the energy for this. "Mom, you know what to do," I say.

"All right, finally some action!" she says.

I hold out my hand to accept her in her blade form…only for her to hover at waist level in her smaller head form.

"Mom, come on!"

"I'm trying," she says, sounding more like a whiney younger sister than a mother.

To my surprise, the blonde girl in front of me snorts, raising her hand to her face, suppressing a laugh. "Are you serious?"

"What?" I say.

"You can't use your abilities in the real world," the girl responds in an annoying know-it-all tone. "They only take shape in Mirages. How do you not know that?"

"What do you want?" I say, too flustered and battered to be embarrassed. I raise my fists. I don't really know if I stand a chance. This girl is bigger than me. She looks strong, and I know she's trained to fight.

Instead, she raises her hands, open palms facing me. "I'm not here to fight. We didn't officially meet. I'm Vero."

I keep my fists raised.

"Not much of a peacekeeper, then?"

"It's hard to be peaceful when everything in the world tries to kill you on a weekly basis," I say. "Actually, that's the first thing you said to me. Remember?"

She runs her fingers through her hair, looking almost like I paid her some unexpected compliment. "Yeah, I know I can be a little intense when I'm on the clock. I'm working on it now with my therapist, okay?" Her smile halts and her face turns stoic. "But you can't blame me. The way you hopped around before, with a Spectre, no less. What did you expect me to think?"

"I can't say your opinion of me ever crossed my mind."

"And after catapulting us out of that Mirage, you then start shacking up with Hiro Hanajima."

"Shacking up?"

"And then," she continues, ignoring my protests, "you start doing his bidding. Hopping in and out of Mirages like there's no tomorrow. You can't expect we wouldn't notice."

"I have no idea who you are. Why would I think you would notice?"

"You're serious?" she says, eyes narrowed, voice suspicious. "You're doing all that and you don't even know...?"

"Know what?"

"How everything works."

"You'll have to be more specific."

"I mean...you can't do what you do without the DOSD taking notice."

"The what?"

"Department of—"

"Oh, right, that thing."

"—Spectral Defe—so you have heard."

"Actually," a voice materializes to my right, causing me to jump. Standing by the sinks is one of the others who I saw in Mom's Mirage—the kid with the dual pistols. "No one else has found you yet. Vero only noticed because she's kind of obsessed with you."

"Seb!" she yells with a stomp of her foot before turning back to me. "I wasn't obsessed with you. We'd found the other Mirage up in the Verdugo Hills."

"*Against* Teach's wishes, let me remind you," Seb says. "He said to steer clear. That there was too much heat on it, what with it being a recent case."

Vero holds up her hand, as if blocking Seb out of the conversation. He only smiles in response.

"What do you know about Hiro?" she asks.

"What's it matter to you?"

"Did you know he's over a hundred years old?"

"Yeah, so?" I say as if she'd just told me he likes his eggs with bacon. "I mean, yeah. It's weird, but look at the stuff we can do. Look at *her.*" I motion to Mom's floating head.

"Hey!" Mom says, somehow offended.

"And commanding a Spectre?" Vero says. "That's dark magic or tech."

"No one *commands* me," Mom says, growing bigger as she says so. "Luna, can we kill her like we should have in the first place?"

"Shut up, Mom."

"Mom?" Vero's eyes widen.

I realize maybe I should have kept that piece of information to myself.

"Okay," I say. "So, you're not here to kill me. Why are you here?"

"I wanna know who you're fighting for," she says.

"Myself. And everything else is my business." I turn to walk past Seb, but he blocks my way.

"What sort of Spectre is in that Mirage?" he asks.

"Why? Are you planning on fighting it?"

The two look at each other. "We need permission first," Vero says. I can hear her clenching her teeth as she does so. "And a...chaperone. And they're too busy right now dealing with other matters to handle local issues."

"Can I leave?" I say, keeping my voice as steady as humanly possible in the process.

Vero nods to Seb, who steps aside. "Just so you know," he says, "I think the Spectre in there is strong. Like it's been around for a long time."

"How would you know that?" I ask.

Seb shrugs. "Just a feeling. The entrance feels...deeper than lower level Mirages."

I open the door to leave when I hear Vero's voice again.

"Be careful with Hiro," she says. "I don't know what you have going on with him, but he's not on good terms with the DOSD. He's persona non grata within the Medium world. He's used others before, you know."

"And where are they now?"

"Dead."

I tense up. "All of them?"

She shrugs.

"Do you know or don't you?"

"I know at least a few are. Just be careful. The Department is interested in you. Thinks you're dangerous. They thought you were dangerous before. That's why they tried to capture you. Now that you're with Hiro, they're worried. Seb and I aren't even supposed to be here."

"Capture me? I think I'd have known if..." I think back to that first awful morning. Those two cops who I thought were trying to break me. Were those...?

"Oh, what did you just realize?" Vero asks, a smile lighting up her face. "I saw your eyes widen. You remember something, huh?"

"Anyone tell you you're too bubbly for what you do?" I ask.

Her smiles fades and eyes narrow. "Now you sound like my mother."

"What would happen if the DSOD—"

"DOSD," Seb corrects me.

I look directly at him. "DSOD. What if the *DSOD* captures me?"

"They'll interrogate you, probably. "

"Vero's underselling it," Seb says. "It won't be the legal kind of interrogation. They may even dissect you. They've been wanting to do that to Hiro for years, but they could never catch him."

"Great," I say, walking out the door. "So I'm staying away from the two of you."

"Just be careful!" the girl calls out to me. "Hiro's using you. You don't know what he'll do once he has what he wants."

I turn around and walk backward. "Did you ever think that maybe I'm using *him*?"

Vero's face wrinkles in confusion as I turn back around and head out the front door of the theater.

I EXPECT Hiro to bombard me with questions the second the elevator opens onto his floor, as if he'd know I'd just had a run-in with the enemy. Instead, I see him seated on the couch, knees curled up to his chest, his netscreen hologram projected in front of him as he scrolls through a browser.

"So," he says, not looking away from his work. "How'd it go?"

"How'd what go?" I say too loudly.

"Your first solo run-in with a Spectre that's *not* your Companion. Kuro told me you made it out okay."

I look to see the crow's dead black eyes staring at me, beak only slightly ajar, as if threatening to caw in protest, though I don't know why. The freakin' bird booked it the second I arrived at the theater.

"I threw up," I say.

"That's delightful."

"That entire theater makes me sick."

"I'm sure it's not that bad."

"No," I say. "The theater literally makes me sick. As in the whole place makes me feel nauseous. And not just around where the Mirage is."

"So you found a Mirage?"

"It's like the lady said. In the men's bathroom and everything. I didn't see her boyfriend, but I'm sure he's somewhere in there."

"Huh, well, there you go. Good for you." Hiro turns off his projector and turns around on the sofa, head resting on his knees. "Don't leave me in suspense. What was it like?"

"So, that's it?" I say. "No apology for how wrong you were?"

"I let you explore it, didn't I? Wouldn't have done that if I expected it to be a total loss. Besides, you can't mess up as much as I do and take things so personally."

"So you admit you were wrong?"

"Oh, absolutely." Hiro waves his hand in front of his face. "You found a Mirage that clearly validates that woman's experience. I've been doing this for so long I only really have my own gut to go off of. It's been helpful having someone else around to push back every now and then, even if it is annoying in the moment."

I don't know how to respond. Dad would have been hanging on to his opinions by the skin of his teeth, even if they'd consistently been proven wrong. I try to resist it, but another emotion flares up in my stomach. It's the first time I can recall being validated for doing something without some snarky comment about me "not being shit" for being right. Any comeback I had ready for him dies in my throat as I swallow uncomfortably.

"So," he says, "tell me about your trip into this Mirage."

I tell him everything. Vero's warning lingers in the back of my mind the entire time, but as I get further into the story, my walls start to come down. His seemingly genuine desire to find the truth without any ego throws me in a way I've never experienced. I don't know what the DOSD or whatever has against him, but he can't be that bad, right?

I push back against drawing any conclusions now. Hiro's been upfront from the beginning. To him, I'm little more than his Spectre's meal ticket. And to me, he's my ticket to freedom from my delinquency. We only need to trust each other until we both get what we want.

When I finish my story—leaving out my meeting with the DOSD agents—Hiro sits back on the couch, face up, eyes closed. "Hmm," is all he says after a solid minute of deep thought.

"That's it?" I say.

"Sorry, just thinking. Why would a Spectre have a Mirage set in one location, but have a memory in a completely different location?"

"Can't they have a memory take place anywhere?" I say. "Mom's Mirage was one setting, but each memory threw me into another setting, depending on what that memory showed. The same with Alan's memory. The high school stage was the main setting, but memories have no limitations."

"That's true. Spectres create complete fabrications as their Mirages, and peppered within them are memories of real events and places. So, let's put the fabrication aside for now and look at the memory. What do we know about the Main Stay?"

"Uh…" I say.

"Oh, come on. You've lived there."

"This version of the Main Stay looked old. The building in the memory looked newer. Less worn down. The cars were different. Every-one's outfits were different. Fancier."

Hiro holds his hand up, mimicking feet walking with his pointer and middle finger. "And our mysterious woman jumps off the ninth floor." His fingers plummet off the back of the sofa. "You're sure it's the ninth floor."

I nod.

"She jumps off the ninth floor and splats down on the hard cement below. Splat."

That's an insensitive reduction of events, but it's true. I nod. "And she got wrapped in wires. There aren't any wires there now."

"Okay. Two things. Did she die right away?"

"I was a little too shocked to notice if she was still moving."

"You're right," Hiro says, oblivious to my disgusted tone. "And even if she did move, who's to say that wasn't just a chemical reaction in her nerves? That aside, if she *was* alive, can you think of a reason her Spectre would be in a different location from where you saw her death?"

My eyes widen. "She didn't die there. She died somewhere else!" I sit down on a barstool, facing the back of the couch. "A hospital?"

Hiro snaps his fingers. "Bingo." He spins back around on the couch and throws up a projection from his netscreen. He types in the movie theater. He taps at a dial on the street view and spins it hard to the left. We see a history of the movie theater's location play out in reverse. The streets around it go smooth, rough, smooth again, rough again, and smooth, the exterior changing from one business to another until the building changes altogether, as though it had been knocked down completely and rebuilt. We settle on one particular iteration of the building in the 1950s.

Just as we thought, we see a sign for the GEORGIA STREET RECEIVING HOSPITAL printed in all caps.

With a few more taps in the air, Hiro pulls up a description. "'Central Receiving Hospital,'" he reads aloud. "'Founded in 1868, was Los Angeles' first public hospital providing emergency care and paramedic services to the people of the city for more than a century.' Looks like it was closed in 1957 when it was moved to a different location."

I read ahead and balk at some of the details. "It used to be a place for them to treat smallpox and other contagious diseases," I say.

"Though something tells me our Spectre was the victim of no such disease."

"Very funny." I turn around on my stool to face the counter, pulling up my own holograph projection. I tap the words "suicide" and "main stay" in, and am met with millions of results. "Oh, goodie, there's a whole wiki article on the Main Stay."

"There's a wiki article on anything. Don't act like it's special."

"No, I mean there's an article exclusively on the number of murders and suicides in and around the building."

Hiro turns on the couch to face me. "That is a tad more unique."

"She said her name was Shelby Wheeler."

"Before she jumped?"

"No, I mean in the Mirage, not the memory. The Spirit there said her name was Shelby Wheeler. I don't know if that was supposed to be her, though. Do the Spirits in Mirages often take the forms of the Spectre before they died?"

"Sometimes. It's worth looking into. If it's not her, it could at least be someone the Spectre knew."

It doesn't take long to find what we're looking for. I tap the article entitled "The Suicide of Shelby Wheeler" and scroll through the details. "She was staying at the DeMille Hotel—that's the old name of the building—while she was sleeping with some sailor on leave. After her death, he was interviewed as a potential suspect, but he claimed she killed herself when she found out he didn't want to stay behind with her."

"Sad," Hiro says, "but not entirely unique. What year was this?"

"1938." I wrinkle my nose at this. I hate these old sob stories. The women in them always seem so pathetic. I didn't know this Shelby, but she probably could have been with anyone she wanted. Instead, she wanted to be with some crusty sailor who didn't even want to stay with her. "Women back then were so dramatic."

"That's judgmental of you," Hiro says. "Things aren't perfect right now, but back then, a relationship with the right man could mean the difference between a life in a nice house and one in the streets."

I bite my lip. I hate that he's right. And then it hits me. "That explains her Mirage."

"What do you mean?"

"The black-and-white look, the gorgeous, quaint houses, the home-cooked meal and all that? That's probably the life she wanted." In an instant, my empathy swings from zero to ten. I may not understand the desire to marry some guy, but I'm the last one to judge someone else for striving for an ideal life. I think back to the cherry blossom tree at the front of her house, the sitting room that smelled of burned tortilla chips, and the perfectly manicured lawns. It melds into my memories of Damien and Lily's home in Burbank.

All she wanted was to be happy.

I continue reading the article. As expected, it confirms that after her suicide, she was transported to the Georgia Street Receiving Hospital, where she died an hour later.

"It *is* her," I say, as if there's any question at this point.

"Looks like it."

"Why did it take so long for her Mirage to form?"

Hiro scratches at the pathetic stubble on his chin. "I wish I could say I know, but there's no rhyme or reason to when or how a Mirage is formed. At least not one I've found yet. But given how old this one is, we'll want to go in with extra caution. There's a chance this one could be out of your league. If she's been wreaking havoc for well over a hundred years, that means she's had opportunities to take in many more victims. I've taken on Spectres from hundreds of years ago at levels in the tens and twenties, back in my prime. She could be *that* dangerous."

That's exactly what Seb had warned me about. That this Spectre was old and potentially dangerous. I groan in frustration. "So, what does that mean?"

"It means the two of us will have to be extra careful the next time we go in."

"You're coming with me?"

"I'd feel terrible if you got killed. Plus, I don't want Kuro to starve." He says that last part with a smile, but it's probably truer than he wants to admit.

I think back to Vero's warning. I can at least trust him to protect his own interest in me until the time is right. That much I'm sure of.

"But," he continues, "we can't go in without a plan. Have you ever tried to commit suicide?"

"That's not something you can just ask!"

"I mean for the Spectre!" he says, defensive. "Remember, you're going to have to get into the right mindset in order to take her down. I need to know if you've had any similar experiences in the past. Have you ever been slighted by a lover?"

"Not so much that I'd want to kill myself." Plus, I've never been with anyone I'd lament much over losing. I don't tell Hiro that part.

I bite the inside of my lip as I think. Hiro does have a point, though. It's not just about the suicide. What is the underpinning of the suicide?

Why did she want to kill herself? Was it as simple as her being infatuated with this man, or something deeper? A lack of acceptance, or general lack of love? Was it about feeling small or helpless? I can relate to that, but is it the real reason?

I scroll through the rest of the article and find nothing. Further research online reveals no more details. We only get the same summary of the sailor, whose name is unsurprisingly Mark. It's clear that everyone who reported on this was only interested in one aspect—the dark trend of murders and suicides in the building. There wasn't much hunger to dig much deeper into this death in particular. It's one of many.

"I hate to say this," I say. "But we need more information. We need to go back to the source."

Hiro smirks. "You're absolutely right." He turns to his Spectre's cage. "Kuro, I hope you're feeling limber today. It's time to play backup."

The bird caws twice in response.

FOUR

"YOU WEREN'T KIDDING about how creepy this place is," Hiro says as we stand on the sidewalk of the black-and-white façade of a neighborhood. His eyes are wide, taking in every detail with suspicion.

"Just wait until you meet Shelby," I say. "She's worse than any horror movie you've seen at this theater."

Hiro gives a shudder, though it doesn't seem like it's in response to what I just said.

"What's wrong?"

"It's this place. The Mirage. This happens with some of them. You come across a Spectre with specific perspectives, biases, or effects on you. For example, the one with your mother. It affected you more than it affected anyone else, because of its connection to you. This one doesn't want me here. I'm unwelcome. I can feel the animosity with every step we take. Stay close, Kuro."

The bird gives two caws and descends from the sky and lands on Hiro's shoulder.

I follow his lead and bring Mom out from my Syncer.

We pass the house with the floral designs and turn to the right. As expected, Shelby is back in her rightful place, out front of the cherry blossom house, waving mechanically, with that same smile carved into her face.

But it doesn't last long. The smile fades as her eyes land on Hiro. Her image flickers, and before we can blink, she's exploded past the front gate and is directly in front of us, teeth bared.

"You're not supposed to be here," she says to Hiro, her voice stiff and unnatural.

"I'm not the one consuming innocent victims."

"Who says they're innocent?"

Without another word, she raises an index finger and spins her hand in a circle. A portal opens up underneath Hiro.

"Shit!" he says as gravity takes hold. "Luna, ru—"

The portal closes around him, and just like that, he's gone. It's not too different from what Mom did with Vero and the others before. I don't know how dangerous this Spectre is, but I'm not sticking around to find out.

Not wasting any time, I make a mental motion, as if I'm pulling bed covers over my head. Instead of being catapulted into the bathroom stall of the theater, I find myself still standing in front of the cherry blossom house.

But Shelby doesn't attack me. She only smiles.

"Don't worry," she says to me. "I'm not mad for what you did to me before. For your *betrayal*. You're just confused."

"Why did you kick him out?"

"Because he's a man. And men aren't welcome here. Now, please. Come join me for dinner. Mark will be here soon."

She walks past the destroyed gate and onto the path that leads to her house.

"If men aren't welcome, why are you waiting for Mark?"

Shelby stops, turns, and laughs. Like every other moment, it sounds and feels beyond unnatural. "Why would you think men aren't welcome?"

"Because you..." I blink. I don't know how to logic with this lady.

"Oh, I mean men who are cheaters. Men who cheat and desert women are the lowest form of human. And that man? He had a cheater's stink *all* over him."

"Right." I don't know what to make of that comment. "Dinner? Sure, I'll, uh, I'll take you up on dinner."

Shelby brings her hands together. "Oh, how lovely. Promise not to run off again like last time. I shall become ever so cross if you do."

"Okay," I say, hoping she doesn't sense the lie.

"Thank you, my dear."

I follow her into the house that smells of burned tortilla chips, tensing up as the door shuts behind me.

"So, what does your husband do?" I ask as we take a seat on the couches.

"Oh, Mark's in marketing. He helps big companies come up with jingles." She raises one finger in the air and starts to wave it back and forth. "'*Go ahead and ring their bell with ImperTel,*'" she sings. "Have you ever heard that one?"

I haven't. I haven't even heard of ImperTel. "Uh-huh," I lie again. "And has he always been in marketing?"

"Oh. Well before that, he was a sailor, if you can believe that."

"You're kidding!" My feigned surprise turns into actual surprise when the ground around me starts to rumble. I involuntarily grab on to the armrest of the couch. I've gone through my fair share of earthquakes, but have never gotten over the lack of control I feel whenever one starts. Plus, this one's in a Mirage, so it's a good bet it's worse.

"Don't worry," Shelby says. "That happens. You know that old saying about your ears burning when someone's talking about you? It's kind of the same thing with Mark."

How is that even remotely the same thing? I keep that thought to myself. I notice Mom cast her gaze out the front window as the rumbling continues. It doesn't take me long to realize this isn't anything resembling an earthquake. It feels an awful lot like what I'd experienced in the other Mirage before Alan Arroyo's Spectre burst through the doors.

"We're not here to have dinner, are we?" I say to Shelby.

"Well, we *were*, but you kept asking questions. Plus, you bringing unwelcome guests into my world is a big no-no."

"How was I supposed to know your no men rule?" I say as I stand up. "Well, that sucks. The food really did look great." Shelby does nothing as I unlock the door and open it. The rumble increases in intensity with each passing second. I stroll down the path to the front gate and out onto the main street.

And then I see her. The Spectre. She's at least fifteen feet tall with telephone wires wrapped around her. They extend on both sides of her body, acting as legs, keeping her hovering several feet above the ground. The way she moves is predatory, like a spider. And I've been caught in her web.

I turn to Mom, only to see her literally salivating.

"Her Essence will be so tasty."

She's not wrong, but in order for her to eat the thing, we'd have to have a chance in hell of beating her. I need to find a way to touch her to see if I do. I take a few steps back as the Spectre approaches, unsettled by how the hovering body hangs in place like a rag doll.

"What are you doing here?" the Spectre finally speaks, her voice almost as rumbly as each step she takes. Already, I can sense the difference between a Spectre like her and one like Alan. I can tell this one has actual intelligence buried under all that ugly. I can't say the same for Alan, who acted more like a feral animal than a human.

"You took someone," I tell her. "A man. His fiancée is looking for him."

"Oh, is that all?" she says. "You're too late. I've already eaten him."

"You killed him?"

"It's the least he deserved. He not only cheated, but was planning to leave her alone with her child."

I resist the urge to point out that her eating the man resulted in exactly the same thing. "So that's it? You bring in unsuspecting victims and eat them?"

"I only eat those who deserve it—those who refuse to take their due responsibility." She stops for a moment, looking me up and down, head tilted to the side. "But what about you? I felt your less than noble intentions in your last visit. I let you go, but you're back. Foolish decision."

May as well go down swinging.

I hold out my hand, accepting Mom, who eagerly transforms into her blade form. I can feel her hunger pulsing.

"If you're not gonna let me leave," I say, "I may as well try to take you down."

Tapping into my familiar emotions with Mom, I take a deep breath and launch at the Spectre. My wrists vibrates, indicating a Spectral Companion sync with her. At least there's that.

I don't know how long I can last against this thing, but I still have a strong sense of preservation. I dart toward her side. Even though she's at a higher level than Mom, my speed catches her off guard. A good sign. I swipe and connect with a wire that serves as a leg. I'm not yet in sync with whatever her core emotion is, so I only hope that slashing a wire will throw me into a memory or allow me to see her level.

My plan is instantly foiled when my blade bounces off the wire with a *clang.*

No memory. No damage.

The impact tosses me backward. My feet rip through my shoes and tear up the asphalt as I skid.

"You didn't do it right!" my blade yells at me.

"What do you mean I didn't do it right?"

"It's supposed to go *through* the Spectre!"

"I didn't do that on purpose!" Besides, I can argue she's just not sharp enough.

I jump to the side, narrowly dodging a swipe from Shelby, whose spare wires have turned into makeshift arms for her to lash out at me.

As I land on my back, I pull at the heel of my shredded left shoe and pry it off. My Spectral powers may make my body stronger, but they don't do much for my clothes. I'll have to ask Hiro about that if I survive.

And then it hits me. I probably won't get a chance to ask him.

I'm not gonna make it.

I dodge another attack and pry off my remaining shoe. I can keep dodging for as long as I can, but unless I connect and get into her emotions, I won't last more than a few minutes. Even if I do sync up, I don't know how much damage someone at my level can cause against Shelby. Still, I have to try.

I launch at her again, this time aiming for an actual part of her body. If I can connect with an arm, leg, or anything that's not a wire...

Thwunk!

I see black for an instant as the impact from a blow connects. I'm somehow able to notice that I've crashed into the house with the floral design, ripping through its roof and second floor, landing in an empty living room. The alarm on my cuff goes off.

DANGER! Defense at 0%!

Shit, that's it. My shield only lasted one hit. I have nothing left to protect me from her.

The dust settles around me and I see the house I'm in has no furniture. I mean, why would it?

With a groan, I reach for my Syncer.

Spectre: Level Two
Class: Attacker

I really don't stand a chance. It may not be as tough as the levels ten or twenty that Hiro feared, but at my current stage, it makes no difference.

The sounds of splintering wood and crumbling drywall shake me out of my tangential thought, and Shelby's figure emerges.

I climb to my feet, shaky. The shield may have protected me, but the impact of it still has my head spinning.

"You shouldn't have come back," the Spectre says.

For once, I have nothing to say. Fatigue has already started to set in, along with an acceptance that I wouldn't be surviving this encounter.

As one of her wire arms descends on me, I close my eyes. This won't be so bad. I just hope it's quick.

A *thwip* followed by the sound of a blade cutting through metal and a monstrous scream. I open my eyes.

One of the Spectre's "legs" has been cut clean off, and she writhes around as though it's a genuine part of her body. A figure lands next to me. Vero's golden hair almost pierces the monochrome palette. Almost.

"Why did you pick the most inconvenient place in the Mirage to fight?" she says. "You had an entire street out there, and you chose here?"

I laugh. It's the only thing I can do to stop myself from hugging her. "What's so funny?"

"You think I chose this?" I say.

She smiles back, but only for the briefest of moments. "Let's get back out into the open."

A few leaps over rubble, and we're back onto the road, away from the thrashing Spectre, who takes the entire house down around her in a few quick seconds.

"Did you catch her memory?" I ask.

"Her what?" Vero says, breathing heavy.

"Her memory. When you cut through the wire."

"What're you talking about?"

I scoff. "We need to figure out her core emotion if we're going to beat her."

"Start making sense! Are you saying you know how to beat her?"

"I don't know. What level is your Spectre at?"

"*I* only have clearance on Level One Spectres on off hours. I don't have a Spectral Companion like you, remember? I've said this before. You're not *normal.*"

"Got it." She's not that high of a level either. I still need to understand Shelby's core emotion if we're going to beat her. I look on in awe as the spidery Spectre rises from the rubble of the house and scuttles toward us. "You need to distract her."

"Me distract her?" Vero says. "No offense, but I'm the stronger one of the two of us. *You* should distract her."

"Look, just trust me. I'm not normal, right?"

Vero gives an irritated growl. "Fine. You hear that Seb?"

"Loud and clear!" A figure calls out from the distance.

I see Seb's figure launch from the top of one of the houses and into the air.

Flash-bang! The sound of machine gunfire breaks through the rumbling, and Shelby stops in her tracks, being pelted by bullets. None of them seem to hurt her intensely, but they *do* work as a distraction.

"You brought a *man* here!" Shelby's voice booms. With a wipe of her hand, a portal opens up underneath Seb.

"What's th——!" He's sucked out of the Mirage before he can even finish.

"Again, Seb?" Vero says.

But I don't listen to what she says next. Seb bought me the precious seconds I need to do what I have to. I jump at Shelby, and with a swing of my sword, connect with her chest.

"You can't just leave me!" a feminine cry echoes in my head before I am zipped into a hotel room.

I recognize it immediately as a standard room in the Main Stay. It's older, and it's decorated differently, but the layout is unmistakable. Shelby stands in front of a man, tears running down her reddened cheeks. This must be him. The infamous Mark. Just as I thought, he's nothing special. Just a thin twig of a man with blond hair. How did someone like him survive as a sailor?

"Listen," Mark says. "We had a good thing, but I'm leaving. I don't know when I'll be back."

"Then I'll wait for you."

"That's not gonna work, Shel. I don't *know* when I'll be back. Or..."

Shelby looks up at Mark, eyes glassy. "Or what?"

"If I even want to. I just..." Mark takes a deep breath. "There's someone else, okay?"

"Someone...you cheated on me?" Her eyes are manic, terrifying.

"It's not cheating. We weren't steady," Mark puts his hands up. "I made it clear when we started that I wasn't interested in a long-term thing."

"But you're interested in this someone else?"

"You were taking this too seriously!"

And Shelby's on him in an instant, smacking and clawing at him. He doesn't put up a fight at first, but when her attacks draw blood from his cheek, he pushes her back, knocking her halfway out the open window.

She reaches for Mark as she starts to tumble out, and he reaches back. Their fingers touch...and then he lets hers slip through his. One extra push is all it takes to bring the whole shot to a close.

And her one emotion is clear.

Betrayal.

Clang!

My sword bounces off of Shelby's Spectre body, and I'm thrown back again onto the ground.

"What the heck?" Vero says. "Your attack didn't work."

"It will next time," I say. "I hope. Just keep her distracted again."

"So you can throw another weak hit her way?"

"Just trust me!" I don't wait for her to argue. I attack Shelby again, this time, keeping vivid memories in the front of my mind. Betrayal. I can work with that.

My own memory comes to me before I can stop it. The day Mom up and left. Not a word spoken. Not so much as a goodbye or even a lie. Just one day she's there. The next, she's gone, leaving me to look after Dad.

How could she do that to me? I still don't know why. I want to know.

Maybe part of me looks forward to the day I feed her to Kuro, so she can feel what I felt.

Spectral Sync: 100%

Shelby doesn't know who to block. She has Vero on one side, and me on the other. Time slows, and I can almost see her making the decision in real time. After surviving two direct hits from me unscathed, she opts to focus on Vero.

With a violent swing, I bring my blade down on her shoulder.

It connects...and cuts! Shelby lets out a scream as I dig into her Spectral flesh. It goes, goes, and it stops hard, partway down her shoulder, as if catching on a bone.

Clang!

I grip my blade tighter as it threatens to be ripped from my hands. Vero descends behind Shelby, her own blade come down on the end of mine like a hammer, pushing it deeper and deeper into the Spectre until, *swish*, it cuts through her entire body.

"How did you do that?" Vero calls out as she lands on the ground behind Shelby. "You're Level Zero!"

"Later," I say, swinging my sword again, this time targeting the gaping opening in the Spectre's side. This time, it cuts through and out the other side with no effort. Vero follows suit, striking Shelby down on her other shoulder. We take turns until all that's left are pieces of decaying flesh.

Shelby's head still hovers in the air, wires sprouting out like legs. Her mouth hangs open, nearly lifeless. "I wanted...to help..."

She disintegrates, the Mirage following suit around us, like a bad dream. Before we know it, we're both alone in the cramped bathroom stall, me standing on the toilet, her on the ground, faces pressed against one another.

Shelby's Essence materializes between us and unceremoniously plops between my feet into the bowl.

"No!" I bend down, feeling pain sprout from the top of my head as I smack it against Vero's. Luckily, I save the Essence from getting flushed.

"Sorry," I say, looking up to meet her red face.

"It's fine," she says. "I just saved your life, no big deal. And now we're a *little* too close for—" She presses up harder against me, and with the extra room, pulls the stall door open. On the other side, both Hiro and Seb stand there, both wearing concerned looks on their faces.

"You made it," Hiro says. "How?"

"Thanks for the confidence," I say.

"What happened?"

"What do you mean, what happened?" I say in heavy breaths. "I did exactly what you taught me and won."

Vero clears her throat.

"With some help."

"And who are these two?" Hiro says.

"Vero," Seb says, his finger pressed against his right ear. "We have to go. Now."

"Darn it, really?" Vero says, her tone turning frantic. "It's our day off."

"*Now.*"

She clenches her jaw and meets my gaze. "This isn't over yet. I want to…*we* want to—"

"Vero!" Seb opens the door to the exit. "Let's go."

Vero turns to leave.

"Hey," I say. "It's Luna. Luna Guerrera."

She smiles. "It's nice to meet you." With one last look, she stomps out the door, leaving me and Hiro alone.

"I thought you were dead," he says.

"Yeah, you made that clear," I respond. "Don't worry. Your meal ticket is safe. For now."

"You make me sound heartless."

"I just know you have your priorities," I say. "And you know what? I have mine, too." I hold up the small marble that is Shelby's Essence, this one the color of metal. "You know, she was pretty scary, but I kind of get where she was coming from. Maybe she saved that woman from a big mistake."

"Food?!" Mom hovers eagerly next to me as I toss the ball up in the air and catch it with the same hand.

"Here you go." I toss it at the giant head, and she snatches it mid-air, devouring it in an instant.

My armband vibrates.

An alert pops up in a projection over my wrist.

SPECTRE LEVEL UP: LEVEL ONE

"That's…one hell of a level up," Hiro says.

"I'll have to thank Vero later."

Any celebration is interrupted by Mom's intense vibrations. Her giant head rolls around the room, and she screams.

"What's going on, Hiro?"

"It's okay," he says. "I should have warned you, but this is completely normal."

"This is *normal?*"

"I didn't think you'd level up this quickly. As a Spectre consumes more, they grow more powerful and more cognizant. But most importantly, they regain memories from their lives, becoming more full versions of themselves."

"So, what does that mean?"

"It means she's regaining her memories."

Mom's screams stop, and her head comes to a halt right in front of me. It shrinks in size and sits at my eye level.

"You okay, Mom?" I say.

"I'm not Mom."

"Huh?"

"You call me Mom. I'm not her. I'm not Mom."

To Be Continued...

HiRO
&
KURO

SPECTRAL | EPISODE 5

THE STREETS OF DOWNTOWN LOS ANGELES...

VERONICA DAUGHERTY BOUNDS down the sidewalk, suffering only the slightest panics over their sudden call. She's gotten used to it. These days, fewer and fewer of her "days off" result in actual days off. The urgency at the DOSD stops for no one. A simple misstep or lack of drive on Vero's part alone can mean civilian deaths.

This isn't the career she wanted, but it's one she's accepted.

Her moments of strife and turmoil are insignificant compared to the rest of the world. She grew up knowing her family in relative peace, with the topics of war and conflict only surfacing in the hushed conversations between Mother and Father behind closed doors or within conference rooms.

Few others have had the luxuries she has, she tells herself, and that point is regularly driven home by her parents.

"We have it easy here," Father would say in their weekly visits. "The least we can do is give back to the country that's afforded us so much opportunity."

For most of her life, though, such pressures *didn't* fall on her shoulders. Those responsibilities had been saddled with her more willing older brother. So long as one member of the family did their part, they were perfectly willing to accept Vero as the artistic black sheep.

That all changed in one short night.

Vero had pestered her parents for months about the Eclectic Charades coming to Chicago. She hadn't expected Mother or Father to pay her any mind—they never did—but she knew John would be home on leave. If she played her cards right, he could take her.

So when John came to Vero's bedroom door, finger resting over his lips, she knew what it meant. They were going out, and neither parent could know.

She wouldn't have it any other way.

The night was electric, the energy infectious. Vero had never been to a real concert before. Had never had the opportunity to scream with fellow fans, to sing the lyrics in sync with the one and only Terra Dvine. Her eardrums and heartbeat pulsed with the rhythm of the drumbeats. She didn't even hear the first gunshots go off.

Like a wave, a sea of bodies flew over her, some falling, some climbing as the sound of rapid-fire explosions rang out. Cheers turned into screams. The lights in the arena turned on full force, only further highlighting the surrounding chaos.

The din of gunshots continued for what felt like a lifetime as she and John scrambled over to the stage, rolling away from panicked concertgoers, finally taking refuge up against one side. Once they were safe, John yelled something, though she couldn't hear what. With a nod of his head, he was gone.

That was the last time she saw him alive.

She still doesn't know for sure what he had said. Probably something about going to help someone else. He was always trying to find ways to help, be it for some less fortunate person or the country itself.

They hadn't even asked her to identify the body, which she'd always imagined looking like an insignificant piece of roadkill. He hadn't been shot by the terrorists, just trampled to death.

Most everyone who died had been trampled. On that dark night, there had been sixty-two deaths by gunfire, and two hundred and thirty in the stampede of human feet.

And all Vero could do was sit tucked away under the stage, pressed up underneath as others push her deeper and deeper. At times she thought she'd suffocate to death, smothered in the heap of equally terrified bodies, or that the shooters would notice her specifically before ending her life with the pull of a trigger.

She'd never felt so helpless. When the police had found her, they had to pull her to her feet before she finally moved on her own accord, and even after she was told it was safe, she could only hobble toward the exit, ignoring the moans of the injured around her. She always wondered how many were dying in that moment and how many would ultimately make it. Had any of those moans belonged to her brother?

Mother and Father never spoke to her about the incident. They uttered no words of accusation. The thought only lingered in the air. Heavy. Overbearing.

If she hadn't pushed him so hard to take her, he'd still be alive. That was a fact even Vero couldn't dispute.

The course of her life changed that very night. Up until then, she'd always been more comfortable at home with a pencil and a tablet than doing drills at a military base. But where everyone else saw tragedy, her family saw opportunity.

"You're starting work with your mother next semester," Father said as he dropped her off at school one winter morning. "You…have the prerequisite now. Don't let your brother's sacrifice go to waste."

Vero clenched her teeth behind closed lips and nodded. She'd expected as much. With the tragedy of her brother imprinted in her mind, it afforded her a unique opportunity: to train in the Department of Spectral Defense program as a Junior Medium. Without firsthand experience in trauma, dealing in the business of souls was deemed impossible. Up until that point, Vero's life had been ordinary. They say everything happens for a reason.

It's not a path Vero would have chosen for herself, but then again, who chooses their own path, anyway?

"Dammit, why today of all days?" a voice rings out in Vero's ear. She sees Seb's lanky form half a block ahead of her, paving a path for Vero to follow.

"I'm many things, Seb. Lucky isn't one of them," Vero says between huffs, dodging a stubborn couple who refuses to move. "By the way, thanks for following me."

"Not that it did much good."

"Still, you were right. I was stupid to go into that alone. Who knows what could have happened?"

"Teach never would've forgiven you, that's for sure," Seb says. "And let's be real. If you disappeared or died, *I'd* get the blame for not being a good partner."

"You're a great partner."

"You can say that again—shit!" Seb jumps to the side as a bicycle nearly slams into him. He flips off the biker as he continues running. "Hey, use the street, you psychopath!"

"But she…she's not normal," Vero says.

"I know. It's like she wanted to kill me."

"Not the—crap!" Vero jumps to the side and dodges the biker, who apparently didn't think one murder attempt was enough for one day. "Not that *crazy bitch!*" she yells the last two words behind her as the biker disappears. "I mean *her.*"

"Your new obsession? The rogue Medium? Any reason we're keeping this a secret?"

"It's not a secret," Vero says. She knows it's a lie the second it leaves her lips. "Okay, it's a secret for now. But only because I know Mom hates half-complete investigations. And she…this girl's…interesting…"

"I'd go with dangerous."

"Maybe. But you weren't there," Vero says, ignoring the first part. "It was like she was speaking to the Spectre."

"Like a Ghost whisperer?" Vero can hear Seb suppressing a chuckle.

"No, not like that! But one second she was attacking it, and the next… it's almost like the Spectre opened itself up to her, inviting her attack. It happened so quickly, but it shouldn't have been possible, right? She was at Level Zero. That Spectre was at Level Two."

Seb doesn't respond for several seconds. All Vero hears are his heavy breaths in her ear piece. "That Essence would have been nice to come back with though," he finally says.

"We can't exactly come back from an unsanctioned mission with an Essence," Vero says with a laugh.

"That didn't make it any less tempting."

"There are countless higher levels in the Essence Bank."

"But how many have *we* caught? On our own, no less."

"None."

"Yes, none!" Seb says with a laugh.

"No one hears about this."

"What was the point of us going if we can't tell your mom about it? That's what this was all about, right?"

"Again, half-baked investigations."

"This is an *open investigation* within the DOSD."

"Which is why it's even more important not to share anything until I have something tangible to give them."

"That's toeing the line. Even for you."

Vero clenches her jaw. "Fine. I'll tell her, but only her. We tell Teach, and he'll just give us janitorial duty again."

"Right, right. Gotta go over the head of your superiors, that's the Daugherty way."

Vero chuckles. "Shut up." She's always hated the cutthroat brand of ladder climbing her family is known for in the military.

Fifteen minutes later, the pair is climbing up the stairs of the X Tower, which sits at the heart of the Financial District in the disappointing downtown of Los Angeles, which Vero always thought should have extended farther than it does. Compared to the other cities she's lived in, L.A. has always felt minuscule as far as skyscrapers go. What a disappointing skyline it offers.

The two attract eyes as they enter through the glass doors, both out of breath, both underdressed compared to the dozens of others on all sides, donning suits, pant suits, the occasional floral skirt and colored blouse, but always professional. Even the marble floors and polished bronze décor of the atrium are more dressed up than them.

Vero always feels self-conscious entering through those doors, but as the two scan their badges and head to the back freight elevator, any insecurity leaves her. Seb runs his watch along a panel below the buttons, and the doors shut quicker than normal, as though to prevent anyone else from entering. In fact, that's exactly what the elevator was designed to do.

In the Age of Infinite Knowledge, that's one way the Department of Spectral Defense managed to remain a secret for the past twelve years of its existence. It's a brief time span given the length of human history, but in modern years, it's practically a millennium.

When the elevator doors open, Jace is already waiting for them, coffee mug in hand, stubble as scraggly as ever, as though he'd just woken up. Based on his appearance, Vero would have thought he'd been called in unexpectedly, but he always looks like he's experiencing a never-ending hangover. She's still not convinced he isn't.

"Know what this is about, Teach?" Vero says with a smile, shoving down any anxiety about their secret. She steps out of the elevator alongside Seb into the brightly lit, wide open lobby that lay out in front of them. Round carbon fiber tables line the sides where office workers chat, a mix of exhaustion and enthusiasm forever permeating the atmosphere.

"Your guess is as good as mine," Jace says, turning around cradling his mug. "Where were you? You're late. The commander won't be pleased."

"Late? It was our day off," Vero says.

"And what do kids these days do on their days off?"

Vero's mouth hangs open as she tries to formulate a lie. "Well…we—"

"Never mind," Jace says with a hand wave and a sigh. "I really don't care. Regretted the question the second I asked."

A few minutes later, the trio stands out in front of a pair of glass doors. On the other side, Vero sees two people—a man and a woman—in police uniforms speaking with her mother, Commander Daugherty.

"Since when are cops allowed down here?" Seb asks.

"The DOSD has eyes everywhere, Kid," Jace says, taking a sip of his coffee. "And those eyes can come attached to many types of bodies."

"That was the weirdest way for you to say cops are useful," Vero says, only half-listening, more focused on trying to read their lips, unsuccessfully.

She locks eyes with the commander, who nods and motions for them to enter.

Jace pushes through the doors with his free hand, holding the door open for Vero with a curt nod.

"Agent Daugherty, you're here," the commander says.

"Commander Daugherty."

"What took you so long?"

Vero blinks and bites the inside of her lip. "It was my day off."

"Hmm," the commander says, lips drawn to a line.

Vero suppresses another groan. If Mother's going to scold her, she could at least wait until the others left.

"Anyway," Commander Daugherty continues, "allow me to introduce the three of you to Officer Gaines and Officer Sanchez. They're informants for us within the LAPD. They've just told me that one of their detectives is trapped in a Mirage."

SPECTRAL

EPISODE 5
AGENT

ONE

VERO INVOLUNTARILY EXHALES at the latest development. Every so often, someone will go missing in a Mirage.

Well, more than every so often. Quite regularly. Most of their targets are found by civilians getting consumed by these monsters. But they rarely find these missing persons while they're still alive. She's heard of cases of Mediums saving some hostages and putting them through memory relocation, but not many. Tens of thousands of people go missing every year, and while a good chunk of those are due to Spectral abduction, the DOSD has only so many resources. Rescue missions aren't a high priority. Usually.

The question here is if this is going to be a rescue mission or something more depressing. Vero keeps her mouth shut and turns her lips upward into a friendly smile as the two cops throw up a projection of Watts, a gentrified and affluent neighborhood just north of the 105.

Officer Gaines points to a block corner near Watts Towers, a series of sculptures that make up a popular local art exhibit. "This is a home that was condemned in 2035. It's been around since the previous century, and is the death place of murderer Derek Kingsley. He was chased down and burned alive inside as members of the community guarded its exits. He jumped through a window and out onto the lawn, where the neighbors watched him attempt to crawl to the sidewalk before he burned alive."

"So he was on fire as he was crawling?" Seb says.

"Correct."

"That's lovely," Vero says. She catches the scolding eye of her mother and looks down at the ground.

Jace lets out a snort, which he also muffles when spared a glance from the commander.

"So, the house survived the fire?" Seb asks, managing to be the sole productive member of the trio.

Vero will hear that from the commander when they're left alone later.

"Survived in structure only," Officer Gaines says. "It's still standing, that is. No one's lived in it for decades and it was originally supposed to be demolished some time ago. For one reason or another, that hasn't happened."

"It's for the best," Officer Sanchez says, speaking up for the first time. "There have been rumblings for some time about Ethereal anomalies residing within the house, but nothing enough to act on. That is until recently. The other day, we received reports of an explosion from neighbors. When we got there, there was nothing. At least initially. Nothing that your standard cops could detect, at least."

"So," Officer Gaines says, "we stepped in. Figured that explosion could be a Mirage bleeding into our world." She gives a sideways glance to her partner, who shrugs. "Turns out we had a tail."

She throws up an image of an Asian man in a suit and tie. Vero doesn't recognize him. "Detective Dan Chu followed us to the scene. After we logged the Bullethole, he confronted us. Started asking questions. One second he was there, and the next, gone."

"And that," Commander Daugherty waves her hand at Officer Gaines to pull down the projection, "is where the three of you come in. Agent Kamil, we need you and your Junior Mediums to engage in a search and rescue of Detective Chu."

"Huh," Seb says involuntarily. Vero can tell because his eyes widen immediately after, and he shuts his mouth, looking sheepish.

She understands his surprise. It's not very often they utilize Department resources to rescue hostages from Spectres. Most of the time, they deem it too late and too high of a risk. In the instances they *do* decide to go in, they don't delegate the task to lowly Juniors.

Does this mean they'll finally start to take us seriously? Vero doesn't know whether to be happy or disappointed at the thought.

"Why us?" Jace says, asking the unspoken question. "Why the kids?"

The corners of Commander Daugherty's lips perked up ever so slightly. As though on the verge of a smile. But if she was, the error was corrected immediately. "You didn't think they could keep the Junior Mediums hunting low-level Spectres in perpetuity, did you?"

The muscles in Jace's jaw tightened. "It's just..." he glanced over at the officers, weighing his options.

A knot tightens in Vero's stomach. Would it be the wisest decision to state outright that she and Seb had no experience in Spectral Hostages? Is that the kind of reputation the organization needs now?

"No, I suppose not," Jace finally finishes.

Commander Daugherty gives him a stiff nod. He'd toed the line, but ultimately made the right decision. At least in her eyes.

But he was right to ask. These missions were more dangerous than the ones Vero was used to. Every Medium, Junior or not, was a precious resource. Plus, if they were to rescue him, he's another potential leak for the Department to worry about. Why risk everything for some city detective? Why volunteer such a risk?

"How did he find out?" Vero asks. "The detective."

Officer Gaines and Sanchez exchange glances, as though weighing the same options Jace had just weighed. Vero can't blame them. No government entity wants to admit error.

Finally, Officer Sanchez speaks. "We think he grew suspicious of us about a week back. There was an incident at the station—something we're still working on," Sanchez directs the last part at Commander Daugherty.

Vero's eyes narrow. She can see the strings being pulled from her mother. These two may be cops, but it's clear their loyalty is to the DOSD.

"We were bringing someone here. A person of interest to the Department. She was also a person of interest in one of his cases, and he's a stubborn man."

"What was the incident?" Vero asks, her stomach turning over. Last week, they'd said. That was around the same time she, Jace, and Seb ran into that rogue Medium—into Luna.

"That's...not important," Officer Gaines says, "but Detective Chu kept a close eye on us after that. A real close eye. Started asking questions, following us around. Frankly, becoming insubordinate to the captain, unfocused in his cases."

Vero is all too familiar with the angry sigh that follows from Commander Daugherty, and she doesn't miss the glare from Officer Gaines. Vero meets her glare with one of her own. It was the most basic of questions. Her mother would have found out one way or another.

"Thank you for coming," Commander Daugherty finally says.

Jace speaks the second the duo shuts the door behind them. "They don't have any experience with hostages," he says in a hushed whisper.

"Don't you think I know that?" Commander Daugherty says, walking over to a coffee nook off to the side of her desk and pouring a mug. "This program has already overstayed its welcome in the eyes of the DOSD at large, and in the eyes of our Commander-in-Chief, we've coddled our Junior Mediums for too long. They need to see some return on our investment, otherwise they see no value. If we don't prove ourselves soon, there may be consequences."

"You mean they'd shut us down?" Vero says, not sure what she's feeling. Panic? Relief? Would Mother deem her a failure if this happened, or could it mean a return to what life was like before?

"I mean, if this doesn't go well, I can't guarantee anyone's security." Commander Daugherty takes a sip of her black coffee. "You have your orders. As you know, with hostages, time is of the essence, so load up with a set of Level Twos and head to the transports."

"Level Twos?" Jace says. "Can't we spare—"

"Level Twos," she says, her voice stern. Her patience has already worn as thin as it will go.

"Yes, Commander. Let's move, team."

I hear him and Seb shuffle out the door behind me. I only wave a hand, and even Jace understands, closing it with a soft click.

"You're still here," Commander Daugherty says, voice cold as she projects a file from her tablet.

"Mother—"

"Commander."

"Commander," Vero says, determined not to be deterred. "About—"

"What took you so long to get here?"

"I was on my day off. I already told you."

"You know better than that, Veronica."

"*Agent* Daugherty," Vero says. It's petty, but she doesn't care at this point.

The commander smiles. "Good. Always be vigilant. Always be ready."

"It's about that other—"

"Do *not* interrupt me when I'm speaking."

Vero clamps her mouth shut, breath heavy but measured.

"I've had enough of your protests. Your childish behavior. And I can feel it rubbing off on your teammates. I've already told you to get on with your mission. Whatever point you're trying to make can wait. I need to prepare your Bank clearance, so do as you've been ordered. I will not ask again." Without another word, she takes a seat and sifts through a projection, mind already far from Vero.

"Yes, sir," Vero says under her breath as she turns away, exiting out the glass door and to the Essence Bank.

SEB THRUSTS his hand into the opening at the side of the Charger, a cylindrical object the size of an SUV with a glass encasing making up the upper half. Inside, a milky, viscous fluid tumbles around, undulating as though in a perpetual state of a rolling boil.

"And what did she say?" Seb asks as he absently punches in his clearance number.

"Level Two clearance confirmed," a disembodied voice announces before the machine whirrs, the liquid bubbling more violently.

"She wasn't interested in hearing what I had to say," Vero says, trying not to let the shame show. Being the commander's daughter has always come with its own difficulties, and the fact that she's twice as hard on Vero while giving her a fraction of the patience of other agents was a never-ending point of frustration.

Vero only has herself to blame. Every time she tries to fall in line, her mother only spits it back in her face. "No one likes an overly eager bunny in the field," she'd said one time after Vero had offered to take on a particularly difficult mission. If she hadn't taken it, though, she knows the ridicule would have never ended. There were two outcomes to every encounter with her mother: bad or worse.

"And what is it you wanted her to be interested in?" Jace cuts in, snapping on his own Syncer, which is strapped to his right wrist.

"I tried to apologize," Vero says, her lie already locked, loaded, and ready for utilization. "I know she doesn't like it when I'm late. I don't know what I was thinking." She follows up the last sentence by sticking out her tongue and knocking on her head softly with her knuckles. "I'm such a dumb blonde," the gesture says without her having to verbalize it. It helps cut the tension in nearly every situation.

"Well, make sure you're on your game today."

"Transfer completed," the female voice announces.

"We heard, Teach," Seb says as he pulls out his wrist from the Charger. "Some hotshot detective is on the line."

Vero thrusts her own arm into the Charger and inputs her own code. *Level Two clearance. What a joke.*

"Level Two clearance confirmed," the voice announces. A vibration tugs on Vero's arm and the liquid in the tank bubbles violently as her randomly assigned Essences are distributed to her Syncer.

It's the bare minimum level required to take on a mission against this particular Spectre. Every so often, the DOSD lets Mediums take higher-level Spectre Essences with them to guarantee success, but they're such a precious resource that they never like to risk it. Plus, with a mission like this, Vero knows the team is justifying its existence. If they can do more with less, it'll mean something to Mother's superiors.

"It's not about the detective," Jace says. "Believe it or not, I'm more worried about you morons." He looks around the Essence Bank and hushes his voice to a whisper. "And I know from firsthand experience this particular Spectre can be a tough one."

Seb and Vero exchange glances. "You've fought it before?"

"I discovered it," Jace says. "Years ago. Could have killed it then, but I was ordered to let it fester and grow until its Essence was more mature. The commander's reputation is on the line. Beyond that and the credibility of the Junior Medium Program, the entire DOSD's reputation could be in jeopardy if this leaks to the president—that a known Mirage led to the death of a police detective."

Vero's face scrunches into a frown. This is probably another reason they were selected. "Why are you telling this to us?"

"Don't the two of you start spreading this around like gossip," Jace says, his voice uncharacteristically stern. "I'm telling you so you understand the true danger. And what's at stake. So, when we get into the Mirage, don't drop your guard. Don't half-ass it. Communicate, communicate, communicate. You may have fought Spectres dozens of times already, but a hostage situation is different. You can't kill a Spectre without freeing the hostage from its clutches first, otherwise the hostage dies with the Mirage. And the hostage can be anywhere. He can be in a specific location, awake, asleep, *dead*. He can even be inside the Spectre itself or inside one of its Spirits. And once we find him, priority is what?"

"Save the hostage," Vero and Seb say in unison.

"Transfer completed."

"Okay," Jace says. "Let's get going."

TWO

THE RIDE in the van to the location is busier than usual. In every other circumstance, they'd sit in silence—maybe even crack a joke or two to keep morale up. But today, Jace's brief takes nearly the entire drive. Most of it is a retread of the details the two cops already told the group, but with a few extra details peppered in as they pertain to the mission.

Included in the brief are the Spectre's general abilities—fire—and its last known level—Level Three. That last part is a given, considering they're cleared for Level Two back at the Essence Bank. With all three of them working together, they can just squeeze out a victory if they're smart.

Or if we're worth the investment, Vero thinks. She's sure that's what's going through the minds of the brass. Can this small unit that makes up the larger Junior Medium program prove they're worth the years of training?

"Remember, it's a *rescue mission,*" Jace emphasized. "We don't need to kill the damned thing. Priority one is to rescue the hostage. Any questions?"

"Yeah," Seb says, looking around the interior of the van. "Do you think anyone gets suspicious about the number of white vans that ride through L.A.? What happens if they look up the company name plastered on the side?"

"So, do you think we should have the word Medium on there instead?"

"I'd settle for SWAT," Vero says. "At least SWAT is cool. And if someone sees us, we're already in tactical gear."

"Kids, not now." Jace's tone is more stern than normal. "I made myself clear before we left, didn't I?"

"Sorry, Teach," Seb says.

"Yeah, sorry." Vero looks down at the ground. Seb copes through comedy. Jace knows that, and the fact that he batted down that innocent exchange shows just how serious things are.

Seb sits up, shoulders stiffening as the vehicle rocks from side to side. "We're here, aren't we?" he says.

Jace looks at his Syncer, which also doubles as a GPS. "We're a couple of blocks out. Why?"

"I can feel it already." Seb raises his hands in front of him, aiming past the driver and passenger seat of the van. "How long ago did you say you found this?"

"Seven years ago, why?"

"It's…not inconspicuous, that's all I'll say."

BY THE TIME they enter the condemned building, even Vero can sense the Spectre's presence. Usually, they rely on Seb, their Tracker, to find the sneakier ones, but here they don't even need him. There's almost a tangible coldness that permeates the charred living room, expanding outward. Vero shivers as she catches sight of her own breath.

"How has no one else stumbled into this yet?" she says.

"Maybe they have," Jace says. He swallows, and Vero can hear the guilt in his breath. "They didn't even gate the damned thing off."

Vero could picture it: a group of kids daring each other to visit the haunted house of Watts, disappearing one by one and being eaten alive by the Spectre.

"We would've known about it," she says. "There would have been reports of missing children or people."

Jace nods and clears his throat, but she can tell he's still not fully convinced. In the years that Jace has acted as their mentor, Vero has never seen this side of him. She doesn't like it.

"We're lucky, then," Vero says with a smile, hoping it doesn't look as forced as it feels. As used as she is to faking her blonde, airheaded façade, she knows it likely looks natural. "It's a nice area. No way these people would go stumbling into a house like this, even if they were bored."

"Or stay silent if anyone was going missing," Seb adds.

Jace nods. "You two ready?" he says with a smirk, insecurity fading away in an instant. If he had suspicions of any missing persons going unreported, he didn't show it, which Vero is all the happier for. Seeds of doubt before a mission are never good.

"Yes, sir," Vero and Seb say simultaneously.

Jace double-taps his Syncer, and the Bullethole, what the DOSD calls openings to Mirages, opens up around them, transforming the scorched remains of the house into an immediate roaring inferno. The air around them practically pulls oxygen from Vero's lungs.

Without hesitation, she pulls a retractable mask from inside her vest pocket and places it over her nose and mouth. It expands and suctions to the outsides of her cheeks, making the air breathable. She hasn't had much opportunity to use it in the past. More often than not, Mirages are perfectly breathable, but there have been a handful of reports of Mirages that destroy the lungs of Mediums. Better safe than sorry.

Vero taps at her own Syncer, and her Spectral Armor materializes around her body, a carbon fiber cuirass enveloping her chest and back. The look had always been decidedly more medieval-looking than she expected, but she didn't have much choice. The armor crafts itself based on its user, and apparently something about Vero led to its look. Regardless, when a Spectre hauls ass in her direction, she'll take whatever armor she can.

Finally, her body-length katana expands out from her right hand, settling between her palm and fingers.

"Seb, Teach—I mean, Agents Mariano and Kamil. You okay?"

"Couldn't be better," Seb says, his voice a lower octave than usual, punctuated by an unexpected shakiness. He'd likely taken a tad too long to put on his mask.

"Okay, Seb. Where is this thing?" Jace says, his voice breathy and weary, nearly drowned out by the sound of flames licking at the surrounding walls.

Seb puts up his hands, scanning the living room for any trace of the elusive Spectre. Jace covers his twelve with his Spectral pistol while Vero covers his six, katana wielded and ready. With the exception of the roaring flames, the house itself is very quiet. Not so much as a wail or moan to draw their attention. In Vero's limited experience, those are the worst kinds of Mirages to be in. In a hostage situation, it only draws things out longer.

"It's not in here," Seb says, directing them out the front door and onto the lawn. Beyond that, they can see neighboring yards and the Watts Towers in the middle distance. As they leave the home behind them, they leave the heat behind as well, the air just a tad more breathable, even with masks on. Vero wipes the sweat from her forehead as she takes in their surroundings.

"This is a one-for-one replication of the real world," Vero says. "I don't think I've ever seen that before."

Seb chuckles. "It's like we're in the dark world of some video game."

"Focus," Jace says. "Still no Spectre? What about the hostage?"

Seb aims his hands down the street. "Both are…that way?"

"Are they or aren't they?"

His question doesn't linger for more than a split second before the ground rumbles beneath their feet. Vero has to widen her stance and plant her feet to keep from falling over.

Bum-bum! Bum-bum! Bum-bum!

It's almost like a one-two punch. A loud rumble followed by a smaller one.

Bum-buuuum! Crash! The sound of metal grinding on metal. A giant, bright red, luminescent ball rolls up the metallic tower structure a couple of blocks down.

"Hey!" I say. "Seb, is that it?"

His hands settle on the ball that sits a hundred feet up in the air. "That's the Spectre."

"Don't forget the mission," Jace says. "Find the hostage first."

"I think the hostage is *inside* the Spectre."

"Well, shit."

"Does that make it easier?"

"If only."

"Why a ball?" Vero says.

"Why anything?" Jace says. "I've given up trying to figure out the why years ago. Just look alive and be careful."

The trio darts down the street, taking advantage of their superhuman speed, hoping to gain the element of surprise, though it doesn't do them much good as a mouth materializes on the side of the ball, letting out a squeal.

Vero takes to her knee and covers her ears. The entire Mirage shakes like an eight-point-zero magnitude earthquake, sending the older houses tumbling in the process. She jumps out of the way of a telephone pole threatening to crush her, and lands on the roof across the street from the highest tower, which is surrounded by two shorter ones.

The ball at the very top melts into a humanoid shape for a split second as it stretches from the top tower to the second-tallest one that sits a bit closer to Vero. As it settles onto the shorter tower, it transforms back into a red slimy ball, though one that rolls and morphs as needed to move.

"I've scanned it!" Seb calls out.

Vero holds up her Syncer and scans the sphere.

Spectre: Level Three
Type: Attacker

"Well, it's stronger than I want it to be, but not unexpected," Vero hears Jace's voice through her earbud.

"It's the strongest one we've ever fought," Seb says.

"They're really pushing us on this one," Jace says. "Don't target its core. You might injure the hostage if you do."

Vero takes a deep breath. "All right, then. Let's kill this sucker."

"I literally just said to take it easy. Don't forget the mission. *Save the hostage*, not kill the Spectre."

"Come on, let's save the hostage, *then* kill this sucker!" A surge of adrenaline runs through Vero's body as she takes a few quick breaths, launching off the roof of the house.

"Be careful, dammit!" Jace's cries are muted by the sound of Vero's pounding ears. It's a weakness. In the thick of battle, she sometimes lets the adrenaline get the better of her. It's served her both well and poorly over the course of her brief career as a Junior Medium.

As her katana connects with one of the tentacle arms materializing from the core of the ball-like Spectre for the first time, she worries this case will result in the latter. There's little resistance in the Spectral flesh as her blade cuts—as though cutting through a marshmallow with a knife—only for it to seize up partway through. The Spectre lets out a shockingly human scream. More often than not, these Spectres emit more animal-like guttural roars, but this one sounds pure human. Like a man who'd just cut his finger with a kitchen knife.

Vero is smacked away from the arm like a fly. She zips through the air and slams onto the concrete sidewalk below. She's a little jostled, but her shield keeps her from feeling much. Still, she curses her stupidity. It was a dumb move on her part to just attacked, but she's worked with Seb and Jace enough to know the creature wouldn't be on top of her.

The sound of a machine gun fire echoes through the Mirage, and Jace's figure clashes with the monster at the top of the tower. The Spectre fights him off, looking like King Kong batting around a fleet of biplanes.

"This is gonna be a tough one," Vero says with a breath.

"Gee, what was your first clue?" Seb says as he continues to pelt the Spectre with bullets. "Was it the Level Three or the murderous backstory?"

Typical protocol was pretty straightforward. Chip away at the Spectre until they take it down. Normally, they can do it in a handful of good hits, but then again, they hadn't taken on a Level Three Spectre together. This would take some time, especially if they have to target the infinitely sprouting limbs to avoid killing the hostage.

And yet, somehow, that Level Zero Medium, Luna, had taken on a Level Two. She hadn't *won*, and surely would have died if Vero hadn't interfered, but still. The fact that she could inflict damage and ultimately kill the Spectre wasn't anything she'd encountered or read before. And the girl had said something strange in the midst of battle.

"Did you catch her memory?" she had asked after Vero had cut through the Stepford Wife Spectre. *"We need to figure out her core emotion if we're going to beat her."* What did that mean?

"They said the man—what was his name again?"

"Who?" Seb says.

"The Spectre man."

"Huh?"

"*This* Spectre man. Who he was before he died. Whatever his name was. When he was killed by all his neighbors, did they say why?"

"What the hell's it matter?" Jace says as he takes another slash at the Spectre's new tentacle, this time slicing through successfully and emitting another bone-chilling, human-esque cry.

"How they die affects how strong they are and what type of Spectre they are," she says. "Can that help us in defeating it somehow?"

"I appreciate your initiative," Jace says, "but I don't think now's the right time to start revamping how we take on a Spectre. I know this is fresh territory for us, but we have our approach. Continue to target and chip away at its health."

Vero nods. "Right, sorry." She did it again. In the thick of battle, she made it all about her and her own journey. She can't afford to experiment based on some strange anomaly she saw. She launches herself at the Spectre and slashes at its exposed tentacle, cutting through it like butter.

Its screams are muffled by the sound of more gunshots from Seb, the bullets of which land on its exposed flesh. And then...

Kaboom! An explosion, and the Spectre is catapulted from the tower through the ground, landing a few feet into a self-made crater.

"Great job, Teach!" Seb yells out.

All three Mediums close in on the injured Spectre on all sides. As she approaches, Vero notices that the spherical figure is now chipped on one side. Out of that side emerges a human arm.

"Bingo," Jace says.

"I take it we can't just hack away at this thing like normal," Seb says with a huff.

"Now that the arm is exposed, we need to chip away at another part of its body. If we're lucky, at a certain point, it'll crack open to reveal the hostage in full."

"If we're lucky?" Vero says.

"That's enough talking," Jace responds. "You two know what to do next."

It takes significantly longer than she would like, but after another several minutes of hacking. The Spectre is a lot less nimble than it was previously, its amorphous, slimy exterior less malleable. After several more minutes, another crack emerges, and with it, another arm of the hostage.

"All right, team," Jace says, jumping into the air. "Clear the way." His Spectral Shield materializes in front of him, blocking his body from head to toe as he descends on the Spectre. A loud thud and crack reverberate throughout the Mirage, shaking the ground beneath them.

Vero is on the Spectre in an instant, not waiting for it to recover or regain its composure. She grabs at the hostage's hand and pulls him out like a yolk from a cracked egg. To Vero's surprised, the man—Detective Chu—is not unconscious. He even manages to stand on his own two feet when she puts him down. His eyes are wide, and his breath is heavy with what she can only assume is pure, unadulterated trauma. But he's still standing.

There are several instances she's read that have to do with Spectral Hostage experiences, but in each case, the experience in question is different. Some hostages revealed it was as though waking from a fitful sleep. Others have indicated it was like being awake but unable to control themselves. Like a twisted form of mind control, only within the body of another creature.

It takes only a passing glance at Detective Chu's eyes to realize which of the experiences he'd just gone through. "It's okay, Detective," Vero says, holding her arm out in front of him. "We're from the DOSD. We're here to help."

"Seb, punch us a Bullethole outta here," Jace says. "Mission accomplished."

The detective opens his mouth to speak, only to devolve into a fit of coughing. Vero keeps an eye on the Spectre, which lays still on the ground, cracked and broken, pieces of its bright red body scattered around the battlefield. Vero places a comforting hand on the man's shoulder. "It's going to be okay," she says. "You're *going to be okay*."

"Wants…wants to go out."

"What?"

"It wants out of here." The detective's voice is raspy and cracked. "The *thing* wants to leave."

"Vero, let's go," Seb says as he opens one of the Bulletholes.

Vero's stomach leaps up into her throat. She casts another glance at the Spectre on the ground, only to see it scurrying at superhuman speed toward the exit. Not really intending to, she tosses the detective to the ground, and with her free hand, casts her katana toward the open Bullethole.

As the Spectre leaps ahead, the sword impales it with a clean squelch, pinning it to the ground within the Mirage. It writhes around, again screaming, tentacles forming and shooting outwards.

Vero picks the detective back up, and bolts through the open Bullethole and out into the derelict home, followed by her two teammates. "Close it, close it!" she yells.

"Ya think?" Seb taps his Syncer, and the Bullethole shuts behind them.

The world goes silent, save for their heavy breaths.

"We did it," Vero says, looking up and catching the eyes of the detective. He looks shocked, scared, bewildered, and a variety of other descriptions, but he's alive. His eyes open wide yet again.

"What's…"

Vero follows his gaze. Floating in the air is a piece of a tentacle. Maybe three inches in length. It hovers, as though still attached to a larger entity, thrashing about, with each whip being followed by a heavy thud, though it doesn't make contact with the ground. Moments pass before Vero realizes what she's looking at. The Spectre hadn't gone through the opening, but one of its tentacles had prevented it from shutting completely.

"It's trying to pry the Bullethole open it," Jace says.

Vero reaches for her katana on instinct, but curses when she remembers it won't work in the real world. None of her abilities work in the real world.

That's the last thing she thinks before the tentacle rips open the portal to its Mirage and throws a fireball into the abandoned house.

THREE

THE BALL of flame collides with the wall and catches instantly.

For the briefest of moments, Vero can only stand back in shock. Spectres have been known to venture out into the real world, but she'd never actually witnessed it herself. At most, they snatch up unknowing victims and gobble them up like gremlins. To explode out into the real world like this…

"Look alive, Kids!" Jace is on top of the situation in an instant. "Hostage has been saved. I wish we could call this done, but it looks like we have to go on to Phase Two—kill this bastard."

"Run," Vero says to the detective, giving him a measured, but forceful shove toward the front door.

He looks back at the group of Mediums, still at a loss. Vero sees the conflict in his eyes. He's used to running *into* these types of situations, not away from them. And then common sense seems to click into his brain as he steps back and through the threshold of the house. He may be used to running into danger, but he's nowhere near equipped to take on what they're about to. At least he's smart enough to realize that.

The Spectre's tentacle slaps around inside the house, taking out a piece of drywall in the process.

"Seb, open the Bullethole," Vero says, without thinking.

"Open it?" he says, his voice shaky. "Are you kidding?"

"Do it," Jace says. "We can't use our abilities out in the real world. The only solution is to take it out *within* the Mirage."

"On three," Seb responds with a nod. "Then you go in. Quickly."

"I'm fastest outside of the Mirage," Vero says to Jace. "Let me go in first."

"You got it." She can tell he's unsure, but he knows it's the best option. Plus, there's no time for a back and forth on this.

"One."

She takes a deep breath, digging the balls of her feet into the hardwood floor.

"Two."

The blood-red tentacle whips back and forth. Back and forth. They all stand just out of reach, Vero keeping her eye on it, timing its lashes.

"Three!"

She charges forward, jumping over the tentacle as it whips back, narrowly missing her calf as it zips upward and down, splintering the hardwood floor. She focuses on the Bullethole, which seems to open in slow motion. Trusting its trajectory, she dives forward, barely skirting its edge as she crosses into the already-flaming Mirage.

It's like diving out of molasses into clean, clear air, and the muscles in her body tighten and almost expand, the power building inside them. She lands on the ground and tumbles, dodging another tentacle that darts out from the Spectre's core, and launches off the ground, katana materializing in mid-air.

There's no need to pull any punches this time. No need for her to aim strictly for its limbs for fear of accidental murder. As her blade sinks into its body, she feels its sponginess. For a split second, she worries about it absorbing her as it did the detective. But she pushes on, thrusting the edge through its body, forcing another loud and disturbing scream from its giant mouth, which forms for the sole reason of expressing its pain.

She emerges from the other side of the slice and glances back to see a third of the Spectre fall, looking like a giant blood cell rocking on the floor. The Spectre is weaker than it was before, but still has some fight left in it. And a goal.

It ignores Vero, limbs materializing and expanding outward to propel its body forward, rolling its core toward the Bullethole at an increasingly accelerated speed. As it nears the exit, Jace jumps through from the real world, materializing his giant shield, and knocking the Spectre away, foiling yet another attempt at escape.

"Close the portal!" Jace yells.

The Bullethole decreases in size, but catches on another set of tentacles that continues to extend outward through it. The Spectre may not have made its way into the real world, but it's determined to keep its proverbial foot in the door.

"Dammit, this thing is smart," Seb says from the other side of the portal.

"Smarter than we're used to," Vero says. As these things consume more people and level up, they become more cognizant. They inch closer to their human counterparts, with their motivations more closely mirroring their real-life selves.

She grits her teeth. "What in the heck did this guy do in real life that makes him want to destroy the house?" She doesn't wait for an answer—she knows they don't have one, and ultimately, don't need one. Instead, she leaps forward, targeting the base of the limbs that stretch out toward the portal. She cuts through them easily, though frustratingly, as she does, more grow to take their place through it, giving Seb no opportunity to close it.

Jace aims his own attacks at the Spectre's main body once again. "Seb, get your ass in here. We're gonna take it down wholesale, and our chances are better if you're in here helping."

"But what about the portal?"

"Hop through quickly, then close it as much as you can."

Vero's stomach lurches at the thought of giving this thing any further opportunity to lay waste to the outside world, but before she can open my mouth to argue, Seb is already heading through the portal, machine guns glazing, peppering the blubbering mass with bullets.

Vero can sense the difference in the tide of battle instantly. Its limbs vibrate and undulate, losing their solid form more readily under the barrage of attacks. She takes it as her cue to continue hacking away at those limbs, further whittling away at the creature's inflated health.

And then, the air around them vibrates, like a tsunami of sound, pulsing Vero's insides and practically putting a stop to her heart. She collapses to the ground, taking a knee, holding herself up with her free hand. Still, she never lets her gaze fall from the Spectre. Better Mediums have been killed while their guards are down. She watches as the creature's blubbery and spherical exterior melts away, seemingly by the fire coming from within. Clump by clump, the pieces fall to the ground, revealing a more humanoid form—a skeleton draped in a trench coat with its skull ablaze. All the while, its jaw hangs open, almost unhinged, with its cries growing louder by the second.

"Closed!" Vero can somehow hear Seb's yell through the domineering vibrations, and a feeling of relief washes over her as she does. The window they'd been working to keep him away from for so long was finally closed.

And then the screams stop. The skeleton's jaw closes, and he locks eyes with Seb.

An eerie silence penetrates the Mirage, in spite of the surrounding flames. And then the sound of bone scratching on cement as the creature bounds toward Seb. Its speed has somehow increased. Sometimes, when being pushed to their limits, Spectres "go feral" as it's called. It's a last ditch survival instinct—one that has the potential to make it significantly more dangerous than it was just moments before.

Though it catches Vero off guard, Jace is on top of the Spectre in an instant, his shield in front of him, knocking him back, protecting his student from the onslaught. The Spectre slams into the translucent shield, but rather than getting bounced back, it presses against it harder, feet continually etching deep scratches into the ground as its teeth chatter.

Vero readies her katana and lays into the skeletal creature, feeling a deep, vibrating crack as she slices through it.

Another scream.

She turns, the soles of her boots sliding on the ground as she shifts her balance and plants her feet, readying another attack. In spite of the crack and snap, the Spectre is still intact. No surprise there. Spectres regularly defy the laws of physics, but she knows there's no way it's truly gone unscathed. She can sense the desperation in its hollowed-out eyes.

She jumps forward, giving it no time to recover. The Spectre's jaw chatters again, and it darts to the side, narrowly avoiding her strike. Vero spins to recover, but is caught by a sharp blow to her face.

The sound of an explosion roars. In an instant, she is transported to the abandoned house in the real world. Only this time, it's no longer derelict. The screams of a mob can be heard outside. The shuffling of socks on the hardwood floor and the panicked whimpers of a man as he peers from window to window. Vero can't hear what he's saying, but she can tell from his tone that it's the sound of begging—begging in the face of a bloodthirsty mob.

Vero's body slams and slides across the floor, her shield taking the majority of the impact. She's back in the Mirage and can hear a renewed scream from the Spectre.

What in the hell was that?

She'd never taken a hit to the face like that from a Spectre before and had never experienced whatever that was either. Was that some form of mind manipulation or an ability of the Spectre? Or maybe a memory, she thinks, again recalling what that girl Luna had said.

Vero bounces to her feet, just in time to block a follow up blow from the Spectre's forearms, which have transformed into blades of their own. The Spectre's teeth chatter again and a long tongue emerges from inside its mouth, extending toward her in a perverted dance.

Whatever that is is interrupted by the sound of gunshots. Bullets smack into the side of the Spectre, punching holes into the bones and chipping away at it. Its tongue retreats back into its mouth and it lets out another scream. Again, the very air around them vibrates, practically debilitating Vero, but she holds her ground, using this distracting moment to attack the creature yet again, this time, burying her sword into its shoulder, cutting through its sternum and ribs with a thunderous crack.

More bullets. More screams. And then a slam from Jace's human-sized shield.

"This thing is not quitting," Seb yells over the sound of exploding gunpowder and bullets.

"It's Level Three, what do you expect?" Jace says. "Keep chipping away at it. It can't be long now."

As if in response, the Spectre jumps backward several feet, avoiding one of Vero's swings. Even as Seb's bullets continue to punch holes in its jacket and chip away at its exterior, it holds out its arms. An unearned confidence seems to emanate from within, and it somehow manages to grin. Vero has no idea how a skeleton can express emotion of any kind, let alone grin, but it doesn't last long. It waves its arms around, as though performing a yoga pose, and suddenly, tens of portals open up all around it.

Its hands explode into flames and it launches balls of fire in all directions. Vero and Seb jump behind Jace and his human-sized shield, holding him up as explosions erupt against it, flames spilling over its sides.

The intense heat bats against Vero's face, forcing her to shield it with her arm and duck her head down. Still, the flames further engulf them, making it feel like she could almost bake alive in her armor.

And then it stops. Once again, silence reigns, only the soft licking of flames and the deep, shaky breaths of Vero and her comrades to be heard. Vero spares a glance, peeking around Jace's giant shield to see the Spectral figure fifty feet in front of them, now a charred black skeleton, hanging in the air like a marionette.

Dozens of small portals to the real world hang around it, flames spilling out from it into the Mirage.

Oh, no. It did it. The house in the real world is officially on fire.

The Spectre's head perks up from its hanging position. Vero can tell it's weak. Weak, but determined. They can't drop their guard now. It's still dangerous.

She materializes her katana and darts toward it, just in time for it to start running. And its destination?

"Stop it!" Jace yells.

Vero picks up her pace, readies her blade, and swings it across. It cuts through the monster with almost no resistance, sending the lower half of its body tumbling to the ground and disintegrating instantly. But the top

half somehow remains determined, floating ahead, unbridled, unbur-
dened with its lower half. It zips through the portal and into the real
world.

Before she can yell, the sound of gunshots fill the Mirage, and bullets
hurtle through the portal as it closes. The last thing Vero sees before it
shuts is the Spectre's upper half collapsing to the floor of the burning
building in the real world.

The flaming red color palette gives way to the mix of dark blue and
yellow flames within the Mirage, and they're left alone. Trapped in a
palace without its emperor.

"Seb," Jace says.

But Seb is already tapping away on his Syncer, frantically attempting
to open one of the Bulletholes. Any one of them will do, but nothing
happens.

"Has this ever happened before?" Vero says, fighting the urge to panic.

"Which part? The Spectre venturing into the real world or Mediums
being trapped in a Mirage?"

"Yes."

And then the world around them starts to melt away like the blubbery
outer layer of the Spectre they'd just fought. It gives way to a roaring
inferno on all sides. As the real world materializes around them, Vero
catches a glimpse of the now-dead monster, upper half dead on the floor,
taken out with Seb's bullets at the very last moment as it finally tasted
freedom.

She shouldn't be sad about it, but for some reason, she is. Her mind
flashes to that brief moment where it felt like her mind was connected to
its—*his*. *He* had been so scared in his last moments, presuming what she
had witnessed *were* those last moments.

And then the Spectral body fades, along with the rest of its Mirage.
Vero can't help but feel like a Ghost herself as Jace collects its Essence, and
the team vacates the fiery building.

They find the detective standing on the street, still alone, still in shock.
But it won't be for long. She can already sense the bustle of curiosity as the
lights start to come on in this quiet neighborhood. A house fire isn't something that slips under the radar.

She looks back as the flames eat up the house from the inside. It almost
seems fitting. Here it was, a relic of a dark age in a polished uptown neighborhood finally meeting its end.

"Let's go," Jace says, his voice stern. "We can't be around when the
firefighters show up."

"Or the nosy neighbors," Seb says.

"They should just let the thing burn," Vero says before she can stop it.

She has no idea why she's filled with such unexpected passion over an abandoned home, but her unbidden thought feels right.

"Well, that's way above our pay grade," Jace says. "Detective, can you walk?"

"Y-yeah," the detective says.

"Good. I know the commander will want to have a word with you about all this."

"The what?"

"Just come with us," he says as he leads the group around the corner to their waiting van.

The detective pauses when he sees the vehicle, every instinct of his clashing with all he's just witnessed.

"I promise," Vero says. "We're the good guys."

"And if it helps," Jace says, "your pals—what is it, Officers Sanchez and Gaines? Is that right? They're on the level, too."

The name drop piques the detective's interest, and his head perks up the slightest bit, though his eyes are still narrowed in suspicion.

"They told us to come find you," Seb says. "To save you from the Spectre." He slides open the door of the van and hops in.

"The what?"

Vero follows close behind, sparing the detective a smile as she settles into her seat. "You were curious about what they were up to, weren't you? Well, here's your chance to find out everything."

"We don't have all day, Detective," Jace says. Vero can tell it's taking all his willpower not to shove the man into the van.

Distant sirens ring out in the background. They need to get going now.

With a final nod and clench of his jaw, the detective jumps into the van, taking a seat next to Vero, who smiles and puts her hand on his shoulder.

"All right, Bruce," Jace says to the driver. "Let's get going."

The van lurches forward and settles into a steady rumble. The group remains silent as flashing blue and red lights pass by, and Vero lets out an involuntary breath.

"Agent Daugherty," a radio attached to Vero's chest piece goes off. Her body tenses at the voice. It's her mother. Always a stickler for protocol, she *never* contacts Vero directly.

"Go for Agent Daugherty," Vero says with a tap on the mic, switching it from speaker to her ear bud.

"What is this radio chatter I'm hearing about a building catching fire in Watts? Please don't tell me that's you."

Vero doesn't answer right away. What would be the best response to something like that?

"The mission's been accomplished," she says. "The hostage has been saved, and the Spectre's been eliminated."

"And in your wake you leave a conspicuous burning building? Did I not impress on to you the importance of this mission going off without a hitch? Did you not realize what was at stake?"

"It's not—"

"No. That's enough," she says. "You know who I have breathing down my throat on this. I knew I should have sent in another Junior Medium unit to take care of this, but..." The commander's voice trails off and Vero can hear her taking a deep breath. "Maybe this will be good for you. Maybe it will be good for me to strip you and your team of your ranks. Maybe you'll finally learn to grow up."

Vero doesn't need to respond. She knows her mother well enough to know she's already hung up.

It didn't take much. One unexpected turn in an otherwise successful mission. It's as though she was waiting for the right moment to prove once and for all that Vero was a disappointment.

So, nothing new.

Vero sits back in her seat, not feeling the relief she expected. As her mind settles on the reality of her Medium career ending, the only emotion she feels is anger.

FOUR

VERO STARES at her reflection in the elevator on her way up from the parking garage into the X Tower HQ. Not just her cheeks, but her entire face is a bright red. And sweaty. *So* sweaty. And it goes beyond the fact that she'd just spent her evening taking on a violent Spectre that set an entire house on fire.

It's a sweat brought on by anger and anxiety—both of which she's feeling a hell of a lot of right now.

Stripped of her team and rank? It's something she's dreamed of almost every day since she took on the Junior Medium role, but to be taken out by her own mother immediately following a successful mission was more than she could stomach.

Blood pulses so loudly in her ears she can barely hear Jace and Seb trying their best to talk her down. Telling her that the commander is under a lot of pressure; that she doesn't mean it and that nothing will change. When she'd scanned her badge to get in the elevator, that it didn't deny her access proved she was still an authorized agent, they said.

But Vero doesn't buy it. Like everything else the commander does, it's all one big power move. Another means of controlling her. By giving Vero hope and stripping it away from her, she maintains control. To what end, she doesn't know, but she's never been one to understand what drives that woman; what reason she has that's pushed her to such continued cruelty following the death of her son.

Vero stomps out of the elevator, ignoring whatever consolation her team tries to provide. When she arrives outside the glass doors of the commander's office, she can see that damned woman sitting at her desk, face stoic and chiseled as always.

"Don't do anything you'll regret," Jace says in a hushed whisper as Vero puts her hand on the door handle.

"I'm way past caring." She opens the door and shuts it behind her, not so much as giving Jace a courtesy indication that he's welcome in whatever conversation that is to follow. He wouldn't like what she was about to do. Vero herself isn't too sure about it either.

"Ah, good. Hello, Vero," the commander says.

"Agent Daugherty."

"Not for much longer. I'm filing your discharge paperwork."

Vero bites the inside of her lip. Filing paperwork for agent discharges is admin work. The commander *wanted* to take care of this firsthand. She wanted to be the one to twist that knife and pull it back out, letting the entrails of her last living child cascade onto the concrete laminate flooring of her office.

"What the hell's the matter with you?" she says, letting it all come out.

"That's no way—"

"Shut up," Vero interrupts. "If you're saying I'm as good as gone, you don't get to wave that stick at me anymore."

This shuts the commander up, and Vero sees the muscles in her mother's jaw tighten.

"What reason do you have for my dishonorable discharge?"

The commander's eyes narrow. "You may think I derive some sort of sick pleasure out of this, but believe it or not, I am protecting you."

Vero somehow stops herself from scoffing.

"You wouldn't believe the pressure I face daily that keeps this ship afloat. The number of fires I have to put out is the only reason you and the other Junior Medium teams can still operate without interference."

"You set me up to fail," Vero says. Her tone is flat, but her voice is confident, full of conviction. "You could have used any other team. You could have used another Junior Medium team, or God forbid a *Senior* team. Instead, you chose mine."

The commander doesn't speak.

"And you knew the strength of this Spectre. That its danger to the real world was imminent."

"Now that's—"

"Shut up," Vero says. "I already know this was a Spectre that you've checked in on every other year since it was discovered. And yet, you kept it around so that it could grow in strength and leave behind a stronger Essence. You set me up as a scapegoat for a Spectre you knew would be out of our league. That could result in real *civilian* damage. Why?"

Vero doesn't need an explanation. The answer was written all over her mother's still-somehow-stoic face. The pressure from above is undoubtedly real, and sacrifices needed to be made in order to keep the machine going. What better way to prove the agency was cutting any necessary fat than for the commander to fire her daughter? That would prove her willingness to make tough decisions. As usual, Vero is just a means to continue her mother's career.

The commander stares back at Vero, eyes still narrow, contemplative, calculating.

"Find someone else to throw under the bus," Vero says, surprising even herself. As much as she'd always wanted a way back to her former life—back before her brother died—things had changed, somehow. She found herself hungry for answers. While the world of fighting Spectres had seemed so straightforward, the presence of this girl, Luna, proved otherwise. There was another way to take on these monsters. In fact, had she known about these methods, perhaps this disaster could somehow have been averted. "If you don't, I'll tell everyone about how you *let* this Spectre fester into the monster it became. That *you're* the real reason why that condemned building is now in flames. You can blame me all you want, Mother, but we all know whose fault this is."

The commander's expression remains passive. And then, the corners of her mouth turn upward ever so slightly.

"What?" Vero says before she can stop herself.

"It's about time you showed some damned guts," the commander says. "I'd given up, but maybe there's hope for you, after all." The commander chuckles to herself. "Blackmail. Didn't think you had it in you, Agent Daugherty."

"I...so I'm not fired?"

"No."

"I...just like that?"

The commander throws up a projection of a document above her desk. Vero can't make out the details, but recognizes what they are: discharge papers with her name filled out at the very top. "What, now you want to be let go? Which is it?"

"No, I..." Vero blinks. "Thank you." She knows the second it leaves her lips that she shouldn't have said that.

As if punctuating her thought, the smile vanishes from her mother's lips. "Thin skin will get you nowhere in this line of work."

"Being polite doesn't mean you have thin skin," Vero says. She has no idea why she's bothering to argue this point, but after seventeen years of life, crossing verbal swords with her mother has become second nature.

"Maybe not, but it'll sure as hell make your enemies think so."

Vero is tempted to say that she shouldn't have to consider her own mother her enemy, but holds herself back. The argument would fall on deaf ears, and it would also reek of a lie. There isn't a single instance she can think of where her mother *wasn't* someone she'd considered her enemy. "Noted."

With a quick motion of her hand, the document disappears into a virtual trash can.

"So, that's it?" I say.

"You see how much easier things can be when you're willing to take risks? Consider this a lesson in politics." Another small, yet distinguishable smile crosses her mother's face.

Vero hates that she feels butterflies flutter around in her stomach. This was it. This was the feeling she'd spent her life reaching for. And yet it came…so easily. She thought she'd be prouder of herself. Vero glances at the virtual trash can on the netscreen and then back up to her mother. "What happens now?"

Commander Daugherty calls in Seb and Jace, and the group debriefs what had just happened down in Watts. It's as though they hadn't just left the building on fire and as if Vero hadn't blackmailed her mother into pretending they didn't.

It's as though nothing has changed.

"I'd like to have a word with the detective," the commander says.

"He's already been debriefed," Jace says.

"Not about the mission. About what put him on our trail to begin with."

"SHE WAS in the interrogation room at the station," Detective Chu says, body stiff as he sits on the other side of the table. "And then…she wasn't."

"So, she disappeared," the commander says, arms folded in front of her, right leg crossed over the left. "Evaporated into thin air?"

"It was more like the air closed in around her." The detective speaks slowly, choosing each word with care, his face still uncertain. Vero can read that look, even through the two-way mirror. He's being honest, but is still trying to decide if he can trust them. "But that wasn't the strangest thing. No less than thirty minutes after she disappeared, I start hearing rumors about how she escaped. It's like someone was purposely spreading rumors to mislead. And no one was even talking to *me* about it."

The commander scratches at the back of her neck with the inside of her right index finger. Vero can tell she's embarrassed. She's always felt like she's worked with idiots her entire career. This was just further proof to her that no one else can do their jobs right.

"And what was the name of the suspect in question?"

"Not a suspect," the detective says. "No one is pressing charges. No one was hurt."

"But the girl was in police custody."

"Not custody. Just for questioning."

The commander sighs through her nose. She's getting tired of splitting hairs with this guy. "And her name is…" she refers to a document that hovers in front of them. "Luna Guerrera, yes? This is her?"

The detective nods.

My mouth hangs open. I catch Seb's eyes, who shares the same dumbstruck expression.

"Am I under arrest?"

The commander chuckles humorlessly. "We aren't a police force. As you've been told, we operate in the shadows regarding very specific matters of national security."

"With Ghosts?"

"Something like that."

"So Ghosts are real?"

"They are."

The detective stays silent, slowly taking in the information.

"I don't like it when our secrets are spilled, Detective," the commander says. "But this is an opportunity. You've been looking for this girl, and so have I. So, maybe we can work together. If you come across her, let us know."

The detective looks at the commander and then back at us behind the mirror. "She's just a kid."

"Officer Gaines and Officer Sanchez say you had it out for her." The commander pulls up a file and flips through some pages. "She's been involved in now *three* arson cases?"

"Did you just open up the police archives?" the detective says, leaning forward in the metal chair.

"Are you just now understanding how deep this whole thing goes? I thought you were a detective."

He sighs and sits back. "Three arson cases. That's correct."

"And some assault charges?"

"Yes."

"They say you pushed her pretty hard. What's changed?"

The detective bites his lip, his gaze combing over the commander and back to us. "During the interrogation…I'd mentioned her mother had been discovered dead. I hadn't realized she didn't know yet. She didn't take it well, I don't think."

"So, you feel sorry for her?" The commander's tone holds little in the way of sympathy.

"I'm sure you can understand," the detective says. "In this line of work, it's easy to get caught up in the mystery. To have a series of boxes and to chase that high of ticking them off one by one. I hide behind mountains of paperwork and bureaucracy, climbing the ladder of the LAPD, just like my dad did. Every year that goes by, it gets easier for me to think of each victim or suspect as an obstacle to ticking off that box—to forget that they're people."

The commander taps her nail on the metal table in front of them, letting the silence permeate the room. "In addition to being a person of interest for a series of crimes on your end, she is a person of interest to us."

"For what?"

"Oh, I don't know," the commander says. "Something about popping in and out of interrogation rooms on a whim. That's our area of expertise, not yours. I'd say that's reason enough to at least bring her in for some questioning, wouldn't you?" She stands up. "You can iron out the details with your captain—yes, he's aware of us, too. And the instant you catch a whiff of this girl, you reach out. I'll even give you my private line." After swiping her information to his netscreen, she slams the door behind her and, a few seconds later, is on our side of the mirror, her thinly veiled frustration even more evident. "I swear to God, this Boy Scout is on my last nerve."

"You think it's the smartest idea not to have his memory expunged?" Jace says.

"Our informants in the LAPD seem to think he's a greater liability on the outside than the inside," the commander says. "That he'll keep on asking questions and prodding. And that he's too much of an asset to relocate. Better to have him on our side and use whatever leads he has. For now, you and your team can go back to your standard duties. If nothing else, I can count on this guy to follow orders. If we find this Luna Guerrera, we'll figure it out from there."

"Commander," Vero says.

"What?"

Vero catches herself staring at the floor, avoiding eye contact with Seb and the commander. "About that girl."

"Eyes up when speaking to your superior, Agent Daugherty."

Vero tries to fight the heat that rises in her face. She looks up, making eye contact with her mother.

"What about the girl?"

Vero glances over at Jace, who gives her a questioning glance. She hasn't even told *him* about their little side mission earlier that day. In fact, he'd specifically told them not to pursue anything. They'd reported the incident to the commander and were to let them handle it. "I ran into her again. Earlier today."

"What?"

"Okay, that's kind of a lie. I didn't just run into her. I've…been searching for her."

Commander Daugherty's expression doesn't change. "Go on."

"You know that rogue Medium the three of us fought?" Vero pauses, though she doesn't know why. She's an agent of the DOSD, for crying out loud. She takes another breath. "Seb and I looked into her today on our day off. And I think…"

"Spit it out."

"Her name is Luna Guerrera."

And for the second time in one day, Vero's mother gave her that special look: a look that filled her insides with butterflies. It was the look that proved to her she wasn't a mistake.

That she was worth something.

"Tell me everything you know."

To Be Continued...

SPECTRAL | EPISODE 6

HIRO'S BACHELOR PAD...

I NEVER KNEW Ghosts could cry. Sure, one of my dad's favorite songs growing up was "La Llorona," which literally comes from the story of a weeping ghost who killed her children, but that's just an old legend.

I'm talking about real life here. I never thought an honest-to-god Ghost —with a capital G—could have tears stream down her face like a character in a *telenovela*, never mind that I never thought I'd see Ghosts period. And yet, as I sit in the living room of Hiro's oversized bachelor's pad, that's exactly what I'm witnessing.

My Spectre's enormous head hovers over the couch in front of me, tears trickling down her cheeks and dissipating before they land on the white leather sofa. She sobs uncontrollably, and has been doing so nonstop since we left the theater hours before.

"How long does this last?" I whisper to Hiro, who sits on a perpendicular sofa, legs curled up into his chest.

"There's no way of knowing for sure," Hiro says. His eyes are glued to the netscreen on his lap, his tone nonchalant. "Every Spectre is different. As they consume the Essences of other Spectres, they regain their memories, and at a rapid speed. It's like having bite-sized chunks of your existence smashed into your brain over a short period. It's, shall we say, an emotional thing."

I nod, though that doesn't make me feel any more patient. I'd spent the past few days calling this freakin' Spectre Mom, only to find out that's not who she is, and I'd be lying if I said I wasn't just a little embarrassed by the whole thing. It feels a lot like hugging your parent in the middle of a grocery store as a kid, only to realize it's some random stranger. Yeah, it's that kind of awkward.

I continue to stare at the crying face in front of me. It doesn't resemble Mom or anyone else I've met, but there's still something *familiar* about her.

For the first time in hours, the sobs slow and the head's vibrations falter. Before I realize it, the crying has stopped altogether. The Spectre takes a deep breath, closing her eyes. When they open, her eyes lock on mine.

Too curious for my own good, I keep my eyes glued on hers. Is it time? Is she in any state to answer the mountain of questions I have?

"What do you want?" she says, her voice thick with an unexpected amount of sass.

"Are you doing okay?" I say. No, I'm not so devoid of social graces that I'd just dive in without getting those annoying obligatory questions out of the way first.

"I'm fine," she says, turning away from me, like a teenager sulking on the couch. It's an absurd sight, with her just being a giant head.

"So, are you done yet?" All right, so I'm a bit of a social neanderthal.

In response, the Spectre devolves into a renewed fit, now wailing louder than ever. I scoot away from her on the couch, bringing my knees to my chin, prepared to hunker down for another three hours.

"Careful," Hiro says, eyes still on a hologram projecting from his netscreen. "You don't want to be on an angry Spectre's bad side. Even your own." After a side glance at the Spectre, he stands and motions for me to follow him down the hall, away from the sobbing head.

Suspicious, I slip from the sofa, around back, out of eyesight of the poor thing, and meet him in the dark corridor.

"You may have questions," he whispers as soon as I turn the corner, "but it may not even be worth asking. I imagine this Spectre will need at least another five or six Essences before her memories come back in a more complete fashion. Not to be insensitive, but if we're to..." he turns his hand into a claw and clamps it into a fist, mimicking a munching mouth, "...we probably want to do it before her memories return completely."

Somehow, I understand what he means, but I furrow my brows at the thought.

"Are you serious right now?"

"What?"

"This is happening and all you can think about is your deal?"

"And why wouldn't I worry about it?"

"We have a..." I stop myself. We have what? A poor, orphaned Ghost with what is likely a tragic backstory? I look at the half-crippled, gaunt figure in front of me. As sad as it is, *he's* alive, and his life is in very real danger. And without my help, he's as good as dead. "You're right," I say. We have a deal. He helps me get rid of this Entity...this Spectre that's been haunting me, and in return, I help build her up so he can consume her Essence and continue living. Without it, his Spectre will pass on, and he'll cease to exist.

"Thank you," he says with a sigh.

"But," I say, seeing his body tense up. "Can I at least get some answers first?"

"Oh, so we're changing things now," he says. "I never promised you answers. An exterminator doesn't promise to give a reason as to why you need their services to begin with."

"I don't think that's true."

"You're right," he says. "It's a terrible analogy, but the point remains."

"Does it?"

"Allow me to remind you of the kind of bloodthirsty animals Spectres become. You've faced some by now. You know the havoc they can wreak."

"What about Kuro?"

"He's an exception. Had someone like me been around over a hundred years ago to stop me from continuing this life, *I* would have taken them up on it."

I look down the hall, listening to the Spectre's continued quieter sobs in the living room. "I want to at least understand her," I say.

"What good will that do?"

"I want to know who she is and why she's followed me all this time. If she's *not* Mom..." I then laugh, frustrated.

"What?"

"I'm so stupid," I press my back against the wall and press my palm into my face. A part of me had still wanted the Spectre to be Mom. "This stupid...she's been following me since I was little. How can she be my mom if she's been around since before she died?"

"That would seem to pose a problem."

I shut him up with a death stare. I don't need his commentary. "Can we at least figure out who she is first? She still needs to consume a few more Essences, right?"

"It depends on their level, but that's right."

"Then just let me figure this out along the way. Once I do, you'll get her Essence."

Hiro nods. It's slight, but it's there. He's probably second-guessing this deal, and I can't say I blame him. But I can't promise to give her up before I find out why.

"So, do we know what she'll know at this stage?" I wipe at my eyes, only just noticing the tears.

"She may technically be gaining memories, but most likely, they're inhabiting her being in a more abstract form."

"What does that mean?"

"Do you ever get that feeling when you wake up and have that twinge in your stomach? You can't remember your dream, but you sort of recall the feeling it gave you? It's something like that."

"I have no idea what you're talking about."

"Luna?" The Spectre's voice from the other room is soft.

I turn the corner and see the hovering head staring back at me. She's never called me Luna before. Not that I recall.

"Yeah?" I say.

"I…I think I remember my name."

I don't say anything for fear of scaring her away from her train of thought. I just nod in what I hope is an encouraging way.

"Well, what is it?" Hiro says.

I smack him on the shoulder. "Shut up!" I yell in a hushed tone, as though the Spectre wouldn't be able to hear me.

"She's taking forever, I just thought—"

"Estrella," the Spectre says. "It's Estrella."

SPECTRAL

EPISODE 6
MY STAR

ONE

ESTRELLA. I've heard that name countless times. I've heard it more times than I dare to remember. It's a name that leaves a bitter taste in my mouth every time I hear it.

It was a fun story Mom and Dad would bring up when I was a kid. If they'd ever attended cocktail parties, I imagined it would be the random fact they'd bring up to entertain everyone.

"Hey," they'd say. "Did you know that we had two names picked out for our daughter? One was Luna, the other was Estrella."

Their hoity-toity friend would gasp in fake amazement, bringing her hand to her chest. I imagine she has glitter on her face, though I don't know why. "Do tell. Why did you go with Luna?" Her voice is stupid and fancy.

And, of course, there'd be a smart and witty reason as to why they decided on my name.

In reality, my parents never really told me the why of it at all. *Why* they'd gone with Luna instead of Estrella will forever be a mystery. I was never very curious, and after Mom's death, I'd never wanted to burden Dad with such pointless questions. Well, that was the initial plan. With the Spectre in front of us laying claim to the alternate name Estrella, it's something I'm a lot more curious about than I was yesterday.

It's the least he could do. *He's* the reason why the pretty name has such a bitter flavor for me. He calls me by it on an almost regular basis.

My entire life, I'd chalked it up to some drug-addled mistake. The man is so infrequently sober, I don't expect common sense from him. I think it's about time I got some answers.

A stray pistachio shell crunches under the sole of my shoe as I meander down the greasy streets of Skid Row. When I suggested to Hiro that we head down to my former and forever home, he offered me words of luck, along with the use of his car, which he programmed to drop me off and pick me outside the gate.

I can't tell if he's bitter or unsure, but I guess I can't blame him. He claims to be researching future targets as I get to the bottom of my own personal affair, but I can sense the uncertainty that our deal is slowly eroding under his feet. I can't deal with whatever shit's in his head right now. I don't even have enough mental capacity to deal with my own.

Crossing Fifth Street, I catch a familiar laugh on one corner. It's Gabe, having some loud exchange with what I assume is a regular customer of his. He glances up, catching my eye as I walk. Our eyes lock for the briefest of moments before he looks away, casting his gaze downward. It's only the second time I've ever seen him truly afraid—the first of which being in the confines of a Mirage. He's full of shit, but there's an undeniable, unbridled confidence he's always exuded. In that moment, it melts away.

I expect him to look back up, but his attention goes back to his conversation. At his side are two goons. One of them I recognize from before, but the other is new. Probably Marco's replacement. I ignore the lurch in my stomach that comes with the memory of his caved-in face and turn my attention to what's in front of me.

Focus. Focus. I exhale, clenching and unclenching my fists. I have my own problems to deal with. Gabe may be a murderer, but he's a murderer who no longer poses a threat.

By the time I'm in the elevator at the Main Stay, that pang in my stomach is replaced with a new one. I never know what state I'll find my dad in. If I'm lucky, I'll get him waning off his last fix, but I'm never that lucky.

The sound of old Hanna-Barbera cartoons bleeds through the thin door as I approach.

Sounds like he's alive.

A smile crosses my face as I jiggle the handle of the door. And he locked the door, too. Even *he* has his good days. Pulling out my netscreen, I type in a code and hear the lock of the door click.

Old slapstick sound effects pour over the threshold as I enter, along with the overwhelming smell of mold and stale body odor. I shut the door behind me softly. I ignore the kitchen this time—I doubt he's touched it since I last visited him—and enter the main living area/bedroom.

Dad lays motionless on the bed, glazed-over eyes cast upward at the cartoons that are projected on the ceiling from his netscreen. He has a wife beater on and a pair of loose pajama bottoms.

"Hey," I say softly. As expected, there's no response. "Hey," I repeat, this time nudging at his foot with my right hand.

His eyes flicker, and a portion of glaze is somehow pulled back from his eyes. He's not all there, but he's *mostly* present. He looks down at me, blinking more glaze from his eyes.

"Luna," he whispers. I can't tell if he's talking to me or trying to remind who I am.

"That's right," I say. "Glad to know you still remember who I am."

"I can never forget you, *mija*."

I stop myself from rolling my eyes. Another attempt to call me by some pet name we've never used. I doubt he even remembers that he hit me the last time we spoke.

"No Estrella this time?" I say. I don't think I've ever been the one to bring up that name first.

He sits up, abs shaking with effort as he does. "Estrella? Why on Earth would I call you Estrella?"

Again, I fight the urge to roll my eyes. I should be winning some kind of award for the self-restraint I'm showing here. "It's my name, remember? Well, one of the names you were going to call me before I was born."

Dad smiles. "And it's such a pretty one."

"Where did you get it?" I ask.

"Get what?"

"The name Estrella."

"I've told you this before," he says. "It's Spanish for star."

"Just like mine is Spanish for moon," I say. "Yeah, I get that. But why one over the other? Why did you go with Luna?"

"They make a good pair, don't they?" he says. "Moon and star?"

I clench my jaw. "I guess so, but..." This isn't helpful. "Did you get those names after anyone in particular?" It takes all my willpower not to pull out my Spectre here and now. Knowing him, he'd have a heart attack and keel over.

"They make a good pair, don't they?" he repeats. "Moon and star?"

"Yes, you've said that already."

"Then what's the question?"

I sigh. "Did you know an Estrella? Did *I* know an Estrella?"

Dad shakes his head. "Of course not. Of course you didn't. Estrella was..." He lays back down on the bed, eyes slowly glazing back over as he stares up at Scooby-Doo eating a giant sandwich. "You would have made a great sister, Luna."

My eyes widen. "A great what?" I say.

"It just wasn't meant to be. It was…too late." Tears well up in his eyes and streak down the side of his head into his thinning sideburns.

"What do you mean?" I shake his leg, but can already feel him slipping away into the nothingness that muze brings. "Dad! What do you mean?" I shake him harder, but he's gone within a few quick seconds.

It takes all my willpower not to punch him in the face or flush his fix straight down the toilet. He'll be out for at least a full day under his normal dosage. Maybe even more. Even when he's present, rarely is he *present*.

I grab a pillow off the bed and scream into it as hard as I can. If I'd just gotten here five minutes sooner. If I'd run instead of walked…

No. I stop myself from taking the blame. Whatever it was he was trying to say he's been keeping from me for over seventeen years, though I can't think of why, for the life of me.

I pick at the skin tag at the side of my neck again. A sister? Could she be my sister? How?

There's one way to find out. I tap my armband, and in a flash of black light, Estrella emerges. She doesn't say a word as she hovers over Dad's gaunt form.

"Do you recognize him?"

She shakes her whole body—which is just a head. "Uh-uh."

"Do you recall who you were when you were alive?"

Again, she shakes her whole "body."

Maybe she'd been alive before me. An older sister who passed away? An unexpected emptiness opens up inside me. I've never felt like I'd missed a sister until this very moment. Every so often, I dreamed of having a sibling to help take care of me, yes. Every kid does that. But to feel as though I've lost one is a different feeling altogether.

"He's hiding something," I say. "And he's too…well, I don't know if I can rely on him even if he does tell me the truth, whatever it is. Do you remember anything right now? I know they're mostly feelings or whatever, but any details?"

"I remember someone picking on me," she says. "There was something on the side of my neck and she made fun of me for it."

My hand instinctively flicks at the skin tag on my neck. "No," I say. "That's *my* memory."

"Oh," she says. Her voice is distant, only the slightest bit disappointed. It's as though she expected me to say that. "Okay. Then no."

"So you've experienced my memories, then," I say.

"I don't know. I remember her making fun of me—you. Then I remember being angry. Most of my feelings are…anger. They're different kinds of anger, but still…" Her breath turns heavy. The giant head puffs up until she's the size of a small cow.

"Hey," I say, my tone soft. "It's okay. It's okay."

"Shut up," she says, tone soft and breathy. "I can take care of this myself."

I try not to get offended or upset. The Spectre's never snapped at me like that before. Not since we first met. The closest thing was her insistence on killing that group of government Mediums when we first met, but that seemed to come more from a place of base animal instinct than a human one.

After several seconds, she's back down to normal size, breathing heavily—I'm still not sure how that works with her being just a head.

"Sorry," the Spectre says. "I don't know what's happening."

"Your memories are returning," I say. "That's what Hiro says. You're getting closer and closer to who you were before you died."

"I hate it."

I can't blame her. To go from base animal instincts to the complex range of emotions that comes with being a human can't be easy. "Any ideas?"

"What ideas?"

"Of how to find out more about where you came from."

She stares at me, not understanding. Until now, I hadn't included her in any of my plans to unravel the secrets of my past. A stupid move, really. Whatever happens going forward will affect her as much as me. "The more we find out about your and my past, the more likely we are to understand why you feel why you do."

"How?"

I don't quite understand it myself. "I guess…it's like learning more about anything."

"What're you talking about?"

She's right. I'm making no sense. "Some people like to learn more about their family. Like people who grew up adopted sometimes go back and try to find their biological parents, right? Whatever's happened to them is done, but they may learn something from seeing why their parents put them up."

"I still don't understand."

I groan. "You're confused. But if we find out more, we can figure out why you feel how you do."

"And that'll help?"

"I…I don't know." I've tried my best to just forget everything that's happened to me. What's happened to me is already done. There's nothing I can do to change that. I'd like to say that it's served me well, but given where I am now, I can't exactly say that with full confidence. "It's worth trying, though, isn't it?"

"I just want this feeling to stop. I just want..."

"To be set free?"

She looks at me. I can almost see the relief washing over her ghostly face. "You can do that?"

I nod. "I want to find out where you come from. Once we do, I can set you free."

"Make it so this feeling goes away?"

I nod again.

"Okay," she says, voice somehow softer and wispier than ever.

"Still no memory of your previous life?"

"No."

I glare at Dad's sleeping body. "Useless." As usual, he goes under when I need him most. Sad, pathetic coward. I clench my fists. If only there was someone else I could ask. Someone more reliable. Someone...

My eyes widen.

"I think I know where we can find some answers."

HIRO SCRATCHES at the back of his neck. I can't tell if it's out of exhaustion, frustration, or if he really has a particularly aggressive itch. Regardless, I can tell he's not on board with my idea. At least not completely.

"Do you even know where she died?" he asks.

"Her body was pulled out of the Salton Sea with her car."

"That means nothing. She could have been killed anywhere and dumped there, for all you know. Plus, there's no guarantee she's turned into a Spectre. She could just be a Ghost or Poltergeist."

"And could I get anything from either of those forms?"

"A Ghost, maybe. Her memories would be spotty, but she would at least be up for a conversation. A Poltergeist would be in zero mood for discussion, and we wouldn't be able to see her. But let's just say she was a Spectre. It's not as though you can have a conversation with her. Estrella is more cognizant than most Spectres you run into, and memories are..." he stopped and thought. "Then again, there are the memories you unlock as you fight them..."

I smile, hopeful. He's starting to see where I'm coming from. "That's it. *If* she's a Spectre, I can relive her memories and understand more about who Estrella is."

"Or you may find nothing," he says. "You can't always predict which memories are shared."

"Who says anything about her sharing?" I say. "If that memory is in there somewhere, I'll find it. There's a way to do that, right? A way to comb through the memories of a Spectre?"

He's still unsure, but he nods all the same. "After you retrieve these memories. After you understand where your own Spectre falls into all this, will you really be able to set her free?"

"It's not just what I want," I say. "It's what Estrella wants, too."

"But she's a Spectre. How she feels now compared to tomorrow can change as she takes in more Essences."

"We had a deal, right?" I say, perhaps more firmly than I should. "She wants to be free, and you need her Essence. Can you help us?"

TWO

I STARE out into the expanse of the desert nothingness. For the first time in my life, I feel like I can see the entirety of the sky. I never realized how *much* there is. At home, the majority of it is blocked by either buildings or hills. Now, only occasionally during our drive do I find it obstructed by a dusty hill on either side of the two-lane highway.

I didn't realize there were parts of the world where people didn't live directly on top of each other. I knew these places existed in theory, but not this close to where I live.

"We're almost there," Hiro says from his laid-back seat to my right.

"We are?" I continue to press my head against the window. "I don't see anything."

"Salton City isn't what one might call…well, a city. It's a city, technically, but it's gone through some rough times over the last hundred-plus years."

"Like what?"

"You'll notice when we get there that the sea itself is…questionable. Back in the mid-twentieth century, it was a huge tourist attraction. Now, the thing is toxic. The businesses that cropped up in anticipation of a new community were abandoned."

"So, that's it?"

"Not quite. When California passed new gambling laws a couple of decades back, they tried again. The nearly dried-up lake was rising, and while it was still toxic as hell, it made for a nicer scenery. New casinos cropped up. You can still find hotels with crappy slot machines, but because of its location, they don't attract the most upstanding clientele. It also doesn't help that the lake's toxicity can make you sick if you stick around for too long, and you can't build a solid foundation of workers while slowly making them sick."

"So, how big is it now?"

"Take whatever you're imagining and divide it by ten. Last I checked, it's a series of abandoned buildings with exactly two hotels that act as novelties. Basically hubs for those who want to explore the abandoned houses and buildings nearby. If you can believe it, it's almost the only industry the place has."

"And they're okay with that?"

"Who's okay with that?"

I stop and think. "Exploring abandoned buildings. What about the police?" I feel stupid as soon as the comment leaves my mouth.

"Not sure you understand the concept of 'abandoned.' No one owns most of the buildings. No one owns most of the land. It's practically worthless. It's less than worthless. I'm sure the State of California would pay good money to have this whole portion of the map wiped from existence."

Even though I haven't laid eyes on this place yet, I feel sorry for it.

"Welcome to the Salton Sea," Hiro says.

I look around, but almost nothing has changed. I see an old house with a caved-in roof, but that's it. "You're kidding."

We head over a small hill, and then I see it. It's surprisingly vast. A blanket of dark brown on the horizon—beautiful in its ugliness. You can almost see the stink lines rising above it. It's no wonder the city never took off.

"That's it," Hiro says. "That's the face that everyone makes when they first smell this place."

I wrinkle my nose involuntarily. "People put up with this?"

"They don't! Have you been listening?"

"But there's a hotel here."

"*Two* hotels. And don't worry about the smell. After thirty minutes, you'll forget it's even there."

"Great."

The car turns off the 86 and onto a small main street. When I'd seen this spot on the map, I'd expected the road to be lined with abandoned buildings. Instead, all I see is more dirt on either side, peppered with the occasional home, almost as an afterthought. Everything here is so spread out. Even I'm jealous of what potential these homes had at one point in history. What's it like to have all of this space to yourself? It's something I can only imagine.

As we make our way closer to the center of the "city," the car slows and pulls into an over-sized, mostly dirt parking lot and parks in an open spot. To our left stands a five-story building with a rickety, gaudy neon sign plastered on its front that reads THE SALTON INN - SLOTS & SHOTS.

"Classy," I say. In the sign's defense, it's at least fully lit, even if it is daytime. The exterior isn't much to speak of. The paint is old, chipped, but not embarrassingly so. I can tell some care went into it at some point, even if business hasn't been good enough to warrant consistent upkeep.

"They tried," Hiro says. "You would not believe the ambition they had for this place. And not just once, but *twice* in its relatively short history."

"You almost sound sad."

"I'm always sad to see people shoot for the stars and fail. In many cases, it leads to success down the line in some new form, but for Salton City, it simply meant more failure."

The inside of the hotel isn't much more to speak of, either. I'm somehow disappointed, and I came in with rock-bottom expectations. The promised "Slots" that the sign hinted at is one lonely machine that sits awkwardly close to the front desk, which I'm sure only makes customers feel like they're being judged by the hotel employees.

The lobby is covered in a gaudy carpet that probably used to be red. Now, it's mostly faded, with only some spots along the edges being left as a reminder of what once was. The smell of cigarettes lingers in the air, though I don't see a single smoker in sight.

The grunginess of this place somehow makes me comfortable. That probably says more about me than it does about the inn. As Hiro checks in using the kiosk at the front desk, my eyes land on the sad, lonely slot machine that sits next to it. I'd only ever seen these things in movies. It looks exactly as it does on the screen.

It takes me several seconds to notice that Hiro is trying to get my attention.

"What?" I say.

"Did you hear what I said?"

"No," I say, not bothering to lie.

Hiro follows my gaze to the slot machine. With a smile and roll of his eyes, he scans his netscreen and pulls the lever on the machine.

My eyes widen as I hear the whirr of spinning wheels, the loud and jangly music, and chime as three cherries line up. Between the sound effects and the blinking lights, it's *exactly* like the movies. I can't help but smile. It's rare when things turn out exactly as you'd expect.

"Huh, will you look at that? I won," Hiro says, sounding only slightly surprised at the recent development. "I'll take a free five hundred-dollar prize, sure."

IT ONLY TAKES me a few minutes after checking in to my room to zero in on where I want to visit first. Mom's car was pulled out at the Salton Sea Campground, which is just a five-minute walk away from the inn. I realize this likely won't get me many leads, but I at least want to see where the body was picked up before I search. It's the one tangible clue I have, and for all I know, she could have created a Mirage there.

At least I hope.

I lay back in my bed, and stare up at the stain-flecked ceiling. I've spent years trying to forget the fact that my mom existed, and here I am actively seeking her out. It's amazing how much can change over a short period.

With a last glance at the map projection, I head down the hallway and knock on Room 316. I wait several seconds before I try knocking again, only to be left with no response. I press my ear to the door, and when I hear nothing, I shoot Hiro a message.

Not wanting to wait any longer, I head down to the lobby, where I hear the slot machine ringing its metallic head off. To my surprise, I see Hiro seated on the red padded barstool in front of it, strawberry daiquiri in hand.

"What in the actual…please don't tell me you have a gambling problem," I say.

"Who's to say?" Hiro says, a rare, giddy smile plastered across his face.

"What's happening?"

"Can you believe it?" Hiro says. "Over a hundred and fifty years old, and I've never once gambled. I always thought it was stupid and pointless."

"It *is* stupid and pointless."

"But it really is *something*. I'm up five hundred dollars."

"How? And that's not even cool gambling."

"Cool gambling?"

"All you're doing is sitting at a crappy slot machine and pulling a lever."

"And cool gambling is…?"

"I dunno. Cards. A felt table. Dice."

"Are you just saying things you've seen in movies?"

I don't answer.

Hiro takes another sip from his drink. "Please, tell me all about your extensive experience in gambling. I'm eager to hear your thoughts."

Rude. "Are you almost done?"

He pulls the lever again. More dings followed by the sounds of coins—

actual physical coins—pouring into a basin at the bottom. "I'm no expert, but I think I may be on what they call a 'hot streak.'"

"You sounded dumb saying that. Are we gonna go?"

"You can go right ahead," Hiro says. He turns around on his barstool. "I'm not much use to you these days. Even Kuro wasn't up for the car ride out here. I'd only get in the way."

He taps his knee and my eyes drop to his cane, which leans against the slot machine. The man drips with so much sarcasm that I sometimes forget that he's actively deteriorating day by day. Given his state, it's hard not to be grateful that he's here at all. Some may even say he's acting against his own self-interest in helping me.

I'd never say this aloud, but what happens if things change? Currently, both my amnesiac Spectre and the decaying frame in front of me are in agreement. But what if she regains her memories and she *doesn't* want to pass on to the afterlife? What if *I* don't want her to pass on to the afterlife?

"It shouldn't be too hard," Hiro says. "I've already asked the receptionist, but they're brand new here, so they're useless. Just find someone else who lives here, and you're on your way. I doubt the news of your mom's body would have gone unnoticed."

"I thought you said no one lived here."

"*Almost* no one lives here. Forcing someone to work here is an H.R. nightmare, but that doesn't mean people don't still live here. And if they do, I'm sure they've heard about your mom." His voice is devoid of any semblance of empathy, though I can tell it doesn't come from a place of malice, but from someone who doesn't bother thinking about normal emotions on a regular basis. "The world is small, and this town is smaller."

Maybe it's for the best. Hiro would probably only judge me if I forced him to visit the campground first.

With a quick goodbye and a promise to give an update as soon as I could, I walk out the front door of the hotel and north toward the beach. Like the drive in, there isn't much to look at outside of a network of power lines on either side of the road and miles of dirt and bushes scattering the landscape.

I make my way down the shoulder of a gray, cracked, poorly maintained road. I pass a plot of land with a "For Sale" sign hammered into it, though there's no way for me to tell where the land starts or ends. With a deep breath, I take in the dusty air, realizing for the first time that I don't smell that rotten stench anymore. I totally get why people would call this place "shitty," but I don't know if I've ever been as far away from human beings as I have in this moment. It's a peace I've never known. Were it not for the occasional car passing by, I'd bring out the Spectre.

Actually…

With a quick glance in all directions, I release the Spectre from her confines. "Estrella," I say as her head emerges in front of me.

"Are we here yet?" she asks, head spinning around.

"Yes, but—"

"So, where is she?"

"We still need to find her. And we don't…listen to me." I have no idea why it was so easy for her to fluster me. "Is there any way you can make yourself…less inconspicuous?"

"What do you mean?"

Truth is I'm not sure. "Hmm…"

"Do you mean smaller?" She shrinks down to the size of my fist. That's better, but I don't know if a glowing head the size of my fist would be any less creepy than a full-sized one.

"Can you disappear, maybe?" I ask.

"Oh, you think just because I'm a Spectre that I can disappear at will?"

"No, it's not that, it's just—how would you even know to be offended by that?"

The small face in front of me presses her lips together. "How should I know?"

"So, you can't turn invisible."

"Hang on." Estrella closes her eyes, and while she phases out a bit, there's still no hiding the prevalent glow outlining her figure.

"That's not working."

"Okay, so no invisible. I have one more idea," she says. "But promise you won't freak out."

I stop walking. "What're you gonna do?"

Without another word, the head floats *into* me. A coldness permeates my chest, as though I've stuck my head in the freezer and taken a deep breath. It feels strange for a few moments, but then the coldness dissipates.

"How's that?" a voice inside my head asks—*her* voice.

"Are you inside me?" I ask. "I mean, are you speaking inside my head or actually speaking?"

"I have no idea what you're talking about. Does this work? Can you see me?"

Seems like I'll have to test her speaking with Hiro when we get back, but I pull out my netscreen and point the 3D camera back at me with my arm stretched out. No Ghost. No glow. "Can't see you," I say. Maybe more important than that, though, this doesn't even feel strange to me. Having her inside me almost feels more "normal" than when she's not here. "Are you comfortable?"

"It's more comfortable than that band you shove me in."

"This is perfect," I say. "That means I can take you out and have you help me search for my mom without anyone freaking out."

"Would they freak out if they saw me?"

"Do you remember what happened to the last person who saw you?"

"Hiro?"

"No."

"The tasty-looking girl with the big sword?"

"No. Gabe."

"Oh."

I can somehow tell she's trying her best to remember who Gabe is. I keep forgetting that as she's consumed more Essences, Estrella has changed little by little. There's no way of knowing how much of her early memories or thoughts have carried over. "Never mind."

"No, I remember," she says, clearly stalling as she continues to file through those memories. And then, out of the blue, I hear a chuckle. An image of Gabe tripping over his pants in the Mirage materializes in my mind. "Right. Freak out."

We pass a sign to the Salton Sea Campground, and I take a deep breath. This is it. This is where the cops pulled her vehicle from the lake. The beach, in its entirety, is a metallic wasteland. Spread across it are deteriorating parts—car engines, deconstructed androids, and chunks of metal twisted beyond recognition. Fifty feet from me, a dark, and almost sludge-like substance runs up along the beach, and retreats, like some dark, demented version of the ocean.

How could they have even found her in this entire mess?

I let any cynical thoughts fall away. I'm here for one reason and one reason only.

"Do you sense anything?" I ask.

"What do you mean 'anything?'"

Interesting. Before, when I'd asked her that, she'd known exactly what I was talking about. Now, it's as though she's starting from square one. Or maybe it's closer to transitioning from childhood to being a teenager. As a kid, things are simple, black and white, but as you grow older, you start to notice the nuances and realize things aren't as cut and dried as you'd once thought.

"Do you sense any Ghosts or Spectres?"

"Hmm…" she says. "Lots of death, but I'm not sure it's the kind of death we're looking for. Nothing compared to home."

Her home or mine? I don't say anything. I'd hate for Estrella to lose concentration.

"I can't explain it," Estrella continues. "But everything here is sad. Not like a proper Ghost. More like ghosts of a Ghost."

"What does that mean?"

"I don't know. But it's sad."

I look across the beach and into the black, sludgy sea, and I can't disagree. Everything about this place is just as she says: sad. As Hiro said, it once held a lot of promise. It was meant to be an oasis amid the California desert landscape.

That dream crumbled.

A small panic forms inside me. What if Mom hasn't even turned into a Ghost, or even a Spectre? What if there aren't any answers for me here?

I stand in silence for several seconds, hearing nothing but the sound of thick water rushing up onto the beach and retreating. My mind runs through everything I've been through over the past few weeks. How this whole journey started. I think back on Gabe once again, but this time, my mind goes further. It goes to that moment after I was spit out by Estrella's Mirage after she'd saved me from Gabe. It was when I saw her Spectral face, staring back at me. There was a malevolence there that I'd almost forgotten about.

"Why do you hate me?" I say without even thinking.

"Hate you?" Estrella responds. "In case you've forgotten, I protect you."

"Maybe now. But earlier, I could have sworn you wanted to kill me." I say it almost as a joke, but I know it's not. I can tell from Estrella's initial silence that she knows, too. "Do you remember what things were like for you before you started pulling me into your Mirage? How you haunted me?"

"I don't know what you're talking about." There's a long pause. It's as though there's more she wants to say. "Okay, I lied," she finally says.

I feel my heart skip a beat.

"I don't hate you," she says, "But I don't know how I feel about you either. When I'm around you, I'm angry, upset. I feel like I once trusted you and that you did something to me."

"Like what?"

"I already said I don't know!" she screams. If someone was around, could they hear her? "You're not the one with memory loss. Why *would* I have some grudge against you?"

"I've already told you I have no clue."

"You've told me I've had it out for you for years," she says, animosity mounting. "So, why would I have it out for you?"

"How could I know that?"

"I don't know!"

"Neither do I!" I cross my arms and huff. If she wasn't inside of me, I'd turn away from her. It takes all my willpower not to spin around.

And then I hear a giggle from inside my head.

"What's so funny?" I ask.

"I've never had an argument with anyone before," she says, her voice full of childlike glee. "At least not one I can remember. It's fun."

"It's not fun."

"It's a little fun. You said I might be your sister, right? Isn't this how sisters act? I think this is how they're supposed to act."

"Is it?" I'm an only child, so I have no idea. I think back to my schoolmates. A few of them got along growing up, but most of them argued with each other constantly. Some even threatened to kill each other, though they didn't mean it. One boy I knew cheated on his sister's friend, and they never talked again at school. Three years of high school, and not a word said on campus. They'd just pass each other in the quad, silent. And they were twins! I'd always thought twins shared some sort of psychic connection or something, but they were adamant that was a stupid myth.

"Do you know where they pulled out Mom?" Estrella says out of the blue, her voice soft, curious. Did she call her Mom on purpose?

I decide not to ask and instead pull up my netscreen, projecting an article from the *Los Angeles Times*. There's a photo of the wreckage. It's hard to tell specifically where it is, but the article itself says it was the Salton Sea Campground. There's not that much in terms of mileage along the campground itself. "It can't be far."

God knows where the hell it really is. The image is too focused on the car for me to make out where, but I walk along the beach all the same, stopping every so often to check in with Estrella. Just more of the Ghosts— or "ghosts of Ghosts" as she called them. I don't quite understand what she means, but I trust her more than I trust myself.

I reach out my own senses, but feel nothing. No sickness or sadness. It's nothing like it was in the movie theater, where death embedded itself into the very walls of the building. Despite its ugliness, I'd dare call the Salton Sea peaceful. Beautiful.

The sun crawls toward the horizon. Minutes pass into an hour, with no Spectral emotions to show for it. Should've known. That would have been too easy.

I turn my attention to the houses that pepper the landscape further inland. Hiro had mentioned looking for someone else—*anyone* else. Now's as good a time as any to start the actual search. I find a random house and head straight toward it.

A stray In-N-Out bag blows past the unenclosed yard, and as I approach, I can't help but notice its resemblance to a lot of buildings in Skid Row. The windows are broken in and graffiti is plastered along one of the walls—an image of a giraffe vomiting a rainbow. I'm sure whoever sprayed it thought they were being profound on some level.

The home looks like the kind of place someone would have been murdered in. I wouldn't be surprised if we ran into *five* Spectres here.

"Still nothing?" I ask Estrella.

"Nothing."

I growl. "That's disappointing."

It doesn't take me long to realize that this house is the norm, not the exception. Hiro had already told me this place was abandoned, but deep down, I thought that meant that people just didn't do much here. I don't care how poor I am. If I had a house to call my home, the last thing I'd do is abandon it. Then again, this is coming from the girl who's burned down three homes.

At first, finding an abandoned home is sort of cool, but by the tenth one, it starts to grate on me. Not only do they all feel the same, but for every empty house, there was one less source of information. And with the sun setting, I realize I should head back to the hotel before the werewolves come out. If werewolves do exist, I imagine they'd live in a place like this.

"One more," I tell Estrella, but I know she doesn't care. This time, I crawl through one of the broken windows. It's not much nicer inside the crummy home. Its carpet is covered in dirt and tumbleweeds, and the graffiti is even less refined than it was on the outside. At least the artist had the grace to save the more phallic representations for the privacy of the living room.

"One more," I say again. It's become a slight obsession. I crawl into the window of another house. When I get to the yet *another* house, I try to kick down the front door for fun, but only succeed at hyperextending my knee. What's the point of having an abandoned house if you can't kick down the door? I throw a rock through the window in revenge. The inside of this home is in better shape than the others. Probably because the door was so rock solid. I feel almost bad that I wrecked the window. From what I can tell, I'm the first one in this house's decades of existence to break in.

Shit. That makes me feel bad. What if—

"Hey!" a gruff voice calls out from the second floor. "What the hell are you doing in my house?"

THREE

I KNEW RUNNING AROUND and climbing into people's houses would lead to something like this. And stupid me, I was having so much fun shattering windows, I completely forgot I was *looking* for a local. Breaking into their houses doesn't really do much to help my case and make me sympathetic, does it?

"Sorry," I say, raising my hands in the air, eyes turned up to the top of the staircase, where the source of the voice stands. The man's hair is disheveled, dirty, and he sports a long, unkempt beard. He's also only wearing a pair of shorts. It would be creepy if it wasn't for the fact that it was still a solid hundred degrees outside, and while the roof blocked a good chunk of the heat, it still wasn't what I'd call cool. And the guy is grimy. His upper body is covered in dirt—not like he's been crawling around in it, but like he hasn't had a shower in weeks. There's a difference. Suddenly, I feel even more guilty than before.

"I said, what're you doing in my house?" he repeats.

"Sorry," I repeat. "I didn't realize anyone was here."

"Hmm…" He descends the stairs, his movements surprisingly graceful. "Don't tell me you're one of those house divers."

My instinct is to say no, but the evidence proves otherwise. "I…I guess I am," I choke out. I don't really know what else to say to him but I keep my eyes glued to him as he continues down the staircase.

"Get out," he says.

I nod, taking a step back. "I didn't realize anyone actually lived here. Isn't this place abandoned?"

"I've been the only one around here for going on five years now," he says, as though it's a point of pride. He trails behind me as I make my way to the front door.

I reach for the knob. Wait, this is exactly what I was looking for. "Do you…" I turn to face the man, who still has a wary eye on me. "Do you know anything about the woman who was found in the lake a few weeks ago?"

"What part of 'get out' don't you understand?"

"It's—"

"I've seen plenty of your kind come by here over the past few weeks."

"What's that supposed to mean?"

The man's chin juts out and he clenches his jaw. He already looked old, but somehow, the movement makes him look even older—like he'll break his own teeth if he clenches too hard. "My home ain't nothing but a playground to you. You hear about a grisly murder, so you run off in search of a dead body of your own."

"That's not why I'm here."

"Good," he says. "Because there ain't nothing to find. The last murder happened years ago here, and he was caught. So you and your friends can just leave me the hell alone."

"You mean there's a killer?"

"*Was* a killer." The man walks toward me, steps smooth and meditated, eyes red and buggy. "And now he's dead. Just like you'll be if you don't get out. Now."

"THAT WAS A WASTE OF TIME," I hear from inside my head.

I sigh and wrap my arms around myself, somehow still shivering in spite of the warm night air. The sun has finally set, and I don't know if I have the guts to stand up to another homeless man shacking up in an abandoned house.

Why did I drag Hiro out here? What am I trying to accomplish?

"What's wrong with you?" Estrella says.

"Nothing."

"You're crying."

"I'm not crying, you idiot. The wind's making my eyes water."

"Oh," she says. There's no judgment in her voice, and I almost feel bad for how easily she fell for it. "Here, let me help." Without warning, her translucent figure emerges from inside my chest and blows up, wrapping around my body like a force field. In an instant, the hot, dry, dusty breeze subsides.

"How…how can you do that?" I say. "I thought you only had powers in the Mirage."

"No. *You* only have powers through me in the Mirage."

"Isn't that the same thing?"

"How is the wind still making your eyes water?"

I scoff and wipe my eyes with the back of my hand.

"What's wrong?" she asks, her voice still the verbal picture of innocence. It's annoying.

"Nothing. Everything's fine," I lie. I just was hoping to finally understand what happened to my mom. No big deal.

"You don't sound fine."

"Thank you." It hasn't stopped. I find myself still wiping away tears trickling down my cheeks and snot that runs over my upper lip. "Stupid, stupid, stupid." Each time I say it, I get closer and closer to screaming it. "Stupid!" This time, I *do* scream it and follow up with an actual scream within the darkening abyss of night, Estrella's glowing acting as the only light in the dim desert.

It all comes crashing down inside me at once. The burning house. Damien. Dad's constant comatose state. Marco's assault and murder. Mom's body being found. I thought she could be the answer I was looking for. After the past few weeks of being steamrolled, I needed something.

I was being stupid. "Stupid, stupid, STUPID!" I collapse onto the street, filled with the urge to roll around and slam my fists onto the tar pavement, but even in this state, I'm too self-conscious to do something so childish. I want to throw a tantrum.

Instead, I close my eyes and curl into a ball. I wrap my arms around my knees and rock back and forth, and finally let the tears come out. I'm silent, save for the occasional breath and sniffle. I'm collected. I'm calm.

Collected. Calm. Smart. Get your shit together, Luna. How'd you even make it this far? How are you not dead already? You're no better than that stupid kid, Marco, but even Marco didn't cry as his face was bashed in.

I take a few deep breaths. The sound of distant wind around me goes still, and then there's a soft whirring. I open my eyes and see the gaudy, patterned floor of the hotel. I jump up.

"What's happening?" I plant my feet and stare around the room, eyes scanning for any sign of Mirage visual trickery.

"We're back at the hotel," Estrella says.

"How?"

"I brought us here."

"Why'd you do that?" I ask, trying not to let panic erupt from my voice. "Why'd you take over?"

"I thought you needed help."

"Well, I *didn't*."

"There was a car approaching," she says. "I kept telling you to stand up and move. You didn't. A man left his vehicle, and I don't think he had our best intentions in mind."

"Oh, no." I searched my hands, arms, and body for signs—any signs—of blood, injury, or worse. "What did he do? What did you do?"

"I ran. We ran."

Rapid breaths again. "And did we lose him?"

"Right away."

I try to slow my breathing. This time, I'm more successful, and the weird buzzing in my ears dissipates. It had happened again. I had lost control.

"So, it *was* you," I say.

"Huh?"

"I thought it was you who took over my body all those other times. When I attacked my foster father. When I burned down the home. It was you, wasn't it?"

"I don't know," she says.

"Don't mess with me." My voice is more emotional than I want it to be. "I know it was you." This wasn't a new revelation. I'd known she was the Entity that had chipped away at my existence my whole life, but as a Medium—or whatever the hell they call it—I thought maybe we were past this whole thing. "So, why did you do it?"

"I told you already." Her tone is defensive. Like a kid's. "I was trying to help you. You weren't moving."

"I mean the other times." I say.

"What other times?"

I smack my head with the palm of my hand. She's frustrating as hell, but I have to remember her current state. She's in child mode. But it doesn't make me any less angry at her. How can a dead person affect my life so much?

Dead. Dead. The word sticks in my head. "Dead," I say aloud. "Dead. Dead."

"Yes, I get it," Estrella says. "I'm dead."

"No. *He's* dead." My mind darts back to the previous conversation with the grifter back at the house. I'd asked about a killer, and he'd said, "And now he's dead."

"Who?"

"That man said the killer is dead. And that the last murder happened years ago."

"So?"

I fumble through my pockets. Thankfully, my netscreen hadn't fallen out during Estrella's body-snatching escapade. I pull it out and throw up a projection. I'm typing before I can lose my train of—

"What're you doing?"

"Shh!"

"But what ab—"

"I said shh!"

I type the words MURDER and SALTON SEA. With so much information at our fingertips, it's almost *too* easy. I skip past the results of my mom's car getting pulled from the water and dive deeper. I modify the word MURDER with the phrase SERIAL KILLER and I'm embarrassed it took me this long to finger the murderer. To finger Donald Westin.

I have to stop myself from snorting.

"What's so funny?" Estrella asks.

"Nothing."

"Why'd you laugh?"

"Because I'm a child."

"Huh?"

"Forget it." I throw up an article from *The Desert Sun*.

SALTON SEA'S INFAMOUS SERIAL KILLER KILLED IN SHOOTOUT WITH POLICE.

I read on, my eyes skimming past the name Donald Westin. Four short years ago, he took up refuge in an abandoned home. It took six long hours, but the whole affair ended with him killing a hostage before rushing out and getting shot by the police thirty-six times.

The piece goes on, chronicling how Westin was suspected of murdering at least seven women over the course of two years, though the actual number was taken to his grave.

My heart sinks. Not so much as a passing mention of Mom. I can't have expected them to know about her. Until a few weeks ago, everyone had assumed she'd just gone missing or run off.

"What's it say?" Estrella asks.

I glance at the floating head next to me, who eyes the text in front of us. "You can't read?"

"I don't think I can," she says. "I feel like I can understand part of it, but it'll be easier if you tell me."

I smile. "Mom was killed five years ago. Four years ago, this man was shot by the police. He was a serial killer with victims here, in Palm Springs, and in El Centro. I think she may have been one of his victims."

"What makes you think that?"

"Pure stupidity," I say. "I don't think as much as I hope."

"Well, then I hope so, too," Estrella says. "What next?"

"We find that house he was shot in," I say, pointing to the screen. "We hope to God he has a Spectre, and use him to find Mom."

Hiro is still sitting on that shitty red-padded stool when I descend from my room. The machine elicits a loud and euphoric ringing, only matched by Hiro's own cries as he extends both arms into the air. A small group of other patrons is now crowded around him.

"This is probably the most energetic I've seen you," I say, squeezing past an oversized man.

"That's because I'm over three thousand dollars up!"

That's more money than I can even picture.

"I mean, I think," he says. "It's all in tokens now, so it's just a guess. But it's nothing in the grand scheme of things. I have over one hundred million dollars in my bank account right now, after all."

The comment elicits a scoff from a woman next to me.

"It's the world we live in, Lady," he says, dryly. "The rich just keep on getting richer. This machine—" he smacks his hand against the metal "— is just a microcosm of the very idea of capitalism." He pulls the lever again and the machine vomits another volley of tokens, which spill into the basin.

The audience lets out another cheer, and Hiro empties the coins into a metal bucket on the small table next to him. My eyes drift to the person behind the front desk, who regards Hiro with thinly veiled contempt.

"Are you coming?" I say to Hiro.

"Heavens, no. Do you have any idea what time it is?"

"It's not that late."

"I'm being serious. What time is it?"

I roll my eyes and ignore the question. "Fine, I'll find the Spectre of the crazed serial killer myself."

The entire lobby goes silent, save for the leftover rings of the slot machine sitting on idle. Everyone in there stares at me like I'd just said *I* was the crazed serial killer.

"I'm guessing you shouldn't have said that out loud," Estrella says, her voice reverberating inside my head.

No one else reacts to the comments, so at least I know I'm the only one who can hear her.

For the first time since we arrived, I see a more serious look cross Hiro's face. He sighs and presses a button at the front of the machine.

Dun-Dun-DUN! An overly theatrical riff plays from the speaker. "Awww! Don't leave!" a voice from the machine says. It's an oddly sexual voice.

With a heavy sigh, Hiro stands up, leaning heavily onto his cane. "You there, stinkface," he points to the woman who'd given him the sour look just a moment before. "The coins are yours."

Her mouth hangs open. Then, without warning, she spits on the ground in front of her. "Go to hell, chinto. I ain't no charity case."

My eyes go wide at the insult.

I don't know what I expect from Hiro. I don't expect him to fight back or even yell, but even still, his response is underwhelming. He only sighs and picks up the bucket of coins. Then, as if changing his mind, he drops the bucket to the carpeted floor. The tokens tumble out in a surprisingly opulent display, and he limps his way toward me.

"Come on," he says to me. "Let's go."

He doesn't look back as the small crowd starts to pick up the coins.

"WHAT IN THE HELL WAS THAT?" I say once we're outside.

"Never mind."

"Was that some power move? Do rich people do that?"

"Sure, we'll go with that."

"What's that mean?"

"Nothing."

I start walking backward, facing him. "What was that?"

"Jesus, your generation is annoying."

"We're about seven generations removed, dude. You pick up the bucket like you're about to do something, and then just—"

"I was going to hit her with the side of the bucket, okay?" He slams the end of his cane on the ground, as if to emphasize his point. "My family was in Japan during World War II, and when she said..."

My smirk fades from my face and I fall in step behind his hobbled pace.

"Anyway, the joke's on her. I'm not even Chinese. I swear, when people are afraid, they look for every way to demonize you. After all this time I've been alive, I'd hoped that's one aspect of humanity that would have changed."

I keep my eyes forward and an awkward silence falls between us. "She's an idiot."

"You don't think I know that already?"

"You could have hit her, but you didn't. It's admirable. I would've hit her. I can go back and hit her if you want me to."

Hiro snorts and shakes his head. "I wanted to hit her. But that damned bucket. It was too heavy."

Again, my gaze falls to his cane and hobbled steps. I want to promise him that his days like that are coming to end. That he'll gain his strength back soon enough once we set Estrella free. Instead, I follow his lead and chuckle along with him.

"So, where are we going? You mentioned a serial killer?"

"That's right," I say. "Headed to a house about half a mile away. Where he was killed in a shootout with the cops."

The house isn't hard to find. While the article didn't pinpoint the address, a lot of other house divers on the net did. It blends in pretty well with every other home I've seen between now and then. Its roof is caved in, and its side has a classy and original male organ spray-painted on it.

The second we're one hundred feet from the home, I can feel its presence.

"That doesn't feel good," Estrella says inside my head. She floats out of my chest, curious.

"I see you and your Spectre have gotten closer," Hiro says. I can't tell if I hear pride or concern in his voice.

We climb through one of the broken windows, and I do my best to ignore the wave of nausea that accompanies me as we near what I assume is an opening.

"Amateurs," Hiro whispers to himself.

"Hey, I'm trying my best here."

"Not you. Think of how easy this was to find. I bet you this thing has claimed more souls than we can count, and that joke of an agency hasn't even found it and secured it."

"They're just kids."

"Wrong. You've only met some of the kids who work for them," Hiro says. "But make no mistake, it's run by adults. So, what's the story behind this thing?"

"I don't know for sure, but I think this guy may be the one who killed my mom."

"And you're basing this on?"

"I've already been through this with Estrella. Pure stupidity. But I want to believe that if he did, I can find a clue here that can narrow down Mom's final location."

"And if you do that, you can find out more about yourself and your Spectre."

I nod, locking eyes with Estrella. I can somehow tell through that translucent blue face of hers that she's just as curious as me.

"Well, you were smart to let me know," he says. "Especially since he's a serial killer."

"Are you sure?" I say. "I thought you said you were beyond useless in your state. Plus, you don't even have Kuro."

Hiro taps the side of his head. "Don't forget my biggest asset. I've freed the souls of many a serial killer. Those who have taken the lives of many people have a different Mirage from most. If you're looking for something specific, you'll need my help. But I can't know for sure which kind until I see his Mirage." His eyes go from me to Estrella. "So, are you ready?"

FOUR

THE MIRAGE ISN'T what I expect it to be. Okay, I don't really know what to expect, but when the words "serial killer" are thrown around, it's hard not to imagine some horrifying hellscape. Dark alleys, sad-looking figures trudging through the streets.

Yes, I fully recognize that I'm describing my home.

Instead, what I'm treated to is a sunny beach. It's not too sunny, though. Not a hot summer's day, but a perfect one set at close to seventy degrees, with the sky slightly overcast. The waves inch up the grains of sand before retreating, the sound as soft as a whisper. So pristine is the scene that I almost don't realize where I am.

"Is this supposed to be the Salton Sea?" The view in front of me doesn't seem to have so much as the *thought* of litter.

"He *does* have the mind of a twisted serial killer," Hiro says. All the same, he takes off his shoes, holding them in his free hand and lets his feet sink into the perfectly warm sand.

"What happened to us being ready?" I say.

"I never said anything about me being ready. I'm already useless without Kuro, so if I'm going to die, I'll at least be comfortable."

I roll my eyes.

"What now?" Estrella says. "Hiro's right. I don't sense anything off about this place. It's almost like we're not in a Mirage."

Hiro nods, his face serene. "It's what I was afraid of. Of course, you've been in the presence of murderous Spectres before, but I don't believe you've been in the presence of someone who's murdered while still alive."

"What's the difference?"

"Regret."

"I'm gonna need more than that."

Hiro growls, annoyed at the need to elaborate. "Say, for instance, you enter the Spectre of a fallen soldier. You'll find chaos and turmoil. The man or woman likely encountered sleepless nights, terrors, and faced a lifetime of self-doubt. Yes, soldiers may be murderers, but they do so in the heat of battle and life-or-death situations, or at the command of a superior officer. And they often regret those murders. On the other hand, a serial killer may find extreme pleasure in their murders. So much so that you end up with a place like this." He motions to the landscape in front of us.

"You sure he isn't just happy?" I say.

"No one who died happy turns into a Spectre. They may turn into Ghosts, but Spectres? No way. Besides, a place like this does more than just reflect the inner peace of such a man. When victims stumble into this Mirage, they're surprised. Put at ease. Put into a false sense of peace and security."

"So says the guy letting sand run through his toes."

"What's more satisfying to a killer than killing someone?"

"Is that a trick question?"

Hiro sighs. "What's the most satisfying type of kill to a killer?"

"Sounds like another trick question. Like you're trying to see if I'm a secret killer myself."

"Do you have to make everything a joke?" Hiro's tone is exasperated.

"Fine. Let me think." My mind goes to just a week back. I've seen a lot of shit in my life, but it wasn't until recently that I saw a murder. I see it again—Gabe's overpowering figure as his cyborg fist lays into the lifeless body in front of him. And yet, I know this isn't the answer Hiro's looking for. Gabe took no pleasure in what he did. He took comfort in his ability to cover up his insecurities. A true killer is different, but there is a core similarity. "It's about power," I say.

"Go on."

"It's all about the effect you have to influence someone's life. Shows your superiority."

"And what better way of showing your true power than luring a victim and putting them at ease before torturing them to death? The power behind a kill has little to do with the end result, and everything to do with the emotional delta between when a person came into your sphere of influence and when you killed them. That ability to influence someone from pure joy to terror is what contributes to the rush."

I look up at Hiro. "Are you speaking from experience?"

His face is as placid as ever. "I've lived through two World Wars, Luna.

Someone who's lived as long as me doesn't leave this world unscathed. But even I feel the pain when thinking back to each death."

I don't know whether to be comforted by the fact that he's on my side. "So, what now?" I almost don't see him reach down to the ground, but by the time I do, it's too late. I close my eyes and mouth as I'm pelted by a batch of sand. "You little bitch!" I yell out as best I can through the grains. "What gives?"

I can hear him running away from me. "You can't sense a dangerous serial killer in his own Mirage. You have to wait for him to come to you."

"And kicking sand in my face will help?"

"The sooner you can find your happy place, the sooner he'll come in and destroy it."

When I finally wipe my face clear, I squint to see Hiro running across the beach, cane forgotten, next to me. "What…?"

"He's a child," Estrella says. I look next to me, and she floats, face solemn, unsure.

"Is it possible for a Mirage to heal someone?" I ask.

Estrella tilts upward, taking in the question. "I don't know. I was able to morph the Mirage around us, wasn't I? What if someone like this killer can take it a step further?"

"Like heal someone's leg?"

"Hiro *did* say killers want to make their victims happy before torturing them." Again, Estrella pauses, as if in thought. "If I had his mind, I'd look at those who entered my Mirage, see what flaws they have, and try my best to fix them before taking them from your plane of existence."

"You're just as devious as Hiro is."

"We Spectres are vengeful Entities," she says. I can almost hear the chuckle in her voice. Was that a joke? I didn't realize Estrella could joke. At what point did she get smart enough to do that?

I watch Hiro as he sprints from one end of the beach to another. "So, we just wait?" I call out.

Hiro makes his way back over to me, out of breath, but smiling. All the same, his voice is hushed, his tone intense. "Don't let him realize you're on to him."

"You mean he doesn't already know what we're here for?"

"He's a Spectre, Luna. He's not a psychic. Why do you think he fixed my leg? He saw a physically evident weakness and fixed it. It was low-hanging fruit—the most visually evident thing he could see I was lacking. The least I can do is show that I enjoy it. That'll attract him quicker than anything else."

"I'm not going to run around here like an idiot."

"Then do whatever you want. Enjoy yourself. Just don't act like a stick in the mud. But once he makes himself known, whatever he does, you have to play along."

"Play along?"

"You'll understand once you meet him, I'm sure. But remember, you can't use your usual approach just yet. You want to find his deepest, darkest secrets, right?"

"And you're sure this is the only way?"

But he's off again, running across the beach, kicking up sand. Against any expectations, Estrella follows behind him. She doesn't run, but floats behind him. She doesn't look particularly enthusiastic, but at least she's trying.

I feel like I should be happy that Hiro has the use of his leg again, even if it is temporary, and to see Estrella at least attempting to return to some form of humanity. Instead, I feel a deep depression fall over me. It's not the kind I get when running through Estrella's Mirage, though. Those usually come coupled with some sort of flashback. A deep, dark feeling fills my stomach as Hiro runs around.

I can't, for the life of me, imagine something that would make me be able to fake as much happiness as I'm seeing from him. I imagine going back to that house with Lily and Damien—a family who actually wants me. But even that doesn't do much of anything for me. My time there was the most comfortable part of my short existence. I'd be an absolute idiot not to reflect back on my time there with nostalgia. But still, nothing.

"Beaches," a voice says next to me. "They're so…simple, aren't they?"

I shake the urge to jump out of my skin and simply glance to my right. Standing there is a tall man—at least six feet tall—his skin light, his voice deep. His arms are folded in front of him, and it's hard not to notice their size. His jawline is broad, peppered by a finely manicured stubble. None of the reports I read had any image of this guy, and it's not like they'd mention he had the physique and charm of a model.

I'm embarrassed to say it, but I feel my cheeks start to redden.

"You disagree?" he says.

I don't even remember what he said. "Uh…"

"It takes a certain kind of person to be gratified by something as simple as a scenic view."

"I guess so," I'm finally able to say.

"And yet, you're not joining them."

"Nope." I can blame my crippling depression on that one, though he doesn't need to know that. "Beaches are…scary." I don't know what I'm saying, but Hiro said to play along. "I mean—uh—where I'm from, beaches aren't so nice. Beverly Hills Beach didn't used to be a beach. Beyond that are a bunch of submerged buildings and houses."

"So beaches remind you of death." It's not a question.

"Yeah," I say. Sure, we'll go with that generous interpretation of what I said.

"I'm making you uncomfortable." His tone softens. "It's okay, you know."

"What's okay?"

"Being different from everyone else. It's what gives us all strengths as human beings. It allows us to be exceptional when the rest of the world settles for mediocrity."

My lips tighten as he speaks. What's he talking about?

"You're just like me. Exceptional."

Ew. This guy's looks clearly took him far in life. His actual game is creepy. God, I hope Mom didn't fall for this guy. "Uh-huh."

"You wanna get out of here? Away from the beach?"

No way. "Sure," I say instead, reminding myself every two seconds that I'm supposed to go along with this.

He reaches his hand toward me, and fighting the urge to actively recoil, I take it. A darkness and depression overtake me for a brief moment. And then it's gone as he lets go.

The night sky somehow darkens. I'm a few inches taller than I was a second ago. The man pulls me along the beach. I look down at my feet. My skin is lighter and my toenails are painted black. That's not even mentioning the garbage that now populates the surrounding area. It's like we've been drawn into an alternate reality.

"What brings you all the way out here?" he asks.

"Does that line ever work for you?" a voice that's not mine somehow responds.

He chuckles. "Ten percent of the time. But even in the other ninety percent, it helps me learn a bit about who I'm talking to."

Damn, I know the guy's a killer, but even I'm having a hard time resisting his charm. "What brings *you* out here?" the voice that's not mine says. Whoever this girl is, I like her attitude.

"Take a look around." The man gestures to the beach to our left. I'm sure it's meant to be a deeply romantic-type gesture, but it's hard to think of romance when the view he's drawing attention to is covered in needles, mountains of rusted metal, and fast food wrappers. Still, I can tell from the woman's chuckle that it's working.

"I don't follow." Her voice is dry, but still captivated.

"The silence."

Creeper.

"It is nice," she says, her voice light and genuine. I can feel the warmth inside her. She enjoys her solitude. "It's why I come out here to begin with."

"Me, too," he says.

I want to reach out and touch the man's face. I'd witnessed a glimpse of his darkness when we'd touched earlier. If I actively touch him, I can tap further into his emotions and memories. But the body I'm in resists.

It's a strange mix of emotions. Part of me is enraptured by him, somehow. He's strange, stupid, clearly playing some game, but he carries himself in a way that makes me want to trust him. I've gone through enough Mirages to know that these aren't my thoughts or emotions, but those emotions of the person whose memory I'm linked to. I try to act on this. To yell out at her to run. This man can't be trusted. But I can only make movements she herself has made.

So when I try to reach out to the man's face, she pulls at me, anger flaring up within.

What're you doing? she thinks. No, it's not her. It's *him*. His emotion is almost childish. Like I'd interfered with some world that he's created. I almost laugh, because that's exactly what this is. As far as I know, there's no way for him to actually know the emotions of the victims he's murdered. Whatever puppet I'm taking the guise of right now is fully created by him, even if it is based on an actual interaction with a victim.

"You're not supposed to do this," he says, his voice confused, yet still charming.

Did I move this woman when I wasn't supposed to?

As though a gag has been removed from my mouth, I can speak. "I... do what?"

"Move her."

"I didn't mean to," I say. It's only partly a lie. I'm prone to pushing boundaries, so even when I realized I couldn't move in the woman's body, I kept on pushing, assuming it wouldn't work.

"It doesn't matter," he says. "You *did* it."

"I'm..." My mind scrambles for anything to cling on to. I was supposed to be playing along. Why did I go and ruin this? "I'm sorry."

The veneer of charm disappears, and his lips peel back, baring his teeth and morphing his face into a sneer. "What are you?"

I want to think in a situation like this that I'd say something cool. Instead, I say "I...I'm Luna." I don't even have the grace to get the two-word sentence out without stuttering. Were it any other Mirage, this would be the time where I'd call out to Estrella and make physical contact with the Spectre. As I stand in front of him, I can tell that he's in complete physical control.

My mind flashes back to the hallway outside of apartment 4C, when

Gabe pressed my cheek to the ground and tried to violate me. The sound of his belt unbuckling still echoes in my mind, but right now, it reverberates even louder as Donald Westin's Spectre further grabs hold of the body I inhabit.

It's gone again. The control.

And I see it, the sneer on his face turning into a sickening smirk. Somehow, the edges of his lips keep on turning upward further, further, further, and further, without turning in on themselves, stretching upward, his entire head expanding to fit the smile until I realize he's taken on a completely different form.

His body is simultaneously wispy, jagged, and made of a pure black sludge. An acidic, tarry scent wafts from his direction, and I try to recoil, only to find my body still completely outside of my control. I can only stare on as he leaps at me.

This was so stupid. What was I thinking? And where's Hiro? He'd told me he'd be here to help. Instead…

A flash of light crosses in front of me, followed by a sharp clang and clashes. A hole is cut through Donald Westin's sludgy body as a blast of energy explodes from a floating blade in front of me.

"What's *wrong* with you?" the familiar voice calls out to me, annoyed and shrill. "You just gonna stand there and let him take you like that? You think we can get to the bottom of this whole thing with you dead?"

It's a blade I'd recognize anywhere. From the glowing neon blue light to the overly aggressive serrations that make up its length, it's the same blade that saved me from the Junior Mediums when I needed it most. The same one who's been with me throughout this entire strange journey.

With an unexpected smile, I grab on to her hilt and grip it with both hands. More than ever, I feel at home holding her.

In the past, with revelations like this, they are usually accompanied by massive trauma and the reliving of moments past, but instead, all I get is this weird feeling. I can't explain it or quantify it, but at this moment, I am sure of one thing. The sword I hold in my hand is more my family than my own father. I know without a shadow of a doubt that Estrella is, and forever will be, my comfort.

My guardian.

With another spin, she slices into the Spectre and smacks it back, knocking him dozens of feet away. He melts into the sand, bubbling up and writhing around the sand.

"Where've you been?" I say, still unable to wipe the stupid smile from my face.

"When Hiro said play along, he didn't mean to run off with the guy all alone."

"Run off?"

"As soon as you started talking to him, the two of you disappeared. He had to punch a hole to get here."

I turn to see Hiro hobbling up not too far behind, cane back in-hand. "Nice of you to join us!" I call out. "You said play along. I played along!"

"And you're doing great," he says. "And because of that, I know what kind of Spectre he is. Once you and Estrella make physical contact with him, you'll be catapulted into his heart, where he keeps the memories he holds most dear locked away. You'll need to navigate it if you want to find one of your mother."

"Navigate? Like a maze?" I cast my eyes back to the bubbling mass on the ground dozens of feet away. I can see the Spectre reforming.

"Yes. It'll be like a labyrinth. It's a way for the human heart to hide away the guilt they feel for taking lives. Think of it like encryption, and only he has the codes."

"Then how can I access them?"

"Because you know one of his victims. The only way you can find anyone as an outside Medium is to know who you're looking for. So you'll need to tap into your memories of your mother as you search. Got it?"

"Not really," I say. "But what else is new?" I grip the blade in my hand. My only family. The star to my moon. "You ready, Estrella?"

I can feel her give an affirmation, and without another word, I launch myself at the bubbling phantom in front of me.

I slice into him, and the world around me warps before fading to black.

To Be Continued...

VERO

SPECTRAL | EPISODE 7

A STRANGE BEACH...

I'D ALREADY THOUGHT I was in the mind of a sick man. I *had* already been in his Mirage. But nothing prepared me for what I'm feeling now as I delve deeper into his heart.

The closest thing I can recall is when a memory in Estrella's Mirage runs through me—that moment of reliving some of my most potent memories, the emotions amplified one hundredfold.

I can feel that amplification taking hold of me here. Except the sensations aren't my own. I only know because the memories that trigger them nowhere near align with my own.

I hear a woman screaming and I know it's an echo of someone he's hurt. The scream is breathy, panicked, terrified, frantic.

My chest pounds and my breathing quickens. Malice and elation course through me at once. It's not two separate emotions as I'd expect, but a single one. They somehow complement each other.

A second scream, the same woman. "No, please, don't!" she begs. The dull squelch of blade through flesh. How do I know what blade through flesh sounds like, and why do I love how it makes me feel?

I exhale, sickened by myself.

Suddenly, that malice and anger come to a crescendo. I want to vomit in my own mouth as I realize what I'm feeling.

Arousal.

What did I expect, jumping into the very heart and soul of a serial killer? That thought doesn't help me stomach the emotion. Suddenly, I want to cry, and I have no idea if this is his emotion or my own.

And then it's gone, as though I've finally made it out of the other side of a thick fog. I can breathe once more. I can feel my own emotions. Thank God. With each passing moment, that elation and arousal are all the more distant. None of them were mine, after all.

I land on the hardwood floor, the sound reverberating as though we're in a room with cement walls, though I can't see my surroundings. Instead, I only see a blinding white light coming at me from all sides.

"See anything?" I ask Estrella, forcing myself past the discomfort.

"Does a white light count?" the blade in my hand responds.

I sigh in what I realize is relief. "Good. Glad we're going through the same weird experience right now."

And then the white light around us ripples, transforming and dissipating into something more solid and tangible. It's like I landed in some coded-off area in a video game. It only just realizes I'm here and is starting to populate the area with assets.

The light disappears.

It's dark. Not completely dark, but it takes a few seconds for my eyes to adjust, and only after do they register the moody luminescence around me. The light is a neon blue, emanating from the surrounding rocks.

I'm in a cavern. The light is soft, and the silence somehow deafening. I can hear my own breath and blood pumping through my ears.

"Estrella?" I say, suddenly afraid.

"I'm here." Her voice vibrates through the blade and up my arm. It's oddly comforting. Her response echoes for several more seconds, traveling farther and farther away until it goes silent.

"Do you sense anything?"

"Nothing." *Echo, echo, echo...*

"Me, neither."

And then, like a violent wave, it hits. Screams ring out. It's maybe three —no, five—no, dozens of screams all at once coming from every direction. Like some twisted haunted house.

The fog within the cavernous scenery around me clears up, and I notice I'm at the very center of a single chamber from which sprouts several tunnels. No, not several—*many* tunnels.

One, two, three, four... twenty-three tunnels. "So, he's killed twenty-three women?" Estrella says, verbalizing my own thoughts.

I don't know if the revelation is comforting, horrifying, or even accurate. At the very least, it's a working theory.

"Which tunnel should we go down?" I say, though even before I finish asking the question, I feel an involuntary tug pulling me to the left. I know that's where I want to go.

"Where are you taking us?" Estrella says. "That's not Mom."

She's right. It's not. "It's her," I say. "It's that woman. The one we just saw—the one I acted as before we got here."

"And?"

I don't have a good answer, but I continue to walk down the tunnel all the same. I need to know what happened to her, even though I know what happened to her. Estrella doesn't fight me on it, so I imagine she's just as curious as I am.

Another scream envelopes me—one I recognize. Yes, this is the same woman.

"Stop it," I hear the woman say. Any sign of flirtatiousness I'd sensed before is gone in favor of anger and outrage. A fury flares up within me once more at one hundred times the magnitude of a normal emotion.

He doesn't want to stop. I see the woman pull away from me—from Donald Westin. He doesn't like the rejection, but anger is quickly followed by exhilaration and the promise of the chase.

He grabs her by the wrist and presses his mouth against hers, and the elation only grows as her resistance wanes.

Somehow, my own emotion escapes the prison of this man's mind, and I know I want to kill this man. I want to kill his Spectre and prevent him from doing this to anyone else again, even after death.

I'm thrown back and my body slams onto the cavernous floor. Any pain I would normally feel is stunted by the armor that Estrella's presence provides.

An orb sits on a flattened stalagmite in front of me. It's the very memory I'd just been catapulted from.

I grip Estrella in my hand and am instantly overcome with a sense of dread. Instinctively, I swing her in front of me.

Out from within the orb pops an ethereal silhouette that resembles a hooded figure. I can sense that this is the "physical" manifestation of Donald Westin's Spectre even as I cut it.

My blade slides through him like it would through fog, and Westin emits a guttural scream.

I know my cut does nothing. I hadn't even tried to sync emotionally with him, but I can still tell the assault surprises him.

The phantasmic figure dissipates and the feeling of dread that came with it dissipates as well.

I let out a breath and can almost feel Estrella sigh in unison.

"Was that worth it?" she says.

I clench my jaw. "No," I respond. I remember all at once that no matter what happens, I can't kill Westin's Spectre until after we find out about Mom. "You're right. I need to focus."

Since when did Estrella become the voice of reason between the two of us?

I walk back to the center of the main cavern and take a deep breath. "So, what are we looking for? A memory?"

"Mom's memory. That's what Hiro said."

Okay, then. I'm full of those memories. Between the two of us, I'm the *only* one with actual memories of Mom. Estrella may be great for sensing Spectres in the real world, but when it comes to—

"I got one," Estrella says.

"You got what?"

"A memory of Mom."

SPECTRAL

EPISODE 7
SERIAL

ONE

"SORRY, YOU WHAT?" I say.

"You said to latch on to a memory, right?" Estrella says. "I think I have one of Mom."

I decide not to question it or show too much shock. The last thing I need is for Estrella to become self-conscious and forget the moment. "What is it?"

"I was five years old," she starts, sounding distant, "and I was sad and confused. Dad had called me by the wrong name. It wasn't the first time, but it bothered me. A lot. But then she said that it was okay. That Dad had always wanted to call me by that other name before I was born, and just gets confused sometimes. She then gave me a hug."

I bite my lip. "That was your memory?"

"I think so."

"What's the name Dad used?"

Somehow, Estrella exhales, despite being both a Spectre and a blade. "I can't remember."

"That's…that's my memory," I finally say, after the pause becomes too long for me to stomach.

"Are you sure? I think it's mine."

"He did that to me my whole life. Mixed up my name with yours. And Mom would lie for him, tell me that it was just an alternate name. They didn't have the heart to tell me I had a sister."

"No," Estrella says, her voice growing more confident. "No. It's my memory. I can feel it."

I want to argue, but know this isn't the time. "Okay, then latch on to it," I say. "Let it guide you." I cross my fingers and pray this memory of hers is enough, because I can tell I'm too distracted to drudge up a memory of my own.

The blade lifts my hand, floating up on its own, and slowly turns me around. With a soft pull, she tugs me toward one tunnel with three stalactites descending downward, blocking nearly half of the six-foot opening. Somehow, this opening is that much more ominous than the previous one.

Still, as I near it, a wave of nostalgia fills me in the same instant a familiar scream cries out. Mom's out there. Or, at the very least, a memory of her.

"Good job," I tell Estrella as I weave between two of the stalactites and descend into the darkness, the blade held out in front of me like a torch. I squint as the light from the cavern behind me fades to nothingness, fighting off the claustrophobia that threatens to strangle me. And then...

There's a scrape—the sound of a blade on rock.

"Ow," Estrella says.

"What's wrong?"

With a grunt, Estrella emits a brighter blue luminescent glow, lighting up everything within five feet.

Directly in front of us stands a solid wall. A dead end. "Hmm." I turn around, holding Estrella above me, thinking that maybe the feeling we had was somehow wrong. My heart stops in my chest as I turn to face another solid cavernous wall covering the direction from which we came. "That's new, right?" I sound dumb to myself, even as I say it.

"Uh..." Estrella sounds equally dumb in her response. At least I'm not alone.

I turn and see an opening to my right. With an exhausted breath, I make my way down the narrow tunnel. It's not like I have much of a choice, anyway.

I keep my eyes wide and attentive with every step I take, eager for any option to turn, feeling anxious every second the Spectre of a psychopath funnels me down a path I don't want to take. And then, the tunnel opens up to another cavern. No, not another cavern. The same cavern we'd just left.

A pang of anxiety courses through me, and I'm aware that it's not my own. It's not Estrella's either. "He's scared," I say. "Or worried. I don't know if someone like him gets scared, but as scared as a sexually depraved serial killer can get."

"About what?"

Another scream. It's a male scream—the same cry I heard when we'd cut through the cloaked phantasm earlier. With a spin, Estrella pulls herself away from me, and her blade again cuts through the same figure, breaking it apart into a mist.

"What do you want?" a disembodied voice asks.

This is different from any other Mirage I've been in. Not that I'm an old hand at this, but every other Spectre felt more…innocent. Like they're victims of their own circumstances, and like Estrella, not even aware of what the hell they're doing. They act on pure instinct.

This is different. This Spectre feels in control. A god of his own little world.

"Help me!" I hear a woman scream from one of the tunnels.

"Estrella?" I ask.

"It's not her," Estrella says, apparently on the same page as me.

There's another wail from the opposite direction to my right. And another behind me. Another, and another, and another. It's a cacophony of cries echoing off the cavern walls, echoing back and forth and back again. Each time it passes is an assault on me that seems to pierce my Spectral Armor.

It stops as abruptly as it started, and silence reigns once again. The only sounds left are the beating of my heart in my ears and my heaving breath.

I blink, and a tear trails down my cheek, another telltale sign of the horrific anxiety that is this Spectre's soul. I blink again, this time to clear my vision as the silhouette of a woman materializes from one of the tunnels. She doesn't look real, but nothing's real in this place.

"Help me," she says.

I recognize her voice as the first voice that cried out a few seconds ago, only this time it's soft and raspy. She limps toward me, wearing only underwear and a white tank top, one strap hanging off of her shoulder. Her entire body is covered in a dark sludge. Oil? I sniff the air. Whatever it is smells like burned tortilla chips—apparently, that's a normal thing in Mirages—and my stomach turns over on itself, almost enough for me to retch in front of the hobbling figure. But I hold strong, licking my lips and clenching my jaw tight. This woman has clearly been through the wringer, and immediately after nearly throwing up onto the cavern floor, I'm overcome with an overwhelming desire to reach out to her. To help her.

Again, Estrella takes control of her own form, freeing herself from my grip and ripping through the woman's body. The poor figure splits in half vertically, and from her body spews a geyser of black liquid. The liquid pools around her splayed fallen body and spreads outward.

"What're you doing?" Estrella says as she whips back toward me.

I reach out and snatch her from the air, taking a deep breath. "She needed help."

"She's a Spirit, remember? She's not real. *Nothing* in here is real."

Somehow, I still have to convince myself that the talking sword is right.

"Now," she continues with a tug at my hand. "We need to go *this* way. The goal, remember? Find the memory of Mom. Find out where she was killed in the real world."

The black liquid splashes at my feet as I push through it, and my mind catches glimpses of sorrow. I feel a deep sense of longing. This woman had a crush on someone, and when it was finally returned, it just so happened to be on the most horrific of creatures.

That twisted pleasure I've come to associate with all things Donald Westin returns, a feeling connected with yet another triumph when he murdered this woman.

The emotion disappears the moment my shoes step back on dry dirt, and my resolve returns.

I stop resisting Estrella's pull and break into a run down another tunnel. "Sorry about that," I say.

Estrella chuckles. "Are you back with me?"

"It's just...I felt her pain." I almost cringe even as I speak. How stupid can I be? The only true emotions in this place belong to me, Estrella, and Donald Westin.

The tunnel turns and Estrella pulls me to the right. We bolt into the darkness, her neon glow lighting the path ahead of me as I struggle not to trip over myself to keep up.

Thwunk, thwunk, thwunk! A rhythmic breeze shoots out from behind me, and I don't have to look to know what's happening. It's like a door directly behind me shutting with each step I take. Westin is closing the tunnel behind us right as we step clear.

"What do you want?" the male voice rings out. It's so loud it feels like it's coming from inside my head. Again, fear hangs in the air, clinging to me like sweat on a hot L.A. summer day.

"What's it matter to you?" I yell, somehow not out of breath, even as I run at supersonic speed.

"Get out!"

An opening appears under me and I feel my body start to slip away, outside of the Mirage. But then an extra yank from Estrella pulls me free and tumbling onto the Mirage floor, skidding hundreds of feet before slamming into something hard. It's only through the grace of Estrella's abilities that I'm not completely pancaked and flattened against the cavern wall.

The fear leaves the air for the briefest of moments, and in its place...curiosity.

As I scramble to my feet, the cloaked phantom slides out from the wall, eyes glowing. I pull Estrella off to the side along the ground, ready to strike again when the Spectre holds up a hand.

"I'll ask again," he says. "What do you want?"

I plant my feet even harder, untrusting, unwavering this time.

His glowing eyes narrow. "You're not here for me."

I still don't speak. He may be right, but I'll be damned if I let him know.

"Luna?" Estrella says.

The glowing eyes turn to the blade in my hand, and they somehow narrow even further.

"You're like me," he says. "Not of this world or any other. Just like in life."

Oh, God. Here comes the narcissism.

"Wrong," Estrella says, but she doesn't elaborate. I can feel her vibrating in my hands, her desire for answers the only thing keeping her from launching at him again.

"You're right," I finally say.

"Huh?" Estrella says.

"Not about the 'not of this world' stuff. But the other part."

The Spectre exhales, practically growling with each breath. The world around us shifts and transforms into another cavernous opening, and at one end is a giant door.

Estrella perks up, pointing herself toward it.

A smile creeps across the cloaked figure's mouth, though I can't fathom how I can see a cloaked figure's smile. And he floats backward, slowly, deliberately. "You want answers? Don't seek out what you're not ready to see."

It's my turn to growl this time, and I punctuate it with a middle finger aimed at the Spectre in front of me. It's not the smartest thing in the world for me to do. In fact, in almost every instance of me flipping someone off, there's a good chance it's at an inappropriate or dangerous move, and I don't know if you can get more dangerous than confronting the Spectre of a serial killer.

Instead of attacking, the Spectre laughs an unexpectedly joyful snort. Like the laugh of a child hearing a terrible joke for the first time.

Again, I growl. Grow up small like me, and it doesn't take long for the patronizing tones to get to you. If Estrella wasn't in my other hand, I'd flip him off with *it* too.

"Go," he says with another laugh. "Just don't say I didn't warn you." With a spin and a wisp, he's gone, leaving Estrella and me in silence.

"I don't like him," Estrella says.

"Good," I say dryly. "You liking him would have been a deal-breaker between us. What I don't like is that he left us." I turn toward a door in the middle distance, standing no less than thirty feet tall. Its size is obscene and almost comical.

"You said he was scared," Estrella says. "I think he's scared of *us*."

"Hmm..."

As we approach the door, I look it up and down, taking in the almost patronizing amount of detail. Ornate gold borders the bright red paint. It's as though he's taken this specific memory and wrapped it for us like a gift. All that's missing is a gaudy bow draped across it.

"This is a bribe," I finally say.

"A what?"

My shoulders slump. Of course, this is the one word Estrella inexplicably doesn't understand. "He sensed what we're looking for and just handed it over. We get what we want and we leave him alone."

"I like that even less."

I snort. "Me, too."

"What do we do?"

"We came all this way to get answers, didn't we? I'm not about to let something like this get in the way."

Estrella shifts in my grip and I can feel her let out an anxious exhale.

I smile to myself. It's nice having someone to share these moments with.

I stand in front of the door and look up. "So, it's behind this door?"

"It seems like it."

It's my turn to exhale as I rest my hand on the golden doorknob. "Are you ready?"

"Just do it."

With a twist of the knob, I swing the door open and walk into the darkness.

TWO

IT FEELS like the air has been sucked out of the room as I enter. I pinch my nose and try to pop my ears, but as I blow out, nothing happens. It's as though a vacuum has emptied all the air from inside my head and whatever pressure is left presses on the back of my eyes.

I wipe away the tears that pool up at the corner and take a deep breath.

In. Out.

Good. I can still breathe. "Do you feel anything, Estrella?"

"The memory is here," she says. "But how do we get to it?"

"This may be the heart of a serial killer, but it's no different from when I run into one of my memory screens, right? As soon as I walk into—"

Thwip, Thwip, Thwip!

A series of gusts blow past me, like lanes of fast-moving vehicles passing on either side. Just like when we'd first entered this maze, pieces of scenery pop in around me, like the Mirage just realized where we are and is frantically loading the surrounding area. The atmosphere returns and I no longer feel like I've taken up residence in a tube.

The sounds of chimes and bells are the first things to break the silence. Except these aren't just the lonely tones of a single machine in a sad hotel, but a parade of spinning wheels, digitized movie jingles, loud dings, and a single, solitary scream of a man way in the distance, followed by the ringing of an avalanche of tokens crashing against a metal container.

"Looks like someone hit the jackpot," I hear someone say. It's a voice

I'll never forget. I turn to see Donald Westin's off-puttingly gorgeous face. He sits at the bar, a half-full glass of dark beer in front of him.

"Wrong," the bartender says with a cheeky smile. "That guy only *thinks* he hit the jackpot. The real jackpot isn't due for another thirty minutes."

Westin tilts his head, looking *through* me and Estrella, to a man at the very end of the aisle of slot machines. He's bald, sporting a graphic tee and a baggy pair of cargo shorts. The smile on his face is nothing short of adorable, and somehow visible from what must be hundreds of feet away.

"Doesn't look like it matters much to that guy."

"It never does," the bartender says.

"I don't think you could sound snobbier if you tried," Westin says with a laugh.

"He won two hundred dollars. With the way he's yelling, you'd think he just won the entire damned casino."

"Let the guy have his fun, you asshole," a female voice enters from the backroom behind the bar.

I'm not prepared for the click in my throat that forms. A weird mix between a sob and a hiccup explodes from my mouth.

Her black hair, tan skin, and barely visible cluster of freckles on her cheeks are exactly as I remember them. Not a single, solitary detail is out of place. It doesn't feel like I've even missed her for the past five years. It's like she's just returned home after a long afternoon.

"Is that her?" Estrella says, her voice desperate, pleading. "That's her, isn't it?"

"It's her," I say. At least, I try to say it. It takes a throat clearing and a few more attempts before the words escape.

Mom drops the box behind the bar, and when she pops back up, my eyes catch the black Guns N' Roses tee-shirt she always wore, and I choke up again. It was one of the few good gifts Dad ever got her. She didn't even like the band, but always loved the logo, saying it had a tackiness that didn't exist in modern graphic design. She'd been thrilled when Dad pulled it out of the plastic bag from the touristy shop right outside of Skid Row. Even then, it made me think of an outside world I'd yet to experience. It was a constant reminder that something existed beyond those barriers and turrets that kept us locked in.

I can only imagine what it meant for her.

Westin's posture changes. No longer is he hunched over his drink, but instead he sits straight up, his eyes only sparing a passing glance toward Mom.

I grip Estrella tighter in my hand.

"So, I was right." It's not past Westin speaking, but the dead Spectre version of him. His figure peels out from under the bar and the scene slows, almost frozen, the ringing of slot machines slowing to a dull hum. "You *were* searching for someone specific."

"Get out of here," I say.

"Don't forget that you're a guest here, and I can have you tossed out on a whim if I need."

"Can you?" Estrella says.

I chuckle, though I can't tell if it's an attempt to intimidate Westin or a need to feel in control of this ridiculous situation.

The comment from Estrella gives the Spectre pause. We were right. Westin *is* scared. In all the time he's been both a predator and a Spectre, I can't imagine there have been many who deigned to fight back or even put him in a vulnerable position. How many victims who fall into a Spectral trap have any capacity to fight back?

As if to ward off any feelings of doubt, Westin floats over to Mom, hovering above her. "Who was she to you?"

"She was a lot more than she was to you."

"How dare you?" he says in what I wish was mock offense. "She's Number Fifteen. I don't have any shame in saying I think back on our short time together...fondly."

I try not to read into the implications as he continues. "What, are you, her kid? She never mentioned having a kid."

I don't justify the comment with a response. After thirty of the longest seconds in existence, he snaps his fingers, letting the scene continue in real-time.

"Come on, Kim-Ly," the bartender says. "Don't act like it's not pathetic seeing these guys pretend they've just split the freakin' atom."

"Where I come from, winning a few hundred bucks may as well be splitting the atom, Freddy."

The bartender scoffs, and I catch the faintest of smiles cross Living Westin's face.

"She had a spark of life, I'll give her that," Spectre Westin says. "It's what drew me to her. I wanted to see what happened when I snuffed it out."

I shudder, but try to hide it. I'm not sure that's even possible in his own Mirage. "And why would she give you the time of day?"

The conversation between Mom and Living Westin turns quiet, and I can't help but wince as I see her smiling.

"For the same reason anyone gives me the time of day. They're lonely. And your mom, while she put up that façade, was so terribly lonely." He pauses. "I'm assuming, of course."

I try to listen to the conversation between Mom and Living Westin and notice it's devolved into gibberish. I tilt my head to listen closer.

"Don't bother," Spectre Westin says. "I don't remember much of anything we said. She was beautiful and charming, but so were ninety percent of my conquests."

I scoff at the last word.

"When I find these women, they're lonely. I offer an escape. A temporary escape followed by a forever escape."

I clench my free hand and I feel myself shake, but know I can't give in. I can't let him get under my skin. I remind myself that this is how he works. He finds something out about your past and uses it against you. Besides, as much as I want answers, I'm not here to learn things second-hand from him. These memories are only his own. The details of the conversation don't matter. It doesn't even matter much how he remembers killing her. I only care about one thing—and that's *where* he killed her.

"What're they saying?" I ask anyway.

"I already told you. I have no idea," he says. "'Blah blah blah, something about escaping poverty, blah blah blah.' I spend most of my time figuring out what I'm gonna do to these girls and how. Contrary to what most of them would say right before I steal away their existence, I'm not really that great of a listener."

"Can you stop messing with me already?" I say as Mom laughs for a third time at something Living Westin says.

"I don't have the faintest idea what you're looking for, dear."

"Don't call me dear."

"If I were still living, you'd be just my type."

I ignore the comment. "Her death," I say.

"Straight down to business, then. You're *definitely* my type." Another snap of his fingers and we find ourselves out on the beach, though not the Salton Sea Beach. I spot a solitary Toyota parked on the sand and recognize it immediately. It was the same beat-up thing Mom and Dad had for twenty years, or so they claim. It was the one real possession Mom had, and one she had few qualms about stealing when she ran off.

The car shakes, and I hear Mom screaming. But it's not the kind of screaming I was afraid to hear. It's worse. As the car shakes, her screams turn to moans—moans of pleasure. I see the two figures, her and Westin, struggling in the backseat, her cries growing shorter with each passing second.

"This isn't the part I wanted to see."

"Just hold on."

As he finishes talking, I hear one of the screams twist from pleasure to pain, though still in rhythm with the shaking of the car. I turn away and look for something—anything—that I can use to place the location. In the distance, I see the signs of two cross streets: Avenue E and Fifth Street.

The beach is littered with art made up of trash and metal. Off to the side is a makeshift bus stop consisting of a park bench, a chalk board, and stray pieces of wood, with the writing ETA: NEVER written on the board.

Snap!

I can tell some time has passed, but not much. We're now somehow *inside* the car, alongside Mom and Living Westin. He's on top of her, breathing heavily, a hunting knife lodged in her stomach, blood pooling outward through her shirt. He twists the knife as he pushes it upward, carving a thick, bloody line up to her chest.

She exhales, and as much as I know I should, I can't for the life of me look away. God, I can't tell you how much I want to look away and be free of this image of seeing life seep away from her eyes.

Even as she spits up blood, and cries a soundless cry, my gaze remains, transfixed. These were her last moments of life, and it was all taken away so thoughtlessly.

"Te..." Mom's eyes flicker as she struggles to speak, pain clear in her face as another wave of blood blankets her chest. "Tell my daughter that I love her." With one final gasping breath, her eyes glaze over.

My own eyes narrow. He'd almost had me. Despite logic, it had been easy to get caught up in the idea that this was how things played out.

"Did she actually say that?" I say, forcing a dry, emotionless edge to my tone. Hopefully, he doesn't notice the fear layered beneath.

Westin's Spectre issues a malicious laugh. "Nah, I thought I'd punch it up for you."

"Hilarious."

"So she didn't say it?" Estrella says, her tone curious, fearful.

"She didn't." I turn to face Westin.

"Are you satisfied?" he says as the scene around us disintegrates. There's a malevolence to his tone. Like with his murders, there's a sexual pleasure he derives from the power dynamic. He loves the feeling that comes from control. I can feel that joy seeping from his core, and I cling to it.

When have I felt this way? The smallest kernel of a memory comes to mind.

"Hey," the Spectre says. "Did you hear me? Is this what you came here for? If you're satisfied, you'll do well to get out of my little world."

This man is nothing. Even in Spectre form, he's pathetic. Less than nothing. I grip Estrella. "Yeah, I'm satisfied." I swing her to my front and, without warning, plunge her into Westin's cloaked chest.

THREE

GUSTS of wind blow on either side of my head, and the disintegrating world shatters like a dome of glass. I'm thrown backward and collide onto a sandy beach. Not the real world beach—the sandy beach still residing within Westin's Mirage.

Right. I'd completely forgotten where we'd been had been one level deeper.

"Did you find her?" Hiro says.

I wipe the sand from my face and glance around the dark, star-covered landscape, finding his gaunt figure standing a few feet to my left.

"Yeah, I found her," I say in between coughs. I stand up and hold out my hand. "Estrella!"

"It didn't work!" I hear her say as she leaps back into my hand.

"That was my fault," I say. "I wasn't paying attention to our Spectral Sync." I flip open the UI on my armband, which reads "Spectral Sync: 85%."

"Forget the Spectral Sync," Hiro says. "You got what you need, right?"

"What?" So much is going on in my head that it's hard to keep it all in focus.

"What you came here for! Information about your mother."

I think back to the sign of the surroundings where Westin had plunged the knife into Mom's stomach. The cross streets and makeshift art are as clear in my mind as anything's ever been. "I think I do."

"You think you do or you *do* do?"

"It's hard to tell how much of what I know is in his brain versus the real world, so I *think* I do."

Spectre Westin's scream rings out all around us. It comes from no place in particular. It's as though every grain of sand on the beach has a built-in speaker.

"That'll have to do," Hiro says. "Let's get out of here."

I know he's right. Westin's given us everything we need. If I leave now, we can try to find mom and get some of the answers we're looking for.

Westin's Spectral form tumbles from the sky, landing feet-first in front of us. "That wasn't too nice of you," he says.

"You were being a dick," I respond.

A dark cloud covers his face, but I can somehow make out a look of confusion, both fear and amusement painted across his entire figure. "You have what you wanted, so get out."

I glance at Hiro, who eyes me pleadingly. He's right. Now that I have an idea of where Mom was killed, I *should* move on.

And yet, I hear myself say the word "No" before I can stop myself.

"That's right, there's no way we can leave now," I hear Estrella say.

Westin's Spectre spares an extra glance toward my blade. I can't tell if he even noticed what Estrella was until this moment.

I lift my Syncer and aim it toward Westin. With a few flicks, I have the barest of information on him.

"He's Level Two," I say.

"He's more loquacious than your average Level Two Spectre," Hiro says. "You think you can beat him?"

I ignore my internal voice that wants to yell out the fact that I'd actually just tried and failed. "I think so. Besides, we need another Essence, right?"

Hiro groans, but steps further to the side, as though those few extra feet would mean much in a fight that moves at the speed of sound. "Okay," Hiro says, "but be careful. You may find him harder to pin down. But just remember his nature."

"His nature?" I say.

"His whole life, he's been driven by one thing. What is it? Every one of his emotions will point back to that."

"What are you talking about?" Westin's Spectre says.

"None of your business," I say, summoning up the sassiness of an overly confident five-year-old. But I can work with what Hiro says. And it makes sense. Most Spectres are complex, and their lives aren't usually driven solely by one emotion. But someone like Westin is different.

Even when he's happy or scared, that underpinning emotion still remains.

"Last chance," Westin's Spectre says, his voice bringing me back. He can try to hide it, but I can tell, like Hiro's, his voice is pleading. It's the only thing that gives me strength as I swing my blade out to the side.

"You ready, Estrella?" I say.

"Are you?" she responds.

And then I launch myself at Westin. He flies off to the side, equally clumsy as me as I try to recall a memory—anything that can sync up with the twisted emotions this guy drudged up in his time on this Earth. I try to mix that in with a dabble of insecurity—an emotion that's worlds easier to cling on to.

He's fast, but I'm still faster, and he lets out another cry of fear as Estrella cuts through him.

Dammit. I cut *through* him again, as though he's mist—not quite what I'm hoping for here. I spin around and swing Estrella, only to find nothing waiting for me.

"It didn't work," Estrella says.

"You think?" I say.

"Hey, Luna," Hiro calls out from hundreds of feet away. "It didn't work."

"Yeah, I know!" I yell back.

"You're supposed to sync your emotion, remember?" he says.

"I know that!"

"Then what's wrong?"

I look down at my Syncer.

Spectral Sync: 80%

I groan. I thought I would have synced by the time the blade cut through him, but nope. "It didn't work."

"Yeah, we know," Estrella says.

"Not helping."

"What's wrong?"

"His emotions are…confusing."

And then Estrella rips herself out of my hand, spinning around behind me, clanging as Westin's Spectral claws clash with her.

The Spectre laughs and dissipates yet again.

"Dammit!" I yell. "It's hard to sync with someone as messed up as he is." I breathe heavily as I snatch Estrella from the air. "He's so erratic!"

"Get out!" Westin's voice rings out from all around the Mirage, and I hop from my spot to another, just dodging an emerging hole to the outside world. Another appears under my feet, but Estrella encases my entire body in a force field that clings on to the outside of the growing pinprick.

"It's not gonna be that easy, Westin," I whisper.

He materializes in front of me, instead taking on his human form rather than his Spectral one. "I thought we had a deal." His voice is also at a whisper, yet somehow entirely audible.

"Dude, you killed my mom."

"And yet I'm giving you the chance to go on living. After everything you've done, you'd be in very rare company."

The heat rises in my face. "You want me to say thank you? Thank you for having the decency not to have your way with me before *killing* me?"

His face is stoic, but I can tell he's clenching his teeth behind those closed lips. He's not used to being told no. He's not used to not getting what he wants when he wants it. Another shift in his emotion. My Syncer vibrates.

Spectral Sync: 70%

I'm no closer to finding a memory with which to sync with him—and the thought of syncing with him still makes me sick—but his mounting anger is enough for me to latch on to. He changes so much.

"Remember," Hiro calls out. "Everything points back to one core emotion."

Then a thought hits me all at once, and I find myself smiling. Suddenly, I get an idea. This isn't just an opportunity for me to take down his Spectre. This is an opportunity for me to live out my greatest fantasy of all: the fantasy of taking down someone less powerful than me.

"You're pathetic," I say to him. "I don't understand how someone like you got away with so much."

"What's that?" Westin growls.

"What's happening?" Estrella says. "Why's your energy so off?"

"Just go with it," I say, leaning further into the very idea of cutting Westin down with her. I embrace the emotion that stirs inside me. His emotions may swing from one end to the other, but it's all rooted in one very core idea, just like Hiro said. Superiority.

My armband vibrates.

Spectral Sync: 90%

"I said you're pathetic." This time, I yell loud enough for him to hear me. "How does it feel being powerless right now? And not just powerless, but powerless to someone like me."

Westin's lips curl upward, revealing his too-white teeth. Normally, I wouldn't indulge like this, but seeing him snarl like that feels *good*. Not just good, *amazing*. It has to be amazing. I tell myself it's amazing. Yes, it's amazing.

He waves his hand to the side, but Estrella and I are already wise to his game. I'm in the air, dodging another pinprick that's just opened up under me. "Keep trying, Westin. Just *try* to get rid of me, you pathetic excuse for a human."

"Shut up!" he yells as he swings a twenty-foot staff that he materialized out of the air.

I catch the staff with my blade, snapping it in half instantly.

Spectral Sync: 95%

It's now my turn to attack. "You ready, Estrella?"

She only grunts her approval, and I can feel through my hands that she's feeling about as amped up as me over this.

I leap toward Westin, knocking the rest of his broken staff off to the side. I need to sync up with him before I make contact. I hate the fact that the emotion in question is a sick and twisted satisfaction that comes with being in power, but my approach has worked so far, so I dig deep into my own memories.

It doesn't take long to settle on to another moment—back when I'd ended up in Estrella's Mirage and saw Gabe, his mouth agape, eyes wide in terror, and his pants around his ankles. Just moments before that, he had me pinned to the floor, and if things had continued, who's to say I'd even be alive right now?

But even as I reflect, I don't know if "pleasure" is the word I would use to describe my emotion.

I swing Estrella. She comes down onto Westin and makes contact.

With a clang, she bounces off him. He's thrown back hundreds of feet and slams onto the sand, throwing trillions of grains forty feet into the air all around him.

Spectral Sync: 90%

"No," I say.

"What happened?" Estrella asks.

"Uh...Hiro?" I try not to let my voice sound too panicky. "What happens if I can't sync my emotions with him?"

"What're you talking about?" he says, running toward me. "You were so close."

"I just..." I can't explain it. He's right. I was so close. It's difficult enough in syncing with someone whose emotions are so all over the place, but even clinging to what I'd found as his core emotion was more difficult than I'd hoped. Just the thought of seeing Gabe like that, of feeling less than happy at the prospect of seeing someone powerless, shattered the emotion. I try to latch on to it again, thinking back to moments before, with Westin practically begging me to leave, but somehow, my mind keeps going back to Gabe.

Spectral Sync: 80%

"Stop it!" I yell at my Syncer, for all the good I know it'll do.

Spectral Sync: 50%

"What's wrong?" Hiro says as he comes to a stop next to me.

"Fifty percent," I say, careful not to give away any context if Westin could overhear me. "What do we do?"

Hiro lets out a sigh, but I can't tell if he's disappointed or afraid. "We need to go—"

The ground gives way beneath him, and he's sucked downward, falling into a black hole that had just materialized under him.

"You should have listened to me." Westin's Spectre is now standing and making his way over to me. "I gave you the chance to live, and you just spit in my face."

"Fine," I say. "You win. I'll go."

Westin chuckles, and I can see that look in his eyes. It's the same look he had as his knife settled into Mom. "You had your chance." One instant he's a hundred feet away, and the next he's on me. Even Estrella is slow on the uptake, and instead I connect to Westin with a sloppy jab from my free hand. It bounces off him, a vibration ringing through my arm and shoulder. If I hadn't been enhanced and linked to Estrella, I'm pretty sure my arm would have been shattered by now.

Instinct kicks in, and I find myself doing what I do best: running. I dart down the infinite beach, trying to quell the panic threatening to rise up inside.

"What're you doing?" Estrella says, her voice chiding.

"What do you think I'm doing?"

"I thought you had this figured out. Weren't you confident and spitting in that guy's face thirty seconds ago?"

"When will you learn that I'm *never* confident?" I say. "Make yourself useful and try to find a pinprick."

"A what?"

"A hole! A portal to the outside!"

"We're running?"

"What do you think I'm doing right now?"

"Regrouping? Coming up with a different plan?"

"Exactly. Regrouping. And the new plan is to get the hell out of here. I don't think I can beat him."

"What do you mean? He's only one level higher than—"

"It's not just the level. I can't sync with his emotions. With the others, there was something relatable, but with him, there's nothing."

"He was scared before," she says. "If you just think back to a moment—"

"It's not the same," I growl. "Don't you get it? With someone like him, it's not about syncing emotions at the moment, but syncing with the emotion that makes up his very being." I don't need to be arguing with my sword right now. On a list of things to be happening while running from a serial killer, it's actually probably somewhere near the bottom.

There's a movement at the corner of my eye and I swing my blade outward. It catches Westin in his hooded figure form, and cuts through him as I come to a halt.

"Nice try," he says. "But do you forget that I can be everywhere at once in here?"

I glance all around us as he speaks, trying my best to feel out an opening. If I can't beat him, I have to find an escape.

"Sorry to break it to you," he says, "but I've closed off all exits."

He's bluffing. I don't think Spectres can close off all exits, even those within their own Mirages.

"But fine, how about this?" His tone has taken a drastic turn. Any semblance of weakness is gone.

Thwip, thwip, thwip! The beach evaporates around us, and in its place are wooden walls that shoot up into an infinite sky. Around me are three openings.

"Ahem," Westin's voice is all around me. "Test, test. Can you hear me?"

"You know I can!" I can't help but blurt out. I curse myself for it instantly. A chuckle from the Spectre confirms that I'd given him exactly the reaction he was fishing for.

"At the end of this maze is a lone exit to the real world," he says. "If you make it through, I'll let you leave."

He doesn't have to tell me twice. Without a moment's hesitation, I dart to the nearest opening.

"Oh, eager are we? Don't even care to hear all the rules first?"

I don't. Even I'm smart enough to know that whatever rules he creates are meaningless. He can create them on a whim and break them just as easily.

Wait, hang on.

I skid to a halt. Maybe there *is* no exit at the end of the maze. And even if there is one, there's no way he'd just up and let me leave.

"He's lying," Estrella says, verbalizing my very thoughts.

"You're right," I say. And then the panic starts to set in. It's the same panic I feel the moments before I disassociate completely—the moments before Estrella usually takes control of me.

There's no way out.

No, no, no! Stop it! I can't be weak. I can't let him do this to me. This is *exactly* what he's trying to do. I will *not* fall into this trap.

But it's no use. I've already tried to take him out, and even my messed up mind wasn't enough to sync up with his.

This is it. This is how I die. Murdered by the Ghost of the same man who killed my mom.

There's a soft sound in the distance. A cry from a feminine voice. It grows louder, louder, and louder.

"Luna!" I'm brought back to the present by Estrella's voice. "What's going on?"

"We're through," I say. God, I hate how weak I sound. It's the antithesis of everything I like about myself, which isn't a lot. "I don't see a way out of this."

"You're not the only one here, you know!" Estrella says, her voice full of frustration. "You think I wanna die...again? If you've given up, then at least give me a chance."

My mouth hangs open and a pit forms in my stomach. I don't know what that means.

"Okay," I say, regardless of my confusion. But if I keep doing things like I am, we're gonna die, anyway. "What do you need from me?"

"You and I are already synced, right? Just attack him," she says, her voice dark, determined.

"Are you sure? What if—"

"Just *attack* him."

Spectral Sync: 75%

What? How did...? I shake my head. There's no point questioning it right now. I turn around and head back the way I came. Down one turn and another.

"What're you doing?" Westin's voice projects from all sides.

"You think I know what the hell I'm doing at this point?" I say. It's the truth, but I take pleasure in him not knowing what it actually means.

A groan from every direction. "Fine. It doesn't matter."

Spectral Sync: 85%

His cloaked figure pops out from one of the labyrinth walls. I slash through him, only for him to dissipate. Nothing yet.

He laughs. "What are you hoping to accomplish here?"

Spectral Sync: 90%

"I thought I'd already made that clear," I say as I continue running down the corridor.

I can feel it. The previous uneasiness from before. Where, for the briefest of moments, there was confidence, it's now been thoroughly replaced.

Spectral Sync: 95%

"I wouldn't be happy until I took you down for good," I finish, trying my best not to think too hard about whatever was happening.

"Stop it," he says, his voice growing more frantic. "Stop it."

Estrella shields my step from a series of pinpricks that open up underneath me so that I'm floating on air.

"Fine!" he yells. "You can't kill what you can't fin—" His last word is cut off, and the labyrinth goes silent.

I emerge from the opening where we'd originally started and planted my feet into the ground.

"He's gone."

"No, he's not," Estrella ways. "This is still his Mirage. Every inch of it is a piece of him."

Not needing any further elaboration, I swing her into the nearest wall, which cascades outward as I demolish it. But I don't stop there. I continue running forward, destroying everything in my wake, and freakin' help me, I can hear the smallest of whimpers with each swing of the sword.

Spectral Sync: 98%

And then I feel that elation returning. It's the one that almost set me over the edge before. I embrace it. Donald Westin is a tiny, pathetic man, and I'll be doing a favor to the world and the entire universe by erasing him from existence.

Spectral Sync: 99%

And, what's more, I'll be taking out the person who murdered my mother, all in the name of a good time.

"Stop!" he cries out, his voice now in a frenzied panic.

A figure pops out from within the maze—one I recognize instantly as that of Kim-Ly Guerrera, my mother. The woman who cared for me for most of my life before leaving me for, what, a life of impulse? I still don't know.

But it takes me less than a nanosecond to see through the ruse. This isn't Mom. This is the last, dying, gasping breath of someone who needs to be killed.

Spectral Sync: 100%

I cut into Mom with every ounce of power I have. I cut into her for every second she was gone. I cut into her for every second Westin stole her away from me. The cut is clean, but I can tell from instant contact that it's a productive one. There's a tension behind it that's satisfying, unmistakable.

And with one last, gasping breath, Donald Westin screams with all his power. He screams with every swing I bring down on him, until the very world around us crumbles into nonexistence.

FOUR

"YOU DID IT," Hiro says as he materializes from out of thin air, along with the rest of the derelict home from where we started. It's probably all in my head, but even with the graffiti and the caved-in roof, something about the house feels brighter, friendlier.

Okay, well, maybe it has something to do with the glowing marble—Westin's Essence—sitting just a few feet away from us. "You sound so surprised," I respond to Hiro.

"I mean, can you blame me?"

"I can't, no. That was…harder than I thought it would be." That's the understatement of the century, but then again, it's not like I've ever been known for my eloquence. I look over to Estrella, who is now in her giant head form, eyes bright for the first time I've ever seen. Empowered. "Thanks," I say.

"Thanks?" Hiro says.

"Estrella. She's the one who synced with Westin." Well, mostly.

"It was easy," Estrella says. "All I had to do was think back to all those times I took over Luna's body."

"What?" And then it dawns on me. Those times when she got me into trouble, all while taking control of my body. In those moments, did she feel the same things that drove Westin? Why would they do that? The thought leaves me disturbed, but that's not all I'm curious about. "Did you know a Spectral Companion can participate in a Spectral Sync?" I ask Hiro.

Hiro's eyes go wide at the revelation. "I'd only been able to do it once Kuro reached Level Five. I didn't realize it could be done so early on."

I narrow my eyes. I don't think he's lying, but I'm still annoyed that he held back a vital piece of information that was the difference between life and death. But like Hiro's insecurity, it's not the highest priority, though I make a mental note to circle back to both points later. I then look over at the glowing orb on the ground, eyeing it suspiciously.

"What're you waiting for?" Hiro says. "Go ahead. The two of you earned it. Take it and you're one step closer to being free."

My stomach clenches at the comment. "One step closer to helping you get back to your previous strength."

"Well, one step closer from death," he says. "I don't know if I'll ever be as strong as I used to be."

I tilt my head as I stare at the Essence on the ground. It's so small, so unimportant-looking. But it's still the last remaining piece of a crazed murderer.

"Is it safe?" Estrella says, expressing my unspoken sentiment.

"Huh?"

"Is the Essence safe?" she repeats. "I don't know if I want to eat something that might turn me even just a little bit into someone like him."

Hiro chuckles, though I can tell he regrets it after the look I give him. "Each Essence may give a Spectre or her Companion unique strengths when in battle, but no, you won't be subjected to any of a Spectre's whims or memories."

Estrella sighs. "Good."

I pick up the marble-sized object and hold it between my thumb and forefinger, staring at its beauty. I can't begin to express how smooth it feels as I roll it between my fingers. You'd think holding an actual marble would feel similar, but strangely enough, it doesn't.

I toss it over to Estrella, who snatches it out of the air like a dog without another word.

My Syncer vibrates, acknowledging an increase in overall strength, but unlike last time, she doesn't level up.

I keep my eyes focused on Estrella, waiting for some sort of indication of a power-up.

"Feel anything?"

"Not really. It's not like the last two times."

"Any new memories?"

"Progress isn't linear when it comes to getting closer and closer to one's living self," Hiro says. "Estrella has made great strides in the past. It was inevitable that there'd be a bit of a stall. Either that or a change can come later, when triggered by some sort of event. Like, say if something happens that reminds her of a dormant memory."

"Well, that's lovely and convenient," I say before turning to Estrella. "Hey, make sure to tell me if you remember anything, okay?"

"Don't talk to me like I'm some kid."

"For all intents and purposes, you *are* kid."

She growls in response. "I'm getting the feeling that I'm the older sibling, and you can't talk to an older sibling like that."

"Fine," I say. I can't tell if this is an actual memory that she's experiencing or just a joke, and she doesn't seem like she's in the mood to clarify, so I just let the statement lie. "Hiro, I was wondering if you could help me with something."

"Oh?"

"It's about my mom."

"Did you find out where she died?"

"That's what I was hoping you could help me with."

I THINK Hiro's been holding out on me. He's been putting the pressure on me to do all the research, and yet it took him all of twenty seconds to pinpoint the location of Mom's murder based on my verbal description.

The Bombay Beach Ruins is where we head next, and while the cross streets were helpful information, the dead giveaway is the makeshift bus stop that doubles as a piece of artwork.

Less than an hour later, we file out of his car and onto the beach. I recall it having some semblance of artwork scattered across its terrain in Westin's memory, but I didn't expect so much to have been added between Mom's murder and now. Then again, for all I know, what I saw in that memory were only the pieces that stuck out to Westin. Maybe I'm lucky he remembered anything important at all.

A breeze breaks across the sand, and a chorus of wind chimes sound off in a wave. Practically the entire beach is covered in them, so while the sound is relaxing, it's also relentless and noisy. It would drive me absolutely insane if I had to stay here for more than thirty minutes. At the very least, the makeshift chime structures and miscellaneous hippie art exhibits make for an interesting sight. I take it all in for a moment before taking a breath.

"Feel anything, Estrella?" I ask as I reach out my consciousness, stretching it as far and wide as I can across the beach.

Nothing yet, so I stretch it out further.

"Anything?" Estrella says.

My stomach sinks. She senses this stuff way better than I do, so the fact that she's asking me is just a little bit troubling. "Hiro?"

I turn to see him standing next to the car, hands in pockets. "I, uh...you always knew this was a possibility."

"I what?" I say. "No. No, we've come too far for this to be how it ends."

Hiro somehow shoves his hands deeper into his pockets. "It's not an exact science, you know. There's no way to know how long it may take for someone to turn into a Spectre—or if they'll turn into a Spectre at all. We talked about this."

I clench my jaw. "So, that's it?"

Hiro slumps his shoulders and he leans against the car. "I don't know. Maybe? Maybe she won't turn into a Spectre for another month, or maybe another twenty years. She can be a Ghost or Poltergeist. The more someone is filled with regret when they die, the quicker they are to turn into a Spectre, if at all."

"You mean we're gonna have to wait out here for five years?" Estrella says.

"I..." Hiro glares at Estrella as if he can't believe what she just said and shakes his head. "I'm saying we have no way of knowing. There are so many factors that go into someone's death that we don't even know if we're in the right place."

"But we are!" My voice rises to a higher level than I'd like to admit. "I saw it in his memory. This was it." I point to the makeshift bus stop, the words ETA: NEVER written in bright red on a faded black chalkboard. "This was in the vision, not a few feet from where we're standing now."

"And maybe I'm wrong," Hiro says. "Maybe this *is* where she died. Or maybe she was killed here but died on the way to the hospital."

"She didn't go to the hospital," I say. "She was only just recently pulled out of the lake, remember?"

"Well, then maybe she only just died *after* she was driven into the lake."

My stomach somehow drops again. I don't know why, but the thought of that makes everything else feel a lot worse.

"Or maybe she's one of those Spectres who doesn't stick around where they died, but links herself to her body. Or a moving vehicle."

"It can do that?" Estrella says.

"Of course it can." Hiro sounds exasperated, as though the rules surrounding Spectres are the most obvious things in the world. "None of this is set in stone. We're not dealing with entities where the normal rules of physics and law apply. Think about Alan Arroyo. Where did his Spectre shack up?"

"In the cemetery," I say.

"Exactly. With his body. Not next to the building where he committed suicide."

"But what about the woman in the theater bathroom?"

Hiro pinches the bridge of his nose between his thumb and forefinger. "You keep trying to apply rules where there are none. There's a reason I don't try to seek out specific Spectres. A Spectre can take up residence *anywhere*. It can be at its body, maybe a place of great importance in its life, or maybe even the middle of the road on the way from an accident to the hospital. Are you seeing how this can spiral out of control really quickly?

"To top it all off, we're not dealing with enough information. Maybe your mom is back wherever they took her body. For all we know, Westin's memory was one hundred percent false."

"If you knew all this," I say, seething, "then why did you let me do this in the first place?"

"Don't act like I didn't try to talk reason to you. Besides, could I have stopped you?" he says. "And you never know. It very well *could* have worked out, and you could have gotten the answers you're looking for. But here we are, and maybe she—" He cuts himself off with a clench of his teeth.

"What?" I say.

"Nothing."

"No, you were on a roll there. What were you gonna say?"

"Maybe she didn't turn into a Spectre at all. Maybe she never will."

I want to yell at him. I want to tell him he's wrong and that he's a piece of shit for suggesting it. That somehow this whole thing is on him and not just a series of circumstances that all point to me having the most miserable life in the world. But I can't.

All this...I should have seen coming.

"What's going on, Luna?" Estrella says, her voice soft, tentative and fearful.

"It's like Hiro said. The more someone dies with regret, the more likely they are to become a Spectre."

In other words, maybe Mom didn't regret anything.

I let out a heavy sigh and collapse, knees on the sand, feet splayed out on either side.

"That's not exactly what I said," Hiro says.

"We're not stupid," I say. "But it's okay. This...this is pretty much what I should have expected when we first decided to go through with this."

"As I said, there are many different—"

"Hiro," I say, my voice as soft as it's ever been. "Just stop. It's okay." And I mean it. It hurts about as much as anything has ever hurt before, but somehow, I know it's okay.

I look over at Estrella. Her giant head is now shorter than normal, squashed, almost as though she's sinking into the sand around her.

"I'm sorry," I say.

"It's okay," Hiro says. "You've been through a lot."

"I don't mean for that," I say with a sniff, wiping away the tears that had started forming around my eyes. "I mean I'm sorry. I can't go through with our deal."

"W-What?" It's not Hiro who says it first, but Estrella.

"Hiro's right. There are a ton of possibilities. For all we know, we can head downtown and find Mom's Spectre there. Or maybe she'll pop up in another ten years. I don't know if I can live with myself knowing we missed out on finding answers." I sigh.

"I...I wanna know what happened, too," Estrella says. "But what about Hiro?"

I look over to find Hiro with his back against the car, eyes cast upward to the starry sky. "This isn't what we discussed," he says.

"Yes, I know," I respond. "But you have to see it from my perspective."

"I'm well aware of your perspective, Luna," Hiro says. "I sympathize. Why else would I have come all the way out here if I didn't? But I gave you plenty of opportunities to change your mind. Chance after chance, and still, you chose to lead me on."

"I wasn't leading you on."

He finally pulls his gaze away from the stars. "I know. Sometimes, I forget that you're just a child figuring things out. You're a teenager. Impulsive, uncertain, untrustworthy. I should have seen this coming. I'd hoped, foolishly, that you'd see reason."

"I know I wanted to get rid of...all of this," I say, careful with my phrasing, "but right now, I just want answers."

Estrella remains silent, but I can sense she's as curious as I am.

Hiro sighs again as he pulls himself away from the car and toward me, leaning forward with an unexpected aggressiveness. "You know your life is only going to get more difficult, right? Becoming a Medium isn't something you can just up and quit on a whim. Like me, you'll be fighting every day of your existence. You'll need to take on stronger enemies over time, meaning you'll need to give existing Spectres time to grow, meaning you'll actively need to be okay with the fact that you're allowing people to die when they fall into their Mirages. And then, at some point, you'll stop fighting, and when that does happen, you and Estrella with both grow weaker together, until the two of you fade away altogether."

I look into Hiro's eyes, and I can tell that he's telling the truth. This is the very fate I was meant to help him avoid.

"No one lives forever," I say.

"This," Hiro motions to himself, "this is hardly living at all."

"I am sorry," I say.

"Well, if you're sorry…" Hiro says, his tone stiff and disassociated. "Good luck to you." He opens the door to the car.

"Wait," I say. "Where are we going?"

"*We* aren't going anywhere," Hiro says. "It's time for Plan B. It's not the route I wanted to take, but here we are."

"At least take me back home."

He stands inside a half-closed door. "Time is already a commodity I've wasted too much of. You have money, don't you? You'll be fine." Without another word, he slips into his car and shuts the door.

I scramble to my feet and instinctively pull at the handle of the door, only to find it locked. "Are you kidding me?"

The tires kick up dust and screech as the vehicle pulls away, leaving me and Estrella alone on the abandoned Bombay Beach.

To Be Continued…

SPECTRAL | EPISODE 8

"CAN YOU BELIEVE THAT GUY?" I kick a rock and watch as it tumbles outside of Estrella's sphere of blue light and into the darkness. "That buttface couldn't even drop me off at the hotel. Had to leave me clear on the other side of the freakin' lake! Who does that?"

"A buttface," Estrella says.

"Exactly!" I have my netscreen in hand, holding it up in the air, spinning around, doing anything I can to find service as we walk. The air is hot, but my face hotter, growing even hotter in the hour it's been since the man abandoned Estrella and me out in the middle of nowhere.

It wasn't just his fault, though. It was mine for trusting him. I should have waited for Hiro to take us home before letting him know that I didn't want to—that I *couldn't*—give up Estrella yet. Not when there were still questions.

And once those questions were answered, I could move on. Leave this whole nasty mess behind me.

Maybe I should have followed through with my promise. It's something Estrella had wanted until I mentioned otherwise. I'd started this entire journey so I could push away my past. So I could go back to Lily and Damien, and into my normal life for the first time.

Oh, shit. Lily and Damien. There's no way I can just ask them if my dead... sister(?) can just tag along, is there? I mean, there still isn't any real evidence she *is* my sister, and it's not like the government would throw them any extra kickback since she doesn't—what the hell am I thinking about right now? Am I considering the possibility that the government would pay my adopted parents to take care of my sisterghost? What sort of crazy, nonsensical garbage is—

"Car," Estrella says, blinking out her light and flying into my chest. At the very least, she understands her need to stay hidden.

In the far distance, I see a set of headlights draw near and flick on the light on my netscreen, casting it in its direction. I don't know what I expect, but my light is overpowered by its headlights, so I shut it off.

I hope whoever this is isn't a complete weirdo.

With a begrudging groan, I hold out my thumb. That's how they do it in the movies, though I can't say I'd ever expected to have to do it myself. Do people pick up hitchhikers these days? Did they ever? Was the whole thing a complete myth and fabrication?

Well, if this guy tries to pull anything, I'll at least have Estrella to scare him off. My heart leaps in my chest as the car slows. On a road where they could get away with driving over a hundred miles per hour, that's a victory in and of itself.

And then a light at the top of the car flickers red and blue.

"Shit," I say.

Whomp-whomp is the one-two punch that sends a spike of anxiety down my spine.

I fight the instinct to run, planting my feet and hold up my fists—to what, fight them? I'm not gonna fight the freakin' cops. I lower my fists. God, I want to run so bad, but with this being a desert, I know it'd be a dumb call.

I can run away. I'm good at that. But then what? That'd put me farther off course and get me lost in the middle of nowhere, and my netscreen's battery can't last forever.

Besides, we're far enough away that I don't think they're looking for me. To them, I'm just some weird girl wandering the desert. Maybe they can even give me a ride. I'm better than some whack job, right?

As the vehicle pulls up alongside me, I give them my most polite wave. I hope it comes off as, "Hey, I'm friendly, and I swear I'm not crazy."

"What're you doing?" Estrella says.

"We might be able to get a ride from them."

"Then why are you scared of them?"

"How do you…I don't…just don't worry about it."

"Okay," she says, her tone uncertain. "But *you're* worried about it, aren't you?"

"Dammit, Estrella. Can you just—"

"Excuse me, Miss?" one police officer says as he exits the vehicle. "What'd you just say?"

Crap. "Nothing. How's…how's it going?" I desperately want there to be something to lean on. That'd look casual. Instead, I put all my weight onto my left leg and lean to the side, my hands on my hips. I feel stupid as I do it and yet can't stop myself.

"It's a bit late for a stroll, isn't it?" he says as his partner also exits the other side of the car.

"My, uh, my boyfriend left me out here," I say in an unconvincing lie. It invites a lot more questions, given how casual I'm trying to look. I swear, I'm good at stuff like this, except it's usually not after having just been in the heart of a serial killer.

"That was pretty rude of him," the cop says matter-of-factly, almost exhausted. He probably deals with stuff like this daily.

"Yeah," I say. "We got in a big fight." I shrug as if him leaving me to wander on the side of the road in the dark of night isn't a whole thing.

"Clearly." He turns to his partner. "Hey, we got another domestic squabble."

His partner pulls out a flashlight and sends the beam of light in my direction, eyeing me up and down. "You okay, sweetie?" she says. It's brusque, but it's not what I could call "unkind" sounding.

"Yeah, I'm fine."

"Do you need a ride?"

I still have no idea. "I…yeah. Are you sure?" I say. "My hotel is on the other side of the lake. Or sea. or whatever this thing is." I point across the Salton Sea in the general direction of where I think the hotel may be, though I can't really tell.

"It's not like we can leave someone out here this time of night," she says. "We'd win an award for worst cops of the year if we did that."

That's a high bar to clear, but I give her a tight smile, anyway. "Thanks."

"Where are you staying?"

"Salton Inn Slots & Shots."

"Classy," the male cop says. I can't tell if he's joking or just condescending. With a flick of his hand, the back door of the sedan opens. "Hop in. Should take us about an hour to get there."

I stare into the backseat and an uneasy anxiety passes over me. I've never gotten into the backseat of a cop car voluntarily. I don't know why, but if I do, it feels like a bell that can't be un-rung.

It's a stupid thought, I know.

"What're you waiting for?" Estrella says in my head.

"Shut up," I whisper.

"What was that?" the male cop says.

"Nothing," I say. "Thanks again." Without another word, I climb into the backseat, taking deep breaths as the door closes behind me.

"What's wrong with you?" Estrella says.

"I can't talk right now, okay?" I say, my anxiety rising even higher as the car dips to one side and then the other as the two cops get into their own seats. The barrier between us is opaque, so I can't see them. I try to prevent it, but my mind flashes back to the last time I was in the back of a police car.

Breathe, Luna. In and out. In. Out.

"Hey," the brusque voice of the female cop cuts into my own thoughts.

I look up to see her looking at me through the now-transparent barrier between us, her voice coming in through a speaker.

I nod my head, taking another breath. "I was just scared. Thanks for taking me in."

She smiles and blinks twice. "Well, you're gonna be okay. You comfortable back there?"

I look around the backseat. "I mean, as comfortable as I can be."

The woman laughs, and it doesn't feel forced. "Good. Forgive us. We're not used to accommodating guests. Did he hurt you?"

"Who?" I regret asking the question as it comes out of my mouth. "Oh, no. It was just a fight. *Verbal* fight. Took me out here for a date, and we just got into an argument."

"He took you to the Bombay Beach Ruins for a date? Honey, you're lucky he left you."

"I really know how to choose them." I plaster on a sheepish grin.

"Affirmative, that's her," I hear a muffled voice from over the speaker. I wouldn't have thought much of it, but it's a voice I recognize as Detective Chu's.

The cop must've noticed the shocked expression on my face because the next moment, she turns the barrier between us opaque once again, the speakers cutting out along with it.

That rush of anxiety returns, rising from my stomach and into the back of my eyes, and before I know it, I'm panicking. No, crying. Why am I crying again? Can't I go five steps without crying? What's wrong with me?

Stop it, stop it, stop it! But the tears are flowing, and they won't stop, no matter how much I yell at them. And I feel it, that lightheadedness. I can feel myself growing distant.

"What's wrong?" Estrella says.

"The cops. Taking...us...in..." I say in between breaths. "Asshole Chu...he was on the radio."

Breath in. Breath out. In. Out. I try to slow it down. In. Out. In out in out *inoutinoutinout.*

There's a flicker. My eyes close, and when they open, I feel the dry, cooling breeze against my face.

I sit up on the ground, head aching. What? When did I get on the ground? My eyes adjust, and everything comes into focus. I recognize where I am—out in the middle of the desert, hidden among the brush.

"Estrella," I say, my voice shaky, upset. "What happened?"

SPECTRAL

EPISODE 8
ISOLATION

ONE

ESTRELLA DOESN'T ANSWER RIGHT AWAY, but I can tell she's inside me.

"What happened, Estrella?" I repeat, sounding an awful lot like someone scolding a child or a dog—is it just me or do those two tones sound similar?

I scan the surrounding area, but don't see the headlights from the police vehicle, let alone the two cops. How?

"I lost them for you," Estrella says, sounding both proud and concerned.

"Lost them how?"

"What's that matter?"

"Tell me what happened. Didn't I tell you not to take over my body?"

"I'm sorry!" she says. "But you were out of it. Like really out of it, and I thought I could help."

"By doing what?"

She doesn't answer.

"Estrella," I say. "By doing what?"

"I popped out and scared one of them in the front seat. They flipped the car—"

"—I'm sorry, they *what*? Are they okay?"

"I think so. So I dove back into you in the back of the car. When they opened the back door, we kicked at it hard, knocked them down, and ran out."

"Great, so you ran away from them after flipping their car?" Relief floods me, knowing they're okay, but ebbs away as I remember that flipping their car doesn't make me innocent.

"I tried to run, at least."

"Huh?"

"Yeah, they're a lot faster than they look, and you're not nearly as fast as I thought you'd be. Short legs and all."

I try—and fail—not to get offended by that drive-by comment. "So what happened?"

"I didn't realize I could do this still—I mean, ever since you and I connected, it's not something I'd even tried. You know, but I guess I've never really been in a position before to—"

"Estrella," I say. "What did you do?"

"I opened up my Mirage, and they fell in after me. And now we're here."

"And they're where?"

"I don't know how to answer that."

"Are they still in the Mirage?"

No answer.

"That's a yes."

"They didn't try to escape."

"They probably didn't *know* how to escape." I want to yell at her. You don't throw people into Mirages and just leave them. "What's wrong with you?"

"Do you want me to let them out, then?"

I open my mouth to argue, but stop myself. No, she's right. I wouldn't have put ourselves in this situation, but now that they're in there, we can't exactly just let them out. Right?

"Are they safe in there?"

"Probably?" Estrella says. "At least physically. I don't know what sort of toll reliving someone else's memories will take. They just need to make sure they don't run into any of those memories, so it's not impossible." She punctuates that last line with a chuckle.

Where did this more mischievous side of Estrella come from? I know Hiro said she wouldn't be affected by Westin's Essence, but she seems a bit off. A bit more...confident? "Are you doing okay?" I ask.

"I'm doing fine," she says. Her tone is curt, almost offended. "You should be happy. I did us a favor."

I'm not so sure. By doing this, we've effectively kidnapped cops. I can't imagine talking us out of this, but the silver lining is that I didn't physically tie them up. In their eyes, I stumbled into the Mirage just like them.

"How did they know it was me?" I say aloud, not expecting any answer or pearls of wisdom from Estrella. "She blinked twice to snap my photo, but why did she bother?"

I guess I was a lone stranger on the side of the road, but they'd reached Detective Chu so quickly.

"It doesn't matter," I say, though I don't believe myself. All that matters is that we find our way back.

It takes us a few minutes to make it back to the flipped cop car, which is off to the side of the road over the hill from where I'd woken up. I run my hand through my hair, anxiety increasing with each second I stare at the overturned vehicle. People don't come back from something like this. I doubt the law would be on my side, even though the circumstances are supernatural.

"What do we do now?" Estrella asks, leaving my body and floating around the car.

I feel my hair stand up on the back of my neck, irritation growing. "We just keep on walking, I guess. I dunno. We can try the hitchhiking again." None of my options sound good.

"You sure?"

"No, Estrella!" I yell as loud as I can. My voice sinks into the vast desert nothingness. "I'm *not* sure. I have no idea what the best next steps are. We can try hitchhiking again, but whoever picks us up could be even worse! Or we can keep on walking and eventually die of thirst." I pull out my netscreen and notice for the first time that I have service. "I can call for a car, but I know the police are tracking every transaction. And all of that is meaningless because I bet you they've noticed this car sitting idle and upside down and are on their way here to make sure their cops are safe. And you know what? They probably aren't! Because you decided it was a brilliant idea to throw them into your death Mirage!" I'm breathless by the time I finish my rant. It feels good to get it all out, but does it even matter?

I expect Estrella to say something, anything, by the time I'm done, but I'm instead met with silence. "Well?" I say. "Do you have anything to say?"

"I..." her voice is soft, taut. "I hate you."

That wasn't what I expected. "Huh?"

"I said I hate you." She sounds like a child whose parents didn't buy her the Barbie doll she wanted. Like some rich, spoiled brat.

My face heats up. "Why?"

"I *saved* you," she says. "You were asleep."

"I wasn't sleeping."

"You were sleeping, and I saved you. I saved you from the bad guys who were going to take you and me away."

"You took over my body again!" I yell. "After I explicitly told you not to."

"But you needed me to."

"Don't tell me what I need. You've only been alive for, what, a week? Maybe two?"

"I've been alive longer than that!" Her head's ballooned to the size of an elephant, towering over me, though she didn't need to be the size of an elephant to tower over me. "And you used to know about me. You used to love me, too. And then you *locked* me away like I was some animal!"

I stand as tall as I can, on my tippy-toes, even, but there's not much I can do to stand up to her sheer size. "What are you talking about?" I say. "Where is this coming from?" And then it hits me. The Essence. Had Hiro lied? "Is this from Westin? Is he the reason for all this?"

"No, you stupidhead!" she wails, though her immature insult undercuts the seriousness of her tone. "This has nothing to do with him!"

Another light bulb goes off in my head. It's not Westin's Essence. I mean, not directly. But it's unlocked a new memory. "Well, what is it, then? Whatever you think you know about me, I don't remember."

"I don't care what you do or don't remember!"

A red light glows from inside her, and I can feel almost a separate presence. It's familiar and unwelcome. The Entity. "You took everything away from me. Even when I begged you not to." She cries. Tears don't run down her ghostly face, but I can tell she's crying.

"I don't know what you're talking about," I say. "You're the one who's the problem. *You're* the one who dips in and out of my life. Uninvited. Unwanted. Unneeded."

"Shut up. You used to want me. We used to be friends."

I want to listen to her—to understand what she's even talking about—but her mere presence is sending a chill down my spine. It's the malevolence I'd feel immediately before another pillar of my life was destroyed. It takes all of my power not to just run as far as I can in the other direction—away from the catastrophe she'll bring with her. But I resist that impulse. "What do you mean?"

"This is just like all the other times. You're too sad and weak to defend yourself. So you go away, leaving everyone else behind, including me, to pick up your mess. To fight your fights and fix your problems."

I clench my fists into balls. I can take most insults, but she's cutting deep. Weak? Sad? I've spent my entire life *proving* I'm anything but those things. And leaving behind messes? I've done a good job not only cleaning up my own, but the messes of my entire family—and that includes whatever the hell Estrella qualifies as.

"You're right," I say, the blood in my face curdling over. "Maybe I am weak sometimes. I *know* I am. The truth is, I felt sorry for you. I let that weakness get in the way when I should have listened to Hiro. I should have let Kuro eat your Essence and put an end to your miserable existence. Then I could finally move on with my life and leave you behind."

Estrella growls. "Then maybe I was wrong, too. All those times I helped, maybe part of me knew you didn't deserve your own body. Maybe there was a reason I kept on trying to ruin your life, after all."

And then she laughs. She laughs loud and long. Wait, no. It's *me* laughing, and it takes up the entire space around us. I wouldn't be surprised if everyone around the Salton Sea can hear me. It's not a fun laugh. It's the kind of laugh you have when no other emotion will do. It's the kind of laugh you have to force out, otherwise the world around you would stop making sense altogether. It's the kind of laugh I laugh to keep from crying.

"What a mistake you ended up being," I say, my voice dry, raspy. "And here I was, thinking that maybe the two of us were sisters. I don't know where you came from, but you should've stayed there—in that somewhere between life and death—because you were *never* wanted here."

And then the world around me falls away like shattered glass, crumbling into a billion little pieces. In its place, I see the dark floors that I recognize as the ones with the chalk-like scribbles across them. Hundreds of netscreens with my memories spin around, dozens of feet in the air, every moment playing out all at once again, and my emotions threaten to overwhelm me yet again. This isn't a feeling I missed.

And yet, here I am, back in Estrella's Mirage. Back in the prison she's crafted for herself and for me.

TWO

"DAMMIT," I say aloud as I'm circled by the now-boring-and-trite memory screens. Who'd have thought I could get bored reliving some of my most integral and painful moments? Okay, maybe boring isn't the right word. In all actuality, I still feel a lot of the same pain—and all at once, no less—but at the very least, they no longer catch me by surprise. I know what I'm getting into now. But I'd like to think I *could* somehow get bored with these memories and that it reduces their power over me.

I'll do whatever I can to avoid pain.

"Miss!" a voice calls out. I turn to see the two cops from earlier running toward me. Right. In the midst of our argument, I'd forgotten they were even here.

"Are you okay?" the male cop says, his feet planted as he nears me. His gun is already out and pointed off to the side with both hands. I wonder how much ammo he's already spent trying to, what, fight off the Spirits and memory screens? Did Estrella's Mirage even have Spirits? I don't recall seeing one.

"I'm...I'm fine," I say. "Are you okay?"

"Hell no, we're not okay," the female cop says. "Have you seen around this place? Where are we?" She holds up her own gun. "I already wasted a whole goddamn magazine on one of these freaky-ass netscreens. Did one of them come flying at you, too?"

Oh, if only she knew. "You emptied your entire gun?" I want to scold her for wasting her ammo, but remember that none of it would do any good here, anyway.

"You would've done the same thing if you were in my position."

She's not wrong. "Did it do you any good?"

"Damn right it did. One of them shattered into a thousand pieces."

"Really?"

"Yeah," the male cop says, "before it pulled itself back together and flew off."

Yeah, that's more like it.

"But it left us alone."

I can't argue with her much there. "Well, I don't think they're gonna do you much good here for long."

"Yeah, about that?" the female cop says. "Where are we? You don't seem nearly as shocked as you should be."

I don't know how to answer. But any attempt to do so is cut off by a loud screech that echoes throughout the stadium-sized Mirage. It pierces my ears and sends a chill down my spine. It's the same unsettling feeling I get both directly before and after Estrella takes over my body. I hug my arms around myself, as though that could prevent anything from happening.

And then a crash erupts from across the stadium, the scenery falling to the ground like crystal shards.

Estrella's giant head emerges, her usual blue luminescence replaced with a bright red. It seems more fitting—like the blue color was a shield or mask. Whatever this is is Estrella's true form. This is the thing that took over my body and actively tried to ruin my life.

She turns from side to side, eyes scanning the Mirage. Of course, since there's nowhere to hide in this flat landscape, she finds me in no time.

"What the hell is that?" the female cop cries out.

Again, I don't know how to answer. A Ghost? A monster? My sister, probably, maybe? That still isn't clear to me. And as if any of those answers wouldn't invite more questions. "It's...it's—"

Any comment is cut off by another scream from the master of the Mirage, and the cops run off. I follow suit, but in the opposite direction. The least I can do is lead her away from them.

Estrella surprises me when she ignores me and heads for *them* instead.

Shit. "Hey!" I screech to a halt and wave my hands. "What do you think you're doing?"

"This whole thing is their fault!" she yells. "If they hadn't shown up, none of this would have happened."

That's a selective memory she has. So long as her memories had returned, this was bound to happen.

"Don't be stupid!" I yell, running in her direction. But gone is my superspeed. Somewhere in this whole mess, she and I lost our connection, and without her abilities, I'm reduced to my normal slow self, no longer casually breaking the sound barrier. "This isn't their fault. Just let them go. Your problem's with me."

"Shut up!" she yells, not slowing down. She's on the cops in an instant.

A surge of panic rises inside me and then, like magic, the cops disappear, dragged into the floor. I freeze mid-step. Who did that? Was it her or me? My unasked question is answered when Estrella turns to face me, face contorted and livid. I forget I have some control over this place. Like I did when I first met Vero and the other government Mediums.

I hold up my hands. "Like I said. I'm your problem."

She wastes no time in charging me. What is she feeling right now? Anger? I've been plenty angry in my life before. I have a goddamned buffet of memories I can pluck from.

That one. I pick at it, then recall my initial instructions from Hiro when I'd first captured Estrella. Match her emotion.

I ball my hand into a fist, plant my feet, swinging my shoulder and throwing my closed hand in front of me as it collides with Estrella's two-story-sized head.

Thwip! Thwip! Thwip! The world around me evaporates. In its place, I'm back home—back in that shithole in Skid Row. The apartment is almost exactly the same as ever. It might be a tad cleaner, but I don't know if anyone other than me would be able to tell the difference.

My vision blurs from side to side. I'm on the bed, arms wrapped around myself. I'm hungry. No. Starving. I can hear Dad's words. They reek of false comfort, lies told to a child to calm them. A promise of safety. A promise of security. That food was coming, and I only needed to be patient. Soon, we would be fed and the world would be better.

Thwip! Thwip! Thwip! Back to the present. Estrella flies over my head, my punch having hit low, sending her tumbling head over heels—or chin over forehead. The stadium-sized room shakes, and the sound of a mammoth explosion ripples throughout.

I hold up my fist and stare at it. I may be without Estrella's powers right now, but I still hold some power over her and this Mirage. But it's not all good news. The last time I punched her, I was able to absorb her into my Syncer, which helped further sync her to me. That didn't happen here. Shit, why didn't it happen here?

What was it that Hiro had said back then? Tame her like a stallion? Treat her like a dog? Dominate her physically? His comments all sounded sexual, but they worked. So why didn't it work this time?

Estrella writhes around on the ground, letting out an animalistic wail that threatens to destroy my eardrums.

Why didn't my punch absorb her? Was I not able to sync with her anymore? I pull up my interface and see that she is no longer paired with me as a Spectral Companion. And yet, I also see no option to test a sync with a normal, non-Companion Spectre. I wonder if there needs to be some connection to a Spectral Companion for that to work. How do the government Mediums fight if they themselves don't have any Companions?

I have too many questions in my head, and not enough time to process them as Estrella charges me a second time. I can't wind up another punch, and instead plant my feet and hold up both of my hands.

A collision, and pain shoots down my hands and arms.

A flash. I'm rolling around on the bed again, my dad standing over me, trying to drown out my cries. His promises continue, and my crying stops. It's like he flipped a switch and I went from crybaby to stoic statue.

"Atta girl, Estrella," he says.

A depressed sigh. "I'm not Estrella," I say.

Dad winces his typical wince whenever he makes that mistake. "Right. I know. Luna. Sorry. Hey, did you know—"

"Yeah, I know," I say. "It's the name you wanted for me."

A growl in my stomach cuts through the silence. "I'm hungry."

Dad nods, his face sad. I don't think I ever realized how sad he was, even back then. "I know you are. Mom's at work. Things'll be better tomorrow."

I nod, as though the entire whining episode didn't just happen. "Okay."

I know now things never got better.

My consciousness zooms into nothingness and then back out into Estrella's Mirage.

I'm holding her back—her entire twenty-foot self by grabbing the bottom of her giant chin. The effort is tiring, but not as tiring as you would think, given her massive size.

Those two memories I had were back to back. Has that ever happened before? "Why do we keep coming back to that same moment?" I say between gritted teeth. What was so special about it that we needed to see it in pieces?

"That was the moment you stopped letting me in," she says.

"What are you talking about?"

"You really don't remember?"

"I'd like to point out that, until ten minutes ago, you didn't either!"

Estrella pulls back and grimaces, almost as though she's assessing if I'm telling the truth. Why would I even lie about something like that?

"What do you mean, letting you in?" I say.

Without warning, Estrella leans in, though not to attack, instead inviting me to touch her chin. With a hesitant move, I oblige and am catapulted into another memory, again set in our home in Skid Row.

I'm young. Somehow, I can tell the inside of my mind is near infantile, the thinnest thread of memory strung to the rest of my thoughts. Mom and Dad are in the middle of another fight, screaming at the top of their lungs about something. It's as though my young mind has scrambled my modern perception, as I can't even make out their words. Just a warbled and muddy mess.

Mom points at Dad and then smacks him in the face before turning around and leaving, making sure to slam the door behind her as she does. Dad is left in a daze. I can only see his back, but his shoulders slumping show a level of defeat that I don't recognize. He may be more pathetic in his modern-day, drug-addled state, but I don't know if I'd use the word defeated. At least not like this.

And then, as if remembering something, he spins around, almost frantic. "I'm sorry you had to see that, Luna." He walks over to me and brings me into his arms. He's still skinny, but nowhere near the skeletal mess he is now. There's a wholeness to him I'd forgotten about.

After a few seconds, he lets me pull back as he gazes into my eyes. "I hope you know that Mom and Dad still love each other. We just disagree."

I nod as though I understand, but I doubt I do. He continues to stare into my eyes and a look of concern passes over him. "You're not my Luna, are you?"

"Who's Luna?" my voice says. But that voice I somehow recognize as someone else's. I mean, it's my voice, but it's not *me*. I don't even think I can explain it, but there's something off about the way the voice speaks.

"Ah," Dad says, his voice softening. "I know you. You're Luna's sister, aren't you? I thought you were in there."

What is he even talking about?

"You've been avoiding me, haven't you?" he continues. "But it's okay. I promise it's okay. I'm *your* dad, too."

"My dad?" young me—young Estrella says, voice vacant.

He stares into her eyes—my eyes—as though seeing me for the first time. "I...I thought we lost you. We'd saved Luna, but my other baby girl. My little star..." Tears well up his eyes. "How do you feel about the name Estrella?"

"Estrella?" she says, her young tongue not grasping the accent just right.

"Estrella," he repeated, focusing on rolling the "r."

"Estrella."

"That's it. Where did you come from, *mija*?"

Mija? Since when did he use that word?

"I..." she says, uncertain. "I don't know."

The memory de-materializes around me, and Estrella's big, red face rests directly in front of me.

My mouth is agape, my mind racing.

"You stole my life from me, Luna," Estrella whispers. "We used to share it, but then you took it from me, and you don't even remember."

"I didn't know," I say, still not believing what I just saw.

"Of course you knew," she says. "Just because you don't remember doesn't mean you didn't know. I remember them now. The conversations. The arguing. We used to be friends, and then you left me. No, you *stole* everything from me." She opens her mouth to, I dunno, eat me? I instinctively deck her with another punch to the chin.

Another flash of a memory, but this time there are no visuals, just the sound of chatter. Arguing. Two young voices—mine and Estrella—and then back to the present, with Estrella's head getting launched back hundreds of feet.

"Shut up!" I say. This time it's my turn to be childish. "I told you I don't remember any of what you're talking about."

Another hiss and a cry from Estrella, who recovers from my hit. "Like I said, I don't care if you don't—"

"I didn't finish," I say, my face reddening by the second. "I don't remember whatever the hell you're saying, and to be honest, I don't care." I let out an angry huff, my mind racing between everything in my life up until now. "You're just like everything else. Like home in Skid Row, like Dad who lies to me, my mom who left me, and each and every other part of my existence. You're just another thing I need to leave behind."

I don't know what I expected from Estrella, but she doesn't disappoint. Another scream and a howl before tearing across the ground in my direction. I know I only have a split second to react. I plant my feet and cock my fist, ready to take her full-on. After everything I've been through, I'm just tired. I'm ready to fight this bitch and take her down if it's what it takes to reclaim my life. I'll reclaim my life or die trying.

I blink. Estrella is now fifty feet away. I blink again, and she's right on top of me. Crap. My fist has only made it partway and there's no way it'll connect in time.

Thwip and flash. I can feel anger, and it's not just my own. Estrella is just as mad as I am, and she has been for a long time—from the very moment I supposedly stole her life from her.

Maybe it's better this way. Maybe she deserves to claim my life. To take my body and live out the rest of my days.

Another *thwip* and flash. I'm brought back to the Mirage and the first thing I see are the familiar locks of hair swaying in front of my face.

The ground shakes and the air thunders as Estrella is slammed into one of the netscreens and walls of the Mirage.

In front of me stands a familiar blonde girl, an exhausted smile on her face. "We really have to stop meeting like this."

THREE

IT TAKES several seconds for me to understand what's happening. Just a moment ago, I was attacking Estrella. No, she was attacking me. She'd pulled me into another memory as she attempted to rip me from the inside. And then...

"Vero?" I say, recalling the name of the girl standing in front of me, her anachronistic armor gleaming and reflecting the lights from the netscreens inside the Mirage.

"Nice of you to join us," she says. "Are you doing okay?"

I just got attacked by some alternate personality of mine. Hell no, I'm not okay. But because I don't feel like explaining any of that, I just nod.

"I'm gonna have to start charging you if we keep this up," Vero says.

I can't help but smile at this comment. I guess it has become something of a habit.

"All right, that's enough flirting," I hear a voice from off to the side. I notice two more familiar faces—the other student whose name escapes me, and their...teacher? Either way, I don't remember his name either. I'm bad with names.

Vero's face reddens immediately. "Shut up, Seb! That's not what this is at all."

Oh, right. Seb.

"That's enough out of you two," the teacher says. "Can someone please explain who we're fighting?"

"That's my sister," I say without even thinking. When I'm met with blank stares, I realize I need to explain a bit more. "Okay, in full transparency, I still don't know what that means. She...she was my Spectral Companion. Now we're fighting. It's been a rough day."

Seb points his hands palm first in my direction, but they're batted down by their teacher. "You can put those away, you idiot. We already know who the Spectre is this time."

"Everything that happens with this girl is weird, Teach," Seb says. "I just want to make sure."

"He's got a point," I say. "I've been around myself for over seventeen years, and I'm still shocked by the amount of strange shit that happens."

A screech fills the entire Mirage, and all our heads turn to face Estrella, who's still recovering from the blow from Vero. Her head flounders around on the ground, shaking away the rubble of one of the netscreens and the Mirage wall. Believe it or not, I still think it's weird as hell that the wall-less Mirage has an invisible wall.

"This is the same exact Mirage where we met you," Seb says.

"Yep," I respond.

"I thought you and this Spectre made nice with each other or whatever."

I sigh. Exhausted. "Yup, one step forward, two steps back. Like I said. A lot's happened. The short version is she doesn't like me right now and is trying to kill me and take over my body." I'm only vaguely confident about the whole "killing" part, but I don't know what else to expect when something that size comes charging at me full-force.

"Get out!" Estrella cries out, piercing our ears. Were it not for the fact that she was a Ghost, I'd be worried she'd just torn out her own vocal cords.

"Oh, yeah," Seb says, hands up, palms facing in Estrella's direction. "No mistake. She's the Spectre."

"Remember," their teacher says. God, what's his name again? "We take her alive."

"Ain't she already dead, though?" Seb says.

"He means don't do what we normally do."

"Or what you failed to do with Derek Kingsley."

"Hey, we kept him alive as long as we were supposed to, didn't we?"

"Weren't you almost fired for—"

"Enough," their teacher says. "I'll take responsibility for starting off that whole back and forth, but we need to focus."

"Ah, it's fine." Seb pulls a pair of machine guns from out of thin air and fires off a couple of rounds, pelting Estrella and knocking her back to the ground. "We got Level Two Essences in the mix here, so we can make quick work of—"

A blur rushes past me and smacks into Seb, sending him in a dark brown streak flying into the air and careening into an invisible wall.

"Seb!" Vero cries out, clenching the hilt of the katana with both hands and throwing herself at Estrella.

And then there's a twist in the air. A mix of malevolence and fear. I've felt this from Estrella before, and I've felt it from other Spectres as well. It's the innate desire to remain in control. To eliminate those who get in the way as quickly as possible.

No, I think to myself. "You're not getting rid of them this time," I yell.

Pinprick portals start to open up and expand around the government Medium brigade, but with a clench of my fists and a gritting of my teeth, I force them close. I can't explain it or confirm that it was *me* who forced these holes closed, but it sure feels like it.

Estrella spinning around and meeting my eyes with her own malevolent glare is the only confirmation I need that I'd done what I thought. And she knows it.

Her anger is cut short by a slice from Vero's sword. Another loud scream fills the air. I want to feel sorry for her. I want to look at her and pity her, but at this moment, I'm angry. So, so angry.

"Luna," Vero says. "Are you going to capture her or what?"

Estrella rises up from behind Vero, mouth opening to swallow the girl whole. A series of rapid-fire pops go off, interrupting the attack and sending the giant head to the ground once again.

I look over to see Seb limping over toward the rest of us, Spectral machine guns smoking, breath heavy. "Okay, so that was on me for letting her attack me there."

I look at Estrella, once again writhing on the ground. These two have barely broken a sweat, and they took her down like it was nothing. Even with those Essences she consumed, in the grand scheme of thing she's...

"Nothing," I say aloud.

"Huh?" Vero says.

"She's nothing." Pathetic. A heaping mess of animosity and anger. I know at this moment that I don't want to continue this mess. This whole back and forth between me and her. Whatever this whole thing is, I've had enough in my life, and I just want her...gone.

"Luna." I hear Vero's voice again, soft and muffled. I can't tell if she's speaking softly or if it's just in my head. "Luna!" Okay, I can tell she's yelling this time, and blink hard.

My eyes rip away from Estrella's pathetic mass, and over to the group of three to her left.

"Capture her," Vero says.

"Can't you just...kill her?" I say. My cheeks start to turn red, and my eyes burn from the back, tears threatening to break free. "Just kill her. Please. Or free her. Whatever you want to call it. Just take her out of my life. I can't take it anymore. Whatever you want me to do, I can't take it." I almost don't realize it, but partway through that, my body starts to shake. I breathe, letting the shaky exhale dissipate.

The three Mediums stare back at me, quiet. My eyes settle on Vero, and her jaw is clenched. I know her answer before she even opens her mouth.

"We can help you," she says. "But not like that."

"Why not?" I say, my voice cracking. "I know what you all do. What Hiro says you do. Systematically eradicate Spectres, right? So, do it!" I'm panicked, manic, and probably sound even more pathetic than Estrella looks, rolled over on her side, panting like a beaten dog. Hiro was right to refer to her as some animal. If an animal could try to kill you and claim your body. I think I missed that part in the picture book about how animals are our friends.

Vero opens her mouth to speak, but nothing comes out. Finally, their teacher speaks up.

"You know we can't do that."

"Yes you can!" I'm screaming now, and the tears are running. God, why can't I stop being so pathetic? Why do I always have to look so weak?

"Because she—you..." He takes an extra second to think. "We need the two of you alive. Peacefully, if at all possible." There's an edge to that last sentence that's somehow a mix between a threat and genuine pleading. I expect him to reach for a weapon, but he makes no movement to imply he'll make good on his unspoken threat. Dammit, I'm so bad with names.

I frown. My face is a hot, wet, sopping mess, tears and sweat steaming off my body. I want to yell at this guy and tell him no.

"No," I say. Oh, I guess it's just that easy.

"No?" he says. This time, he does reach for a weapon, but out of the air—a baton with serrated edges. "Are you sure you don't want to rethink that?"

I smile and wipe my face with my forearm. "You think you can threaten me?" I say. "You already admitted that you need me alive."

He clenches his jaw and throws his serrated club into the air. It disappears at its apex. "You're right."

I don't even see the attack until after my vision goes black and the taste of metal fills my mouth. Before I can even regain my composure, I'm on my back, looking at the spinning memory netscreens floating hundreds of feet in the air.

"Teach," I hear Vero scream. "What're you doing?"

"We can't wait all day for her to listen."

A *whoosh*, and my body is in the air. And then I'm standing back up, a pressure pushing against my back. The world around me *whooshes* by at supersonic speed. Man, I'm so slow right now. It's a wonder my body isn't ripped apart by him pushing me forward like this.

It takes me too long to realize what's happening. He's pushing me over to Estrella and forcing me to capture her with an outstretched hand.

No way.

"Get out," I say, and as I do, my body slows down. My foot catches on the ground, and I'm propelled forward, flying head over heels toward what is likely to be my death in my own Mirage.

But rather than smashing headfirst into a wall, I feel my body being cradled into a gradual stop. Vero stands in front of me, hands outstretched, a translucent force field between us.

"Teach!" I hear Seb say. "Where'd he go?"

Vero's eyes narrow. "You threw him out again, didn't you?"

My stomach is still turning circles, and I do my best to smile and shrug, still not sure if whatever I did worked, but willing to take credit for it, anyway. The next second, I wretch, propelling a stream of vomit toward Vero. Luckily for her, the force field she's wielding catches it all, though it still looks plenty gross seeing liquified chunks floating between us.

And then I see her. A giant head rising up behind Vero. "Look out!" I cry out, holding my hand out in front of me.

Vero's body slips downward and out of sight, out of the Mirage. But at least she's safe.

I hear Seb's voice call out Vero's name, but I'm a bit preoccupied by the chunks of my vomit splashing to the ground and onto my ankles and pants. Oh, and not to mention Estrella's giant head careening toward me.

There are two pops, and Estrella recoils, falling into my hands, which I push forward and up.

Thwip! Thwip! Another flash of darkness.

"I'm sorry," I hear a voice say. It's Estrella's. Her tone is slight, innocent. *"Please don't lock me away. Not again."*

And then the memories start to flood back again. Well, not memories, per se, but the *feeling* of memories. The ones you get after waking up. You don't remember the dream, but you're left with a lingering feeling.

I...I did know her.

Thwip! Thwip! Estrella slams into my hands, and with a subconscious thought, I absorb her body into my Syncer. She lets out a scream, and I can feel that same exact fear I felt moments before, when she begged me not to lock her away again. I ignore that feeling and suppress my empathy as she's sucked into the device, a faint hiss locking her in place.

I'm left breathless, heaving with my shoulders, head spinning. This place was not made for normal people. And then, several short seconds later, a pressure grows inside my stomach, pulsing outward. The muscles in my body tense up, and the grogginess and nausea that plagued my head subside almost as quickly as they came.

My sudden burst of clarity is interrupted by the sound of cocking guns, and I turn to see Seb's dark face looking back at me, eyes bloodshot, and Uzis aimed squarely at me from just a few feet away.

My shoulders slump, and I feel almost guilty, setting this kid off like that. I hold up my hands. "It's okay. I...I surrender."

His face shows the slightest hint of relief, but his body remains tense, and his weapons don't lower. His eyes scan the Mirage. "Why didn't it disappear?"

"Oh, right," I say. "You're used to killing Spectres, aren't you? Estrella isn't dead, so her Mirage is still here." It's an odd feeling, knowing more about this stuff than everyone else. It feels pretty good. "Hold on to your ass." I snap my fingers—mostly in show—and both me and Seb slip through an open pinprick, emerging back into the open air.

My feet land on rocky ground, the hot desert air blowing around me. I'm met by a flood of red and blue—my worst nightmare—and see an entire fleet of police cars parked on the road ahead of me.

A wave of guns cock in my direction, as every man and woman in blue locks on me. Just a few feet away, I see Jace and Vero standing by, arms crossed, faces cold.

Against every instinct, I hold up my hands. "I already told this to Seb," I say. "I surrender."

FOUR

"HOLD YOUR FIRE, EVERYONE!" a voice calls out from amid the parade of police cars. I know who's speaking before I see his stupid golden boy face peek out from the crowd. "Hold your fire," Detective Chu repeats, hands in the air, motioning for them to all lower their weapons.

A few of the men look at each other, and I can't tell if they're confused by his orders or by the fact that I'd just fallen from a void in the sky. Either way, their guns lower with no further drama, and I catch myself letting out a heavy, shaky breath. No matter how many times I have a run in with the cops, it never ceases to be a terrifying experience, especially with their weapons drawn.

As Detective Chu makes his way toward me, I scan the dozen officers behind him, catching sight of the pair that had just lived through Estrella's Mirage. They look the most confused out of the entire squad, and stand off to the side, baffled expressions etched on their faces. I wonder if part of their confusion stems from how casual everyone else is about this whole thing. Girl falling from out of nowhere in the air? No big deal! Just another freakin' Tuesday.

How widespread is this whole thing? I'd just assumed only select government agencies would be in the know, but now I'm not so sure.

My eyes settle on Detective Chu, who stops a short six feet away from me. I don't quite know how to read his expression. Is it disappointment, relief, or something else that I'm seeing in the crow's feet around his eyes?

"It's good to see you," he says, and I'm instantly annoyed at how genuine he sounds. His eyes take a few moments before they settle on my own. "I feel like I owe you an apology."

What's happening now? "Huh?" is all I'm able to say.

"I spent...a lot of years assuming the worst," he continues. "When you do what I do, you see the uglier sides of people, and you think...I thought I knew everything there was to know about you, your past, and where you were headed. I expected the worst, and I probably wanted the worst. As if it'd justify all the time I spent chasing you around. I didn't realize that..." He holds hands up, motioning to the sky—I'm assuming to the invisible Mirage I was just spit out of. "...you were a part of all this."

Neither did I.

I open my mouth to speak, but nothing comes out. I'm still reeling from everything that had just happened within the Mirage—about how one of the government Mediums almost killed me, and that I still had no godly idea what the future had in store for me.

"You don't have to say anything," he continues, "but I wanted to let you know that whole thing about you running away from the station—"

"I didn't run away!" My voice comes back the instant it needs to defend me. I guess that's a start.

"I know," he says. "This is all new to me, and I can only imagine what you've been going through."

This whole thing is making me uncomfortable. I almost liked it more when Chu hated me and assumed I was out to murder each of my guardians one by one. Almost against my will, I frown at the detective in front of me. "Don't think this fixes everything," I say. "All the visits, all the doubts, the check-ins, and promises of getting to the root of my problems." My heart quickens as I speak, and I want to yell at this man more than anything else in the world. "You made my life a living hell, you know that? You made me want to..." I can't even finish my statement, though Detective Chu doesn't interrupt. He just stares at me, silent, understanding. Damn this guy.

"Ms. Guerrera." The teacher's voice distracts me from the anger, and while his tone isn't light, I'm all too happy to pretend Detective freakin' Chu isn't human. My eyes settle on the Medium, and he's just a few feet away, his hand is out, palm facing up.

"What?" I say, tone harsh.

"Your Syncer," he says, his annoyance thinly veiled.

"My what?"

He sighs, letting that tolerance fall to the desert floor. He points to his wrist.

"Oh," I say, realizing. I look down at my wrist and notice the pulsing blue light, a sign of Estrella's presence. "So, what happens now, teacher guy?"

"You can call me Jace," he says.

Oh, right. That's his name.

"Like I said," he continues, "you two are not normal. We want to—we *need* to study her and find out what makes her tick."

"So, you find that out, and what happens next?"

"That all depends on what we find out," he says.

I nod to myself and snap the Syncer from my wrist. With one final regretful look, I toss it over to him. "Are you going to kill her?"

"She's already dead," Jace says, his voice clinical as he snatches the Syncer from the air. His whole body changes its posture once he has it in his hand. He's looser, less anxious.

"So, can I go?" I say.

A pained expression passes over Jace's face, and I see it's shared by everyone else, including Chu and even Vero, who's standing off to the side, her typical Mirage armor now just reduced to a dark tactical jump suit.

"Remember, it's not just her who's unique," Vero says. "It's you, too."

"Hang on a second."

"I've seen how you work with that Spectre," Vero says. "It's night and day from how we work at the DOSD. We only use the Essences, but you… you work hand-in-hand with a Spectre."

"Not very well," I say. "You saw what she tried to do to me."

"Doesn't matter," Jace says. "You have a Bond with her, and it's something the Department is determined to learn more about."

I rub at my eyes, letting out an exhausted breath. Once again, I feel like crying, never mind that I'd just finished throwing up a few moments ago. This whole thing is never-ending. "I thought I was done. That I'd hand her over and can move on."

"If you cooperate with us," Jace says, "then I promise I'll do everything in my power to make sure that's what happens."

"And how much power do you have?" I say.

He doesn't respond.

"It's not just me, you know," I say, growing more and more desperate by the second. I'm not proud of what I'm about to say. It's not in my nature to rat someone out, but considering I was left out in the middle of the desert, I try not to be too tough on myself. "Hiro can do it, too." I turn to Vero. "You know Hiro. You've mentioned him. And you've all mentioned him, too."

Vero doesn't make eye contact with me. "We've known about Hiro for a while. For as long as…well, for many years. If we could have caught him and studied him by now, we would have. Right, Teach?"

Jace shrugs. "Let me tell you that this is a situation we all prefer not to be in."

"Well, gee," I say. "That changes everything. Sorry to have inconvenienced you and your team here, Mister Teacher Sir. Since you'd *prefer* not to be here, I guess I'll just make the job easier for you." I hold out my hands, wrists against each other. I know my tone is sarcastic, but given where I am, I understand that this isn't a request, and now that they've taken away my only means of escape with Estrella, there's no point in me fighting it.

"Don't be like this," Vero says.

Her tone prickles my skin, sending goosebumps down my back. "Don't talk to me like that." My voice cracks. "Don't talk to me like you're my friend. Don't act like every move you made hasn't been to get me to drop my guard and move along with whatever plan your twisted secret club has in mind."

"This whole thing is so much bigger than you," Vero says, her voice now pleading. "It's bigger than Teach, than me, than all of us."

"Isn't everything?" I say. "That's just a stupid line people say to get people under them to sacrifice themselves. It's what they say when we go to war, and it's what they say to make you nuke your own happiness. I'm tired of everything in this world being bigger than me. I'm sick of everyone's own wellbeing taking priority over mine. I've lived my entire life being told that everything is bigger than me, that I should be more understanding, and make sacrifices for the greater good. It's only the case when all of this is happening to someone as minuscule and unimportant as someone like me. Some nobody growing up in Skid Row. Someone with a sad past, a pathetic father, and no future!" I'm not even yelling by the end. I collapse onto the dirt, letting the tears escape from behind my eyes, relieving the burning sensation that threatened them.

"Fine," I say. "I give up. Go ahead. Take me away, and let's get this whole thing over with."

To Be Continued...

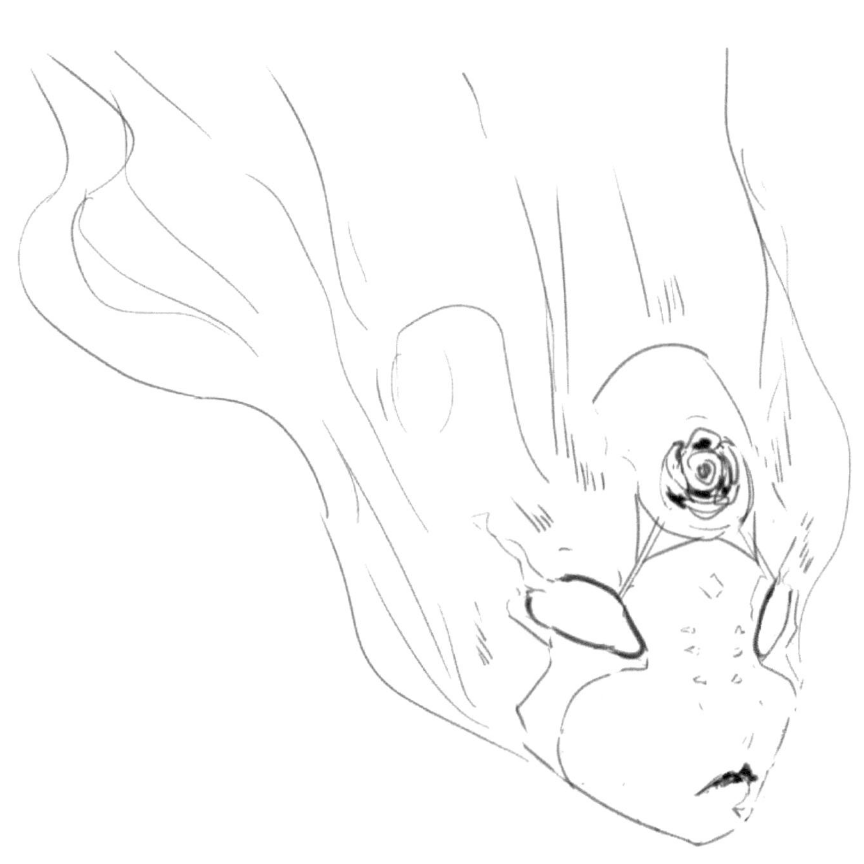

ESTRELLA

SPECTRAL | EPISODE 9

A LOADED VAN...

THE VAN ROCKS as we make our way down the pothole-ridden desert road. You'd have thought that a heavy-duty military grade vehicle would have killer suspension to match, but no. I can feel every bump and piece of gravel as we make our way back to Los Angeles.

The van is silent, dare I say awkward. I'm not too happy with everyone in here, and I can tell they don't want to say another word for fear of setting me off—the weird, temperamental Ghost girl. I can't tell if it gives them any solace that my Syncer is with the driver in the front, blocked by what I imagine is a bulletproof barrier. I also wonder if they're relieved that I'm handcuffed to my seat. That part doesn't surprise me too much. Law enforcement is always all too happy to throw on a set of handcuffs, whether I come quietly or not.

Seb sits across from me, feet up on his seat like a goblin. His face is illuminated by a handheld console. He's been playing the thing nonstop since we climbed into the back of this thing, silent, with buds in his ears. I can't tell if he's purposely avoiding eye contact or if he's just ridiculously introverted.

To my right, with his back to the barrier dividing the cargo and driver's seat of the vehicle, Jace sits, arms crossed and a sleeping mask over his eyes. His mouth hangs open, his breathing rhythmic. He hasn't said a word to me this entire time either. After a quick thank you for agreeing to what I consider to be legalized kidnapping, he piled everyone into the van and set about getting his eight hours in.

Good for him, I guess. I only wish I could sleep half as well as that guy. I guess that's what the mask's for.

Across from me and to the left, on the other side of the cage full of intimidating-looking weapons—assault rifles, pistols, and grenades, if you can believe it—Vero's legs poke out, one crossed over the other.

Everyone seems to be avoiding me, but she's the one who's distancing herself *physically*. Her face is blocked by a Kevlar vest hanging in the cage, so unlike the other two, I can't so much as make eye contact, let alone initiate a conversation.

"This is bullshit," I whisper, though I don't know why I bothered. Between the sleeping teacher, the FPS fanatic, and the girl trying everything in her power to avoid confrontation, it's not like anyone would have heard me, anyway.

I raise my hand to snap at Seb in front of me, only for my hand to be yanked down by its cuff, which I keep forgetting is locked to an anchor attached to the floor between my legs. I curse at the unexpected pain that comes with the jerk, but it doesn't stop me from snapping my fingers at Seb.

"Hey," I say. "Heeeey..."

His dark eyes only steal the briefest of glances before focusing back on his game. At most, I can tell from a crease in his brow that I've annoyed him.

I frown. "Don't any of you have anything to say?"

Another quick glance from Seb is the only response I get.

"I have some questions," I continue, even though I'm not sure anyone is listening. "First off, why am I being treated like a prisoner when I came of my own free will? Second, where are you taking me? And third, for the hell of it, how long have you all had Detective Chu in your pocket? I know it can't be too long, but how many of those LAPD jerkwads do you need to bribe to have them work as your lapdogs? Sorry, I guess that's four questions. We'll call that four. Five, if you knew about Hiro for all these years, then why haven't you tried to take him in? The guy's been alive for over a hundred years and I would have imagined that with the resources of the U.S. governm—"

"He's been alive for over a hundred years?"

I look up and see that Seb has lowered the console from his face, his eyes wide with curiosity.

"We're not supposed to talk to her." I hear Vero's voice for the first time the entire drive.

"But she's talking about Hiro," Seb says. "Admit it, Commander Daugherty would give her left nut to get details on him."

"And she'll get it when she meets her," Vero says, her voice sterner than usual. Since when did she become such a hard-ass?

"Fine," Seb says, though as he pulls the console back up, I see him mouth something to me.

I tilt my head and shrug, mouthing the word "What?"

"How old is he?" I can see him mouth. At least I can tell he's *trying* to mouth them, but between his earbuds and what I imagine is a slight case of stupidity, he whispers it.

"I can hear you, Seb," Vero calls out from her corner.

"Oh, come on, Vero," Seb says, putting the console down on the seat next to him. "You know you're just as curious as I am. Besides, what'll it hurt if she just shares a few things?"

"We were told to bring her back to HQ. Commander Daugherty wants to question Luna herself."

"Ms. Guerrera," a deeper voice interjects. I look to my right to see Jace, arms still crossed, mask still on, but I think he's looking at Vero. "If we're going one hundred percent by protocol, then you call the target by her last name."

"Ah, dammit," Vero says, her stone-cold façade falling away. "Don't tell Mom I said that, okay, Teach?"

A smirk crosses the man's face. "I'm sure I can keep your minor lapse in protocol between us."

Vero's head pops out from behind the cage, eyes narrowed at Jace. "You're making fun of me, aren't you?"

"Yes."

"It's easy to do with that Florida-sized stick up your ass," Seb says.

"Watch it, now," Jace says.

"What's your problem?" Vero leans over further, peering at Seb from around the cage.

"What, I'm just supposed to pretend you didn't recently have a massive stick shoved up your—"

"She's in a tough spot right now, Seb," Jace says.

Vero crosses her arms and leans back into her spot, out of view again. "I don't need you to defend me, Teach. I get it. I've been acting different lately. But I have to make sure we handle this right. If we do..."

No one completes her thought, and silence stretches on as the van rocks back and forth.

"Can I have my netscreen back?" I ask, breaking the silence.

"No," Jace says, eyes still hidden behind his mask.

Damn. It was worth a shot. "Then can I at least get a few of my questions answered?"

Jace takes a deep breath, lifting the mask for the first time, revealing a pair of half-open, bloodshot eyes. "If you promise to let me sleep for the rest of the time, sure."

"Teach..." Vero's tone is cautious.

"Vero, I'm gonna need you to trust the fact that I've been doing this longer than you and understand protocol better than a Junior Medium such as yourself."

She frowns and sits back in her seat, once again out of sight. Again, we fall into an awkward silence.

"So, what can you tell me?" I ask after too much time has passed.

"You'll have to remind me what your questions were, Kid," Jace says. "You threw a lot at us at once. That's not even taking into account that I wasn't listening."

I sigh. "Where are we going?"

"Department of Spectral Defense HQ."

"And where's that?"

"Los Angeles."

"Where in Los Angeles?"

"That's classified. Next."

I groan. "What's with the handcuffs?"

"We don't trust you. Next."

"I came quietly, didn't I?"

Jace tilts his head and runs the back of his hand along the scruff of his jawline. "Only after you tried to kill us in the Mirage."

"I didn't try to kill you."

"You fought back, endangering our lives and yours."

"I gave myself up in the end."

"That's right. You changed your mind. You'll forgive me if I can't trust that you won't change it again. Nothing personal."

"I hate when people say that."

Jace shrugs. "People say it because it's true. Next question."

"What do you want from me?"

"I thought we already made that clear. You're a special case here in the world of Mediums. We need to understand *why* you're different."

"To what end?"

"That's above my pay grade. Next question."

"Do all cops know about...all this?"

"They do not. It's more on an as-needed basis."

"How long has Detective Chu known?"

"Why do you care about him?" Vero says, breaking her silence.

"He's had it out for me for years now. Always trying to prove I was dangerous. If I was to go to prison someday, I'm sure it'd be because of him."

Vero and Seb exchange glances before looking at Jace.

"He..." Jace says, pausing a few moments, as if deciding how best to continue. "He's a fresh recruit to the cause."

"From what the commander's said," Seb cuts in, "he actually found out about this while looking for you."

"Huh?" I say.

"Seb!" Vero says. "Too far."

"Sorry."

I nod. It all seems to be coming together, but I feel like I've only scratched the surface here. "The DOSD. What do you all do?"

"Classified," Vero says.

"I can put two and two together!" I say. This new, hard-assed Vero is starting to get under my skin.

"Do it, then," she says.

"You fight Spectres."

"We fight Spectres in the name of national security," Jace says. "Following the influx of Spectral activity after the Second Civil War, Ghosts were confirmed by the U.S. government as a very real threat, though that remains a secret from most folks. The Department was formed as a response to that threat."

"Okay, so after all this time, and considering how old Hiro is, why haven't you talked with *him* about his own Spectral abilities?"

Both Jace and Seb look over at Vero.

"What're you looking at me for?" she says. "I don't have an answer for that. If you want to know, you'll have to ask Commander Daugherty."

"That's who I'm about to see? Commander Daugherty? Who is she?"

"She's an original agent of the DOSD, the first registered government Medium, and my mother."

SPECTRAL

EPISODE 9
GOBLIN KING

ONE

THE DRIVE GOES silent after the mention of Commander Daugherty. I can't tell for sure, but I get the impression that they don't have too many prisoners like me. Seeing as they're Mediums, I'm sure they *kill* most of their targets, so who knows if they've ever been put in the position where any of their secrets could be revealed?

It's not too much longer until the car comes to a stop—maybe thirty minutes, though I can't be sure because I have no netscreen, watch, or any semblance of time.

After unlocking my cuffs and shifting them to behind my back, the cargo doors of the van swing open. I'm guided—or guarded—by an escort of six other men and women, in addition to the three I've been sitting with for the past two hours. I catch a peek at their wrists and notice they each have Syncers as well.

Unlike Seb and Vero, though, these men and women are closer to Jace in age, in their late twenties and early thirties.

We march through an unmarked parking garage, any semblance of how deep or high up is left ambiguous by blank walls. I'd like to think we're at least a mile deep, just because it sounds cool.

The whole experience is marred by the time we enter a freight elevator. Its walls are covered by hanging moving blankets, and it's hard to tell if this was intentional to help further hide any clues as to our actual location, or if I just caught them in the middle of moving day.

I have to squint when the elevator doors open as an overwhelming bright white light pours in. There should be a freakin' warning on the inside of the doors and a pair of sunglasses to go with them. I'm pushed forward by a rough hand before my eyes can even adjust, but I trust my feet not to trip over the threshold. Every fifty yards down the narrow, bright, white hallway, we pass an offshoot to another open space, though unlike the hallway itself, the rooms look to be dimly lit. Whether it's just because of the stark contrast between them and where I am, I'm not sure.

After a solid five minutes of walking, we reach a turn and follow it to the right. We turn one way, then another, and wrap around a few open and empty bullpens, and by the time I'm already good and lost, we reach a set of glass doors.

Vero takes the lead, opening the door and peeking her head in. With a motion of her hand, the guards at my front part.

I take a step back, bumping into a guard behind me. "Oh, shit, sorry," I say before I can stop myself. Nothing like being polite to your captors.

Vero gives me another wave forward, this one more frantic, anxious even.

The office I step into is ornate, almost obnoxiously so, I'd say. It's at least three times the size of my entire Skid Row apartment. The first thing I notice as I enter is the deep brown leather wraparound couch taking up the left half of the room, large enough to seat a group of six. At its center is a coffee table that's the shape of a tree cut in half vertically, with the round part at the bottom and the flat cut on top. To my right, on the other side of the room, is an equally rustic-looking desk that's almost big enough to be a bed. It's covered in desk decorations, including a figurine that resembles the Washington Monument and one of those hanging metal ball toy thingies that go tick-tick-tick-tick. Behind the desk, against the brick wall, are a bunch of certificates and medals framed and hung, telling a story of privilege and ridiculous accomplishments.

A woman stands up from her desk. At first glance, I think she might be in her thirties, but as she walks toward me, I can see the experience and fine lines that only come with age. I have no idea how old she looks. She could be sixty. Her hair is wavy and graying, peeking over her shoulders as she walks.

"What's all this?" she says, motioning to my wrists. Her voice is sweet, a contrast from what I expected based on her appearance which, while put together, has the look of a woman who'd rather get down to business than engage in meaningless small talk. "There's no need for that here."

The guard at my rear reaches into his breast pocket and pulls out a key card. With a beep and a hiss, my wrists are free, the slightest impression on my skin being the only sign that they were ever there. Rubbing my wrists with my hands, I look up at the woman approaching me. Yes, like everyone else in this world, she's tall—at least a head taller than I am, though I feel like that's pretty much everyone I've met other than Mom.

"So, you're Luna Guerrera," she says, looking me up and down.

A part of me wants to stand on my toes, as though that would impress her. "And you're..." I try to think back. What was it they called her again?

"Commander Mia Daugherty. I'm the head of the DOSD. You can call me Commander or Commander Daugherty."

I furrow my eyebrows. "Uh...are you...am I...? Why would I call you Commander?"

She smiles at this. "Well, I hope you don't think me presumptuous, but given your abilities, it would be the smart thing for you to do. Can't let your gift go to waste, now can we?"

I look from Vero to Jace and Seb. "So, you want me to be one of them?"

Commander Daugherty waves her hand in front of her. "I wouldn't worry about that just yet. First things first, we need to understand what it is we're dealing with. What skills do you have and how can we best harness them? Those are the questions we want to answer."

I blink, using up all my willpower not to vomit in this woman's face. "And why would I want to do that?"

Commander Daugherty's smile lingers, as if she's deciding if she should continue. The sides of her lips pull up higher, her smile deepening. "Did anybody tell you about what we do here?"

She waves her hand, and the surrounding guards pull back, heading toward the exit. Jace, Seb, and Vero follow suit. "Uh, not you, Agent Daugherty. Please stick around."

With an extra glance toward Jace, she stays put.

Commander Daugherty motions to the couch. I follow her lead. "Agent Daugherty, would you mind preparing some coffee or tea? Ms. Guerrera, what would you prefer?"

Vero's face falls ever so low, but she recovers, eyes falling on me.

I'll admit, I'm pretty damned tired. "Coffee," I say.

"Cream? Sugar?" Vero asks, her voice softer than normal.

"Uh, no. Just black."

"Excellent," Commander Daugherty says. "Not enough kids your age drink it black. It's the best thing in the world to do when you start drinking coffee."

Is she complimenting the way I take my coffee? "Okay?"

"Start when you're younger and you can drink coffee in any country with no accommodations. It causes you less headaches when abroad. Plus, it doesn't get you used to too much sugar. It's the biggest problem facing the U.S. right now. Did you know?"

"Drinking sugar with coffee?"

"Sugar in general. *One* of the biggest problems. As you can imagine..." she lifts her hands up, motioning to the rest of her room. "...none of this would exist if we didn't have other problems, too."

"Okay," I say, uneasy, not sure what the whole point of this conversation is.

"Please, take a seat." Commander Daugherty, for a second time, motions to the couch, this time taking a seat at one end. I take my spot at the opposite corner with the other armrest. Her smile seems to perk up even more as I do.

"Back to the initial question. What do you know about what we do at the Department of Spectral Defense?"

I think back to when I'd first spoken with Hiro. He'd mentioned that there was an uptick in Spectral activity after the Second Civil War, but only mentioned one thing. "You fight off Spectres to protect the public?" I say.

"Correct," Commander Daugherty says, but then she pauses and tilts her head to the side, thinking. "But it doesn't stop there. Yes, protecting civilians from Spectres is important. I think that goes without saying. But it wasn't just the U.S. that saw Spectral activity arise following the Second Civil War. It was all over the world. More specifically, they arose in Asian countries. China, Japan, India—they all had massive upticks in CBS incidents."

"In what?"

"Consumed by Spectres," Vero says from the coffee nook on the other side of the room. "Like that man from the movie theater."

I nod. "Right." Or like that Isabel girl who was consumed by Alan Arroyo's Spectre before we freed her. Even amid this interrogation, I wonder how things ended up between her and Colin.

"And what they won't tell you on AIN is that it's those three nations who recently signed an under-the-table agreement to share resources to fight off their own infestation of Spectres."

"And that's bad?" I say, no longer following her train of thought.

"Of course it's bad." Commander Daugherty smacks the coffee table in front of her, leans forward and gazes into my eyes from across the table. "Make no mistake, my dear, this is an arms race. I promise you, China, India, and Japan didn't get into bed with each other for the general well-being of their public. They did so because as we fight against these Spectres, we're seeing massive potential in what Mediums can bring to warfare."

Commander Daugherty's comment is interrupted by Vero, who places a mug of dark coffee on the table in front of me.

"Coasters, dear," Commander Daugherty says without looking up.

Vero rolls her eyes, but retreats to the desk, pulling a set of ceramic coasters from a holder and placing them neatly under our mugs. After pulling another soft leather chair from in front of Commander Daugherty's desk, she places it on the opposite end of the short side of the table. She collapses into it and takes a sip of her coffee, either not noticing or refusing to notice the annoyed glare from her mother.

"I'm sorry," I say, cutting the awkward silence. "You said warfare. Do you mean soldiers?"

"That's exactly right," Commander Daugherty says. "You've seen it, haven't you? Forgive me, based on the reports I've read—"

I steal a glare toward Vero, who sips at her coffee, avoiding eye contact.

"—you have your fair share of miraculous abilities yourself. Moving at high speeds. Super strength. Pulling weapons out of thin air. For Christ's sake, it's like Genghis Khan's wet dream."

That's an interesting way of putting it. I think back to my own experiences. How fast I move, how strong I am, and how intimidating Estrella is in her blade form. Okay, I can see the appeal there. "But," I say, "these abilities don't extend to the real world. Outside of Mirages, I mean."

"Ding-ding-ding-ding!" Commander Daugherty says, pointing to me and smiling as though I'd just won the lottery. "Very, very good, Ms. Guerrera. You're right. At present, your abilities *don't* extend to beyond Mirages. And if I can let you in on a trade secret, the same can be said of our own homegrown Mediums. My own beautiful daughter here, as lovely and capable as she is, is nothing but a normal girl out here in the real world."

Vero mumbles something.

"I'm sorry, what's that, Agent Daugherty?"

"I come from a military family and know three types of martial arts, M—Commander Daugherty."

"And yet, you'd be no more effective against a Spectre than a newborn puppy."

Vero only sighs in response.

"My point is," Commander Daugherty says, "that there's an opportunity there. What if we could harness these abilities in the real world?"

"And you think I can help?" I say.

Commander Daugherty sits back in her chair, crossing both her arms and her legs. "I don't know. Frankly, we have had little contact with someone with your abilities. Well, there's one. I believe you know him, but he's not the most cooperative of men."

"Uh-huh," I say, thinking back to him leaving me to rot in the middle of the desert. "Yeah, I guess you can say that.

"But you give us a unique opportunity. Unlike any other of our Mediums, you can sync with at least one Spectre."

It's something Hiro always highlighted, but it's not something I understood all too well. "And government Mediums...they can't do that?"

"Agent Daugherty, can you please raise your left hand?"

Vero obeys, and I look at her wrist, where her Syncer rests.

"You know what this is?" Commander Daugherty asks.

"It's, uh...a Syncer?" I say, proud that I could remember the most basic of terms.

"That's right," she says. "We use it to store the Essences of freed Spectres." She stands up and makes her way across the room, behind her desk. "Our agents can then use any innate skills or abilities to fight when they're in a Mirage. The more Essences we have, and the higher level those Essences are, the stronger our agents are. Before each mission, we assess a threat and send them off with the requisite number and level of Spectres to take on their targets. But you..." From behind her desk, she raises another Syncer. This one I recognize as my own.

It takes all my willpower not to scoff at the reveal. This woman is all about theatrics. Did they rush my Syncer over here ahead of time just so she could have it at this exact moment?

"You don't use your Syncer to store Essences. You use it to store entire Spectres. I'll be honest. Outside of Mr. Hanajima, I didn't know if there was another person on the planet who could do that."

"And that's important how?"

The woman shrugs. "Your guess is as good as ours. It can mean everything or it can mean nothing. Call me an optimist, but I'd like to think it means everything. But we won't know until we take the time to look. Mr. Hanajima has never been cooperative. He's never given us the time of day, and he's gotten in our way a hell of a lot over the past fifteen years. So, what do you think?"

My eyes widen. I'd been waiting for the part where she lets me talk, but now that she's asking, I don't know what to say. "What do I think about what?"

"You've been given an amazing gift. And now you have the opportunity to help people with that gift."

I blink at this. A gift? If she knew anything about my life, she'd know that whatever this is is anything but a gift. "I just want this to go away," I say, perhaps too honest for my own good.

Commander Daugherty's smile falters for a moment, and I can see the gears turning in her head. And then she smiles again. "I understand," she says. "But this isn't something that'll work without you. Without you to harness her abilities, the Spectre in this Syncer is just your average Ethereal Entity. There's nothing special about her. There may be nothing special about *you*. But together, you can do a world of good for your country."

I frown. "I'm sorry, my country?" I say.

"That's right," she says, as though it's the most obvious thing in the world. "Don't you want to give back to the men and women who protect you from our enemies? Who keep America great?"

I snort. I try to hold back, to keep her from seeing the smile crossing my face for the briefest of moments, but it's too late. "I spent the first five years of my life trapped. And I don't mean figuratively. Literally trapped. Did you know unless you have a job, an interview, or assigned reason to leave Skid Row, you can't step foot outside the barriers without the androids turning you into Swiss cheese?"

Commander Daugherty says nothing. I can't tell if she didn't do her research on where I came from or if she genuinely didn't know the protocol around where I grew up—the cage they put us in.

"I could only leave after I was sent on runs or to a foster home. Even now, the only reason I can go in and out is because I'm still technically adopted by someone on the outside. And you think I plan on paying it forward to the country that condones my imprisonment?" I snort again, this time out of derision, not humor.

She meets my glare with her own. I'm not sure what she expected. How else does she expect a normal human being to react to a proposition like that?

"Okay," she says. "So that's how we're going to play it? Fine." She taps in the air and throws up a holographic image of my upper body. "I'll admit, I've been playing coy with what I know about you and your kind."

"And my kind being...?" I swear to God, if she says what I think she's about to say...

"Those with Spectral Companions."

Well, at least she dodged that bullet.

"One working theory revolves around what makes you and Hiro tick. Why are these Spectres linked to you like this? Can we replicate it? In Hiro's case, I know his connection, and in yours, I have a solid suspicion of why you're linked to your Spectre."

My eyes widen and my heart quickens. Against my will, I lean forward in my seat, and her smile deepens. Shit.

"It looks like I have your attention now," she says.

I groan, sitting back in my seat, my finger picking at the skin tag on my neck of its own accord. "So, why?" I say. "Why *do* I have a connection with her?"

Commander Daugherty's eyes land on where my finger flicks at the skin tag at my neck. I force my hand back down to my lap.

"No so fast," she says, eyes once again boring into my own. With a wave of her hand, the image of me floating in the air disappears. "It sounds like the two of us need to come to an agreement."

I look over at Vero, who glares at her mother almost as intensely as I do.

"What's the deal?"

"You agree to let us study you, and I tell you all about our theory as to why you have a connection with your Spectral Companion." She takes a moment, as if letting it sink into my brain. "So, Ms. Guerrera, do we have a deal?"

I grind my teeth behind closed lips. "Your mom's a real bitch, you know that?" I say.

But it doesn't matter. I already know the answer to her question.

TWO

"SHE'S RIGHT, MOM," Vero says, leaning against the console in the small control room. She doesn't even bother hiding the disdain in her voice. "You really are a bitch."

This only makes her mother laugh. "You don't get to where I am without making a few enemies."

Vero looks through the two-way glass into a large white room.

At one end, Luna leans against the wall, impatient and bored. "How long is this gonna take?" she says, her voice coming in through the speaker.

"Just be patient," Commander Daugherty says, pressing the red button in front of her. "They're running a few tests, and then you'll be reunited with your Spectral Companion."

"Yaaayy…." Luna says, her head hanging to the side, punctuating her dry tone.

"Don't you feel at least a little bad for her?" Vero says. "She wasn't in a good place when we found her. Her and her Spectral Companion were literally fighting to the death."

"You think I get my kicks this way?" Commander Daugherty says. "We've been hitting the same wall in our research for almost a decade now. Throughout the entirety of your tenure—and longer—we've learned nothing new. Congress doesn't fund programs with little to no progress. We continue hitting this wall, they shut us down, and there's no line of defense when the next World War breaks out."

"World War?"

"It's only a matter of time before the East has a breakthrough of their own. They already trounce us in terms of population, and they have triple the resources between the three of them. They'll be knocking on our doorstep before we know it, and that'll be the beginning of the end of Western Civilization." She pauses, as if to punctuate the point. She turns to stare Vero in the eyes. "But at least we were nice to this one girl. Am I right?"

Well, that's dramatic. Vero doesn't know how to respond. She's always known her mother to be Machiavellian, but it's one thing to know something and another to *see* it in action. Until just a few days ago, it's something Vero had been able to keep tucked away at the back of her mind.

"That doesn't make it right," she says, almost in a whisper.

Her mother frowns. "And here I was getting my hopes up thinking *you* had a breakthrough. That you were finally understanding how this game is played. It's okay, dear. You'll get there soon enough."

"Am I supposed to be doing something in here while I wait?" Luna says from inside the white room.

Commander Daugherty smiles. It's not a smile that has ever given Vero any comfort. "Ah, yes. While we wait for your Spectral Companion, there is something we need to do." She picks up a Syncer from a table nearby and pulls a tray that comes out from the barrier between them and Luna, places it in, and slams the door shut. With a few taps of the button, the drawer opens on Luna's side. "Please put on that Syncer."

Luna sidles over to the drawer and peeks in, picking it up as though it'll bite her. "This isn't mine," she says.

"Yes," Commander Daugherty says. "I'm aware of that. Just another quick experiment we're going to do before your Spectre returns. Please put it on."

With a suspicious glance at us through the two-way mirror, Luna obeys, strapping it to her left wrist.

"What's happening now?" Vero says, heat rising in her face, though she can't tell if it's from fear or anger. A little of both, she supposes.

Commander Daugherty ignores her daughter and presses the red button next to the microphone. "Okay, Luna. As I've already mentioned to you, you're not a run-of-the-mill Medium. You don't just use the Essences of freed Spectres. You capture *living* Spectres. Or, at the very least, you've captured at least one living Spectre. I wonder what you can do if you came across another one in the wild, *without* your Companion."

Luna shrugs. "I have no idea."

"Great," Commander Daugherty says. "Let's find out together." She lets go of the button next to the microphone.

"What do you mean by that?" Luna says, almost in unison with Vero.

Click. "We will be releasing a low-level Spectre in just a few moments. So please, hang tight until then." *Click.*

"What do you mean 'release a low-level Spectre?'" Vero says, her pulse quickening. "Do we keep Spectres here?"

"Oh, my dear sweet innocent flower." Commander Daugherty's tone could not have been more patronizing. "They do keep you kids in the dark, don't they?"

"How do we capture them?"

"We technically don't *capture* them. The process is fascinating. We think of our existence on two planes—life and afterlife. Once you die in one, you pass on to another. But, of course, the mere existence of Spectres sort of puts a hole in this whole thing, doesn't it? It's not so cut-and-dried. With enough trauma and unfinished business, they linger behind, sometimes forming into what we know as a Spectre. This should have been a hint to all of us." Commander Daugherty's tone is lively, almost girlish with excitement. Vero's never seen this side of her before. "Even when they are 'freed,' as we like to call it, they aren't freed. Not completely. There lingers a subatomic thread, linking its Essence to its freed spirit in the afterlife."

Commander Daugherty taps a few more buttons and a there's a hissing sound from inside the white room.

"Uh..." Luna says. "What's happening?"

Click. "Oh, don't worry. We just released the Spectre into your room. Now do your best to capture it like you've done with your Companion."

"You know I've only done it once, right?"

"Sometimes with science, we have to sink or swim."

"Are you crazy?" Vero says. Her voice is almost embarrassingly high-pitched. If she wasn't so mad at her, she'd be ashamed that her mother saw this weak side of her.

"Don't be so dramatic," Commander Daugherty says with a wave of her hand. "It's only a Level One Spectre. It'll take some time before it kills her, probably."

"Probably?"

"Maybe. Anyway, back to the 'how' behind everything. We've found that if we put an Essence under enough pressure, it may pull at that thread linking it to the afterlife, reviving a freed Spectre. And the best part is that they come pre-captured in our containers where their Essences are being held."

"So, this is what we're doing now?" Vero says. "We're bringing Spectres back to life? I thought we were trying to free them to help them pass on *and* keep people safe."

Commander Daugherty sighs, and Vero recognizes that disappointed tone. "Don't make me repeat what I said to Luna. This whole thing has gotten bigger than that. The most important thing we can do is learn as much as we can, because when our enemies do, who knows what they'll do to us?"

"Are you kidding me?" A scream comes from the other side of the two-way mirror. The once-invisible Spectre reveals itself to be a goblin-looking abomination, a tongue sticking out and its head cocked to the side. No, it's not just cocked to the side. Its head is halfway sliced off and just sort of hanging there. "You're just going to stand behind that mirror like a couple of damned psychopa—"

With a twist and a *thwip*, Luna and the Spectre both disappear, the room left empty and silent.

"Where'd they go?" Vero's hands smack down on the console in front of her as she yells.

"What are you, some novice?" Commander Daugherty says. "They're in the Spectre's Mirage, of course." She says it as though it's the most obvious thing in the world, and if Vero's being honest with herself, it is.

She's never seen anyone jump into a Mirage herself without going with them, but she should have at least been able to put two and two together. "So, what now?" Vero says. "We can't see them. How do we know if she needs help?"

"Two steps ahead of you," Commander Daugherty says, throwing up a screen with a few different real-time graphs. "That Syncer doesn't just act as a storage device, but it also tracks her vitals—even in Mirages. If she's in distress or near death, we'll know. And then you can go in and lend her a hand. You don't think I brought you in here just because you're my daughter, did you? I needed someone who's ready to act and act fast."

Vero bites her lip, a well of anxiety rising from her stomach and into the back of her throat. "Why me, though?" she says, though the potential answer turned her stomach in on itself. "You could have had any other Medium. You could have had Jace. An adult. Is it just because I'm your daughter?"

Somehow, Commander Daugherty's face darkens.

"I don't think I need to tell you that trust is a hard commodity to come by. It's why I never married your father, even after all these years. I don't trust anyone. Not even you. But I trust adults far less than I do kids. Every single one of them has their own morals, preconceived notions, and agendas."

"You've just described people."

"And I'll be damned if I let any single one of them interfere with this program. You may have your own problems and thoughts—don't think I haven't noticed you tackling your own inner demons recently. We all do. *I* have. But it was your last mission where you caught my eye.

"You stood up to me, proving that you'd developed a backbone, and then told me about this girl. This tool. This person who could be the savior of this great nation. It proved to me you're willing to stand up to authority when needed, but that you also understand and respect our greater mission. I knew it was time to bring you into the fold more, because, apart from myself, there's no one on Earth I'd rather trust more than you."

Vero's stomach turns in on itself again and again, emotions turning from anger to confusion to guilt, and then, of all emotions, flattery. She can't help but smile.

Vero swallows a click in her throat, overcome with emotion, but desperate not to show it. After several long seconds stretch between them, she says the last thing in the world she thought she'd say to her mom.

"Thank you."

IT DOESN'T TAKE LONG for me to get my bearings within the Mirage. In fact, compared to most, what I see here is downright quaint. The house is big and beautiful. Like how I imagine those enormous mansions in England, the ones that require an impractically large staff to be kept functioning. So large that it's easy for kids to get lost in, to find secret passages and go on adventures.

It reminds me of this old movie, *The Secret Garden*. I know it was a book first, but I never read it. But the movie? The movie was the perfect way for me to escape. I spent way too many hours scouring the streets of Skid Row, pretending they were the passages within Misselthwaite Manor. It's these memories that run through my mind as I make my way through this house.

"What was this person's life?" I can't help but say aloud. How did they live that would warrant such an elaborate and ornate Mirage? And why did the Spectre take the form of such a creepy monster?

I push open a swinging door and enter a dining room. At its center sits a wooden table with enough seats to fit ten people. Light floods in through the tall windows, illuminating thousands of dust particles floating the air.

"Ready or not, here I come!" a little girl's voice cries out from the room on the other side of one of the two doors. Before I can so much as breathe, a girl runs into the room, breath shallow and excited. Any excitement she has is gone the instant she lays eyes on me. "What the...you were supposed to hide!"

"I...forgot?" I answer without realizing. I know my Medium skills aren't as attuned without Estrella's help, but nothing about this girl gives me Spectre vibes. So, what is she, a Spirit? Something else?

The girl pouts her lips at me and grabs me by the hand, pulling me back through the swinging door she came from, which leads into the main entrance of the home. The "lobby" of this mansion is large and empty, its wooden floor creaking with every step we take, the smell of damp earth filling the air.

"Okay," she says, frustrated. "We have to do this again. But it's okay. Just make sure you do it right this time."

"Do it right?"

"I'm not supposed to find you so fast," she says. "So you have to hide good. Real good." She turns around to press her face against the wall before spinning around again. "But not *too* good. I need to find you, remember? If I can't find you, it's not any fun. And we're supposed to have fun. Got it?"

"Right," I say. "I'll try to keep that in mind."

The girl turns back around, pressing her eyes against the back of her forearm. "Now I'm gonna count to a hundred, okay? Make sure you run and hide this time. Because last time you didn't do it, and it was really sad."

I don't bother trying to suppress the laugh that escapes my lips. "Okay, then."

"One. Two. Three." She doesn't even give me any time before she dives back into the count.

As her counting continues, I try to get a read on her. Even though I don't think she's the Spectre, I try to understand why she's here. Why is this little girl in this Mirage? What does she represent, and who is she to the actual Spectre? More importantly, how does she reflect the state of mind of the Spectre?

I look down at my Syncer, swiping through a few menus until I come across the Spectre menu. The girl had grabbed my hand, and if she was the Spectre, her information should now be accessible.

"Dammit," I whisper when nothing pops up.

"Oooooh!" the girl says, interrupting her own count and looking back at me. "you said a bad word!"

"No I..." Oh, wait. I guess I did. "Sorry."

A loud pounding echoes down the staircase from a room above, a heavy fist splintering a door with every fall. "Dammit, Tawny, you better let me in, ya hear?" a man's voice booms, almost as loudly as the pounding itself.

"What was..." I turn my head to look up the stairs, but a pair of soft hands pull my head back down.

"Shhh...that's okay," the girl says. "That's just Daddy. Yeah, he shouldn't swear either, because it's a sin, but it's okay, because he's Daddy."

The pounding continues. "Tawny, I'm sorry, Baby Girl. Please, just let me in."

The girl's soft hands are guiding me again, away from the stairs and into another room. "Let's go," she says, her tone frantic, at odds with the confidence she's shown up 'til now.

The door we enter *doesn't* lead into another room, but into the middle of a forest. I blink. No, wait, it's not a forest. My entire surroundings are so covered in vegetation that makes it *feel* like a forest. She pulls me into a thick hedge, and we emerge on the other side to a trickling creek, surrounded by a kaleidoscope of flowers. It's like something you'd see in a documentary, not in actual real life.

The girl probably notices my gaping mouth, because she lets out the smallest chuckle. Holding up a finger to her lips, she shushes me. "Don't tell anyone. This is my most secret of secret places. It's where I can go that no one can find me."

"Tawny!" the man's voice calls out, almost as if to taunt her last statement, though he's not as close as he was last time. It's more distant, as though he could be miles away.

This doesn't stop the girl from flinching. She's quick on the recovery, and before I can even comment, she's clutching my hand with both of hers, dragging me through the garden and through another hedge on the other side of the creek.

When we emerge, we're no longer out in the sunlight but in the middle of a dank, dark cavern, illuminated only by green geodes set in the walls.

She continues to pull me down the dark tunnel, going so fast that it's a miracle I don't trip over her feet.

"Tawny!" the voice grows louder, echoing through the tunnel and reverberating off the walls, somehow feeling closer with each echo. How is that even possible?

Oh, right. Mirage.

The cavern opens up, and we emerge into a large chamber that splits off into at least seventeen different directions. Without missing a beat, the girl pulls me toward an opening to the right.

"Where are we going?" I ask.

"Away," she says.

"Away from your dad?"

But without another word, she pulls me into a corner—the only one that isn't lit up by the luminescent rocks.

"Shh!" How loud she shushes me seems at odds with her goal.

We both crouch into the corner and a second later, we're quiet, the only sounds her shallow breaths. For someone who's trying to hide, she isn't that quiet.

"Tawny!" the voice booms from a distance, sounding less and less human with each scream.

Is that still her father? "Who is that?" I say.

"Shh!" Again, her shush is way louder than my voice.

The entire cavern shakes and booms, the sound of a monster's footsteps.

"It's him," she says. "It's the Goblin King."

As if on cue, I feel an uneasiness in my stomach, and the hairs on the back of my neck stand up. Before I even see his ugly face, I know what he'll look like—like that abomination I saw back in the lab.

It's the master of this domain. The Spectre.

THREE

I SUCK in a quiet breath of air as the Goblin King comes into view. He's almost as horrifying as he was when I saw him in the real world. Except, he doesn't have his head half-hanging off his neck. I guess I should be relieved by that, but the rest of him is still terrifying enough to make up the difference.

The beast is at least eight feet tall, his head almost skirting the ceiling. It's as though this cavern was created to fit his exact height. Of course, this *is* his Mirage.

He stops a few feet away from us, sniffing the air, and I hold my breath. I was given one instruction from the mean, psychotic commander back in the real world—to capture this thing. I wasn't so confident about it then, but I'm even *less* confident about it now that I'm facing this ridiculous monstrosity in front of me. Not only do I not have the same abilities with Estrella nowhere near me, but I'm only just realizing that I've never faced another Spectre without them before.

I swallow a click in my throat and immediately regret it when the Goblin King looks in our direction. Both me and the little girl slink even further into the darkness. He stares for several long seconds before turning and walking past us, down the corridor.

"He can't see very well," the girl whispers in my ear.

"Who is he?" I ask.

"He's the Goblin King," she repeats, as if that answers my question.

"THE GOBLIN KING?" Vero asks as she flips through a file in the air.

"He's not a real goblin, dear," Commander Daugherty says.

Vero glares at her mother from behind narrowed eyes. "But *why* is he called the Goblin King?"

Commander Daugherty flips open her netscreen. "So, this one's interesting. The Spectre, Dewayne Brown, was an alcoholic and serial abuser. One day, back in the late 2030s, he almost beat his own wife to death. But his little girl, Tawny, killed him. Sliced the bastard right through the neck."

"I'm sorry?"

"Yeah, I know," Commander Daugherty's tone betrays the severity of the comment. "Most would have settled for stabbing him through the back, but she went straight for the neck, cutting most of the way through."

"Oh, my God!"

"Don't be so soft, Agent Daugherty."

Vero sits up straighter and clears her throat, flicking through the files. "So why the Goblin King? And why the constant shift in settings in his Mirage?"

"His case was a big deal when it happened. Made the news, hit the feeds, and there've even been a few documentaries about it.

"Tawny Brown is still alive, and has spoken about it at length. During his episodes, she'd check out altogether. Disappeared into her books. Turned every aspect of her life into a fantasy, just to cope. She called him the Goblin King—even wrote it down in her online diary. In his world, he is the Goblin King, and his daughter is forever on the run."

Something isn't quite adding up. "Why would he craft a world built around his daughter's fear?" Vero asks.

Commander Daugherty shrugs. "You're asking me to get into the mind of an abuser. How would I know? Maybe he feels bad about the whole thing and is looking to make amends. Or maybe he gets his kicks chasing his daughter around, instilling her with the fear of God."

"So, what would you do?" Vero almost asks her mother as much, but restrains herself. Instead, she stands, hoping her mother doesn't notice the awkward silence falling between the two of them. She's almost relieved when an alarm goes off.

"Oh, there she goes," Commander Daugherty says.

"There she goes what?" Vero says. "What does that mean?"

"She's on the run, in combat, or just flat-out scared. There are no issues with her other vitals, so I'd assume either running or scared."

"She won't last long in a fight without her Spectral Companion."

"Which is why you should be on high alert. We'll know pretty quickly if she succeeds or not."

Vero doesn't waste another second. She's out the door, through the giant chamber adjacent to them, and into the white room where Luna disappeared.

"YOU SAID A BAD WORD AGAIN," Tawny says as we run through a set of ancient ruins, turning around the corner to hide behind what I'm imagining is an ancient tomb. Her tone is matter of fact, and the girl doesn't seem bothered by the fact that the Goblin King is right on our heels.

"Yeah, I did. So what?"

"And it was the F word."

"Not now, Kid!"

I hadn't had the guts to attack the beast outright, but you can't blame me for that. Right now, I have little to no idea what emotion I need to resonate with. The creature may be big, but he's fast—though, not Spectre fast. If this was any other Mirage, we would have been caught ages ago. What, is he having fun chasing us? I can't get a read on the freakin' thing.

"Tawny!" it calls out for the millionth time. "Where are you, Baby Girl?"

"This is stupid," I say aloud again. "He knows where we are. He's right behind us!"

"Shhh!" Tawny puts her finger to her mouth again. "You can't ruin the game."

"Ruin the game?"

"SO, IT'S A GAME THEY PLAYED?" This time, Commander Daugherty asks the question.

"How much of this report did you read?" Vero asks, flipping through the file. She sits cross-legged on the floor, back against the wall in the white room. The smallest of Bullethole portals is next to her, and she's ready to jump into the Mirage at a moment's notice. But in the meantime, she wants to learn more about the Spectre.

"I only read what was necessary."

"I thought your story about her calling him the Goblin King in secret didn't quite match up. If she kept it to herself, then how would he create an entire Mirage about it?

"You're saying it's not something she wrote in her diary, then?"

"It was in her diary, and she called him that during his episodes, but it's also something she called him when they played a game," Vero says. "He'd chase her around as the Goblin King, and she'd go off hiding. But as you said, it wasn't *just* a game to her, but a representation of her fears of him. At least, that's what Tawny Brown wrote in her memoir. Huh."

"What're you thinking?" Commander Daugherty's voice rings out from the speakers.

"Something tells me Dewayne Brown didn't know his daughter was afraid of him until the very end. Maybe this Mirage is a weird tribute to their relationship, but also a way for him to chase his daughter forever. Both reliving a fond memory and fulfilling a weird form of revenge."

"I DON'T THINK I understand this game," I whisper to Tawny from behind a white tree atop a cliffside city.

"Shhh!" the girl shushes me again, and if I'm being honest, it's kinda pissing me off.

"But he can *see* us," I point to the giant goblin, who peeks from behind a giant brick wall, his lower body visible.

"That's the game."

"What is this *game*?"

Again, Tawny pouts at me, though this time, her brows are furrowed. "You're ruining the game."

"She's ruining the game!" the Goblin King calls out from the distance. The scene would have been funny if his voice didn't sound so gravelly and painful.

"I don't understand you two at all," I say, still not bothering to lower my voice. "But I'm through playing games." I step out from behind the tree. I don't have the faintest idea what emotion to sync with for this Spectre, but this whole thing is running us in circles.

"Come back," Tawny whisper yells out at me, as though still trying to keep her presence secret from the Goblin King.

I ignore her, remembering that this girl is still very much a part of the Mirage, not some separate human entity. Listening to her will probably result in me falling deeper and deeper into whatever all this is. "Let's go, big guy," I say. "You and me."

The ground shakes as he steps out from behind the giant wall. Dude is only eight feet tall. Why is the ground shaking? I don't know what to take from his expression. It's a mix of anger, confusion, and satisfaction. I think. But which emotion can I latch on to? After the hours I've spent running through this Mirage, I haven't touched a single thing that's triggered a memory. I'm flying blind here, but I don't care. "Come and get me!" I pound on my chest and then run at him.

After spending so much time running at the speed of sound, it's hard not to feel let down by how much effort I'm putting into my sprint, and how long it's taking me to reach him.

With a vile smirk, he bounds toward me with the speed of a gorilla, closing the distance between us.

I bunch my hand into a fist, timing my run. I need to make sure I connect. If I do, maybe it'll trigger a memory. Maybe I'll be able to get a peek behind those dull, thick eyelids of his.

With a swing, I connect. A pain shoots up my arm, and my vision goes white.

I WAKE to a blinding white light. A face comes into a focus above me. I blink a few times, only to recognize that face as Vero's. Her face is a mix of confusion and concern.

"Are you with me?" she says.

"With you where?" I say before I can stop myself. It's not a response that would have inspired any confidence in me if I were in her shoes. "Wait, are we in the Mirage?"

Vero shakes her head.

"She wisely pulled you out," Commander Daugherty says, her voice circling from all sides.

I try to sit up, but Vero places her gloved hand on my chest, gently pinning me to the ground. "Not yet," she says, her brows furrowed in concern. "Stay still. Your body is still in shock."

"From what?" I say, trying to look down at the rest of my body, but she clutches the bottom of my chin, keeping me from doing so. "What's going on?"

"Trust me, you don't wanna see."

I feel panic rising inside me. "See what?"

"Your arm's been shattered," Commander Daugherty says. "Right now, it looks more like a deflated tube than an arm."

Vero rolls her eyes. "Mom!"

"She was going to find out eventually. At least now she'll know what's happening when she can't move it."

As if to prove them wrong, I try to move my arm. But no, nothing. Not so much as a phantom pain.

"It's okay," Vero says. "We used a numbing agent on it, so you won't be able to feel it."

"And your Spectral Companion is still on the way," Commander Daugherty says.

"Which I still think is a dumb idea," Vero says. "We should call the medical team."

"Dumb how?" Commander Daugherty says. "Dumb to work toward a solution that results in instantaneous healing or settle for the slow method?"

My mind swims as it catches up with my current situation. I'm on the ground, my arm is a blubbery mess, and I can't so much as move a muscle in it. How did I end up like this again?

"If nothing else, we can learn something from this," Commander Daugherty says, her voice calm.

"I haven't learned anything!" I say.

"Yes, you have. You've learned that you are either incapable of capturing other Spectres that aren't your own, or you're doing something wrong."

"Mom!" Vero says. "Now's not the time—"

"That's where you're wrong, *Agent Daugherty*," she emphasizes her daughter's name with a hiss. "We are in the process of a potential breakthrough. This is exactly the time to debrief on what we know. This will only serve Ms. Guerrera well as we move on to the next phase."

"Which is what?" I say.

There's a click in the room—a sound I recognize. I turn my head to see a drawer pop out from under the two-way mirror. Vero stands up and steps past me, taking care to step around me and not over me, though over me would have been quicker. She exhales as she looks inside the drawer.

"Really?" she says.

"I thought you wanted her to heal as quickly as possible," Commander Daugherty says.

Vero doesn't respond, instead turning to reveal my Syncer, its blue gem pulsing with Estrella's presence.

"She's right," I say. My mind feels like mud, but I'm connecting the dots. I'm connecting them *slowly*, but connecting all the same.

Back when Jace had tossed me around my Mirage, my wounds were quick to heal as soon as I captured Estrella again. I lift my left arm with the Syncer on it. "Can you switch this out with mine?" I say.

I can tell Vero still doesn't understand, but she's quick on the uptake, and is unlatching the empty Syncer moments later. As she slides on Estrella's Syncer, I spare a glance at my other arm. The visual is worse than I'd feared. A part of me had expected to see bones jutting out at hard angles, but my mind wasn't prepared to see my arm resting, looking like rubber, laying almost flat on the floor. Commander Daugherty hadn't been exaggerating in her initial description.

"Oh, Jesus," I say with a breath. I feel tears well up in my eyes. Why tears? I'm not even sad—just freaked out. My breath quickens, and the panic sets in. Please, not now. Not now.

But my chest heaves up and down, and the tears free themselves from the confines of my eyes. God, I wanna make it stop. Please, just make it stop.

There's a click. I can tell the Syncer has been placed, but I feel no different. My arm is still numb, my mind rattled.

"Luna," I hear Vero say, but my mind can't focus. "Luna, look at me."

Tears are blurring my vision, but I still settle my gaze on Vero's face. It's placid and strong.

"Breathe," she says. "Follow my breath." She places my free hand on her chest. I feel her heart beat. It's beating as fast as mine, but her chest expands and contracts slowly. I swallow and try to follow her breath. It's difficult at first, but after what feels like several minutes, I can feel my heart slow, and my breathing even out.

For the first time since I can remember, I'm relaxed, my body feeling like it's on some sort of drug.

"Okay, I'm going to need you to stand," she says. "We need to go back into the Mirage, but I need you to stand and be ready in case the Goblin King is still there."

"You know about the Goblin King?" I say, my mind still slow.

She chuckles. "Yes, I know about the Goblin King. Now I need you to focus. Are you okay to stand?"

"His game is really stupid," I say. But I nod, blinking away the last remnants of tears. She grabs my right hand and cradles my back with her other free hand. With a quick movement, I'm on my feet. I take another deep breath and swallow. My right arm feels heavy. It's like all of my shattered bones have piled up into my hand and are weighing it down like a giant mallet. I push the image from my head, refusing to look at it, and breathe again.

"Are you ready?" she says. "I'm about to take us back."

"Do it," I say in a shaky voice.

A breeze rushes past me, and I'm back in the lush garden from before. The air is crisp, and the sun bright, cutting through the branches and leaves.

And then it starts.

A large series of cracks run up my arm, starting from my hand all the way to my shoulder. It's both painful and liberating and I can't help but scream as bones crunch into place. Whatever numbing agent they used rushes from my system in the blink of an eye, allowing me to feel every crack and pop. Though as excruciating as it feels, it's gone in a few quick seconds, and normal feeling returns to my hand.

I hold up my hand in front of me, clenching and unclenching. I swear to God I'll never take this limb—or any limb—for granted ever again.

"It worked," Vero says. She looks over at me, mouth agape.

"You can at least pretend you thought it was going to work," I say, my voice still shaky and uneven. I can't blame her. Last time when we were in Estrella's Mirage, I didn't have my abilities. I don't know what's changed. Maybe it had to do with her power over the Mirage. Either way, I'm grateful for the use of my hand again.

Vero smiles back at me, but doesn't say anything, an immense relief painted across her face.

"Shhh!" a girlish voice calls out from behind a bush of purple flowers. "Quiet! You're ruining the game!"

"Oh, my God, Tawny," I say, exhausted. "I've had enough of you and your fucking game."

The girl's mouth hangs open, and she gasps. "Oooh! You said—"

"Yes, I said a bad word. So sue me."

"You're ruining the game," I hear another voice from the opposite side, this one deeper, still terrifying. Behind a tree, I see a pair of yellow eyes peek out—though the rest of his body peeks out as well from both sides of the tree. The dude isn't svelte.

"Yes, I know," I say. "It's what I do." I tap at my Syncer, and with a burst of blue light, Estrella emerges. She's in the form of a large head dozens of feet away and is about as large as the Goblin King. "Estrella." I'm stern and cautious when I speak.

She spins around, eyes narrowed. "You!"

"I know you're mad at me," I say. "But we're in trouble right now. I need you to help."

Without so much as a warning, the giant head bounds straight toward me.

FOUR

"ARE YOU SERIOUS RIGHT NOW?" I say as I wind up to punch Estrella's big stupid head. My blow plows into her chin, the impact running up my arm—though not as painfully as before, when the Goblin King decimated my arm. She flies off and to the side, through the hedges and exploding into a tree. "I did *not* need this part of my plan to go wrong!" I can't help but yell. It's impossible for me to catch a break.

Though as I stare back at the landscape around us, which is peppered with chunks of mud and flora from our impact, I can't help but notice one big development—that I didn't have a flashback when I hit Estrella.

Huh.

I have little time to think though, because the Goblin King is only two steps from beating in my face. Shit, I'd only just gotten back and I'm already—

I see her before I hear it, the impact of metal on rock, and before I can blink, the monster flies backward, soaring hundreds of feet away, his body splitting through trees along the way. Vero's golden locks spin as she whips around to face me.

"Are you good to fight?" she says.

"I...yeah. I think." My body may be up to speed, but my head still has a lot of catching up to do.

"Good, because now that you're back to normal, Commander Daugherty wants you to try to capture him again." Her expression is almost apologetic, but I can tell she doesn't want me to fight her on this one.

I nod back. Commander Daugherty isn't the only one who's curious about this. Ever since I looked into the eyes of Alan Arroyo's Spectre, I also wondered if there was a better way. Despite what Hiro had told me, was there an alternative to just "freeing" every Spectre we come across? "Fine," I say, "but I need to have a word with my sister."

"I'll hold off this guy in the meantime," Vero says, cracking her knuckles. "He's only Level One, so it should be a piece of cake." And with that, she's off, knocking the goblin back another few hundred feet. Hopefully, she doesn't kill him before I can patch things up with...

"Estrella!" I yell out. "So, where did we leave things out in the desert?" I leap over to her fallen Spectral head of a body. She looks deflated and defeated, but I'm still mad. "Right, you said I was trying to steal your life."

"Wrong," she says. "I was saying you stole *my* life."

"Okay," I say. "I stole your life. But right now, we're dealing with another Spectre that will kill me—kill *us*—if you don't help."

Estrella scoffs, face turning into the ground, like she's trying to hide from my gaze.

"If I die, you'll *never* be able to steal my body back."

This gets her attention. She looks back up at me and after several long seconds, she tilts herself back up, her head floating up a foot from the ground. A low growl emanates from her, like how I imagine a grizzly bear sounds.

"Do we have a—" My vision goes white again and a pain shoots down my back as I break through ground, clumps of dirt and rock exploding around me. Dust settles, and when it clears, I find myself in a giant cavern, larger than any other cavern I've been through in this Mirage. I can't believe Estrella sucker punched me.

"You guys are *so* loud," a girlish voice calls out from the darkness. Tawny's tone is no longer condescending, but upset and screeching. "You're ruining our game!"

"Oh, my God!" I yell in no direction in particular. I can't quite tell where that little shit is calling me out from, but she's getting on my last nerve. "Shut up about your stupid game! None of this is a game!"

The dust in front of me wisps into a spiral, and from it, Estrella emerges, mouth open, Spectral brows furrowed in anger. I jump to the side, just fast enough to feel her brush past me and into a cavern wall.

I launch off the ground and run straight into the elephant-sized hole in the wall. I emerge out into an open space. The sky is a bright blue, and the leaves around me an autumn orange and yellow.

Estrella comes to a halt, spinning around to face me.

"I don't want to do this all day," I say. "Can't you just listen to me for once?"

"Listen to you?" she says. "You think I should just listen to you? I've had to listen to you for my entire life. Imagine what it'd feel like to be locked in a cage every single day. You could see and hear everything. But you couldn't move, you couldn't speak, you couldn't do anything but watch as every decision is made for you."

"What you're describing is *my* life!" I yell. "Imagine making decisions that never matter, because something is always there to snatch it away from me!"

Estrella growls and we collide head on, a loud explosion berating my ears as we do. I punch her and she retaliates with a full body blow. I reciprocate with a half-assed super-powered kick. And back and forth we go, neither of us making much headway as we continue to fight like children. We're one step away from pulling at each other's hair and leaving nail marks along each other's arms.

And then I tackle her, knocking her farther and farther back until we… fall off the edge?

The ground is now thousands of feet below us, and I spin back and glance above from where we fell to see the bottom of what looks like an island floating the sky. This place has a freakin' sky island, too?

But whatever shock I have Estrella doesn't share. She bites down on me, trying to rip my arm apart. Ironically, were it not for the shield that protects me from her abilities, she would have succeeded.

I smack the side of her face and kick away from her, launching myself upward and away from her as the two of us crash into the hard ground.

The wind is knocked from my chest, and while my vision doesn't go white this time, the surrounding and ascending clumps of land and dirt block my vision. "This is a stupid fight!" I say. I may be reliant on her abilities to survive, but it's clear that her own strength is just as useless against me as mine is against her.

"You're right." I hear Estrella's voice cut through the dust. "But I don't care."

The wind is once again catapulted from my lungs, and I'm thrust through the ground and up into the air.

"You stupid…" I'm through wasting time with Estrella, and as I see her big dumb-looking head flying up to meet me, I give my Syncer a few quick taps. The Syncer beeps, and with an inelegant squeal, Estrella is sucked in. With a click, the gem embedded within the device glows a faint blue.

My feet land softly onto the dirt ground, despite the amazing height from which I'd just fallen—a perk of the abilities from Estrella. I try my best not to feel bad that I'd just captured her against her will. It's easy to rationalize it, given that she's still out to kill me. I only regret that I don't know how to take her out myself. Besides, it's not like I *need* her. I'm pretty freakin' certain that she's pissed at me, and if I just sync with that emotion, along with whatever emotion this mysterious goblin is feeling, I can't be too far off from a solid capture attempt.

If capturing another Spectre is even possible.

I'm shaken from my thoughts by an explosion, and the Goblin King's bulbous body emerges from an equally-bulbous plant the size of a house. I swat at him and he bounces off my hand like a bouncy-ball, careening headfirst into the mouth of a giant flytrap-looking monstrosity, which clamps down on him.

Wait, can a Spectre be killed—sorry, "freed"—by its own Mirage? My question is answered when the flytrap explodes into a thousand slimy pieces, covering my entire body in a green goo.

"Did the two of you make up?" Vero says as she lands next to me, giant katana slung over her shoulder.

I wipe the goo from my mouth and eyes. "Not quite," I say. "Or at all."

Vero plants her feet on the ground and looks around. "Where is she?"

I hold up my arm and point to the gem. "I'm sorry, but I have no idea how I'm supposed to control her."

Vero's shoulders slump, and I can't help but feel a lump grow in my stomach. Like I've failed her. "Can you capture another Spectre without her?"

"I don't even know if I can capture another Spectre *at all*," I say, unable to hide the irritation.

"Right, right. Sorry," Vero says as she scratches the back of her head sheepishly. It's the ditzier side of her I first met, back when she introduced herself as the person who was going to kill me.

That feels like a lifetime ago. How long's it been? A week-plus? I don't know anymore. I don't even know what day of the week it is. And here she is, fighting alongside me against this stupid Goblin King. "Wait," I say. "Earlier, you said you knew he was the Goblin King."

"Yeah."

"That means you know a bit about this guy, right?"

"Right?" Then Vero's eyes widen. "Right! Core emotion! I remember you saying that before. Core emotion? Is that what you're trying to get at? I don't even know what that means, but it sounds promising."

The Goblin King lets out a loud roar, his scream blowing off more of the green goo that covers my body, like I'm in some old cartoon.

Without another word, Vero tackles the monster, throwing him back hundreds of feet.

Light footsteps pad up beside me. The hair on my neck bristles, annoyed at the mere presence of this kid. "Don't even say it, Tawny," I say. "I promise you I can kill a fake little girl."

She opens her mouth to speak, but stays silent.

"That's better," I say. Another explosion, and Vero's next to me again. "You're not even breaking a sweat."

"It's a low level. I just need to get him out of the way while we figure out..." Her gaze falls on Tawny. "Is this Tawny Brown?"

"What's it to you?" the girl says in response, her voice filled to the brim with an unnecessary sass that would have gotten me smacked in the face at her age.

"Yes, it's her." I speak quickly to cut through any small talk the two may engage in. "What do you know about her?"

"Oh, you wouldn't know, would you?" she says.

The story is heartbreaking. A father who beat a young girl's mother until near death, only to be decapitated by his own daughter. By the time Vero's story is done, Tawny Brown's mouth is agape.

And then, over the course of a few seconds, the light goes out and the entire Mirage around us almost seems to dip, and I realize the reality of what's just happened.

"He didn't know," I say. "Dewayne Brown didn't know. Until just now."

"You're lying!" The Goblin King emerges from the darkness, swinging a makeshift club in his hand made from a small tree.

Vero dodges the attack with little effort and hits him with the back of her sword, sending him to the ground. "It's true, you abusive asshole."

The Goblin King vomits green bile onto the floor in front of him, and it glows, lighting up the darkness around us. "She...she loves me."

"Of course she loved you," Vero says. "You were her father. But that doesn't mean she was unwilling to protect herself when you...just look around. Where do you think you are?"

He does as she says, and the darkness disappears, illuminating the ever-changing fantastical landscape, made to please this imaginary version of his daughter.

And then, the world evaporates, and even Tawny Brown, mouth still hanging open, dissolves into nothingness. The only thing left behind is a dull gray room, so uniform that I can't even distinguish the ground from the open air.

A hundred and fifty feet away, the Goblin King sits, hefty but spread across the floor, chest heaving in and out. Slowly, steadily, sadly. His eyes are wide, and as he sits, his very body dissolves away, leaving behind a husk. No, not a husk. Left behind on the floor is a man, eyes still wide, clothing baggy, dreadlocks unkempt and frayed, and face vacant.

I don't know what this Spectre has gone through or what his core emotion was prior to this moment, but I sure as hell know what it is now.

I take care to sync with Estrella first. That's easy enough. If I were her, I'd be pissed. My wrist vibrates.

Spectral Companion Sync: 100%

I smile to myself. Even when she's in her confines and against her will, I can sync with her. She wouldn't like that, but that somehow makes the moment that much sweeter.

It doesn't take much for me to sync with the poor soul sitting in front of me. I'm an old hand at feeling betrayed. It may as well be my middle name.

My Syncer vibrates again.

Spectral Sync: 100%

I walk up to the braindead husk of a Spectre in front of me. The husk of a person who just had their entire world turn upside down. He'd created this entire Mirage to relive some of his fondest memories. It was an homage to his daughter who he played with. He created an entire world where he could relive those memories again and again. Forever.

Spectral Sync: 80%

"What the hell?" I say.

"What's wrong?" Vero asks.

I don't answer, but I know what had happened. His core emotion had shifted. Betrayal is now the farthest thing from his mind, replaced by what I imagine is self-loathing, the desire of self-harm.

"I...I don't want to capture him," I say.

"What?" Vero says.

"I can't," I say. "I mean, I don't even know if I can. But this isn't the time to try. He wants to be freed. He needs to be freed."

Vero bites her lip. I can feel her glare, but I can somehow feel it soften as the seconds tick by. "We can tell her we failed," she says. She cocks her katana to the side. "I don't want her to...I'll tell her it was my call. That I had to free him."

Without another word, she darts forward and cuts straight through the hapless Spectre. He doesn't even let out a scream as it slices through his neck. His face is almost content, relieved.

A brief second passes before the world explodes into flashing bright red and white lights. The Mirage is gone. We're back in the plain room at the DOSD headquarters.

An alarm blares in my ears.

"What's happening?" I say, though my voice is lost in the chaos.

Vero holds up a hand and puts a finger to her ear. The seconds stretch by as she stands in silence, and then she looks over to me. "We're under attack."

To Be Continued...

SPECTRAL | EPISODE 10

A DIFFERENT LOADED VAN...

HIRO WIPES away the beads of sweat that form on his forehead. His breath is steamy, even in the warm California air. It's yet another sign of his condition. A reminder that his time is ending, unless he does something quickly.

But he *is* doing something. That's why he's here in the first place, double-parked in a no-parking zone outside the Downtown Los Angeles Library and across the street from X Tower. He doesn't have much longer to wait, but that doesn't stop the goosebumps from prickling along his skin, his hair from standing on end. It's either his anxiety or impending death. Either way, he prays to God he doesn't believe in that some overzealous cop doesn't flash his lights and start asking questions. The last thing he wants is to kill someone else.

The faint sound of flapping catches his ear, and he turns to face Kuro in the back. The crow rests on his perch, wings outstretched, beak open.

"Do you feel bad about using the girl?" Kuro says. Well, he doesn't *say* it, as he's long lost his ability to speak. All anyone apart from Hiro can hear are the annoyed squawks of a dumb bird. Hiro misses the sound of Kuro's voice, but he's grateful he can at least understand him.

"Why would I feel bad?" Hiro sends to the crow. *"She's the one who used us."*

"As if you wouldn't have done the same thing in her shoes."

"They would have gotten her one way or another," Hiro insists, punctuating his comment with a glare.

"Maybe," Kuro sends, *"but you didn't need to be the one to send her directly into the hornet's nest."*

Another stab of guilt assaults Hiro's stomach. The opportunity was there. When he realized she wasn't going to follow through on their deal, tipping off the DOSD of her whereabouts was the only thing he could think of. *"It's not like they're gonna kill her. They can give her more answers than I ever could."*

"And you still think this is the best approach we *should be taking?"*

Hiro bites down on one of his knuckles. He knows what Kuro is getting at. He wants to know whether they should act at all. *"I've been ignoring the DOSD for too long,"* Hiro says, dodging the question.

"Out of pure fear. And it's only because of fear that you're here in the first place."

"It's hard not to have a bit of fear when you can feel your life slipping away from you," Hiro says. The outburst causes him to descend into a coughing fit, even though he wasn't even speaking aloud. This is another thing that's been happening too often over the past twenty-four hours. His health has been declining for years, but the issues have gotten worse for the past month. Knees going out, kidney issues, heart palpitations. Mother Nature is trying to make up for lost time.

"Have you forgotten you're speaking to a Ghost?" Kuro sends.

"You had it easy," Hiro says.

"I think you're first person in history to refer to death in an atomic explosion as 'easy.'"

"You were killed quickly."

"Was I?"

"You were barely conscious when I showed up," Hiro says. *"I'm saying you didn't have to sit by and feel it drain away."*

"What do you know about how I felt in my last moments?" Kuro says. *"Besides, what's more human than feeling the slow embrace of death close in around you? You're not special, Hiro. You're human. You've always been human."*

Kuro lets out another squawk. Hiro can tell it was involuntary—like a nervous tick that's increased in frequency at about the same rate as Hiro's deterioration. Hiro can sense it. Kuro's hold as a Spectre on this plane of existence is slipping away, too, and in those moments, the crow, whose form he takes, is reclaiming control.

Hiro doesn't mention this to Kuro. They both let the unspoken thought pass between them. Kuro's already died once, and this entire process is like dying all over again, Hiro's sure.

Thankfully, a soft beep interrupts any need to continue the conversation. "She's in," Hiro says aloud.

"You sure you wanna do this?"

Hiro opens the door, leaving it open for Kuro, who flies out without instruction. Hiro ignores the cries of surprise from a random passerby about the bird with the top hat. He doesn't even bother turning off the hazard lights or turning off the vehicle. It doesn't matter what happens to the van. He won't be coming back when they're done. He won't need to come back here. If the night goes his way, he'll run home.

Hiro pulls up his phone and wipes away another bead of sweat from his forehead as he limps down the sidewalk and up to the main building, only vaguely regretting his decision to leave his cane behind. No time for a stupid stick when you have a plan in motion. Besides, the cane would only draw attention.

"Well, it looks like your plan is working." Kuro almost seems disappointed.

"The girl is like me. I knew she'd draw their interest."

Hiro also knew that if they took Luna into their HQ, her Syncer's safety would be guaranteed. Before he'd even met her, Hiro realized the interest Luna would hold with the DOSD. So he planted a special microscopic chip into the device. The whole thing cost him a pretty penny, not that money means much of anything to him these days.

But it'll give him exactly what he needs. If all goes well, the instant a Medium near Luna scans their card, it'll clone their credentials and send them to the dummy card strapped to Hiro's belt.

Of course, the second it's clear there's an intruder in the building, the flaw in their system will be easy to pinpoint, but unless they're scanning for wireless cloning in the moment, it'll give him plenty of time to get the hell out. One positive of having lived for over a hundred years is that it gives you more time to figure shit out, and X Tower has been a target of his for almost a decade, ever since Mia Daugherty took over.

His netscreen beeps again, and the words "clone received" cross his vision.

With an icy breath, Hiro steps through the revolving doors into the lobby. His boots thud a-rhythmically in step with his limp stride.

"You should have brought your cane," Kuro says.

"You should focus on sneaking in."

"Already two steps ahead of you, Hopalong."

"You okay, sir?"

Hiro's head jerks to the side, and he catches the eye of a bald security guard. The man has his hands outstretched, not threateningly, but more like he's ready to catch Hiro if he collapses. While sweet, the gesture makes Hiro's face heat up. He can't tell if it's from embarrassment or anger.

"I'm okay," he says with a chuckle. "It's this bad hip of mine." He punctuates the statement with a soft bump of his fist to his side. "Old running injury."

"Would you like a hover chair? Or an android escort?" He motions to an ancient-looking machine seated at the corner of the booth.

"Oh, no," Hiro says. He stands up straighter, knowing he needed to prove his ability to walk. Otherwise, this guy'll just tail him or insist on taking him to whatever floor he needs.

The guard nods and gives a stiff smile. Hiro knows the man will remember him, but when this is all done, none of this will matter much.

Hiro hobbles as best as he can without drawing attention to himself. He skips the main elevators that most office workers head to and toward the freight elevator.

"You around here somewhere?"

"Right above you," Kuro says. Hiro hears flapping above him. He looks up to see his crow form making his way above, way out of sight of most people.

"I didn't realize you'd keep your crow form here."

"Call me sentimental," he sends to Hiro. *"It's the form I've had for the past five years. Plus, when I let this guy go, he's gonna be pretty confused. Even hold a grudge against you for holding him hostage."*

"If anything, you held him hostage."

"He doesn't know that. It's your face he saw every day."

Hiro can almost hear Kuro sigh before there's another flutter of feathers. It's the very sound of Kuro shaking free of his mortal coil in favor of his more Spectral form.

Hiro's heart thunders as he approaches the scanning station by the freight elevator, which is manned by four guards. This'll be the moment of truth.

Was this whole operation money and time well spent?

With a swipe, the machine beeps, and the turnstile opens, allowing him to walk through the opening that doubles as a weapon detector.

He waits for sirens to go off, or for one of the cyborg security guards to give him a second look, but nothing.

"Where are you?" Hiro says.

"I'm in your head," Kuro says. Even though their communication is nonverbal, Hiro can tell that Kuro is close, taking up residence inside his body.

He nods at the guards on either side of him. All it takes is one call to the rest of the building for this whole mess to fall apart. And Hiro's life would end with a whimper.

Under normal circumstances, they may recognize him as persona non grata in the DOSD, but in his Spectral form, Kuro can fudge some of Hiro's features, allowing him to pass through undetected.

A shaky sigh escapes Hiro's lips as the elevator doors close behind him.

"Well, that was disturbingly easy," Kuro says in Hiro's head. *"It almost makes you wonder why we didn't do this years ago."*

"That's enough out of you," Hiro says. *"You know why."*

"If you had kicked the bucket, wouldn't things have been better? We'd be one step closer to being together forever."

"One of us is dead, the other a near immortal, and yet neither of us knows what the afterlife holds. I'll take my chances on this *plane of existence."*

"And you're still afraid of Daugherty? She really did a number on you."

"If by number you mean almost killed me, then yes. I'm only here because I have no other choice," Hiro says.

"Ever the moral high ground with you."

"And it doesn't bother you they store Essences here?"

"It bothers me that if you'd acted against your fears, you could have either been better off by now or dead like me."

Kuro sounds a bit too cheery about the whole thing for Hiro's liking. Then again, he was always the crazy one between the two of them. At least, that's how he was in the two years he knew him when he was alive.

Hiro tries not to think about it, but every so often, he dwells on the fact that he practically didn't even know Kuro. The number of years he's known him dead versus living outnumbers the latter by a factor of, what, ninety? Maybe eighty-five?

This connection between the two of them that unites them even in the semi-afterlife…how genuine is it, really?

"You know you didn't have to let me stick around for so long," Kuro says. Somehow, he can always tell when Hiro gets inside his own head.

"Don't be stupid," Hiro responds. *"I mean, who else on this gray planet would put up with me?"*

The elevator dings and the doors fly open.

"If we're doing this, let's do it right," Kuro says. *"We'll secure some Essences and get your geriatric ass out."*

SPECTRAL

EPISODE 10
VICTIM/KILLER

ONE

IT'S ALMOST TOO easy for Hiro to weave his way through the DOSD headquarters.

Is this really happening?

When things are too good to be true, there's a reason why. But it's not like it's easy for no reason.

He may have decided mere hours ago that he was going to follow through with this infiltration, but this has been a plan in the making for well over a decade. A part of him knew this day would come. After his initial clash with Mia Daugherty and the fallout that followed, it was only inevitable they'd face each other again.

As such, he's been laying the groundwork on a near monthly basis. Sneaking blueprints here, bribing a low-level worker there—it all made it so that by the time those elevator doors opened, he would be familiar with every square foot of the place.

He knows which places will be crowded, which will be empty, and most importantly, where to go in this maze of a headquarters to hit the most important room of all: the Essence Bank.

Ironically, this was one of the first places he learned about when the DOSD was first formed. A few encounters with Daugherty taking on miscellaneous Spectres proved a lack of consistency in her level, as well as the levels of her colleagues. They seemed as strong as they needed to be, no more, no less, taking one a Level Five Spectre one day, and a Level One Spectre the next.

And this was before he'd made enemies of them—when their tongues were looser than they should have been. He knew they'd want to recruit him to their ranks. In this narrow window of time, one of them revealed the truth behind their strength, and the coveted Essence Bank.

Hiro's always hated the idea of storing Essences, though, given that he doesn't know what happens when an Essence is eaten, he had no way of knowing whether what they did was causing any harm. So what if they're storing Essences? The Spectres are still free and the territories around the Mirages that much safer without a lurking ethereal presence.

Really, what's the downside?

Hiro's spent the better part of a decade wrestling with that very question. Though every internal thought led back to some variation of, "It feels wrong."

"*Left,*" Kuro sends to Hiro.

He follows Kuro's direction and turns into a somehow even longer hallway. The DOSD's offices are a freakin' labyrinth. If he didn't know any better, he'd think it was a maze on purpose.

"*Right at the dead end, then go straight until you approach a set of double doors.*"

Hiro pulls up the profile of Doctor Jeremy Huang, a DOSD employee, and throws it onto the periphery of his vision. "*You have the irises memorized?*"

"*I know how to do my job.*"

"*You said he's out for the day?*"

"*We sent him home with a case of food poisoning,*" Kuro says. "*Last I checked, he was still hugging the sides of his toilet at home.*"

"*Will anyone ask questions?*"

"*Do I look like a mind reader? Anyway, if they do, we'll have to rely on your amazing improv skills,*" Kuro sends. "*It ain't that hard. Just say you're new.*"

"*That's a stupid excuse. It'll never work.*"

"*Then just pretend you're filling in for him. This building alone employs hundreds of people.*"

Hiro approaches the set of double doors, exhaling. "*You sure you got this?*"

"*I'm sure I'll try my best,*" Kuro says. Hiro hates that after all these decades, he can't tell if he's kidding. "*And don't worry, I'm only sixty percent joking.*"

"*Shut up and get to work.*"

Hiro can almost feel the weight of his head change as Kuro shifts his presence to the font of his face, right behind his right eye. With a few taps on the keyboard outside the double doors, the console clicks, and a small slot level with his head opens up. Hiro sticks his eye in front of the slot, holding it open as a red light scans his retina.

"Identity confirmed," a male voice says.

"*It worked!*"

"Like I said," Kuro sends, *"I know how to do my job."*

Hiro opens the door, taking care not to slide in—that would only make him look suspicious. He opens it harder than he should, allowing it to swing open and hang for a few seconds before shutting. Anyone who works here would be used to going in and out, after all.

Hiro's eyes widen at the sight in front of him. It looks almost exactly like he pictured it would, but there's something upsetting about seeing tall, capsule-like tanks knowing they're packed full of Essences of departed Spectres. The warehouse-sized room is immense, with every few feet taken up by a large, ten-foot-tall tank. There's just enough space for an average-sized man to walk between them, meaning there's more than enough for Hiro.

"That's a lot of Essences," Kuro says. Somehow, even *he* sounds impressed by the sight. *"Is it weird that I'm feeling hungry?"*

Hiro smiles. He feels it, too. *"So, any of these will do?"*

"I'd go deeper," Kuro says, floating out of Hiro and into a nearby console. *"They organized them by Level, with the lower-Level ones on the outside. But no need to go too deep. We're not looking to get up to Level Twenty or anything. Try enough to get me up to Level Ten."*

Hiro steps forward, keeping his eyes open for anyone else in the room. Considering how big it is and how important it is, he expected there to be more people walking in and out. Maybe he got lucky and stumbled in during an off hour.

As he makes his way deeper, he notices the placards on the side.

LEVEL ONE
LEVEL TWO
LEVEL THREE

How high do these get? Hiro thinks. It's not a figure he ever came by in his research.

He makes his way to the center, noticing the spacing between the level gaps getting smaller as he goes, with the very center of the room capping out at Level Fifteen. It's a high level, but not as high as Hiro was in his prime.

And what happens in a few years if Essences even this high aren't be enough to ward off death for him? Does he break back in?

"He has clearance only through Level Five," Kuro says.

"Huh?"

"Doctor Huang's credentials only give him clearance to pull out Level Five Essences."

"That's it?"

"*And only three at a time,*" Kuro says.

"*I forgot how useful you were in your Spectral form,*" Hiro says. Maybe going forward, he should have Kuro take over an android or computer instead of a crow. That way, he has access to the net at all times.

Hiro circles back toward the Level Five tanks. He's never seen one of these in person before, but he's done enough reading to know what it is and how to use it.

With another scan of his badge and another retinal scan, he sticks his Syncer arm into the opening of the large tank. He only recoils slightly as he sees the milky fluid inside tumble around.

The keypad in front of him glows. He types in the forever changing code—he's had Doctor Huang's verification fob cloned for years, in case of such an occasion.

"Level Five Clearance confirmed," a voice says. And then Hiro's arm vibrates as the liquid inside the tank boils even more intensely.

He taps the keyboard a few more times, confirming the desire for three more Essences, and lets the machine do its work. The task only takes ten seconds, but it's the longest ten seconds in his entire existence.

In those brief moments, he can see it all happening again in front of his eyes. The moment he'd heard the news about Nagasaki, and the careless trek that led him out there.

He was so stupid. So young. He couldn't imagine a life without Kuro. All the while, he swam in a sea of Spectres and radiation.

"Transfer complete," the disembodied voice says.

Hiro waits a few moments before pulling out his arm, as though remnants of Essence may spill out if he disconnects too early. He licks his lips. He can feel the hunger emerging from Kuro inside him as well. It's ravenous.

"Excuse me?" someone says down the line of SUV-sized tanks.

Hiro looks up to see a man in a dark blue jump suit walk toward him. He must be one of the techs, Hiro realizes, though he doesn't recognize the man from any of the research he did.

"Yes?"

The man looks Hiro up and down, trying to place him. "Sorry, I didn't recognize you," he says.

"I'm...new," Hiro says. He can almost hear Kuro snickering inside his head.

"And they already have you working Level Fives?"

Hiro shrugs. He hopes it's casual enough that it doesn't come across as suspicious.

"Well, just so you know," the man says, "Charger number five-two-eight," he points to a tank just a few rows down, "is having some problems.

So make sure you avoid using it, okay? I've got a ticket in and will get to it in the next hour."

Hiro holds up his arm. "I've already got what I need," he says. "Thanks."

The man nods, and with a wave, disappears behind one of the tanks, making his way down the rows.

Hiro lets out a taut breath. To him, there's nothing scarier than the prospect of having to kill someone. He unclenches his hand and scans the catwalks above them. This place wasn't very crowded, but he still feels very exposed just standing in the middle of the tanks.

"Do you remember where there's an isolated room?" he asks Kuro.

"What, don't wanna hobble out?" Kuro says, his mental voice somehow deriding.

"I can't take another minute like this," Hiro says. *"We need to take this. Now."*

"Follow the edge of the room way to your left. There's a chamber that only five other employees in the building have clearance for."

"Let's hope none of them are here," Hiro says. He follows Kuro's instructions, leaning on the tanks as he walks to the end, and using the wall even less as he approaches a large metal sliding door. It's as though his body knows what's coming, and is giving him the last bit of energy he needs to make it.

Another annoying eye scan and PIN is all that stands between him and the rest of his life, and by the time he's on the other side of the door, he's sweating again, his breath shallow. Black feathers the edges of his vision, and he almost doesn't have the energy to tap on his Syncer to release the Essences, which tumble to the ground, only just large enough not to fall through the grated floor.

He wants to yell at Kuro to tell him to hurry. To eat the Essences and get it over with, but he doesn't have the energy to communicate telepathically, let alone speak.

A flicker of light crosses his vision. His body feels colder than ever, as though the cogs in his body are no longer moving, no longer giving him warmth. It's a stupid, delirious thought that makes no sense, but it's not as though he's in any state of mind to...

...

...

...

Hiro's eyes flicker open and he inhales a high-pitched breath, the air whistling through his constricted windpipe. The oxygen brings with it an unexpected warmth. It might be the warmest he's ever felt in his entire life.

Has his body always felt this warm, or is he about to burn alive?

Jesus, it's so DAMNED HOT!

His chest inflates with each breath, his ribs cracking as it expands, but not in a bad way. It's as though his bones are snapping into place for the first time, even though there was never a single bone out of place. But somehow, he knows this is right. As foreign as it is, this is how he's supposed to feel. This is how *normal* people feel.

He sits up, his eyes coming into focus. Even his vision is sharper than normal. Greater than twenty-twenty vision, as it should be. He can see a fly on a wall from hundreds of feet away, like he used to.

"*Welcome back, Hiro,*" Kuro says. Even the Spectre's voice is livelier than usual. The very thought is enough to make Hiro cry.

No, it's enough to make him laugh outright. So he does. From a low moan to an almost maniacal cackle, he lets it all out—months of pent-up anxiety released in a short sixty-minute spree. It's enough to dislodge with it a waterfall of tears that explodes from his eyes, dripping through the grated catwalk flooring.

He thought this was it. That his time had come to an end. He's over a hundred and fifty years old, and he's still not ready to go. And he doesn't have to. Not yet, at least. He has another chance. A chance to...

Hiro blinks. The room he's in is bigger than he expected. In fact, it's bigger than shown in the blueprint he'd stolen. What, did they renovate the place when he wasn't looking? He steps down the stairs and onto the laminated cement floor.

In front of him stand what look like giant versions of the Charger tanks in the other room. The same milky liquid sloshes around inside, but there's something different about it. It's somehow...fuller. He can't explain it. The liquid isn't thicker, but he can still tell it has more substance to it.

There are only four tanks, but they all also have giant pipes that lead into another pair of rooms placed in each corner, with each pair comprising of two adjacent doors.

"*What is this place?*" Hiro says, circling one of the giant tanks.

"*There's no label in the room,*" Kuro says, his dark, translucent form darting around the room in search of clues.

"*Do you think—*"

Hiro's comment is cut off by a series of beeps on the other side of the entrance. Without a second thought, he sprints to one corner of the room, behind a giant metal barrel. It feels good to run without having to think about each step.

The door slides open just as he takes cover. Peeking around the side, he captures a glance, and between the rigid voice and the graying hair, it doesn't take long for him to peg the owner as Mia Daugherty's.

"I've never been in this room before," another voice says—almost sounding like a younger version of Mia. Hiro realizes it must be one of those Junior Mediums. Her daughter. Though he can't remember her name.

"You can fill a library with the secrets you'll never see in this building," Mia says, sounding almost proud.

"It's so...big." That last voice is unmistakable. Luna. So, she was just walking around with them like they were friends? Hiro expected it would at least take a few hours for that to happen. Mia wasn't what he would call the hospitable type.

"Yes, it is," Mia says.

"What does it do?"

"Just move along. We have experiments to perform."

Luna elicits an audible groan, but allows herself to be shepherded through one of the two adjacent doors farthest from where Hiro hides. "We'll be in touch on the other side," Daugherty says. "Just stay put and don't touch anything."

"You don't need to talk to me like I'm a five-year-old."

The door shuts behind Luna.

"Unnaturally short, that one," Daugherty says.

"What're we doing here?" the daughter asks.

"All in due time."

The entrance opens again, and in walks a man in a white coat. Mia glances up at the man from down below.

"Where's Doctor Huang?" she says.

"He's home sick. Food poisoning, I think," the bespectacled man says.

Hiro can make out an annoyed frown on the woman's face. "Very well, you'll have to do, then. When I give you the okay, funnel Spectre Number Five into the adjacent room."

"Why?" the man says. "Didn't we just—"

"Don't ask questions. Do as I say. Have him prepped and send his file over to the control room while you're at it." She disappears through the door with her daughter in tow.

Hiro can tell from the man's body language that he wants to argue, but thinks better of it. He mumbles to himself as he retreats to a console attached to a tank.

"Shit," Hiro whispers to himself. He hadn't expected to be locked in the same vicinity as Luna when she was here. He leans back against the wall, eyes peering around one of the giant metal barrels.

No, he thinks. *We're too close.*

"*Kuro*," he sends to his Spectre. "*Find me the best way out of here.*"

"*You're not gonna do anything?*" Kuro says.

"*What do you mean, do something? We just reclaimed our lives.*"

"We've just entered a top-secret room within a top-secret base. Aren't you the least bit curious about what this may all be for?"

"There's nothing we can do."

Somehow, Hiro can feel Kuro frown. The Spectre's unhappiness emanates from within Hiro's very core. It was one of his least favorite parts about their sharing lives. Their emotions are never far from one another.

"Bullshit," Kuro says.

Before Hiro can react, he feels Kuro floating across the room and descending into another open console attached to one of the unused Chargers in the middle of the room. Hiro grits his teeth and retreats behind the barrels.

"What're you doing?"

"What do you think I'm doing? I'm getting to the bottom of..." Kuro's mental signal goes silent for several seconds, and Hiro holds his breath.

"This is stupid. Get back here." Several long seconds pass. Almost a minute. *"Kuro!"*

For the briefest moment, Hiro almost loses all connection to Kuro. It's almost as though the two of them never had one to begin with. As though a pair of scissors are in the midst of cutting it between them.

And then the connection returns, slight as it may be.

"Kuro!" he says again.

The connection between them strengthens. Hiro can feel him, though the Spectre remains silent. He can sense that he's troubled.

"What's wrong?" he says.

"They're...they're bringing them back." Kuro's mental communication is frazzled. It isn't something Hiro's ever felt from his partner before.

"Who?"

"Spectres," Kuro sends. *"They're using their Essences to...pull them back into this world."*

Hiro's stomach clenches. *"They what?"*

"It's what I said."

Hiro's eyebrows furrow, his mind caught between confusion and anger. Anger for the resting Spirits they yank back into our miserable existence. *"Can they do that?"*

"According to this, they can. According to this, they have. One hundred and seventy-two times."

"This isn't...they shouldn't be doing this."

"Since when has anything gotten in the way of people doing what they want?"

A blink, and the sight of the mushroom cloud in the distance flashes into Hiro's vision, but disappears just as quickly.

"Well?" Kuro says.

"*It's…it's not our problem,*" Hiro says. He hates himself for sending that thought to Kuro, but it's how he feels.

"*Then whose problem is it?*"

"*No one's, Kuro! It's nobody's problem. Those Spirits are dead. Passed on.*"

Again, Hiro can feel Kuro's frown. It deepens. He's furious. And Kuro is never furious. But it doesn't matter. This *isn't* their problem. This *can't* be their problem. They'd just gotten their lives back. He can't—*they* can't—spend the rest of their lives fighting forever and ever.

"*So, that's it,*" Kuro says. "*After all this time, this is how you feel.*"

"*It's not about how I feel. It's about what's realistic.*"

"*You coward.*" Hiro can tell Kuro's last comment is a whisper. "*You're a coward. You always have been. Too afraid of death to even live with the life you have. Too scared to take any risks.*"

"*I risked my life, Kuro. I risked everything. I gave everything up for you.*"

"*Then I hope the hundred and thirty years of extra existence is enough compensation,*" Kuro says. "*If you don't do this with me, I swear I'll never eat an Essence again. And I'll wait for the two of us to die for good.*"

"*Jesus, Kuro.*"

"*Jesus, God, Yomi, Allah, or whoever—we have no idea if any of them exist because you refuse to let us die.*"

Hiro wants to say something, but can't so much as think, let alone retort against Kuro.

"*You and I have lived three lifetimes, and we've accomplished nothing. We were finally on death's door, and again you brought us back. If I'm going to keep on living, I'm going to need you to promise me we'll do something with the time we have left.*"

One tank hisses, and the white fluid within bubbles violently. A gunshot —or the sound of a gunshot—propels one of the big white amoebas through a tube and into a pair of rooms where Luna and Mia reside.

"*Hiro!*" Kuro's plea brings Hiro back. "*Please. You have to do something. We have to do something.*"

Hiro fights back the nausea that threatens to pour from his throat and takes a deep breath.

"*You've always had a bleeding heart, you know that?*" Hiro says. "*But, let's be honest, so have I.*"

TWO

IF THE FLASHING red lights weren't enough of an indication, I realize things aren't normal. The moment we leave the small white room made of nightmares, goblin kings, and annoying little girls, we emerge into the larger chamber from where we came. My eyes are drawn to the four giant tanks that sit at its center. When we'd walked through before, they'd been bubbling with a disgusting white fluid that's the stuff of punchlines.

Now, those tanks sit empty.

I scan the area below the tank, expecting to see the stuff spilled out onto the floor, but no, the room is unchanged, save for the flashing lights, the deafening alarms, and the absence of white fluid.

"Oh, no," Vero says next to me, her mouth hanging open, eyes focused on the now-empty tanks.

"I take it that's not good?" I say. Even in moments of dire circumstances, I can't seem to give a serious response. It's a flaw, I know. Trust me, I really do know how to read the room.

"I think those are where they keep the…" She stops herself, biting her lip. "Never mind."

"Keep the what?"

"Nothing. This is all new to me, too, you know."

"What is?"

She doesn't so much as open her mouth to respond when I feel a chill run up my spine. It's a familiar feeling to when Estrella and I are in search of a Mirage.

"There's one in here," I say.

"One what?"

"A Spectre. A Mirage." Another stab. "No, a few." I can feel it. A small series of explosions within the chamber. It's as though they're all fighting for the space itself. "What happens if there are too many Spectres in a small space?"

Vero shakes her head. "They rarely form close to one another."

That makes no sense. Battlefields are littered with dead bodies. It only makes sense that at least some Spectres would form close to each other. And if there are too many within a given area…

"They're fighting each other," I say with confidence, though not understanding how I know this. "There are three Spectres in this room alone, and they're fighting. Or maybe their Mirages are all trying to claim the space." My curious self wants to open a pinprick. To dive in and see what it is we're dealing with. But Estrella and I still aren't on speaking terms, and I'm sure there are more important things we need to be dealing with.

Ignoring whatever feelings I'm having, I let Vero guide me out of the room.

As we enter the adjacent Essence Bank, the wailing of the alarm stops, though the obnoxious flashing red light persists. I almost run into somebody standing in front of us right outside the threshold. I open my mouth to yell at whoever this is before I notice the stiff posture and the graying hair. It's Commander Daugherty, and she's not alone.

Within this giant chamber with rows and rows of Essence tanks, there are at least a dozen Mediums dressed in black tactical gear, not unlike what I've seen Vero wear under her armor in Mirages.

"Is the room secured?"

"Yes, Commander," one of them replies.

"Good. We can't let any more of them escape."

I want to ask her how they can keep a Spectre from going through walls, but then I remember the Goblin King, who had somehow been confined in the small white hellish room we'd fought in.

"What's going on?" Vero says.

"There's been a breach. Some fool let the damned Spectres out," Commander Daugherty says, as though she's talking about a pack of coyotes.

My stomach drops. "How many?" I ask.

Commander Daugherty spares me a glance, and in it, I get the sense she wants to say something like, "Who told the little brat she can speak?"

Instead, she says, "That's classified." I guess that's a more efficient way of saying the same thing. "It's under control. Dozens of our Mediums are on the case."

"Dozens?" I say. "But what…" I stop myself as I grow to understand what she's talking about and get a pulse for the rest of the room. I may only see about a dozen Mediums, but I can sense a lot more in the room. "They're in Mirages, aren't they?"

Thwip! Thwip! Two of the Mediums several feet away from us disappear in an instant, no doubt jumping into a Mirage.

Amid all this, Commander Daugherty scoffs at me. "Stay out of our way. Go back into the other chamber if you have to. Agent Daugherty, keep her out of our way."

"I can help," Vero says.

"And I just told you how."

"I mean I can fight."

"I know what you meant," Commander Daugherty says. "Charger systems are down right now. All you have are a couple Level Two Essences in your Syncer, right?" She glares at Vero, who nods in response. "Then you're useless here. Just keep this girl out of the way and *alive* until we get this sorted out."

"How'd this happen?" I say.

Again, she gives me another petty and condescending look. "That's classified."

Thwip! Thwip! She and three more Mediums disappear in front of us, looking like a set of two-dimensional images getting sucked into a straw.

"Hanajima," Vero whispers to herself.

"What?" I say. "What's he got to do with this?"

She opens her mouth to speak, but after a split second, shuts it again.

"Let me guess," I say. "Classified?"

"Probably," she says. "We should listen to her."

I want to tell her that there's no way I'm just going to stand by as whatever's happening happens. In my experience, in times of crisis, if you sit still, you get killed. Even with Estrella and me not cooperating, I refuse to sit off to the side and wait for these Spectres to attack.

I start to argue when I'm hit with an overwhelming sense of nostalgia. It's like when you hear a song after so many years, and a door is unlocked in your brain to a very specific moment in time. This one, though, I can't pinpoint, because it's no one memory, but a cascade of them, as though cycling through many moments of my life at once.

Mom and Dad fighting when I was too little for them to acknowledge me in the room.

Mom buying me a candy bar at the corner store on her way back from work.

Her saying goodbye to me for the last time, neither of us realizing this would be the last time. A quick hug and a kiss on the forehead, with promises of being back after her shift. I barely even turn my attention away from the netscreen to acknowledge her.

"Hey, are you listening?" Vero says.

"She's here," I reply.

"I don't think...wait. Who's here?"

I hold up my hand for her to shut up. I hate it when people do that to me. I usually want to punch their teeth in for shushing me, but I know that if she keeps talking, I may lose that feeling. I can't lose it. Not again.

I take off in a sprint, weaving in and out of the tanks. A breeze passes me by as I avoid a Mirage pinprick. And then another. And another. Damn, these things are all over the place, worlds and Spectres colliding into and clashing with each other in the back of my head. I can hear Vero calling out to me, swearing up a storm as she begs for me to listen to her.

Mom gets closer. Or I feel her *presence* getting closer. It's like stepping into my Mirage, only about one-tenth as impactful. Whatever this Mirage is isn't affecting my emotion as much as it's just rekindling some vague memories. I guess it's a lot closer to a typical Mirage, only this time, I share a connection with this Spectre.

I'm so caught up in my own thoughts I almost miss a Medium popping out of a pinprick in front of me. In fact, all around me, Mediums pop in and out of these things, the *thwipping* sound somehow overpowering the flashing red light that threatens to drive me insane.

I dive to the side but pop back up. I'm used to outrunning things, living or not. There's no way any of this is gonna keep me from finding answers.

That feeling of nostalgia edges. I find myself praying that no one is fighting her, or that no one "frees" her before I get my chance to get what I need.

I almost miss it, but my shoes screech across the laminated cement floor, and I sense its location right next to me. My stomach does somersaults, though I can't tell if it's from excitement, fear, or a recollection of some distant memory.

Either way, I'm at the Mirage.

"Luna!" Vero's voice has gone past pleading and has transitioned to abject anger. "Listen to me. If you don't—"

"It's my mom," I say.

"What?" Vero's tone is annoyed, though it lacks the condescension of the commander's.

"It's my mom," I repeat. "This Mirage. It's hers." I look at the pinprick that sits at my eye level. The butterflies continue to flutter around in my stomach. I can almost see *into* her Mirage. "I'm going in," I say, sticking my finger into the opening. And without giving Vero any time to stop me, I pull the Mirage over us.

The nostalgia intensifies, but the scenery itself is kind of a letdown. Like with every other Mirage, I had hoped to see something—I dunno—more visually stimulating? Something that'll confirm who it is I'm dealing with here. Instead, all I see in front of me is a black void. I guess it's like my own Mirage in that it's dark, and has very little in terms of…self-expression? Though, at least in my Mirage, I had circling memory screens. This one is just a vaguely lit void of space.

"Are you crazy?" Vero screams behind me, though I can't tell if it's because she's loud or if it's just because there is no other sound filling the Mirage. Other than my breath, all I can hear is the pounding of blood through my ears and the sloppy smacking of my own lips.

"Have you ever seen a Mirage like this?" I almost whisper, not wanting to berate our own ears.

I feel Vero's glare turn from me to the rest of the Mirage. "I haven't seen one like this before, no," she says. "We rarely see Mirages when they're in their formative states. By the time we get to them, they've developed more, taken on a personality that fits their Spectre's emotional state. I've heard about them, though only in theory. The closest I've been in was yours."

"Huh?"

"Your Mirage. Or the Mirage of…what is it, your sister?"

"Not important," I say, "Go on."

"Sorry. Your Mirage was the plainest of any I'd seen. Even so, there was more to it than this."

"So, why is this Mirage practically blank?"

I can hear Vero's breath hitch, as though deciding whether or not to say what she's going to say next. "It means this is new."

"New Mirage?" I say. The entire void seems to spin around me. "What do you mean new Mirage? This is my mom's, isn't it?"

"I don't know. Is it?"

"It is!" I insist, though I don't have any way of backing it up. "So why does it look like this?"

Vero bites her lip. Again, uncertainty paints her features. "It's cl—"

"Don't you dare say it's classified."

"Luna."

The hair on the back of my neck stands up. "Don't say my name like that."

"Like how?"

"Like you're talking down to me! What does it mean?"

Vero presses her lips together so hard it almost makes her look like a chimp. Not the most attractive of expressions, but at least she's not refusing me outright. Several seconds pass in the void. It may as well be hours, and every moment that ticks by has me clenching my fists harder.

"Fine," I finally say. "I don't have time for this."

"Are you sure this is your mom?" Vero says. Her voice is taut, anxious.

Her asking a second time makes me doubt myself. I look around at the empty space. There's nothing here to show any semblance of a personality of a life lived. But still... "I don't know how, but I can feel her here. It's different from my connection with Estrella, but somehow the same. I can't explain."

Vero stares at me for another long moment before nodding. "Mother's going to kill me," she says in almost a whisper. And then, after a few paranoid looks behind her, she drops a bombshell on me. Not only was the DOSD actively using Essences to engage in combat with Spectres, but to *revive* Spectres.

Vero looks out into the void. "When a Mirage is newly formed, it looks like this. And if this is your mom..." her voice trails off. Her implications are clear enough, though she still refuses to say it. Probably too afraid that I'll get mad and...yell at her? Hit her? Impale her with my sword? I guess that last part isn't possible so long as Estrella is acting the way she is, but it sure as hell seems like she's scared.

Regardless of her fears, the truth is obvious even without the explanation of the forming void. Mom was killed—or rather "freed" by a Medium —and was later brought back to life by the DOSD. Recently.

"Shit, I'm sorry, Luna," Vero says. Her voice cracks. It's not the kind of "I'm sorry" people use when they just feel bad for the situation you're in, but the kind they say when they did something wrong.

Any questions I have are drowned out by a wail that comes at us from all sides, bringing a gale of wind along with it. This I also recognize. It's a scream I heard countless times in the shouting matches between Mom and Dad.

"Mom?" I call out. I don't know which way to yell. Normally, in a Mirage I can sense a direction where the Spectre resides. But here is different. It's like she's a legitimate god and the Mirage is her entire being. I stare into the nothingness and am at a complete loss. With my Mirage, there were images I could touch that acted as vessels for memories. Others had different objects act as catalysts, or sometimes even full rooms.

But there's nothing in this void. Nothing to walk toward. Nothing to cling on to. Nothing to trigger a memory.

And then I have an idea. I kneel to the floor, and with a moment's hesitation, press my hand against it.

There's a small spike of emotion that runs through me, and then it disappears. "Come on, Mom," I whisper, closing my eyes. "I'm here. Please, just come out."

The deep silence breaks and is replaced by the ambient bustling of Skid Row. I know the screams and smells by memory. When my eyes open, they fall upon the Main Stay, and standing in front on the sidewalk, not a few feet away from Hank's sleeping form on the ground, is my mother.

She's as thin and as graceful-looking as I remember, even dressed in her jean shorts and graphic tee.

She stares back at me as though she's seeing a ghost. Her mouth hangs open, her hands lifted, as though she wants to reach out and make sure I'm real. The irony isn't lost on me.

I blink, and the very next instant, she's gone. No, wait. I squint and see her fluttering away. That's right, fluttering. I can barely make her out, but she's transformed from my mother into a small bird—what kind, I don't know. I don't know a freakin' thing about birds. It looks like it could be green? I don't know how normal it is for birds to be green, but this one is. Given what I know about Mirages and Spectres, I'm sure there's some deeper meaning, but I don't have any time to think about that.

I take chase, only remembering my own speed at that moment. Even in its own Mirage, I catch up in a matter of seconds, plowing through the facade of Skid Row. I'm just an arm's reach away, but the moment I reach out, she pulls ahead, slipping through my fingers.

Flicker.

There's an argument in an apartment I don't recognize. Mom and Dad scream at each other. Any doubt I had about where I am fizzles.

Flicker.

I'm back in the black void.

I reach out again, and this time the bird pulls ahead so far that I don't so much as touch her.

Flicker.

A memory falls into place, though I don't think it's from the Mirage itself, but my memory being triggered. I was six years old. Wow, I'd forgotten about this moment until now.

I'd come home to our apartment. Dad laying on the bed, breath smelling of beer. He didn't drink as much then, so this time caught me off guard. The apartment was dirtier than usual. Ignoring him, I looked around the apartment in search of Mom. Mom was the one who dealt with him. She'd know what to do. But she was nowhere to be found. For ten minutes, I searched. Ten minutes in an apartment the size of a shoebox.

"Don't you worry about her," he said, eyes closed on the bed. "She's always been flighty, that one. She'll be back."

And he was right. She came back just a few days later, though it wouldn't be the last time she had one of her disappearances.

I reach out and snatch for the little green bird and feel its soft feathers grace the pads of my fingers.

Another flicker, and we're back to the same argument as before. I still can't make out what they're saying, but I realize Dad isn't screaming at her, just placating her as she unloads on him.

Wait, she's not screaming...at least not in anger. She's scared.

"We'll make it work." I see him mouth the words, but I don't believe his expression.

I continue my superhuman run through the black nothingness, closing the gap between me and the bird by the second.

Dad was right. She *was* a flighty one. I think back to my memories of her, and they range from amazing to nothing. When she was home, she was amazing—the perfect mother. But every so often, she'd leave for months at a time. How had I forgotten?

Dad had assured me she wasn't leaving because of me, and you know what? I believed him. This whole time, I thought she was running away from *him*. Her pathetic excuse of a husband.

He was the reason she was tied down, and the reason we couldn't live free. So, how could I blame her for running off like she did? I wanted to do the same.

I thought that I'd grow up to do just that. I'd drift from place to place, seeking excitement and purpose. I'd find the purpose in me that Dad never allowed Mom to find.

I trip.

I fall head-over-heels, my head scraping against the dark floor, my hand snatching out in front of me, grasping a soft object that I know is the magical green bird.

I'm catapulted into a hospital. This time, I hear it all. Mom screams, swearing up a storm, expelling words I didn't realize could be used as swear words until this very moment.

I close my eyes. This was a lot more graphic than I signed on for.

When I open them, I see the baby. I see...me?

I catch only the briefest glimpse, but it's unlike any baby I've seen. There's something off about its shape. There is no ceremony. No congratulations from anyone in the room. The doctor is out the door, carrying the figure, leaving my parents with the nurses.

I can see from Dad's body language that he wants to follow. Instead, he stays behind, holding Mom's hand.

Suddenly, I'm filled with the deepest sense of dread. It's like I somehow know what's going on despite *not* knowing what's going on. My hand reaches up to my neck, and I pick at my skin tag again.

I flick it back and forth. Back and forth.

The scene changes again. The doctor is back, his head low.

I can barely make out the words, "We couldn't save her."

Dad's fists are clenched in front of him. He doesn't say it, but I can somehow sense his thoughts. Even worse, it's something that could have been avoided if we'd checked in with a doctor throughout Mom's pregnancy. If only we'd had the money to.

"I'm sorry, Estrella," he whispers.

I look over at Mom, whose eyes stare into the distance. As the doctor hands the swaddled baby that I assume is me, she looks on, face red, a blank expression on her face.

I release the green bird from my clutches. It tosses me from the memory, and I roll onto one knee.

Somehow, the bird that is my mom knows the chase is over, and rather than fly away, she hovers just a few feet away in the air.

She lets out a loud chirp. It shouldn't make any sense, but I can somehow make out the words. "You killed her," she chirps at me.

"What?" is all I can say. I've relived that whole memory, and still, hearing it come out of her beaked mouth, I can't believe it.

"You killed her," she chirps again. And again and again.

"You killed her! You killed her! You killed her! You killed her!"

My hand is at my neck again, fingers no longer just picking or flicking, but tearing at the tag at my neck—at the place where my sister was removed. Where she'd once been a part of me, only to be murdered by me.

The bird's chirping grows deeper with each repeated line, and the bird itself growing larger and larger along with it.

I want to apologize to her, but I also want to scream at her. To tell her she's wrong.

It wasn't my fault. I wasn't even born yet. I wasn't even a child. How could any of this be because of me?

At some point, the bird reaches the size of a bear, and I only just realize that she's stopped chirping accusations and has transitioned into full-throated apologies.

"I'm sorry! I'm sorry! I'm sorry! I'm sorry!" her voice continues to deepen and warp.

I can feel the mix of resentment and regret. That she tried her best to look past this, but still couldn't see me as anything other than the one who ruined our family.

She wishes I were dead.

She wishes I were happy.

She wishes that I'd had a chance with *anyone* else to ensure I grew up with a better life.

She regrets it all.

Without warning, she explodes. Thousands of feathers and blobs of coagulated blood are thrown in every which direction, though somehow avoiding me.

Her voice echoes within the void, simultaneously whispering, "You killed her" and "I'm sorry" on repeat.

"Luna!"

I turn to face Vero, who stares back, eyes soft. "Are you okay?"

"Where did she go?"

"There's no one here," she says. "It's just us." She opens her mouth to continue, but then stops. "What did you see?"

"Am I going insane?"

"You're in a Mirage," she says. "Anything you see in here is bound to drive you a little insane."

I nod with each breath, taking in her comforting words. I know this is a Mirage, and that things in here don't obey any laws of logic, but I'm surprised how good it makes me feel to hear her say that. To hear someone else understand how I feel for once. It's not something I get very often.

"I'm sorry," she says, her voice somber.

She said it again. "For what?" I say, realizing for the first time that my cheeks are wet from tears. "It's not your fault I'm so messed up."

"No, but it's my fault that you're such a nervous wreck right now."

I'm not sure if I should be offended by that, but given what's just happened, I choose not to. "How?"

"I'm the one who told my mother about you," she says. "About you and your abilities, I mean," she follows up. "I don't know for sure, but I think that's why your mother's here now. My mom always wants leverage, and this was who she'd use against you. To understand where you came from."

"I always thought she was running away from Dad," I say.

Vero's eyebrows raise, but she doesn't question me.

"She...Mom was running away from me." I'm talking nonsense, I know. I mean, to her, it seems like nonsense, but it's anything but.

"Do you...do you want to go?" I can tell she wants to get out, and far away from any trouble I can get her in, but I commend her for at least trying to make it look like she was doing me a favor.

And then, without warning, the Mirage around us disintegrates, making way for the Essence tanks surrounding us.

Before I even realize it, we're back in the real world, and all that's left behind to remember Mom by is a glowing, marble-sized Essence.

THREE

I STARE at the glowing marble between my fingers, only half-understanding and half-believing what had just conspired. I hadn't so much as lifted a finger against Mom, but that didn't stop her from blasting to a million pieces in front of me. Now, she was truly dead, and I'd somehow been the one to kill her.

I'd thought learning about my past would bring closure—that it would make me feel better—but it only makes my stomach feel that much emptier. The void Mom had already left behind expands, making me feel even more lost and somehow regretful. Not only did she run off and get killed, but it had been me who had driven her away.

It's stupid, but then again, a lot of emotions are stupid.

And what does any of this change? So Estrella had died in the womb. So what? It doesn't take away the loneliness of a life having to raise yourself and care for your nearly invalid father. And it doesn't make me feel any better about anyone trying to take my body from me, no matter how much ownership they claim to have over it.

That dive into Mom's past only confirms what I've been too afraid to admit to myself all along. Everything in my past needs to go. Everything in it needs to be buried and left behind.

I can forget Mom.

I can leave Dad behind.

And Estrella…my sister, whose life I had taken…

I tap at the Syncer on my wrist, and with a blast of blue, Estrella emerges.

"What're you doing?" Vero says.

"This is it," I say.

"This is what?"

I don't need to say a single word to Estrella for her to understand. Her giant lips spread into an eerie smile. "This is it," she repeats.

"What are you—"

Vero's comment is cut short as she disappears from view, replaced by a near blackness filled with a smattering of memory screens. In spite of the emotional anguish each moment brings, this Mirage feels like home.

"Mom says hi," I say, holding up the Essence for Estrella to see.

Her eyes narrow. "And?"

"And...you were right. Sort of." It's easier to say than I expected. "The two of us? We're twins. At least, we were supposed to be."

"Before you stole my life from me."

"It was an accident," I say. "It was less than an accident. Things just happen." I sound cold, but I don't know how else to say it. I can't be blamed for anything as much as a person can get blamed for stepping on a lone ant on the sidewalk.

"How is that fair?"

"I've been saying that my entire life," I respond with a chuckle. "Trust me, my *entire* life. If it makes you feel any better, you didn't miss much while being locked inside me. But don't think I'm going to just stand by and watch as you take me over."

"Then why let me out at all?"

Good question. It was stupid of me. But then I think back to Damien, and his declaration that he and Lily still want me in their lives, even after everything.

"Believe it or not," I say, "I have a life I want to get back to. I have parents who actually want me." And until I get rid of everyone in my past, I don't think I can ever be free. I don't say that last part, but I sure feel it, and I think Estrella is smart enough to pick up on the subtext.

I toss the Essence into the air. It lands in front of Estrella, who eyes it hungrily. "You want your answers?" I say. "This is your chance. Eat that, and you'll have all the answers you need."

With a wary eye, she snatches it from the ground like a half-starved pit bull. As she swallows, I can feel the energy course through my veins and my muscles tense with an unexpected surge of strength. As I see her contort several feet in front of me, I can only assume she's feeling the same thing. I don't know if me giving that thing to her is a good idea, or even if her memories will return right away, but if we're going to do this, the least I can do is let her know the truth—that my body was never meant to be hers.

A few seconds pass, and when Estrella stills, her ghostly eyes come into focus, resting on me.

"Did it work?" I say.

No response.

"Are you still mad?" I say. I don't know what I hope to accomplish by asking this, but I desperately feel the need to know. How slighted can she feel after learning that, yes, this body belongs to me?

"This doesn't change anything," Estrella says. "Do you know how long I've been trying to break free? How long I've felt trapped?"

I sigh. This again. Nothing's changed. "So you're still determined to make my life miserable?"

"Do you really not remember?" Estrella says before launching herself at me.

I'll admit, I didn't expect her to attack right away, so when she slams into my chest, I'm not in the best position to absorb the blow. It doesn't much matter, though, because my mind plummets into a memory.

Darkness surrounds me.

I can hear my younger voice giggling, my surroundings muffling my voice. No, wait. I can hear two voices. Near identical.

As my eyes adjust, it only takes a moment for me to recognize the space beneath Mom and Dad's bed. It's messy. No, *dirty*. Half of it is packed with spider webs, with the other half made up of dirty socks and Dad's old tee-shirts. But we're young. I'm young. I've yet to understand how terrifying spiders are. In fact, I'm filled with the vaguest sense that people who are scared of spiders are idiots.

"Ew!" I hear my voice say, though it speaks of laughter rather than genuine disgust. I can tell the voice doesn't actually belong to me. "Under the bed!"

More laughter. One is physical, the other in my head, but both somehow real.

And then I see a change in my childish face's eyes, and my smile widens.

I crawl out, breath ragged and panting from excitement. I duck under the sink, knocking what few bottles we have of soap and Windex out of the way. My expression changes again.

"Oh, that's easy!" my voice says. This one, I can tell, is me. "We're under the sink!"

Again, my pupils dilate, and I crawl out from under the sink and look around from hiding spot to hiding spot within the confines of the small apartment.

My eyes fall to the door leading outside our apartment. I know—*she* knows—I'm not allowed, and as if keeping myself from snitching, I hold my index finger up to my own lips before opening the door and closing it behind me. I'm filled with a sense of elation—a thrill. We've never been outside of the apartment by ourselves before.

"You're not supposed to be out here," I say. This time, the voice is me.

"You're not supposed to be cheating!" she responds, her voice bratty.

"*You're* cheating!" Mine is equally bratty. "We're not supposed to hide out here."

And then, this moment falls into place. Something about that feeling of excitement of being outside of our apartment for the first time. It's not even a surprise when I hear his voice.

"Who's cheating?" His voice is like silk, his face gaunt. Creeper Carl from down the hall. He's one of a thousand reasons Mom and Dad don't let us out of the apartment without them. He's weak, sickly, and only has a few years left before he ODs in his apartment. But right now, he's the most terrifying figure in the world.

His figure is thin, frail, and broken, but he's fast and on us in the blink of an eye. I want to run, but can't. My legs are frozen, as though stuck in place, and I want to do nothing but cry.

I recoil, throwing myself from the memory and back into the Mirage. I have no recollection of the moments following, but wake up inside the apartment, blood in my mouth and under my fingernails.

The memory jets forward. Dad scolds me for going outside, but tells me I did the right thing in fighting back.

"I'm sorry," I say. Though I remember only feeling anger. Anger at the position Estrella had put us in.

Years passed, and any memory I had of Estrella retreated into my subconscious. She became nothing but distant recollections of an imaginary friend.

"You took everything from me!" Estrella yells at me as I slam into the chalk-ridden floor. I feel the force field take the brunt of the damage, but that doesn't stop the wind from getting knocked out of me.

With a hop, I'm back on my feet. I swing and punch Estrella on the cheek and send her flying. This time, no memory interrupts our fight as I follow up with a series of punches.

Those memories. They only bring back the worst feelings. It brings it all tumbling back. The apartment. The danger. And the only way to ensure a better future for myself is to keep fighting.

"It used to be you and me," Estrella says. "And then you *left* me. No, you trapped me in this prison. Why?"

It's in that moment that I realize she's genuinely asking. Even the most vivid of memories haven't brought her the answers. Only I have the answers.

"Because," I say. "Even when I was little, I understood I knew I had to move on."

I leap at Estrella, and for the first time, strike *her* with a memory of my own. Of those exact moments following the attack from Creeper Carl. The intense panic that followed, and the never-ending desire to do whatever it takes to leave my hellhole of a life.

"Even when I was little," I say, "I knew I couldn't live a normal life so long as I had you...this malignant tumor of a human being attached to me, undercutting me at every step."

I have no idea how true my words are. I don't know how conscious I was about blocking Estrella out from that point forward. Most of my memories are still foggy, uncertain, and terrifying, but I feel a desperation inside I've never felt before. It's as though my very future is slipping away from my fingers in every passing moment, and that if I don't fight back, I'll lose it forever.

Because, between the two of us, Estrella has always been the strong one, and if I'm going to win this fight, I'm going to have to give it everything I have.

Like it or not, this is the fight for my life.

FOUR

ESTRELLA OPENS HER MOUTH, letting out a high-pitched scream that threatens to destroy my eardrums. My hands clamp to the sides of my head, but it doesn't seem to do much against the auditory onslaught.

And then I feel her inside my chest. Not only is she ripping apart my organs from the inside, but she's twisting and pulling my emotions along with them. I'm sobered by the reality that while I may have *some* ownership over this Mirage, it's still very much Estrella's. She has the dominant power, and that includes the ability to more easily run my brain through a cheese grater.

I tighten my stomach, then my chest, and somehow, pulling from within, my Spectral powers pull outward and form into a force field. Estrella's ethereal form is catapulted from my insides and thrown back.

Her giant head hisses. "Why?"

"Why what?" I say, my hands up in defense of an inevitable incoming attack.

"Why do you hate me?"

"I don't like it when Spectres dedicate their non-lives to ruining mine." I take slow, meditative steps toward Estrella, hands raised into fists. "I get my shit in order one day, and the very next, you throw it all into chaos."

Just then, I'm berated by an unsettling image—Estrella's giant head sprouts thin, almost stick figure-like arms from its cheeks. One of them waves from the outside in, as though swinging a small club.

A stabbing sensation punctures my back, but my pain is cut off by a blackness. I can't even tell if my eyes are open. And then it all comes into focus. Above me, I see the crisscross patterns of two-by-fours interspersed with the ruffles from the mattress coating poking out in between.

It's the bottom of a top bunk. It's where Casey slept before she was adopted. I don't need to look around to know right away where I am. This is my second foster home—the one I burned down. Whoops, I guess? It was a miracle I didn't spend the rest of my young years behind bars after all this.

I don't remember the night it happened—only waking up amid a burning living room, a fireplace poker in hand. You know, typical psychotic shit.

Now, I know better. I know that Estrella was behind it all. That she'd spent part of my life lashing out against me in desperate hopes of wresting control of my body.

"Luna?" I hear Casey's voice from above.

"Yeah?" I call back up, but I can tell this isn't me speaking.

"You awake?"

"What do you think?" Estrella responds in my body, speaking for me. How often had she done that without me noticing?

"Sorry," Casey says. "I can't sleep. Excited for tomorrow." There's a long pause, like I can tell she wants to say something else.

Estrella doesn't try to fill the void. I can tell she doesn't have a full grasp of the context of the situation, and doesn't want to give herself away, even though no one would be stupid enough to think I'd been possessed by a long-dead sister.

"I'm...I'm also scared of what'll happen when I'm gone."

Casey was always too sweet for her own good. She was the big sister to everyone in our foster home—even the older kids. "I'm sure you'll be okay," Estrella tells her.

"I'm not worried about me. I'm worried about you. You and the others. Antonia. Ben."

"Why?"

"Did...did Mr. and Mrs. Segal never do anything to you?"

"Like what?" Estrella's confusion is thinly veiled. I'm confused, too. In my time at their home, the Segals were nothing but nice to me. It's what made it all the more heartbreaking for them when I set a torch to their home. The judge made sure I knew how saddened they were by the whole mess. I mean, I'd be sad too if my house was razed to the ground because of some mentally disturbed child.

Another pregnant pause. "That...that's good." I can practically feel Casey nodding in the bunk above me. Like she's convincing herself more than responding to me.

A knock at the door. I recognize the rhythm immediately. One quick knock followed by three rapid ones. It's soft, but audible.

I can somehow feel Casey tense up in the bunk above me.

"Luna," she whispers. "Please don't let me go with them."

"What?"

"Please don't."

"Casey," I hear Mr. Segal's soft voice through a crack in the door. "Do you have a minute?"

Casey's breathing above me has gone from frantic to steady in the blink of an eye.

"Casey?" Mr. Segal's voice is still soft, but a touch sharper, as though he can aim his voice at the bunk above mine. His footsteps are muted, his socks squishing down on the soft carpet.

The bunk sways lightly as he shakes her above me.

"You have a few minutes?"

"What time is it?" Casey says, feigning sleepiness. I can hear her voice shaking, though I don't know if it's because I'm listening for it. Can he hear it, too? Does he care?

My pulse quickens as Casey climbs from her bunk and follows him out the door. I can hear her silent plea in her look back as it closes behind her. Is that pulse mine or Estrella's?

The next moment, I'm—or rather, Estrella in my body—sitting up in bed and tiptoeing to the door. She opens it a few inches.

The sound of a crackling fire in the living room is interrupted only by a dull click down the hall. It's the door to the Segals' room.

I can feel Estrella's fear. I can feel her inner turmoil, but as she steps into the living room, the kernels of a poorly thought out plan unfurl in her mind.

My mind flashes, and I'm back in the Mirage, but the memories don't stop.

Every horrific instance where control is snatched from my hands, leaving my life in greater shambles. I don't relive the memories, but experience the emotion in each moment simultaneously.

That time where I beat the hell out of that devious bitch who made fun of the "mole" on my neck. Back then, I didn't realize that she was making fun of a part of me. A piece of me that lay hidden inside. It's no wonder Estrella took control and beat her senseless.

In every instance where I was frozen in fear—where my fight-or-flight response was to freeze—Estrella was there.

In every life or death situation I was in, I wasn't the only one making the decisions. She was there, every step of the way—sometimes dipping in and out of my body, and other times acting as a soft voice in the back of my subconscious.

"*I'm sorry,*" I hear her voice say. "*Please don't lock me away. Not again.*"

I don't know how, but I remember this moment now. And my response was to push her away. I shoved her back into my subconscious.

It's no wonder she finally decided to break out and culminate into her Spectral form. It's no wonder she finally fought for her freedom.

I'm back in the Mirage, only this time, it's no longer the black, stadium-sized void I've learned to recognize.

Instead, we now stand at the center of a ring of flames—layers upon layers of flames on all sides, like the rows of teeth on a great white shark. It's fitting, considering how this all started.

Estrella is no longer a giant. For the first time, she takes on a more standard physical form. She looks like a slightly taller version of me. Her chest heaves with each breath, her face painted with an ugly scowl. But this version of her highlights something I never acknowledged. For the first time, I recognize her humanity.

"I gave you everything," she says. "I tried to be a good sister. I tried my best to be good, but none of it was enough for you."

I want to argue with her that I didn't know, but at some point, I know I did, and at some point, I chose to forget. Because what I said earlier was true. Memories of her didn't just disappear. I forced them out. I actively chose to leave her behind. I actively chose to keep her suppressed and trapped.

Because that's what I always do.

Because I always choose to run away from the pieces of my life that don't fit some perfect vision of my future, no matter how much they are a part of me.

I let my arms fall to my sides, even as Estrella bounds toward me, mouth open, screaming in frustration—screaming as she prepares for the fight of her very existence.

And this time, I don't fight back. I don't run. I don't try to talk my way out of it. This battle with Estrella, like every other aspect of my life, is a part of me.

"I'm so sorry," I say.

I close my eyes and give her what she deserves.

I give her the life she never had.

To Be Continued...

SEB

SPECTRAL | EPISODE 11

A DARK MIRAGE

MY EYES OPEN TO BLACKNESS—NOT the blackness of the Mirage, but something darker. If I didn't know any better, I'd think I was blind. Wait, am I blind?

I wave my hand in front of me and snap my fingers, but I see nothing. I can't even tell if I moved my hands. Can I move my hands.

"What's wrong with you?" Estrella's voice is raspy, but somehow fuller than normal. It's like her voice is coming from an actual body. Still, it's unmistakably hers.

"*Me?*"

"Yeah, what's wrong with you? What kind of idiot just stands there and lets herself be attacked?"

"I just...I dunno." I don't have an answer for her.

"Of course you don't know. Because you don't think."

I'm almost caught off guard by this new tone of hers. Whereas before she came across as young and...feral...this new voice of hers is different. Different, but the same.

"Well? Why'd you do it?"

I shrug, or I think I shrug. I still don't know if I still have a body, and it's not like she can see me. "I'm..." I sigh. I can't be dead, can I? Death would be a lot less exhausting than this. "What do you want from me?"

"I want to know why you just stood there."

What am I supposed to say? That I felt sorry for her? Something tells me she wouldn't take that well.

"What did you expect would happen?" she says, her voice persistent.

"I didn't think it through. I just did it."

"Of course you didn't think it through. You never do. You froze again."

"Is that what I did?"

"Like usual. You can either fight someone head-on or you can outsmart them. Only you decided to stand still and take the fight head on. Except you don't fight."

"Freezing is a completely normal thing to do in scary moments!" I yell at her.

"That doesn't make it any less stupid!"

I smile. Somehow, in the dark, and without a body, I smile. A warmth grows inside me. It's a feeling I haven't had in years. It's a feeling I didn't realize I was missing.

"I don't freeze all the time."

"That's true. Sometimes you run. Most times, you run."

"And?"

A pause. What is she doing? Thinking? "So, why didn't you run this time?"

"I'm...I'm sick of fighting with you."

Another long pause. "Well, that makes two of us."

"Listen," I say. "I still don't know everything that's going on. In my head, you're still just some Ghost that's threatened to steal my body from me, but in my gut..." I don't know where that sentence is going, so I just stop, hoping she'll interrupt and complete my thought for me.

She lets the moment linger for way too long. I can't tell if she's angry or just messing with me, but either way, it's awkward.

"Did you know?" I say.

"What, that you killed me in the womb? I can't say it's crossed my mind. Being with you like this is all I've ever known."

"And now that you do know?"

"I don't know, Luna," Estrella says. "I'm still figuring all this out."

"So am I." Another awkward pause between us. "I'm sorry," I say, "for trapping you inside me for all those years. I think I was scared."

"We're always scared," she says.

I chuckle, and a sob escapes my mouth. "We are. I didn't know what to do. I was so desperate to find happiness that I tried to run as fast and far away as I could."

Silence. Not so much as a breath to pull me out of the blackness. No chuckle. No cry. Just ear-piercing silence.

"Thank you."

The darkness brightens, and I'm standing face to face with Estrella, my sister. Her face is thinner than mine, and she's a tad taller than me, but there's no mistaking it. This is the girl she should have grown up to be.

I feel my wrist Syncer vibrate, and I don't need to look down to know what it signifies.

Like a puzzle piece, her presence fills a void that hadn't been filled for almost as long as I can remember. But I *can* remember a time when it was once there.

I swallow, choking back another sob.

And then, like a glass dome, the world around us shatters.

SPECTRAL

EPISODE 11
SPECTRAL

11

ONE

THE LIGHT'S ALMOST BLINDING. Scratch that. The light's blinding as hell. Literal hell. If Jace lives through this, he's confident he won't see the same for the rest of his life. Then again, that's the way it feels in many Mirages. You almost can't imagine feeling anything other than what you're feeling at that exact moment.

It's the reason so many Mediums crap out of the program early on, and why their ranks are still thin, even after existing for fifteen years, and why early exposure to trauma is an essential prerequisite. To be a Medium is to deal in trauma. Either the trauma of the Spectres themselves or the trauma you'll experience as you progress in your career. You don't go far in this line of work without becoming a hapless victim. You don't go far without being scarred for life, either mentally or physically.

The Mirage he's in is *hot*. Melting your skin hot. Piercing your eyeballs hot. Nuclear explosion hot.

Jace sits up.

In the distance, a series of mushroom clouds rise above and around the old city. Or town. It's some awkward in-between. Not quite a city, but not a town, either. Whatever it is isn't important. What *is* important is what's happening in front of him. No less than a dozen other Mediums zip around, coming from every which direction. They wield weapons of absurd sizes—blades, guns, bats—there's even one with a heavy chain—all converging on one solitary silhouette in the distance.

Jace recognizes the almost gaunt figure in front of him as Hiro Hana-jima—the anomaly—and a pain in the DOSD's side. He can't count the number of meetings they've had about him, and how much mental real estate he took up in the commander's mind. But he's a far cry from the badass Jace remembers from previous encounters. Last he heard, Hanajima was on a downswing, likely mere months away from disintegrating into nothingness, along with his Spectre. Looking at him now, he looks anything but weak.

"Teach!" Jace hears a voice call out from beside him. He turns to see Seb standing over him, hand outstretched. *God, he's so young.* "What'd I say about calling me that?"

"Sorry," Seb says as he pulls Jace up. "Force of habit."

Jace groans. "Well, make a new one. At some point, you have to accept me as a peer, not a mentor."

"What happened?" Seb says. "Where are we?"

That's a good question. Where are we? Last he remembered, they were answering a call. An emergency revolving around escaped Spectres. It was always a risk, dealing in the business of reviving Spectres. It's one that drove a wedge between him and the commander. The threat these Spectres posed was immense, but no threat was too great in her eyes.

He, Seb, and dozens of others had poured into the Essence Bank, putting a stop to the flood of Spectres and their Mirages. He and Seb took down two escaped Spectres with ease. Then they were back in the Essence Bank, only to get tossed back into this violent Mirage involuntarily.

Jace can't remember the last time he was thrown into a Mirage against his will. Actually, he knows for a fact that he's *never* been thrown into a Mirage against his will. If you're a Medium, it's just something that doesn't happen. Not unless you're up against an exceedingly strong Spectre. Though, it's fitting that the Spectre in question is over a century old.

Hundreds of feet in front of him, Hiro Hanajima spins, sending four Mediums flying in every direction. Acting quickly, Jace holds up his arms. A force field shoots outward, and catches one of the Mediums flying toward them, slowing her to a halt just a few feet away.

"You okay, Maria?" he asks.

"Who is this guy?" she says, whipping her hair out of her face and ignoring the fact that he pretty much saved her from getting liquidated against an invisible wall within the Mirage.

"What, Lazarus never told you about Hiro Hanajima?" Jace says. "I'll have to have a word with him about that."

"He's a Spectre?" Maria says.

"No. He's a Medium," Jace replies. "You don't know him?"

Maria gives him an irritated glance with her piercing green eyes that are at odds with her dark skin.

"Okay, you don't know, but I'm willing to bet good money that this Mirage is his Spectre's doing."

"What do you mean his Spectre?" Maria says, slinging her shotgun over her shoulder.

"I need to talk to Lazarus when this is all over. That you don't know about Spectral Companions at your level is criminal. Have you found the Spectre of this Mirage yet?"

"We've been a bit too preoccupied with the rogue Medium to think about that, Boss," she says.

Jace's eyes scan the skies. Last he heard, Hanajima was donning a crow for a Spectre. Then again, that was in the real world. Who's to say if that would carry over into the Mirage?

"Seb!" he yells over the sound of sonic booms and collisions that make up the fight between Hanajima and his fellow Mediums.

"Yes, Tea—Agent Kamil?" The kid sounds so stiff, Jace almost expects him to salute along with his response.

"Get to tracking," he says. "This is the Mirage of Hanajima's Spectral Companion. He may be strong, but the two are linked. If we take down his Spectre, we take down the Mirage."

"Is he not fighting with his Spectre?" Seb says with a puzzled expression.

"You're the Tracker, not me," Jace says. "Either way, look at him fight." Jace casts his eyes over to Hanajima, who is taking on the squad of over a dozen Attackers and Defenders with his bare fists. "He's strong, but it doesn't look like his strikes are amplified by a Companion."

"But what about—"

"That's enough. Do what I say."

In response, Seb holds his hands out in front of him, starting with his palms facing toward Hanajima ahead of them, and slowly turning to the mushroom clouds in the distance and a pack of zombie-like bodies limping toward them.

"Dammit!" Jace says. "I can't stand Spirits. Seb, keep up your tracking. I'll cover you." He summons a scimitar and runs full-force at the small group of Spirits threatening to take Seb down. "Maria, you do the same!"

"Understood!" they say in unison.

HIRO WINCES as a blade cuts into his arm.

Dammit.

He'd been distracted by a Junior Medium again. It sickens him how the DOSD still throws teenagers into battle, but he's already committed to taking down anyone stupid enough to attack him.

"*Something tells me you bit off more than you can chew,*" Kuro sends to Hiro.

"*I'm fine,*" Hiro says, stomping his foot into the ground. This sends a shockwave in every which direction that throws back another volley of Mediums who threaten to take him down. "*Besides, who's the one who wanted us to stand up for the wellbeing of all Spectre-kind?*"

"*You think I expected you to lead a mass prison break of all Spectres in the facility?*"

"*Don't act like you weren't one hundred perce...*" Hiro stops and chuckles. "*You're messing with me, aren't you?*"

"*Even in your wise old years, it still takes you far too long to catch on.*"

Hiro ducks down, dodging a blade attack from a Medium who threatens to cut him in half.

"*You sure you don't want my help?*" Kuro says.

"*I'm sure,*" Hiro says. "*I may be stronger with you, but we can't risk you getting freed. That happens, and it's...*"

"*Over, got it.*"

Hiro stomps again, just as another Medium threatens to impale him with a staff, and rebuts with a punch to the chest. He feels the man's sternum crack beneath his fist as he's thrown back, and a piece of him feels guilty. He doesn't want to kill these people, but they've left him no choice. It's them or him.

A buzzing goes off in his head, and he wraps a force field around himself just in time to block bullets from another overzealous Medium. "*This is never-ending.*"

"*Of course it is,*" Kuro says. "*You didn't expect everyone would just roll over and take it while we destroyed the very foundation this organization was built on, did you?*"

"*That's why we hid here. In your Mirage.*" Hiro holds out his hands all around as a swarm of no less than fifteen Mediums close in around him, pressing in on his force field. "*That's why we...*" And then he sees it. Out of the corner of his eye, he sees another handful of Mediums pour in through a previously hidden Bullethole. They slam into the ground.

Hiro swallows a lump in his throat, and he feels a void expand inside his stomach. "*What're you doing, Kuro?*"

"*What?*" The Spectre sounds confused. Hiro almost buys it.

"*What're you doing bringing them in here? I thought they were following me.*" Hiro doesn't know why he bothers asking. He knows the reason, and Kuro's silent response is all he needs as a confirmation. "No. No. No, no, no, no."

"*I'm tired, Hiro.*" Kuro's voice in Hiro's head is reserved. "*I'm ready to move on.*"

An explosion bursts inside Hiro, and with it, his shield explodes as well, throwing the incoming Mediums in every direction, hundreds of feet away. *"You may be ready, but I'm not!"*

"You've had over a hundred and fifty years."

"It's not enough."

In the distance, Hiro sees a few Mediums jumping farther away from the epicenter of the battle and toward one of the many mushroom clouds that pepper the post-apocalyptic landscape. Toward where Kuro hides.

"It looks like someone wised up and sent a Tracker after me," Kuro says.

"Kuro."

"I promise to at least pretend to put up a fight."

"Don't do this."

"Goodbye, Hiro. I know it doesn't feel like it right now, but I wish we could have had a life together. A real life."

IT DOESN'T TAKE much effort to fight off the horrifying zombie corpses that pepper the Mirage's landscape. More than anything, it feels like they've been put here for set decoration, crumbling at the smallest show of force. Jace knows even non-Mediums can take down these bastards with a half-decent punch.

"Are you sure about this, Agent Kamil?" Seb says, running ahead.

"Just shut up and listen to your abilities," Jace says. He usually tries to rein in his temper when dealing with his students, but nothing about this situation is normal. Besides, even as they descend deeper and deeper into the pack of mushroom clouds, it's impossible not to notice how they move as they approach them. It's like they're not mushroom clouds at all, but a pack of tornadoes, twisting and turning *away* from them, like a parting sea.

The Spectre is inviting them in. Seb is right to be suspicious, but Jace is suspicious enough for the both of them. Right now, they need to focus on taking out Hanajima's Spectral Companion and putting an end to whatever this charade is.

"I think I see something!" Seb squints through the whipping wind, and Jace follows his gaze to a dark shadow sitting in the middle of the mushroom clouds. It's large, malevolent, and almost seems to smile back at them as they approach.

And then, with each step, like a real mirage, it appears to morph and billow, shrinking all the while. Jace almost doesn't notice that the air around them comes to a standstill. By the time they're within a hundred yards' distance, the shadowy Spectre is reduced to the size of a bird.

A crow, Jace thinks. *A large crow, but a crow, nonetheless. Unless its size makes it a raven.* Jace brushes the thought aside as they near the Spectre. Unlike most he's encountered, this one feels calm. Inviting.

"Seb, you sure that's it?"

As they come to a stop dozens of feet away, Seb holds out his hands in front of him, palms facing outward toward the crow. "That's him."

The crow's head tilts to the side. "Now, why'd the two of you stop?" The bird flaps its wings once, covering the distance between them in the blink of an eye.

Seb's guns are out just as fast—at least Jace trained him well enough to do that—and the sound of machine gun fire goes off. Feathers flutter and explode as the bullets make contact. The crow lets out a squawk of pain and pulls back.

"Seb?"

The kid is on it quick, pulling up the stats on his Syncer in an instant.

"Yeah, I got it," he says. "He's...Level Twenty?"

Jace looks at the crow as it hovers in the air above them.

Seb continues his assault, and more feathers erupt out of the Spectre as it continues to get pelted.

Jace clenches his scimitar, and leaps into the air, cautious as he comes down on the bird. It squawks, but doesn't move as his blade moves through its body, though it doesn't pierce its strong hide.

More gunshots. More swings of his blade. It's like a never-ending parade of feathers and squawks. All the while, the crow doesn't so much as lift a talon to fight back or protest. At Level Twenty, he could decimate both Jace and Seb if he wanted to, but there is no resistance. With each passing second, Jace can see the Spectre weakening, each attack contributing to a slow and painful death.

"No!" the Spectre cries out, his silence ending.

Jace jumps backward from his planned continued attacks and holds out his arm for Seb to follow suit.

The crow writhes and twists in front of them. "Stop it!" he yells. "Just stop—"

Then the Spectre flies sideways, hundreds of feet away, as though being pulled by an invisible string. He transforms from his crow form into a translucent black Spectral form, before turning into a long blade.

The blade's hilt lands into the open and waiting hand of Hanajima, whose faced is contorted into a pained grimace. The man is weak. On his last legs. And behind him, a swarm of Mediums follows. This is the end of Hanajima, and he knows it.

"You!" Hanajima growls as he points his blade at Seb.

Poor Seb takes an involuntary step back—in spite of the weapons he wields. Jace knows the kid was always too soft for this. If he wasn't so gifted, maybe Jace could have convinced the commander not to recruit him into the Department.

Jace moves before he can second-guess himself, and before Hanajima can move. After all, this is *his* Mirage. It'll be hard to get to Seb before Hanajima does. But Jace tries his best anyway, pushing his feet off the dirt with each stride.

Hanajima's already halfway there. Jace knows he has to pick up the pace.

So he does. He could never forgive himself if something happened to one of his students. Time and time again, Commander Daugherty tried to beat that instinct out of him, telling him they stopped being kids the instant they signed on.

But that's not true. He's seen how they interact, how they fear the Mirages they set foot in, how even after all these years, a Spectre can catch you off guard and make you feel smaller than the smallest of creatures. They may be gifted kids, but they're still kids.

The soles of Jace's boots skid as he comes to a halt in front of Seb. He holds out his hands as he brings the shield up in front of him.

But it's too late. He can feel the sharpness of the blade for the quickest instant. It's the most painful thing he's ever felt.

And then it's gone.

SEB DOESN'T WASTE his breath on a scream. He doesn't waste it on so much as an extra breath as he sees Teach fall in front of him, his body getting cut in two in a single swing. A *single* swing. He's never seen that happen in a Mirage.

If only they'd been allowed to hang on to higher-level Spectres, this wouldn't have been a problem. He could have taken a hit, even from the sharpest Spectral blade.

Seb stops himself from following that train of thought. Hanajima is Level Twenty. There isn't a world where every Medium on duty right now could get anywhere close to Level Twenty all at once using the limited Essences available in the Bank.

Seb swallows, his breath catching at the same time.

Mourn later. He can almost hear Jace's voice saying it. And he's right.

Seb jumps backward and to the side, getting a good vantage of the Medium and his Spectral Companion, and lets loose. The bullets spray both Hanajima and the writhing blade, though the damage done is nonexistent. Almost embarrassing.

Seb's never felt prepared to take on a Spectre before. No matter the target, there's always some factor that keeps him from feeling competent in his work. But Jace was always there for him, and when he wasn't, Vero was.

But neither of them are here now. He takes another leap back, keeping his fingers pressed down on the triggers of his weapons, continuing to pelt Hanajima from a distance. It's times like this that he appreciates his long-range weapon—and to think it originally materialized because he thought it was cool.

He somehow dodges a swing from Hanajima, the sound of screaming permeating the Mirage. But it's not his own, nor the Medium's. It's the Spectre. He can't make out what he's saying, but he's fighting back against his Medium.

Seb doesn't let it distract him. He continues his strategy: jump back and unload. Stay clear of the long, Spectral blade. It's like a test of endurance in his video games. Dole out one hit, then jump. Rinse and repeat. He'll have to do this a *long* time if he wants to survive.

And then Hanajima's figure recoils in front of Seb, as though attacked from behind, opening him up for a few more direct hits from the bullets.

The entire thing moves in a blur. One second, it's just Seb and Hanajima. David and Goliath. And the next, there's Maria, her shotgun all but punching a hole through the Medium. And then there's Lazarus and his claymore. And then there's a mountain of other Mediums who descend on Hanajima.

Still, over the bustle and chaos, the Spectre's cries ring out all across the Mirage, even as the entire thing dissolves around them, the mushroom clouds fading into nothingness.

TWO

ESTRELLA and I emerge from the Mirage, and with it, her human form melts away into a more translucent form. It holds the shape of her as a young woman, but her detailed face has reverted to the abstract look I'd grown accustomed to.

And when the tanks of the room around us come into view, I notice the difference in atmosphere instantly.

"Luna!" Vero's voice cuts through the noise of my thoughts. "What were you thinking?" She shakes my shoulders, a mix of frustration, anger, and concern.

"I'm fine," I say.

"Are you? Because that was beyond devastatingly stupid what you did. You had no backup, and no means of reaching out to us if you needed it."

My brow furrows. I never like it when people call me stupid. "Hey, it worked out." On cue, Estrella shrinks down to the size of my hand and hovers over my shoulder.

Any anger on Vero's face disappears in an instant, replaced by confusion and curiosity. "Is that...?"

"Vero, I'd like you to meet my sister, Estrella."

"Stop acting like I haven't met her before," Estrella says, her arms crossed. "I'm still the same person, only now I have all of my memories."

A *thwipping* sound catches Vero's attention. It's like she's reminded of the situation we're in. "Look, I'm happy for you—and I know the commander will be happy, too—but things are insane here right now."

I cast my eyes around the room. It's a far cry from the tense, quiet intensity of before. Instead, all of that quietness has exploded into a frenzy, with hundreds of staff and Mediums bustling around the room.

Thwip! Thwip! A Medium pops in from a random Mirage and runs over to one of the Essence station tank thingies and jams his arm into one of the slots. The machine whirrs and the liquid visible at the top rises.

Past him, I can see several stretchers loaded with Mediums being carted away, and several bodies litter the ground, pools of blood trickling out from them.

"What's happening?"

"I thought I told you two to get out of here," Commander Daugherty's voice is just as ragged and unpleasant as usual, but with an anxious edge I didn't expect.

"What happened?" Vero says.

"What do you think happened? We've been fighting dozens of Spectres nonstop, trying our best to reclaim them. We're almost there, but I've lost ten men, and there's another twenty-five injured. And the rest of them, I don't even know where the hell they are."

Thwip! Thwip! Another handful of Mediums materialize around us, each running to one of the Essence stations. Commander Daugherty only gives them the briefest of acknowledgements as she continues to walk. Vero and I follow behind. Well, Vero follows her, and I follow Vero, too curious not to get a handle on what's going on.

"How many are missing?" Vero says. I can hear the shift in her tone from before. It's stiffer, and somehow deeper.

"Eighty-three so far," Commander Daugherty says. "Before each one jumps into a Mirage, they're supposed to log their intentions and general location within our HQ team, but eighty-three of them are MIA, including Agents Kamil and Mariano."

"What?" Vero says.

"Keep your voice down, Agent Daugherty."

Vero clamps her mouth shut, but follows up with a whisper. "So, what are you doing about it?"

"Right now, we're worrying about what we can. We're providing medical attention to those who are here and sending remaining agents off to sweep up the rest of this mess. Though, on the plus side, it looks like the vast majority of Spectres have been accounted for. If any of them are to escape now, it's likely not to cause any more issues than a standard CBS incident."

"Great," I say. "Way to reach for the stars."

Commander Daugherty turns her attention back to me, as though remembering for the first time that I'm even there. "It's the best we can hope for, given the circumstances." She stares at me for an awkwardly long time. I can tell she's deciding what to do with me—it's a look I've gotten often growing up.

"*Luna,*" I hear Estrella whisper in my head. I look around, not realizing she'd retreated inside of me amid the chaos. "*Do you feel that?*"

I've been feeling an awful lot lately, especially in the last few minutes with everything that's been going on between me and Estrella. So much that I haven't had much room or space to feel anything else. But the second she asks, I know what she's talking about. It's like listening to a familiar song, and I feel a flood of nostalgia for recent moments—the first time I "caught" Estrella, the theatrical Mirage of Alan Arroyo, and more recently, the time at the Salton Sea.

I didn't even realize it was possible to feel nostalgic for memories that recent, but here we are. And I understand what it means.

"He's here," I say. "Hiro." It shouldn't have surprised me. Vero had mentioned him before the scuffle with my sister, but now the feeling hits deeper. And I can tell something else. "Kuro. His Spectre. He's dying."

Commander Daugherty eyes me with suspicion. "How can you know that?"

I shrug, equally confused. "Hiro mentioned something about my abilities being more than your standard Mediums. I don't know if that's a part of it, but I can tell right now that he's in trouble."

"More than likely, he's the one causing the trouble," Commander Daugherty says.

And then I feel an overwhelming surge of emotion. It's like an explosion, and I push back the urge to cry. God, I hate crying, and this whole Spectre thing makes it happen way too often.

And then that metaphorical explosion breaks out into the real world, as dozens of bodies materialize out of the air, slamming onto the hard laminated cement floor.

Most of them land on their feet, but more than a handful aren't so lucky. It's only after a second look that I realize it's either because they're injured or…are they dead?

In any other circumstance, I'd expect to hear screams, but I almost forget that I'm among heartless, seasoned Mediums, who deal in randomly appearing figures on a near-daily basis. They move fast, picking up their fallen or injured and set to work, taking them where they need to go without so much as a word. I wouldn't call it quiet, but given the number of people who had just erupted out of thin air, it still feels like it.

The first one to speak is Commander Daugherty, who turns to the nearest agent. "What happened? Where were you?"

"Hiro Hanajima, Commander." He doesn't so much as elaborate on the name. It's clear it carries weight among the DOSD.

"He's in one of the Mirages?"

"His Spectre *created* one of the Mirages."

Commander Daugherty pinches her lips together, the fury clear in her narrow eyes. For the first time, I notice the prominent trail of crow's feet that outline them. "And where is he now?"

"Dead," the Medium is quick to add.

My stomach drops, and I let out an involuntary gasp.

Daugherty's eyes widen, untrusting. "You're sure?"

The Medium smiles. "We're sure. Agent Mariano saw to that. Ain't that right, Seb?"

The room breaks out into an unexpected eruption of cheers from the formerly stoic figures. Everyone is turned away from me, facing a figure several rows down. I can barely see him, but he's one I recognize, and as I sidle down a row, I see him on the ground, bent over a body.

"Is this true, Agent Mariano?" Commander Daugherty says, though her voice fades out as she notices the blood spilling out from the body he's kneeling over.

All it takes is an extra look from me to realize that I'm not even sure I'd classify it as a whole body, but two distinct pieces. I look away, trying to purge the sight from my mind.

"Teach?" Vero whispers before she runs over to the other boy and the body. Me? I hang back, keeping my distance. I'm in no mood to see a mutilated corpse. Call me old-fashioned.

I swallow as saliva floods my mouth, and I try not to think about who the poor soul might be. It doesn't work. Between Vero and Seb's reaction, it's clear who it is.

"Dammit, Hiro," I whisper to myself. And then I remember the news that Hiro had been killed—by Seb, of all people. My stomach does somersaults and backflips, somehow at the same time, and I don't have the faintest idea how to deal with the emotion coursing through me.

I'm still angry at Hiro for leaving me, but heartbroken that he's gone, upset at him for killing their teacher, and somehow, I have room to feel conflicted about Seb's involvement in the whole mess.

"Breathe, Sis," Estrella whispers to me. "Breathe."

Sure, it's easy for her to say. She's a Spectre. She doesn't breathe at all —though I keep this insight to myself, hoping all the while that she can't read my mind. Instead, I follow her instructions and breathe. It doesn't help much, but it doesn't make things worse either.

I just hang back as the pieces of the man's body are hauled onto the stretcher and carried off. Vero and Seb only look on, expressions blank, before turning back to face the commander. Ever the obedient soldiers.

Only when the body has cleared the area, do I have the courage to step closer and eavesdrop on the discussion.

"Yes, it's true," Seb says, his voice clipped and sharp. "Commander," he adds when he realizes his error.

But I can tell Commander Daugherty isn't as preoccupied with his tone as I thought she'd be. Instead, I see an anxious smile cross her lips. It's not the kind of smile when someone is anxious, but one where they're almost too worried to smile. Like if they smile, it'll somehow jinx the whole thing.

I decide I hate this woman.

Hiro may not have been working with the DOSD's interest in mind, and he may have screwed me over, but he didn't deserve death. At least I don't think so.

I can't tell anymore if I want Hiro to be alive or if I just want everything in this woman's life to go wrong.

"Ms. Guerrera!" she yells. Had she been yelling my name for the past few seconds?

"Yes!" I say too loudly.

"You share a special Bond with Hanajima."

"I don't know if I'd call what I have with him a special Bond."

"Well, whatever you have with him, use it. I want you to sense him."

"You what?"

"Like you did before. You knew he was here. You knew his Spectre was in danger. Now I need you to sense him."

And then I remember. She still thinks she has something on me. That she can order me around like another one of her Mediums.

"I...I don't think I can do that," I lie, for no other reason than I hate her.

She turns her head to the side, keeping her eyes focused on me. "Don't you lie to me now. Don't forget, this is all that stands between you and the truth of your past."

"Which part?" I say, my heart racing. "The part where I killed my sister in my mom's womb or the part where my mom left to get away from me?"

Commander Daugherty's mouth hangs open for the briefest of moments before shutting once more.

"You don't know anything more than that," I say. "You still don't understand why I can do these things and your other Mediums can't, or why I can't seem to do it with other Spectres. So why should I listen to you?"

Commander Daugherty crosses her arms. "Okay, then. Let's play. While I may no longer have any information to keep you obedient, you're still in my building. With a single word, I can have you reprimanded or even locked up. Make no mistake, I have no qualms with taking what I need from you and throwing away the key."

I tense up, though I hope that I don't show my anxiety on my face. I can feel the remaining Mediums closing in on me from every direction.

"But I'd much rather do this the civilized way," she says.

"You mean where I do exactly what you tell me to?"

"You have five seconds to comply."

"Commander Daugherty," Vero says in a scolding tone.

"Don't you talk back to me, too. Five."

I'll admit it. I'm curious. With everything that's going down, I want to know if he's behind everything, and if he's survived. Somehow, I'm able to let my pettiness subside. "Fine," I say before closing my eyes. I don't even wait to see the smug look on Commander Daugherty's face.

It takes no effort to do what Commander Daugherty asks. Every Spectre in the immediate surrounding area is in turmoil. They're angry, violent, and confused.

But none are Kuro, or Hiro for that matter.

"*Estrella?*" I send to her.

"*I don't sense him either,*" she sends to me. "*No Hiro. No Kuro. Either they weren't here before or they really are dead.*"

"*Way to sugarcoat it.*"

"*Sorry, Hiro is dead and Kuro is 'freed.' Does that help?*"

I can't for the life of me tell if she's being serious or ironic. The reality of the comment hits me. He's gone. I hadn't known him for long, but I don't know if there's a way not to feel something after spending most of your time with someone else for a week or two before their untimely death.

"He must've been scared," I say aloud. I can tell my voice is shaky. I know, more than anything else, the man feared death. You don't live as long as he did without being terrified of your fading existence. I wipe away a tear that threatens to break free from my eye.

"What?" Commander Daugherty's stupid voice interrupts my thoughts.

"Nothing," I say. "He's not here."

"You're sure?" She looks around, perusing the floor. "Did his body emerge from the Mirage with the others?"

"It disintegrated," Seb says. His voice is distant, more disengaged than I remember. "The second he and his Spectre were killed, he exploded into dust."

Somehow, this elicits a chuckle from Commander Daugherty.

"Why would it do that?" Vero says.

Commander Daugherty eyes her as though she were a child. "Give it some thought, Agent."

"It confused me at first, too," Seb says, his voice rigid, and his hand wiping a tear from his eye. "But we don't have any precedent for a Medium who's been alive as long as he was, let alone one who had a Spectral Companion. His Companion gave him an unnaturally long life. This means whatever power the two of them shared linked them. When his Spectre was free, any life-giving powers it offered him were cut off, and his body returned to its most natural form."

"Exactly, Agent Mariano," Commander Daugherty says. She exhales, and I swear I see her smile genuinely for the first time since I've met her. Gone is the apprehensive one I'd seen earlier, and in its place is the smile of a warrior who's scored an impressive victory. It's the same smile I've seen the likes of Gabe wear when he first joined Alethra's crew. It's probably a lot closer to a release of anxiety than a happy smile. But it fades as quickly as it appears. "Well, that's one golden goose gone." Her eyes fall on me, and I take a step back.

I feel more like a piece of meat than I ever have before. I resist the urge to cross my arms, and a second later, her eyes are now back over to Seb.

"Where is the Spectre's Essence?"

Seb tosses the marble-shaped object over to Commander Daugherty, who snatches it from mid-air. She holds it between her thumb and forefinger, closing one eye and staring at it with her other. "What Level was the Spectre?"

"Level Twenty, Commander," Seb says.

"We may have lost one key subject, but we have this, at least."

"Isn't it just a normal Spectre?" Vero says.

"We won't know until we analyze it. We still don't know where the anomaly lies. Is it within the Spectre itself, the Medium, or both?" The commander's glance again settles on me. She's not even being subtle about it at this point.

"Commander," Seb says, his voice still uncertain and rattled.

"What is it?" she says, her focus now back on the Essence lodged between her fingers.

"How long do you think it'll take for Hanajima to turn into a Spectre?"

"I don't think that's a concern for today."

"You're sure, Commander?"

Her eyes narrow and she faces the boy, who doesn't shrink back. "Teach—I mean, Agent Kamil had us study the life cycles of Spectres."

"We all study the life cycles of Spectres, Boy."

"But," Seb continues, unperturbed by her condescending tone, "I know the angrier someone's condition, the more likely they are to come back as a Spectre, and the older they are, the quicker it'll be. The only question is how quick." He pauses, as though waiting for her to interrupt. When it doesn't come, he continues. "We don't have a precedent for something like this. No one's ever been older than eighty-five on record for the Spectres we've freed. And I can tell you right now that Hanajima was...well, I don't know if he was angry or scared. But he was emotional at the end."

Commander Daugherty nods, and any relief that had stretched across her face fades as she takes in Seb's comments. The implication was clear. Any victory against Hiro is only temporary. At some point, his Spectre will emerge, and it'll be a whole new problem to contend with. "Well, we can't ignore warning signs that are dangerous, can we? And remind me, the highest level Spectre found in the wild?"

"Level Thirty-five, Commander. Though—"

"—though we have no way of knowing how long that Spectre was around consuming victims before we found it. Yes, I remember now." She flicks her wrist, and a screen emerges from it. On it is the face of a chubby, pale-faced woman.

"Commander!" she says. "What's going on? Everyone's saying—"

"Not now, Hanh. I need you down here in the Essence Bank ASAP. Set up Spectral sensors at every point here. You're gonna love this. A new opportunity for our research to get another breakthrough. Whenever that may be."

"How do you mean?"

"I'll explain as soon as you get down here with as many sensors as you think this room'll need. What do you think, fifty? Will that be sufficient?"

"We only have three hundred in our inventory, and two hundred and seventy-five are—"

"This takes priority over all other missions they're earmarked for."

The woman's mouth opens and closes several times before she nods. "Yes, Commander. May I ask—"

"I'll brief you when you get down here. You have ten minutes." Without waiting for a response, Commander Daugherty ends the call.

Before she could even divert her attention to something else, another Medium approaches. "All Mediums accounted for, Commander."

She nods. "And the casualties?"

"Thirty-five injured and twenty confirmed fatalities."

"Damn you, Hanajima," she says, bringing her hand to her forehead. She then turns back to the Medium. "Have everyone clear out. We have work to do, and we can't have this place crowded up. The Essence Bank is off-limits for the next twenty-four hours. Any missions within that window will require my approval first."

"Yes, Commander," he says before turning around and barking orders at the remaining Mediums, who continue to scramble, quietly and efficiently picking up wounded and uploading remaining Essences into their respective tanks.

"And you," Commander Daugherty says, her attention settling back on me. She's somehow gotten more exhausted in the past thirty seconds. "I need you to—"

Thwip!

I blink and the commander is gone. My mouth hangs open in confusion for the briefest of moments. I'd been ready to argue against whatever she was going to say, but her sudden disappearance leaves me rattled and confused.

And then another Medium in the distance behind where the commander stood disappears.

"Look alive, Mediums," Vero says, her voice back to its more stern version. She and Seb step back to back, feet planted as I see more Mediums disappear around me.

"Estrella?" I say, trying my best to ignore the overwhelming emotion that surges inside me. An anger I've never felt in my entire life.

"I feel it, too," she says.

"It's him," I say aloud as Seb disappears. "It's Hiro's Spectre."

And then the world twists and turns in a blur.

THREE

I OPEN MY EYES. Wait, they're already open. Still, I'm surrounded by darkness, as though I'm in a lightless vacuum. I move my legs, or at least try, but I can't tell if I'm stuck or paralyzed.

I somehow don't even hear my blood pulsing in my ears. When I release my held breath, I don't hear the exhale. My entire sense of presence has been robbed. It's unsettling. Horrifying.

"Shit." I say the word, but can't hear it. If I say a word, but can't even hear myself, did I actually say the word? Philosophers, bow down and worship me.

"*Estrella?*" I send.

"*Luna?*" her voice reverberates in my head. *That* I can hear, and I release a soundless exhale of relief. So I *haven't* lost all my senses after all. At least not all of them.

"*Can you hear anything? Or see anything? Or...sense anything?*"

"*No. Can you?*"

"*What the hell's going on?*"

"*I basically just burst into full existence twenty minutes ago.*"

Even in times like this, she has to be a smart-ass. There's no doubt about it, this Spectre is my sister. I'd be proud if I wasn't terrified of the overwhelming darkness.

"*Do you think this is really Hiro's Spectre?*" I say. "*I mean...Hiro as a Spectre?*"

"*It feels like him,*" Estrella responds. "*Even though he's dead, there's a piece of him that persists. But I always thought his Mirage would be more...anything. Yeah, just any amount of anything would be more than whatever this is.*"

"*What is this?*" a voice cuts in through the silence, and then the silence itself erodes. Suddenly, the vacuum feels like an actual open space. And then I recognize the voice.

"Vero?" I say.

"What's going on?"

"It's his Mirage," Seb's voice rings out. "But why is it...?"

"It's forming," Commander Daugherty responds. She's as stern and stiff as ever. "This Mirage is brand new. It'll take time before it forms any real identity."

"That's right," I say, understanding the realization. "It's like with Estrella. Even days after it formed, it was still a black void with screens circling around."

"Oh," Seb says. "So that's why it looked like that." It's almost as though his curiosity at the situation alone is enough to override any anxiety over being locked in a black void for an indefinite amount of time.

"How long will it be like this?" This is a voice I don't recognize.

"It could be seconds, hours, or days," Commander Daugherty says. "Probably no more than that."

"Oh, great. Days," another voice says. "I'm glad that doesn't put us in any *real* danger." Apparently, all hierarchical etiquette flies out the window as soon as you enter a black void where you can't so much as see—or even move—your hand in front of you.

And then the chatter rises. A few voices turn to several dozen. Weaved throughout all of them are a myriad of emotions: curiosity, fear, anger, shock. These are the type of people who are usually calm under pressure, but I'd bet it's because they can at least control their own actions. Here, they can't so much as control the snapping of their own fingers.

"*Luna, make them stop,*" Estrella sends to me. Her voice cuts through the chaos like a knife, and somehow drowns it all out without it feeling like she's yelling.

"*You think they can hear me through all this?*"

"*Won't you at least try? They're giving me a headache.*"

"*How?*" I say.

"*I'm new to this whole sentient thing, remember? I dunno.*"

I don't have time to try before I hear Commander Daugherty's voice. I don't know how, but even amid a dark room of confusion, she manages to be heard. "Silence!" she bellows, her call lasting several long seconds.

The chatter subsides. Any lingering cries or calls fall silent. Several more seconds pass, and I can almost hear Commander Daugherty reel in a long breath. "You are all professionals, and I expect you to act like it. We're all in a situation we'd prefer not to be in, but I assure you, this will not last long. The longest a Spectre has ever lasted in this formation stage is a short few weeks. And before any of you highlight the fact that this is an unprecedented event…well, you're right. This is an unprecedented event and a challenge to the status quo.

"But consider the role you took on when you signed up to be a Medium. Your very existence is a challenge to the status quo. Fighting Ghosts. Stealing their powers. These aren't the type of battles our founding fathers had when they created this country. But here we are, dealing with the unexplained on a daily basis. I'm not saying you can't be scared, but I urge you not to lose your wits when there's nothing you can do." The entire Mirage is silent when she finishes, but I can almost hear the words tumbling over and over again in their heads.

"Now!" she yells. "What we *can* do is take stock of who we have here. Junior Mediums? Sound off!"

"Agent Cunningham, present!" a voice says.

"Agent Daugherty, present!" Vero follows up.

"Agent Mariano, present!"

"Agent Jones, present!"

"Agent Pham, present!"

One by one, agents ring out, from Junior Mediums all the way through the A-Ranks.

As each Medium speaks, I feel my body's presence take shape. It's a weird thought, but you know how sometimes you can feel your tongue sitting in your mouth? It's kind of like that, only with your entire body.

Gravity starts to pull down at different parts of my body, and before I know it, my body's full weight returns, resting my feet on what feels like a cement floor. At the very least, I can tell it's not dirt. A faint dawn glimmers on the distant horizon of the Mirage, though I can't see a source of light. As the glowing intensifies, I make out dozens of silhouettes all around me, and the breaths of each and every person becomes even more apparent.

The glowing light intensifies, and with each passing moment, a presence floods my mind. It doesn't take me long to realize what that presence is.

"He's here," I say. My breath escapes my lungs, and I'm overwhelmed with exhaustion and emotion. It's nowhere near the same level as my first Mirage experience, but it's enough to bring me to one knee, my body now *heavier* than usual. It's like Estrella all over again. A malevolent presence. An anger.

It seeps into every square inch of the Mirage.

"Luna!" Vero says as I feel a hand rest on my shoulder. "What's wrong?"

"A presence is forming," I hear Estrella say, floating in her small human form. "It's stretching throughout the entire Mirage, and is focusing itself over there." I look up and see where her finger points. As I should have known, there's nothing there to see, but I *can* sense Hiro's presence gravitating in that direction.

"Pull back, agents," Commander Daugherty calls out to the Mediums loitering in that direction, and they follow her instructions without so much as a question. "Those of you with Essences at the ready, you know what to do."

A series of clicks and hisses, and the entire crowd around me changes. Agents' black tactical suits disappear behind capes, plates of armor, force fields, and over-sized weapons.

As I rise to my feet, I meet Estrella's tiny eyes hovering at my level, and nod. With another series of clicks, my armor locks into place. While before, it had only covered my top half, I now find my entire body covered from head toe, an invisible force field shielding my head. Estrella does a flip in the air and settles in my right hand in her blade form, her gem at the hilt glowing brighter than ever before.

Oh, right. A lot has happened since the last time we fought together. I tap at my Syncer, and my eyes widen as I see the words "Level Ten" glow back at me.

I suppose I should never underestimate the power of a fully synced Spectre.

But there is little time to celebrate. The atmosphere within the Mirage is tense, everyone's breath light in anticipation of what's coming.

"Seb," Vero whispers. "Can you find an opening?"

"What do you think I've been doing this whole time?" he responds with an uncharacteristic annoyance. "But this place is sealed off airtight. Not a single Bullethole to be found."

"Well," I say, "he's angry. He doesn't want us to escape."

"You can even sense his emotions?" Commander Daugherty says.

"It's the one thing I could do without," I say, only half-lying. Sure, I'd prefer the ability to switch my connection to a Spectre's emotion, but it's the only reason I've stayed alive through the handful of Mirages I've fought my way through.

"Sounds like torture," Commander Daugherty says.

"For you, I'm sure it is," I say. I'm not joking, but I hear an agent snort in response.

"Well," Commander Daugherty says, "now is as good a time as any, then. How do you do it?"

"What?"

"I can tell from what little we've seen that you don't use the same techniques when fighting within a Mirage."

"Are you trying to gain intel right now?" Vero says, but she's quick to follow up the comment with, "Commander."

"We're about to take on what may be the strongest Spectre on record. I'd prefer to know ahead of the fight what sort of secrets we may have up our sleeves to help us survive." Commander Daugherty turns back to me. "So, Ms. Guerrera, what can you tell me about your abilities and how they allow you to take on Spectres stronger than you?"

I almost hate to admit it, but even I'm not petty enough to let my hatred of this woman ruin the lives of dozens of people. So I tell her as much as I can—or at the very least, as much as I understand for myself.

Specifically, how I sync my emotions with Spectres and use that to take them down in a moment of weakness. When I'm finished explaining, she almost seems...disappointed. It's like she had all of her worst theories confirmed in one fell swoop.

"But it helps, Commander," Vero says. "I've seen it. Once, a Spectre who was a few times her own level was weakened, she was able to take her down."

"It was a Level Two Spectre," I say, adamant that she not oversell my own abilities.

"At that level, every ounce of strength makes all the difference."

There's not much time to argue. Before Commander Daugherty can so much as open her mouth, another lurch in my stomach catches my attention. I can feel Hiro form in the distance. And then the slow and steady rumble that comes with a stomping giant.

"Who here is housing Level Thirty Essences?" Commander Daugherty says.

No one says anything.

"Level Twenty?"

Nothing.

"Level Ten."

This time, a few voices ring out near the front of the pack. As I'd debriefed her on my abilities, it looks like the rest of the team had already arranged themselves by strength. Only a handful of Mediums sported above Level Ten abilities, with most hovering in the high single digits. I'm sure the commander is regretting her orders for everyone to reupload their Essences, but the obvious gaff isn't even mentioned. For all her flaws, it doesn't seem like the commander is much interested in dwelling on things they can't control right now. Maybe she'll change her tune once they're out of the Mirage, but for now, she's focused on solutions.

As Vero and Seb take their places in the middle of the pack, I take my place near the front.

"What're you doing?" Commander Daugherty says.

"I'm Level Ten, old hag!" Estrella says, turning back into her head form, though still only the size of a normal one.

Commander Daugherty spares her an annoyed glance, but directs her comments at me. "Why in the hell would we risk losing our best hope of survival?"

I stare back at her, not really sure how to respond.

"We don't know how strong he'll be when we face him, but if what my daughter says is true, we may need you. Especially when this is all over."

"I'm one of the highest levels here," I say. "I can help. And I know Hiro better than anyone."

"True," Commander Daugherty says, "you may be one of the highest levels here, but you have next to no training, and you're also an asset I can't afford to lose. Just because you *think* you're the only one who knew Hanajima, doesn't mean you are. Vero, Seb. Keep an eye on our trump card here, will you?"

Stomp. Stomp.

I feel a hand land on my shoulder. I look to see a random Medium looking at me with kind eyes as she pulls me back behind her. Fighting the urge to wipe off my shoulder, I let her do it, and I even let the others guide me back, deeper into the mob.

Stomp. Stomp.

I settle in between Seb and Vero, biting my lip and clenching my left fist. I want to disobey her. To prove her wrong. But I also know it would be suicide to lash out without understanding what I'm up against.

Stomp. Stomp.

Emerging from the shadows is a large silhouette. Not quite human, but not altogether animalistic either. The creature's shoulders are hunched as he walks, almost gorilla in nature, and only as he draws closer and closer do I realize what I'm looking at. The thing that approaches is an oversized version of Hiro at least ten feet tall. The main difference apart from his size? Bulbous tumors protrude from all over his body, from his shoulders to his back, and his legs, making his gait uneven.

His mouth hangs open, widening with every breath, a string of drool stretching down, eyes red. The poor man could not be more obviously in pain.

As his eyes settle on the mass of Mediums in front of him, he lets out a roar, shaking the entire Mirage.

Commander Daugherty stands out in front of the group. "Jesus, Hiro," she says. "What have you done to yourself?"

Hiro only roars again in response. Maybe roaring is all he can do in his current state.

He pounds at the ground in front of him, causing all of us to recoil, though it doesn't seem like he's trying to attack anyone as much as it seems like he's just trying to get out his rage.

With a few taps of her Syncer, a light explodes outward from Commander Daugherty, and she's covered in plates of bright purple armor, wielding a scythe that can't be any less than eight feet tall.

"That can't be practical," I say, but am quick to look down at my own weapon, which I realize doesn't obey any laws of practicality itself. "Never mind," I say to no one in particular.

Stomp. Stomp. Hiro steps closer, and while everyone else around Commander Daugherty takes a few steps back, she stands firm.

"Is it smart of her to do that?" I say.

"She's not only the most experienced living Medium in the DOSD," Seb says, "but she's also the only one who's never discharged any of her Essences in her career."

"You mean she makes everyone else discharge theirs, but gets to hang on to her own?" I say.

"It's more like she was grandfathered in as the most senior Medium," Seb says. "Believe it or not, she fought against the ruling that forces Mediums to discharge after missions, but she was overruled."

"By who?"

The Mirage shakes once again, and Hiro is bounding for us. The mass of Mediums do not disperse as I expect, but hold their ground. Commander Daugherty doesn't waste a single moment, launching at Hiro, though she doesn't go straight for a kill strike, instead, jumping over him, bringing her scythe down in a vertical strike that only just grazes him.

Hiro tries to swat at her, but is distracted by an attack from another Medium. And another. And another. None of them land a single hit, but they confuse him enough that he's not sure where to focus his attention. Before I can even blink, the Mediums have circled back behind the Spectre in a defensive formation.

Commander Daugherty sinks the base of her scythe into the ground and taps at her Syncer. A chorus of beeps goes off almost simultaneously all around me.

Vero flips open the screen on her Syncer, and her mouth hangs open.

"Level Twenty?" Seb says in disbelief. "This can't be right. Right from the outset?"

"Stand strong, agents!" Commander Daugherty calls out, sensing the confidence draining from everyone within the Mirage. "Don't forget, there are dozens of us and only one of him. And he's stupid at this stage in his cycle."

Hiro roars, as if in protest, though it's clear it's based more out of confusion than anger.

Commander Daugherty launches an assault on the hapless Spectre, who tries his best to swat at her, only to again be distracted by other members of the group.

Her scythe cuts into his side, but the damage appears to be minimal. This is no all-out attack like I'd originally thought. Everyone here is playing the long game. The Mediums cycle in and out, playing a game of distract-and-attack. Only a handful do so at a time. The only one involved in each wave is Commander Daugherty, who cuts at Hiro with each run. First with a flip and an attack at his shoulder, then a somersault and swipe at his side. The strategy is smart, but almost boring, especially given that Hiro doesn't seem to be smartening up. He falls for the same trick each time. Someone feigns an attack, and by the time they dart off to the side, he suffers yet another wound—a tiny, almost imperceptible wound, but a wound all the same.

Several minutes pass, and while Hiro looks increasingly frustrated, he doesn't seem to have gotten any weaker—or any smarter.

And then, his eyes flicker for the briefest of moments and the energy he emits changes the slightest bit. He launches off the ball of his foot, his speed increasing as his hand thrusts to the side, catching a Medium by the throat and slamming him into the ground.

The man is dead on impact. I don't need to look at his motionless body to know that one hit is all it took.

"He's getting smarter," I say, covering my mouth with my hand.

"What're you talking about?" Vero says. "It was just a lucky hit."

"No, she's right," Seb says, his eyes focused on the Spectre. Even from a distance, I can tell he's taking in a lot of information. "That last move wasn't random. It was a conscious one. He's getting better at predicting movements."

But that's not all. Even beyond looking at Hiro's movements, there's something else more than that. "Did you feel that, Estrella?" I say.

"He's getting smarter," she agrees. "It's like how I grew after consuming an Essence. Only he's *not* consuming Essences."

"Check your Syncer," I say to Vero.

She listens without question, and her eyes widen. "Level Twenty-two," she says, looking up. "Mother! Watch out! His level is growing!"

Commander Daugherty aborts an attack just as Hiro lashes out, missing her by inches. A group of Mediums all jump backward, giving the Spectre a wide berth as they reassess the situation.

"What was that?" Commander Daugherty calls through her Syncer. I can hear her irritated voice through the speaker on Vero's own wrist.

"His level is growing," Vero says. "It's like he hasn't settled into his final Spectral form yet."

Commander Daugherty flicks open her Syncer. "Shit."

"Oh, he's another level higher," Seb says. "Level Twenty-three."

"It's not just his level," I say.

"What do you mean?" Vero says. She holds her wrist closer to my face so Commander Daugherty can hear me.

"I don't know what you know about my abilities, but mine grow as Estrella eats Essences. Each time she ate one, she didn't just grow in level and ability, but she also got smarter. Like she regained her memories. So with Hiro—"

"He's not only going to get stronger by the minute, but he'll get smarter too and more aware."

"At least until he hits his equilibrium," Seb says.

"I'm sorry, what?" Commander Daugherty says, her tone dry as she jumps back, dodging an attack from the Spectre. "I've been here since the inception of this Department, and I've never heard that term used."

"Sorry, I just made it up now," Seb says. "It's just a theory, but his Mirage is still developing into what it's supposed to be, right? Come back in a few weeks to a month, and it'll show some reflection of his base personality and base memories. An equilibrium of sorts."

"So you're saying there's some predetermined starter level he's heading toward?"

"It's just a theory," Seb says, his voice losing its luster by the second. It's as though verbalizing his theory aloud is making him realize how ridiculous it all sounds.

"Well, true or not, we need to take him out as quickly as possible," Commander Daugherty says. "He's already at a ridiculously high level for a Starter Spectre—that's a new term I just coined myself, by the way. You don't get to be the only one who has all the fun." I can't see her face from here, but I'm almost confident she's winking in our direction.

I bite my lip as another wave of Mediums descends on the Spectre, still confusing him with their sheer numbers before Commander Daugherty gets another quick, but shallow slice into his neck. If this were any normal fight with a normal real-world creature, he would have been dead after the first hit, but of course we're in a Mirage, where monsters have an ungodly amount of resilience and nothing makes sense.

Hiro whips around in pain and anger, and throws his body backward, launching himself into another Medium, smearing her body across the floor and leaving a blood streak on the still-forming ground. She didn't have a single moment to so much as scream before he cracked through her shield and her head was caved in.

I let out an involuntary breath and feel my stomach clench as Seb says, "Level up," almost too calmly.

Without thinking, I run to the front lines, ignoring the cries from Vero and a few of the other Mediums.

"What are you doing, Guerrera?" Commander Daugherty yells out from the other side of Hiro, who spins to look at me. Shit, he's way uglier and more terrifying than he looked from a distance. From where I stand now, I can see that almost all of his tumors are oozing some green goo, and that his eyes have gotten even more bloodshot as he's gotten stronger.

"We don't have time," I say.

"No kidding," Commander Daugherty says, jumping into the air, and taking this opportunity to get in another slice at Hiro before landing tens of feet away from him. "I don't have time to deal with your shit right now. I get you want to help, but the best way you can help—"

"—is to do what I'm supposed to do," I say. "He's a high level, right? And I'm our only hope of defeating him this century, right?"

"So you say."

"So do Vero and Seb!" I'm screaming now, but I don't care.

Commander Daugherty doesn't say anything, so I continue.

"If this was any normal Spectre, I'd agree. Wear it down until I can get into his mind and sync with his emotion. But he's not. He's only getting stronger, and we only have so many Mediums, and so much time." I don't even mention the fact that Commander Daugherty is already looking exhausted. "If we're going to use my abilities to get an edge, we need to use them *now* before they no longer make a difference."

Commander Daugherty lets out a growl, but nods. "Stay close, but stay out of his range. You wait for *my* mark before you jump in like an idiot. Got it? Just because we want to go faster doesn't mean we have to be stupid about it."

"Agents Kent, Meyer, Matsuda, and Eberle, join the front lines. If we're going for maximum confusion, we need more bodies."

None of the four agents she calls out flinch at her poor choice of words, and before I know it, there are ten Mediums on the front line. Hiro looks around at all of us in confusion and lets out another angry roar.

"Okay, you ugly bastard," Commander Daugherty says. "Time for round two."

FOUR

AS WITH MOST EVERYTHING, Commander Daugherty doesn't wait to act, and the rest of the Mediums are quick to follow suit. They enact the same strategy as before, only this time, dialed up to account for the increase in their numbers.

"Formation 6-C!" she cries out. As the next group of nine shuffles in, they arrange themselves in a circle, and they attack. Some Mediums go high, some low, some to the left, and some at an angle. Their trajectories miss each other by mere inches, though none of them flinch.

And this time, with each pass, Daugherty isn't the only one landing attacks. Every group is matched with one higher-level Medium, who takes a cut or shot at the Spectre, with long-range Mediums shooting in spurts in between these rounds.

"Level Twenty-six!" Seb calls out.

This sends a pang of anxiety through my stomach. I want to attack Hiro now, but know the time isn't right.

The Mediums cycle for a few more rounds, somehow avoiding any more fatalities before Daugherty calls out, "Okay, Guerrera, file into the rotation. You'll join Agents Daugherty and Mariano. Formation 3-A."

"That means nothing to me," I say.

"Just slide at ground level and attack him at his right thigh," Vero says. "We'll handle the rest. Just make sure you get what you need."

"What can we expect from you?" Daugherty says.

"I need to get at least a handful of hits in," I say, shocked at how confident and competent I'm sounding as I speak. "First, I'm just going to touch him. This'll allow me to get a feel for emotions."

I hear Daugherty sigh in what I imagine is disbelief or annoyance.

"Did you just scoff at the word emotions?" Vero says.

"I scoffed at her uncertainty."

"Every Spectre is different," I say. "And I'm still new to this, so I can't be a hundred percent sure. Plus, like you said, Hiro's not normal."

A growl escapes Daugherty's lips. "Just do what you have to do, Guerrera. And try not to get yourself killed."

As one round of Mediums finish an attack, those of us in the next set line up.

"Okay, Luna. You ready?" Vero says.

The truth is I never am, but I take my spot and answer, "Yes."

Commander Daugherty yells out a command and I run toward Hiro in concert with the rest of the group. He still doesn't know who to attack, and I'm sure he's perplexed when both me and commander Daugherty land hits on him—me just slapping his leg (gross, I know) and Daugherty taking a slice at his opposite shoulder.

There's a flicker in my vision, and I'm transported to a desolate landscape. No, that doesn't describe it quite right. It's a flattened landscape—rubble. Like an entire city had been decimated by an atomic bomb. In the distance, I hear the wails and moans of injured, along with the sound of voices screaming for help. I don't understand what they're saying, but I recognize the language as Japanese.

Shit. This isn't *like* an aftermath of an atomic bomb. This *is* the aftermath of an atomic bomb.

And then I see him. I'd recognize his face anywhere. A younger-looking version of Hiro running through the rubble. It throws me off. I would never describe how he looked before as old—maybe in his thirties—but at the very least he was a lot more world-weary than he is here. His skin here is smooth, and his face devoid of his trademark stubble. His face is red, dirty, and wet with tears, his expression frantic—panicked.

My body slides forward on the hard ground and I'm back in the Mirage. I jump away, narrowly escaping a swing from his closed fist, and circle back around, falling back into line with the rest of the team.

The next pack of Mediums press on, attacking the confused Spectre once again.

As we fall back to our waiting positions, I tap my Syncer:

Spectre: Level Twenty-seven

Great. He's leveling up. I shift my mind to something more important:

what I'd seen in the memory. What it could mean for the emotion I'd need to sync with.

"When was Hiro born?" I ask.

"What?" Daugherty says after dodging an attack from the Spectre. "Why the hell do you need to know that?"

"Can you please not ask me to explain every single time I need a detail explained?"

"He was born in the 1920s in Japan," Seb says. I can't quite tell, but I think he's as annoyed at Daugherty as I am.

"Where in Japan?"

"A town in the Nagasaki Prefecture."

And just like that, the entire scene clicks into place. My mouth hangs open as I consider the weight of what I've discovered.

"Did we know he was an atom bomb survivor?"

"Not true," Seb says. "From what I've been able to find on him, he was in a neighboring city when it went off."

"Then how do you explain that?" I point at Hiro's Spectre, whose tumors grow larger with each level he gains.

Seb doesn't have a response. Regardless of whatever he says, I know what I saw in that memory. Maybe it could have been the remains of any great battle, but the feeds I've seen of the aftermath line up with what I saw.

Another attack from a wave of Mediums, and we step into place. We launch another attack and I cut him with Estrella, this time on his other leg.

I'm thrown into a memory that begins with the sound of someone crying.

Hiro's crying.

He kneels over a charred corpse. I gasp as the blackened head lets out a breath. All the while, I hear Hiro's strained cries. he's not speaking English, but I can still somehow understand him.

"Don't leave me, don't leave me, don't leave me," he says again and again, the words only broken up by the occasional sob.

In an instant, I can feel their history. Hiro and this man grew up together, but it was much deeper than that.

And no one else knew. They couldn't know.

At that moment, I see something. It's a smallest flicker rising from the charred remains of the body latching on to Hiro. A shared trauma. An eternal connection.

A flash, and we're somewhere else altogether, in a countryside town. Hiro is throwing up outside of a battered building, welts pepper his face like aggressive boils. But more than just his pain, I can feel his terror at his imminent death, coated with a heavy cloud of regret.

Blackness envelopes him, and I can tell that he's entered a Mirage. It forms around him, several mushroom clouds circling him all at once. A figure emerges from the high contrast shadows within the Mirage, and Hiro's face lights up, accented with a mix of happiness and confusion all at once.

As I emerge back in the real world, I can tell that I've still only scratched the surface. Whatever this is, it's not yet the emotion I seek, but only just the beginning. In that moment when Hiro had been vomiting outside the building, I'd felt it—the slightest glimpse. It was a fear of death.

As the Mediums and I circle back around, I tap into this emotion, even though I'm uncertain. A fear of death is something I'm far too familiar with. I can reach back to something as recent as Gabe's unhinged assault on his lackey. At the time, I was almost sure I was going to die.

My wrist vibrates.

Spectral Sync: 35%

I groan. Not even close.

"Level Thirty," Seb says.

I clench my teeth. I don't need him to keep on announcing this, but I know it's more than just for me. It's to help the other Mediums reassess their strategy.

I find myself anticipating my next go at Hiro, eager for the rest of the story.

After the next hit, I am launched into the familiar Los Angeles bachelor pad. I have to blink several times to make sure I'm not mistaken. Why would I be cast this far into the future?

"It's starting," Hiro says. He sits on the couch in the sparsely decorated living room. He massages his knee, gritting his teeth in pain. I can tell he's the same age as when I'd first met him. There's a weariness in his eyes that I recognize.

"You're getting old, Hiro," I hear a voice say. The voice, I realize, is coming from Kuro as he stands in his cage. "It was bound to happen."

"It was never supposed to happen."

"We couldn't keep doing this forever."

Hiro bites down on one of his knuckles, trying to block the pain.

Kuro sighs. "I'm...I'm sorry, Hiro. I wish there was something I could do."

Hiro wipes at his eyes. "Don't be stupid, Kuro. There's nothing to be sorry for."

"I know that—"

"I'd do it all over again," Hiro says. "And again and again and again."

Kuro doesn't respond, but there's an unspoken tension in the air. And I can feel it again. The regret.

When I emerge back into the Mirage, I change my emotion. Regret. But a different regret—a regret for something I've done. Though, I can't, for the life of me, make it work.

As we approach the front lines of our attack, I pull up my Syncer.

Spectral Sync: 50%

It's closer, but still not anywhere near enough. "What am I missing, Estrella?" I say.

"We need more," she says.

I bite my lip. "Seb. In Hiro's life, do you know of anything he regretted? Something to do with Kuro, his Spectral Companion?"

Seb only shakes his head. "Some of us have seen him pop up while on missions, but none have had more than passing interactions."

When I launch into another memory, I grit my teeth when I'm treated to the same memory as before. Beat for beat, line for line, Kuro and Hiro repeat the same details, and the same feeling of regret lingers in the air after.

"What are we missing?" I ask Estrella.

"Kuro apologizes. Why? That his life is linked to Hiro's and that both of their times are running out?"

I cross my arms, staring at the two figures in the memory, and at the way Hiro looks at Kuro. My stomach stirs, and I swallow, feeling a click in my throat forming. A sob escapes my lips.

Spectral Sync: 80%

"What'd you do?" Estrella asks.

"I thought about Dad," I say.

"What? Dad how?"

I pause, hesitant to say it. To admit it to myself, let alone someone else. "I feel trapped. No matter what happens, I feel like I have to come back home and take care of him."

Estrella doesn't say anything for several seconds as the scene between Hiro and Kuro plays out.

"I'm sorry," Estrella says, sounding an awful lot like Kuro.

I'm about to tell her not to worry when I'm launched from the memory.

"Look out!" One of the other Level Ten Mediums jumps in front of me as a fist comes down on me—well, her. She forms a force field around herself, holding him off for a brief moment before it bursts and the woman is crushed under his fist.

Several other Mediums unleash volleys of bullets and arrows, but it's too late. I can already tell her crumpled body is lifeless, and when a few more Mediums break formation, Hiro's fists connect with them as well, sending another three flying.

"Stay in formation!" Commander Daugherty says. "Stay in formation!"

The next wave of Mediums follows orders, backing up and out of Hiro's way, but the loss of life has taken an effect on morale, and I can tell from the panting breaths and red faces that we don't have much longer.

"Are you any closer to beating him?" Commander Daugherty says. "We can't take all day."

The truth is, I have no idea. I have no idea what I'm doing most of the time in the normal world, let alone when it comes to all this Medium shit.

"I...I don't know," I say, my breath ragged.

"Well, you need to figure it out," Commander Daugherty says.

"Luna," Estrella says. "You're almost there."

"I am?"

"Think."

"I can't."

"*Think*. I can sense you're close. I told you I'm sorry, right?"

"That had nothing to do with it."

"But it did," Estrella says. Her voice is soft. "You know it did. Don't feel bad."

"Oh, my god, shut up," I say. "You burst into sentience like a few hours ago, remember?"

"You know I'm right."

And I do. As much as I hate to admit it, I know the exact emotion I need to tap into. It's the most complex emotion I've ever used to fight a Spectre. A mix of regret, fear, and the feeling of being trapped. Like the entirety of your life is passing you by without your say so. In many ways, it resembles Alan Arroyo's emotion, but it goes much deeper.

I jump back as Hiro attacks me, instead taking out another Medium. Formation has broken again, and any semblance of organization has been lost. The Spectre is now a meaty Level Thirty-five, and few of us can so much as take on Hiro's pinky, let alone his entire body.

But then my wrist vibrates again.

Spectral Sync: 100%

I leap into the air. His attention is focused elsewhere. I swing Estrella down onto him...only for his fist to swing around. I can see it coming, but I can't dodge it. I know that if he connects, it'll be the end. Even if I tap into his emotions perfectly, it doesn't do much good if I'm getting bludgeoned to death.

And then a figure in a force field catches my eye. An explosion erupts near me as his fist connects with the force field, and Commander Daugherty's body is sent flying hundreds of feet away, diverting his fist enough for me to sink Estrella into his neck.

Against any proper sword use techniques, I close my eyes.

Whatever happens, I know this will be the end.

To Be Continued...

SPECTRAL | EPISODE 12

HIRO'S BACHELOR PAD...

THIS TIME, I'm not thrown into another memory. I find myself in Hiro's bachelor pad, sitting on a barstool, surrounded by his lifeless and nonexistent decor. I spin around and see Hiro leaning against the back of the couch, facing me. He's the same age as he was when I last saw him, but that same weariness I remember is now gone. He looks rested and almost peaceful.

"You made it," Hiro says. "I guess that means I'm..."

"A Spectre? Yeah. You're kind of going nuts out there."

"I'd apologize, but I don't have control over myself. Or...over whatever form I've taken out there. At least I won't until I consume enough Essences. Right now, he's going off pure instinct."

"Yeah," I say. "I can tell."

"But if you're in here, it means you've found a way to sync with my emotion, right? Maybe this is a stupid question, but what is my emotion?"

"It's complicated."

His face drops. "And what does that mean?"

"You...loved Kuro," I say. I don't say it as a question, even though I almost want to. There's no question, but I'm still not sure.

"I did," he says. "I do."

"But you hated him, too."

"No."

"Regretted. I mean regretted!"

"I thought you fully understood my emotion. Now it seems like you're just stabbing in the dark."

"Like I said, it's complicated!" I say. "But you loved him."

"I did. I do."

"And you lost him when the bomb dropped in Japan."

Hiro crosses his arms and stares at the floor for a few moments. "I did," he says. His eyes gloss over. It's as though he's thinking about this memory for the first time in years. "When I'd first heard about the bomb dropping, I didn't know what to do. I was beside myself. So I made a single rash decision. I waded through that…mess to find him. It was stupid, but we didn't know the effects of radiation back then. Can you believe it? My entire life, I'd taken the safe route, but this one action dictated the rest of my existence. I was young. Just nineteen years old and couldn't imagine a life without him." Hiro smiles. "And once he emerged in Spectre form, I didn't have to."

A flurry of dark clouds wisps around me and Hiro is nineteen again, swinging Kuro around in dual baton form, batting at a Spectral figure. The Spectre explodes in a burst of light and shrinks down into an Essence. Kuro, turning from batons to half-human form, consumes the marble-shaped object.

"And for most of my life, that was okay." The vision disappears and we're back in the living room of his condo. "I thought it was *okay*."

Another flurry of clouds and we're at that point in time where Hiro massages his knee.

"It's starting," he says to Kuro, who resides in his cage.

"But then the escalations started," present Hiro says. "A Level Two Essence no longer gave the sustenance needed, and I saw the end in sight. And for over a hundred and thirty years, I'd fought. It had twisted my soul apart dozens of times over. And I'd never known what my life would be without Kuro. What life I could have lived if I didn't have to…" Hiro's lips tighten, and that weary look I recognize returns in an instant.

"So you were scared of death," I say.

"I was scared of missing out on a normal life."

"Yeah, most people go through that. It's called being scared of death."

"And you?"

"What about me?"

"You're here. You're in the same boat I was. And like me, you have a choice. It's not too late for you, you know? You're young enough that if your sister leaves, you won't explode into a handful of dust in an instant."

I find myself smiling.

Hiro's eyebrows furrow. "What?"

"For most of my life, I've been trying to get rid of her. I think…I think I'm at a place where I'm ready to accept that, no matter what, she's a part of my life. That no matter what, she'll always be a part of who I am."

"Even at the cost of your entire existence?"

"Okay, drama queen."

"I'm serious," he says, and his tone darkens. "Don't end up like me, spending the last years of your life alienating the only person you loved because you couldn't let some stupid decision go. I made Kuro's life a living hell. I made it clear, in no uncertain terms, that part of me wished I hadn't run after him. I put myself in a situation where I needed him to survive. I could have let him go and just moved on. I don't want you to live with the same regret."

I clench my jaw, but his comment only solidifies my decision. My entire life, I've been running, and not just from Estrella. I've been running from any part of my life that didn't fit into what I wanted it to be. But now?

"I think I'm okay, Hiro," I say. "But what about you?"

He lets out an exasperated sigh and hops over the back of the couch, laying down and facing away from me. "I don't regret what I did, no matter how much Kuro thought I did. He was my entire world. But I'd be lying if I didn't say I still wanted an idea—some idea of what my life could have been like..."

"Without Kuro?" I finish.

"I sound terrible."

"No," I say. "You sound human. You gave him a second chance at life. I'm sure he appreciated that."

"I know he did," Hiro says. "He told me more times than I can count."

"I'm sorry he's gone."

"He was ready," Hiro says. "Unlike me. Just do me a favor. When you make it back into the Mirage, make it quick. Kuro always said I was too attached to this plane of existence, but what the hell does he know about what comes next?"

"Well, he knows now," I can't stop myself from saying.

Hiro sits up from his seated position and looks at me.

"Too soon?"

Instead, he smiles and then breaks out into a laugh.

"So, what happens next?" I say,

"What happens next is you get back into the Mirage and plunge your sword into my heart, bringing my sad existence to an end. While I can't control my Spectral form, I'll do my best to hold back and keep him from attacking. I can buy you a few seconds. Are you ready to make them count?"

I nod. I'm ready.

He holds out a hand. "Well, Luna. It hasn't been long, but I can say that, of everyone else I've met in my hundred and fifty-year existence, that you may be the person I regret least meeting." He smiles.

I take his hand, and he shakes it.

I pull myself toward him and hold his frail form in an embrace. I sense him resisting at first, but then his body softens, and he lets me. I feel his arms wrap around my back, pulling me close in a shaky hug.

"Thank you," I say. "You gave me my life back. I only wish I could give you yours back."

"I've already had mine."

He breaks our hug and looks at me. For the first time, he shares a genuine smile.

"You ready?" he says.

"I'm ready."

"Oh, and give Daugherty my regards, eh?" He holds up his hand and snaps his fingers, and I feel my consciousness being catapulted from his condo and back into the Mirage.

Estrella slices through the Spectre's neck. It cuts through and exits the other side like a knife through butter. Unlike other hits, it doesn't just cut through, leaving his skin intact. Instead, the creature's entire head slides off, tumbling to the ground in a bloodless heap.

Of course, if this was your average creature, they'd be dead on the spot. Instead, Hiro's Spectre lets out a blood-curdling scream that sends shivers down my spine. I can't even tell if the scream is coming from the head or the opening at his neck, but either way, it resonates throughout the entire Mirage.

"She did it!" one Medium yells. And like flies to a wound, they descend on the Spectre, weapons drawn.

Contrary to what I expect, rather than try to hit back, Hiro's Spectre stays still, despite getting shot, stabbed, diced, and battered by dozens of Mediums all at once. It's sad to watch, but I know it's Hiro's doing. Just as he promised.

"What're you doing?" a ragged voice calls from the other side of the body. I look up to see Commander Daugherty panting, shoulders heaving with each breath and hobbled step she takes. "Now's your chance."

I nod. She's right. I've given everyone an opening, but the Medium whose attacks would be most effective would be mine. I look down at my Syncer and see my Spectral Sync still sitting at 100%.

"You got it, Commander," I say, leaping at the prostrate body. I cut through his torso, and an explosion of green bursts like fireworks, and with a flicker, I sense his fear. Hiro may have understood where things stood, but his Spectre doesn't. Instead, I sense the same fear as before, highlighted by a complete lack of understanding.

Why are these Mediums trying to kill me? I can sense from the Spectre. *Is it so wrong to just exist? Can't they just leave me alone?*

I make another pass, cutting him deeper. The other Mediums are making slow and steady progress, but I can feel every one of my hits adding several times more damage than the whole mess of them, his body growing more and more lifeless with each pass. And with each pass, his emotions grow. Overbearing and desperate. He just wants to live. He doesn't say it, but I can feel it every time I connect.

He's begging me to give him another chance.

Like Alan Arroyo's Spectre, I can almost hear him pleading inside my head.

"Do you hear that?" Estrella says.

"You hear it, too?"

"He's practically screaming."

Another flash of emotion as I cut off a leg.

"You want to save him, don't you?"

"Save him?" I say. "He's been alive for over a hundred years."

And yet it hadn't made him any more ready.

I think back to that moment of weakness with Alan Arroyo. When I wanted to save him. Even then, Hiro stopped me, ensuring it wasn't possible.

"Guerrera!" Daugherty yells at me. I turn to see her closer, clutching her shoulder, a trickle of blood running down her face from her forehead. "Take him down before he regains his composure."

I look at the body on the ground. He's split into several pieces, but each body part moves as though they're still connected. They convulse on the charcoal-black ground, evidence of Hiro's diminishing power by the second. Any moment, the Spectre will regain full control and endanger everyone around us.

I bite my lip. "Tell me I'm not an idiot, Estrella." I place her on my back, and she snaps into place on my armor like a magnet.

"Now why would I lie?" she says.

"You're no help."

"I'm here to help?"

"What're you doing, Guerrera?" Daugherty's voice is raised, almost frantic. "Are you trying to get us killed?"

"I can save him."

"What?"

"I can save him." That's not quite right, I realize. "No, We—Estrella and I—can save him."

"What are you talking about?" she says.

"Now you're bringing me into this?" Estrella says, though I can tell she's on the same page as me. I can feel her presence dissolve from the sword, through my back, down my arms, and into my hands.

We don't know if this will work, but I try it anyway. I run straight for Hiro's dismembered Spectre body, Estrella's own form encasing my fist like a flame. I try to envision Hiro as I did with Estrella when I'd caught her both times.

My mind flashes back to the first time I caught Estrella. "And when you get closer," Hiro had told me, "*punch* the Spectre!"

I clench my fist. My emotion is synced, and I *punch* it. "Are you ready, Estrella?"

"Damn right, I am."

I bring my fist down on the split chest, and it starts to disappear. A light bursts from the scattered body parts around me and starts to twist and turn inward, as though my fist is a black hole.

The blackness around us spins and I feel it. I feel Hiro's strength running up my arm and throughout my body. A cape and a set of smaller, more intricate plates line my body, replacing what's already there. With it comes…confusion. He's insecure. Unsure. He thinks he's unworthy.

And then I feel the resistance.

"*No,*" I can hear him say. "*I've had my time. More than any one man deserves.*"

"Then what's a few more years?" I say. "Right, Estrella?"

"Right," she says. I don't need the Syncer to tell me that the two of us are in sync—that no matter how this turns out with Hiro, we're ready to face the consequences together.

The world explodes and we're back in the room with the giant tanks, the liquid still boiling over within. The Mediums land on their feet all around me, breaths heavy as their supernatural abilities leave their bodies.

As my feet hit the ground, I wait for that same feeling to strike me, as it does every time I transition from a Mirage to the real world. For my abilities to atrophy almost instantly.

But it doesn't. If anything, I feel my body expand and my muscles in my core tightening.

"Oh, God, what have we done?" Estrella says, her tone giddy.

SPECTRAL

EPISODE 12

MOON & STAR

ONE

"I CAN HONESTLY SAY that today has been a myriad of firsts, both for me and the DOSD as a whole." Commander Daugherty sits behind her desk, legs crossed and hands folded on top of her knee. She'd sustained a bit of an injury in her deflection of Hiro's attack on me, but had mostly healed while in the Mirage thanks to the high level of her Essences.

Though not everyone was as lucky as she was.

"It was the first time we've had an infiltration, an outbreak, and the first time on record that we've seen someone take control of not just one, but *two* Spectres." She eyes me on that last one, and I can see the eagerness and curiosity in them. "Under normal circumstances, I'd ask that you hand them over to me for analysis, but even I know both your sister and your former mentor are more valuable in your hands than they'd be in ours."

She sits back and crosses her arms, avoiding the unspoken truth—that there's nothing she can do, even if she wanted.

When I'd come out of the Mirage, my abilities remained intact. I found myself just as fast, just as strong, just as dangerous in the real world as I'd been *within* the Mirage. Another first for her and the DOSD, I'm sure, though she won't highlight that part.

Even as I sit in front of her, in her building, in her office, I remain clad in my armor. I feel pretty ridiculous sitting in a cushy chair wearing it, but I'm not stupid enough to think the second I deactivate my abilities that she and the rest of the DOSD won't be on me.

"Let's talk," she says.

"Isn't that what we're doing now?" I have a clinical problem. I can't approach even the most serious of conversations without being a smart-ass.

Her eyes narrow. She doesn't enjoy being on the wrong side of a negotiation. "I'm going to put it all out on the table. We need you." It pains her to say it. I can tell. "I'd...*we'd* like to hire you as an agent of the DOSD."

My jaw clenches at the prospect. A part of me knew this was coming. After everything that had happened, I'd be a jewel in the crown for this agency—a boon of information in whatever impending war they were gearing us up for. But there was one big, gaping problem. "And what makes you think I'd trust you?"

"You can trust us to protect our investment," she says. "I'm pragmatic. If we do anything that leads to your death or your running off—and trust me, with your abilities, we understand just how real of a prospect it is for you to flee—it only means bad things for our nation. We can't afford you to go missing or fall into enemy hands."

She sighs and stands up. "And so the U.S. government will go to great lengths to secure your services as a member of our ranks—though your duties may be changed to ensure your safety. At least until you're trained." She flicks at the air with her wrist, and a document pops up in front of me. At the top, I see the presidential seal and in the first paragraph, a ridiculous number of dollars to work as a Medium.

I want to scream out and say no. Why should I trust them to hold my best interests? Until now, what have they done for me? And that's not even mentioning the shady operations they created that led to this whole mess. But I think for a moment and consider the opportunity for what it is.

If I say no, they won't just leave me alone. This whole mess would follow me no matter where I go or what I say.

"I need to think about it," I say. "Need to talk with my...parents first. After all, I'm still a minor."

Commander Daugherty rolls her eyes. "Fine, then. But this offer expires in forty-eight hours."

"And if I say no?"

"Let's just say it's not just for show that it was our Commander-in-Chief who signed your offer letter. I can't speak for him, but I can't imagine a world where he wouldn't move the Earth to find where you're hiding."

As I leave the office, I catch Vero's glance, sparing her a smile. She returns it, her own looking just as uneasy as I feel. Almost apologetic.

"I'd say she grows on you, but that'd be a lie," she says.

"You put up with her your entire life?"

"Well, not all of it," she says. "She spent more of her time working than she ever did at home. I didn't really know what she did until I started here myself." She chuckles awkwardly, though I can't tell if she's being awkward or I'm being awkward. "So, are you joining?"

"I...need to think about it," I say, though a part of me already knows the answer. I don't think a normal life is a possibility for me anymore, as much as I wanted it, but there is one option that's a hell of a lot closer to it than the other. "A lot's happened, and I think I'm overdue to speak with my parents about this."

It feels weird to say it, but now that this whole mess has been resolved, I feel a pang of excitement at what's to come. The opportunity to discuss an important decision with parents is something I've always wanted. This was the whole reason I started this journey to begin with.

Damien and Lily have been patient enough as I worked through uncovering the truth behind the Entity. The very least I can do is do the normal family thing and talk over these options. After all, going forward, I am still legally their daughter.

VERO CAN'T STOP the butterflies from fluttering around in her stomach as she enters her mother's office. The mix of anxiety, depression, and adrenaline boils around in her like a stew. A lot has been happening—too much of it today. Between the whole mess in the Essence Bank, the death of her mentor, and everything going on with Luna and the DOSD as a whole, it's enough to bring any human being down, let alone a teenager who already had to grow up too fast.

What she hadn't been prepared for, of all things, was the call with the President of the United States, and what news he brought.

"Oh, good," her mother says, looking up from her desk. "Just the person I need to see." She stands up and makes her way to the front of her desk, leaning against its front, facing Vero. "As I don't need to tell you, everything's kind of a shit hurricane right now."

"SOURCES close to me have said that you have an interesting relationship with your mother," President Ruiz had said. "She doesn't trust anyone as far as she can throw them. Not even me. But she trusts you."

"THAT GIRL, GUERRERA," Commander Daugherty says, "is joining up with the DOSD, and the president is going to want to keep a close eye on her."

"But…she hasn't signed yet," Vero says.

"Oh, she'll sign," Commander Daugherty says. "Trust me, she'll sign."

Vero put on her best professional smile—close-mouthed, so as not to show any weakness, just as she was taught. "What did you want to discuss?"

Commander Daugherty nods. "When she signs, she'll need to be assigned to a Medium task force. I know it's a bit earlier than you planned, but I'd like her to be teamed up with you and Mariano. With Kamil gone —sorry for your loss, by the way," she throws in that last line as an afterthought, "you'll need a third."

"We need a Defender," Vero says. "I don't think that fits Luna."

"She has two Spectral Companions. She can play whatever role she needs."

Vero wants to bite her lip, but she resists the urge to telegraph any of her thoughts.

HER CONVERSATION with President Ruiz had been brief, but his perspective was clear. After this incident, which was of Commander Daugherty's own doing, she could not be trusted.

It's a wonder the guy thought Vero could be trusted to keep the secret at all. Perhaps he hoped the order coming straight from the President of the United States would be enough to keep her lips sealed. Or maybe he, like everyone else, assumed someone like Commander Daugherty would raise a daughter just as cutthroat as she was.

"We need someone we can trust," he said to Vero. "And I hear on good authority there are few who are as by the book as you."

He paused, as if trying to read her. "We need you to monitor Commander Daugherty."

"Monitor her, Mr. President?"

"Alert my office of any major moves she makes. You know what she does, and I'm sure she confides in you on some level. If she does something out of the ordinary, we want to know about it."

Vero cleared her throat. "And what is it I'm supposed to be looking for?"

"Like I said, anything out of the ordinary."

"With all due respect," Vero said, "I'd be more helpful if I understood what you were so afraid of."

The president looked up, biting his lip. "After this whole fiasco," he said, "we're concerned she may grow more desperate. I'll be frank with you. We've wondered for the past few years if the DOSD is even worth our tax dollars. Security from CBSs is great and all, but not high enough in frequency considering the investment. We need something more tangible, and with Ms. Guerrera, we have it. But this incident has proven Commander Daugherty's aversion to risk."

"So, why not fire her?" Vero asked. She had no idea how she gathered the courage to ask such a thing, but it escaped her lips before she could overthink it.

To her surprise, the president laughed. "And here I was told your mother's no-nonsense approach skipped a generation."

Vero didn't know if she should be offended by that comment, but stayed silent.

"Well," the president continued, "after the discovery of Ms. Guerrera, your mother is bulletproof, at least from a political standpoint. Even I'm not foolish enough to tempt ruining my career over this. But her approach to running this Department still concerns me. It was the decision of my predecessor, who I respect, but it has its issues. Your mother...she's para-noid. It's like she's—if you'll forgive the pun—chasing ghosts."

Vero chuckled, half at the awkward joke, and half at the awkward situ-ation she was in. "You don't think our rival countries are a threat?"

"Of course they are," he said, "but she's moving too fast. It's like she's waving a beacon at them, emboldening them. We can't afford to be as reckless as they are. Your mother thinks I'm a fool. That I'm too conserva-tive, but now that we have an asset like Luna Guerrera, we can't afford to be careless. If we leave her to her own devices, Guerrera will be killed in a lab before the year is up, all in pursuit of 'knowledge' as she'd call it. Either that, or she'll be in the hands of our enemies."

"AND SO," Commander Daugherty says, "I want you to keep a close eye on Guerrera."

Vero clenches her jaw tighter.

How did she get caught up in reporting to two different superiors?

"You mean, we're no longer Junior Mediums?" she says. "Mariano and me?"

"After everything you've been through, it would be foolish to keep you suppressed in the ranks. It'd be nothing more than going through the motions. Besides, you only have a few months left before you were set to graduate, and we need all the help we can get."

"And Luna?" I say. "Is it...smart to promote her to Medium rank this soon? She's only been doing this for a week or two."

"And yet she is the only one to wield a Spectre—and not just one, but two." Commander Daugherty looks to the side and sighs, displaying a rare show of emotion. "It's a damned shame Kamil is gone. He may have been a grumpy asshole, but he was the best instructor we had. I'm comforted by the fact that both you and Mariano have gone through his tutelage. If, between you and Mariano, you can add up to half the teacher he was, then she'll be well taken care of."

"Seb?" Vero says. "Him teach?"

"He'll learn on the job like most of us," Commander Daugherty says. "So, what do you say?"

So, in addition to being a double spy, Vero can now add Medium Mentor to her list of duties. If she hadn't spent an entire lifetime suppressing her ever-present anxiety, she'd scream. Maybe she'd even cry.

Instead, she continues her forced smile, meeting her mother's eyes, no longer suppressing her emotions over some misplaced sense of duty or devotion. Now, the future of her entire country relied on her ability to keep the waters between her and her mother smooth, and though it had never been an easy task in the past, Vero had a feeling the most difficult phase of their relationship was still to come.

"I accept," she says.

What have I gotten myself into?

SEB IGNORES the constant foot traffic in and out of the Essence Bank chamber. He ignores the conversations as other Mediums file in and out, loudly jamming their Syncers into the Essence Chargers, as though they hadn't just spent the last few hours fighting for their lives.

He shouldn't be surprised. Life is fleeting, nothing is permanent. Not even the sorrow or empathy following the death of a loved one, or the relationships created between loved ones. It's why he'd always spent most of his life with his head in a screen.

When you made progress in a game, you kept it. There was no one from the real world who could come in and steal your accomplishments or party away from you.

Jace had been the only one who'd understood. Well, Vero does, too—to some extent—but she has her own shit to deal with, so Seb had never felt like he could burden her with so much as the knowledge that he had a goldfish at home.

He sits cross-legged in front of a vase of flowers planted on the spot where Jace's body had fallen after the Mirage had disappeared.

The room is full of vases, each one honoring a fallen Medium. It's a rare sign of compassion from the commander to allow a decoration that gets in everyone's way, but it's one Seb appreciates.

Growing up, no one had understood him, and even in his early days at the DOSD, he was convinced that no one ever would. Jace changed that, and had often told his pupils that he would give his life for any one of them. Seb believed him, but never thought he'd be the one the man would die protecting.

Seb wants to cry. His therapist tells him he needs to let himself cry, but he can only stare at the vase of white lilies, as though they maintain some connection to his fallen mentor.

"Miss him?"

Vero's voice almost makes him jump, but he's able to suppress that instinct.

"What do you think?" he says. He hadn't meant for his comment to be so mean, but he doesn't have the energy to backpedal on it.

"I miss him, too." There's a shakiness to her voice.

He refuses to look back, because he knows he may start crying, too. "Do you think he'll come back as a Spectre?" he asks.

"I don't know," she says, her voice cold. "As far as I know, he had no family. Little to leave him clinging to our plane of existence. I think we were as close to family as he had."

"That's sad."

"Yeah. It is."

Seb catches sight of Vero in his peripheral vision as she sits down next to him. She closes her eyes and bows her head. He's surprised to see her face red and eyes wet. How does she do that? Seb thinks. How does she cry like that? Some sad part of Seb judges her for it. She's a Medium. She should maintain composure at all times. But another part of him is envious. If only he could wear his emotions like she did. How is she able to be so strong and so vulnerable at the same time?

Vero's arm wraps around him, and she pulls him to her side, resting her head on his shoulder.

The sudden show of intimacy makes him anxious and uncomfortable. But, as usual, he lets himself settle into the moment. Like an older sibling, she's always able to force his emotions into submission when needed.

"You know you can cry, right?"

As usual, she reads him like a book.

"What're you talking about?" he says.

"He was important to me, too," she says. "And I also don't have any real family."

"You have your mom."

"You're kidding, right?"

"It's more than I have."

There's a pause. Shit. He made it awkward. He didn't want to make it awkward.

"You're right," she says after several seconds. "All the more reason for you to cry. I promise I won't judge you."

That's not the point. It's not that he doesn't cry. It's that he can't. Not anymore.

"Would it be okay," he says, "if you don't judge me for not crying?"

She pulls him closer, and he can feel her warmth at his side, and with it an added comfort he'd always had around her.

"Yeah," she says. "I can do that."

IT FEELS like a million years have passed as I leave X Tower and get spit out into the Financial District of Downtown Los Angeles. The darkness is gone and the blistering sun peeks through the skyscrapers.

I know my life will never be the same. Not that it's ever been normal, but in addition to gaining a sister in the form of a Ghost, I now had the infant Spectre of a former mentor. I look down at my Syncer and see the soft glow of his presence.

I want to let him out, but I don't know what to expect from him yet. If I set him free, will he just cause trouble? I only just started trusting Estrella. Am I gonna have to go through the same thing with him again?

It's a lot to think about, and I can't say I'm quite in the mood just yet. For now, I can focus on reclaiming whatever husks of my life I have left.

I smile as I think back to Damien and Lily. My new family. My road to a better life. At least that's what I'd seen them as. But now that Estrella and I are on actual relationship terms and I have this strange new job at the DOSD, I don't know what they're supposed to mean to me anymore.

A father and mother figure? At most, that'll be it. In just five short months, I'll legally be an adult, and living off the generous government salary I'll be making, I don't need their support anymore.

But then I think back to the million-and-a-half vizmails Damien had left me and what he had said to me outside the Main Stay.

I may be going too far, but a part of me feels like I deserve them. Even if it's not entirely practical, I *deserve* to have a family like them.

With Estrella no longer out to destroy my life, this is something I can finally claim. I deserve it and I can *keep* it this time.

An uneasy feeling passes over me.

"What the hell?" I say aloud. I've never been good at keeping my emotions in check.

"What?" Estrella says. She doesn't even bother keeping her voice down since there's no one else around.

"Why did you..." I start to speak, but my voice trails off, mulling over countless possibilities in my head. When Estrella and I had gotten into our big fight, I'd relived almost all of my big life incidents. The fires, the violence, all of it caused by Estrella, but in the name of protection. But what about the incident that set this entire sequence of events into motion?

Why had Estrella burned down the home of her adopted parents?

"Burn down the house? What're you talking about?" Estrella says when I ask, her voice placid and innocent. "I thought you were the one who did that."

TWO

IT'S an odd feeling entering a police station without feeling like you're stepping straight into a frying pan. In one hundred percent of every other situation, I'd be worried about saying something that'd give Detective Chu exactly what he needed to put me away for good—or at least *threaten* to put me away for good. Maybe he couldn't put away a seventeen-year-old for good, but that doesn't stop me from freaking the F out every single time.

This odd feeling is heightened when I hear myself asking for Detective Chu at the front desk. Me, asking for my goddamned nemesis like I'm picking him up for lunch. The guy who I imagined sitting up late at night plotting for ways to ruin my life.

It's all the stranger when Chu walks out from the back and he's...smiling. And no, it's not in the "I got you, bitch" kind of way, but more in the "I'm excited to see you" kind of way. I didn't even know until this moment that someone like him was capable of that kind of smile. I'm tempted to tell him to stop, but that would just be weird, right?

"Listen," he says when we're back in his office. For once, we're having a conversation *not* in an interrogation room. Will the strangeness ever end? "I...need to apologize to you."

Nope, not yet.

"I thought you already had," I say, thinking back to our conversation in the desert. I don't remember if he said the words "I'm sorry" as I was busy with a million other things, but it kinda felt like an apology.

"Something tells me," he continues, "that once will never be enough for what I've put you through. The constant fear of imprisonment for something you didn't do is no way to grow up. It's something my parents went through growing up in Chinatown, and it was…stupid of me. I was hyper-focused, as my therapist would say. Bordering on obsessive."

"Awww," I say, "you talk about me to your therapist? I don't know whether to be flattered or weirded out."

"It's…weird," he says. "And if I'm being honest, it's weirder that I told you about it. Forget I said anything. Except the part where I said I'm sorry."

I can't wipe the grin from my face. I relished the thought of seeing Detective Chu, someone who I saw as unflappable, squirm. Ever since Estrella came into my life, I've seen it happen in almost every single encounter we've had. And yet, somehow, seeing him more human felt less satisfying than I had hoped. It almost makes him more endearing. Am I getting caught up in the web of his golden boy persona?

"Anyway," he says, "I'm happy everything worked out with you and you-know-what." He leans in conspiratorially. "I don't know who knows what around here, so I'm trying to keep things quiet."

I nod my head. The existence of Ghosts and an entire Department dedicated to their handling isn't something you can just scream out to everyone without making headlines. But considering how widespread it feels like it is, it's a wonder it hasn't already. Especially considering other countries have also made similar breakthroughs as us. I guess all the more reason to keep things silent.

"Thanks, but that's not why I'm here," I say. "I…I wondered if you could tell me more about your investigation into the fire."

Detective Chu raises his eyebrow. "Which one?" It's not met as a jibe, but it kinda feels like it.

"Fair point," I say. "Uh, the most recent one in Burbank. I was just curious about what you uncovered. Is that…something you can even share?" I feel stupid as I ask. This was a dumb idea.

"Is there…something else I should know?" he says. His tone is still friendly, but it's hard not to see a glimpse of the old Chu. You know, the one who hated me and wanted to see me locked up for the rest of my life?

"I…I'm not sure. Is it okay that I ask about this?" Of course it's not okay. This is a freakin' police investigation.

"Well," he says, "the instant our friends got hold of the case, it became a closed one, with the cause being classified as an accident. The details became public record. So, you didn't even need to come to me. You could have just logged into the LA County database."

"You say that as if that's something normal people know how to do." I punctuate the line with an awkward chuckle. I'm such an idiot.

He waves his hand in front of him. "I'm happy to help. Plus, if you have any more details you're not telling me..."

"Nothing definitive," I say. "Just a hunch."

Chu's gaze lingers on my eyes for a moment longer than I prefer before he swipes up a screen in front of him. He flicks his wrist, blacking out the back of the screen for privacy. "So, what are you curious about?"

"Were you able to find out where the fire started?"

Another glance in my direction before his eyes resettle on the screen in front of him. Several long seconds pass.

"Looks like there were scorch marks in the trash can next to the door inside of your room. It spread onto the clothing on the carpet and up the door." He looks up at me, his eyes scanning my face. He'd make an intimidating poker player.

My heart sinks. Not because of his look, but because of what he said. I pinch the bridge of my nose, the frustration mounting with each passing second.

"Are you okay?" he says.

No, Chu. I'm not okay. That's what I want to say. Instead, I sigh. I just wish there was one thing in my life that could be easy. For once. It'd be a nice change of pace.

"I never kept a trash can next to my door," I say.

LILY STARES outside the window of her parents' West Hollywood apartment, her eyes following a mama bird as she hops into a nearby bush, a worm dangling from her mouth. She can't hear the chirping of the baby birds, but she's heard them enough over the past few days to know they must be going nuts.

She's....envious of her. She and Damien could never have kids—something he always held against her, though he never said anything. Even though it was a long shot, and even though she was already nearly an adult in her own right, Lily had hoped the time they had with Luna would be enough. That it would make her happy. That it would make *him* happy.

And now she's gone.

Damien had assured her she'd be back, though he'd been tightlipped about where she was.

Her lip trembles at the thought of that small girl out there. Alone. For all they know, she could be dead. Damien had transferred a ridiculous amount of money into her private account, so there was no way of knowing when a transaction was made or where she was. Another stupid decision she agreed to was to allow the girl to have her own bank account. Damien told Lily that it would help build trust—whatever that meant.

She hears Damien before she sees him. He lets his body collapse onto the couch, rather than sitting down like a normal person—even though she's told him time after time that the couch feet will slide across the floor and scratch the hardwood. He promised he'd buy footpads to prevent it from happening, but days had passed, and still nothing. With a few flicks of his wrist, he could make it happen, but he just sits.

There's something frustrating about him lounging around the house as though it wasn't the house she grew up in and the biggest thing her parents had left behind when they'd died.

"How you doing?" he says for the seventeenth time.

Lily grits her teeth behind closed lips. "It's the same as it's been for the rest of the day, honey. It didn't change in the past hour."

He sighs behind her, sounding more annoyed than concerned. Their relationship's never been perfect, but even Lily had to admit that things plummeted the moment poor Luna moved in. Even though he'd promised they'd get better. And after she ran off following the fire, the pair of them may as well have been separated.

"She'll be fine," he says. "I promise she'll be back."

Lily doesn't bother responding to his one hundred and eighty-seventh comment of reassurance. He's as in the dark as she is. Lily had read the girl's profile. She knew the circles she'd run in before they met her. They knew the issues she'd caused and the risk she posed. They'd gone into her adoption eyes wide open, and that was all well and good before she disappeared altogether.

Lily is so caught up in her own thoughts that she almost misses the briefest glimpse of a girl wearing a black shirt, a vest, and a pair of pants with oversized pockets cross from the front hedges and make her way to the front door.

Against all odds, Luna looks the same as when she'd last seen her. Her clothes may have been dirtier, but she looked healthy and well fed, at least.

"Damien!" she yells out before she can stop herself.

WELL, this is more awkward than I'd hoped it'd be. For starters, I was hoping to get to speak to them one at a time, but both of them greeted me at the door, and Lily was quick to subject me to the biggest hug I've ever had in my entire life. It made it even more heartbreaking for me to tell them I wouldn't be coming back.

I die inside as Lily stares back at me, face sagging, eyes distant. I'm sure this is one of the many things she didn't want to hear. Though it's a little better than hearing that I'm dead. I know the answer to my question at that moment.

Several long seconds pass, and with a swallow, she reaches out and holds my hand. "I'll admit it's not what I wanted to hear, but at least you're okay." She sighs, I'm sure holding back a lot more than she's saying. "And besides, we knew this would be a short-term situation. You turn eighteen in, what, four months?"

"Four months and three days," I say, looking over at Damien, whose face is placid.

Adoption isn't something that any normal minor can just weasel their way out of, but you'd be surprised what someone even my age could do when you're in my position—the position being someone with a direct line to government agents in high places. And, to their credit, neither Damien nor Lily argue when I show them the paperwork emancipating me from their custody. It's almost too easy. I could even ignore Lily trying not to cry as I tell her the specifics.

But even as we sit there, I know I'm getting what I need. After an awkward lunch of takeout paninis, I can tell Lily is ready to retreat to their room. It's something she did now and then when the stresses of the day were too much for her to handle, and I can't help but feel guilty as she gives me one final hug goodbye, trying her best to put on a show of affection.

"Are you sure you can't stay?" she whispers.

My heart twists in my chest. "I...don't think that'd work with my new job." And it's not a lie. No, I haven't signed all the paperwork yet, and yes, I already called in a favor to get emancipated, but it's still not a lie. There's no way I could do the work I do without causing a stir. She'd ask questions, I'd be up and about at inconvenient times, and worst of all, I wouldn't be able to tell them anything.

"You're welcome back anytime," she says. "Even if you're not legally our daughter anymore, you're still family." It reeks of obligation, but it's still nice to hear. And this reaction confirms my initial thoughts. It's not her.

My eyes settle on Damien, who had been silent throughout most of that exchange.

"Can we talk?" I say. "Outside of the house?"

"I'M NOT GONNA LIE, KIDDO," he says, "this isn't the homecoming I'd expected."

"What did you expect?" I say, hands shoved in my pockets as we walk, my forehead sweating from the hot California sun. Even in the shade, the heat is sweltering.

"I guess an actual *home*coming would have been preferred," he says. "I...I understand why, but after everything we've given you..." His voice trails off as he realizes his error, and I can feel my face heating up in response.

"Okay, so we're going there," I say, my pulse quickening. "Fine. Then tell me why you started the house fire."

Damien's eyes widen. This is the last thing he expects to hear.

"What?"

"The fire," I say again, keeping my voice casual. "It started in the trash can next to my door."

"Okay."

"I didn't have a trash can next to my door. I didn't even have a trash can in my room."

"And so, naturally, I started the fire?"

I don't respond. I don't know how to respond to such a pointed question. He's right. It could have been anyone. It could have been Lily who placed the trash can inside my door. In fact, I'd come to their house expecting to prove just that, only to come home to Damien's silence. I haven't known Damien for that long, but I know enough to know that he is *never* silent. Not only that, but everything Lily had said felt so genuine and melancholy.

I shrug. "Did you?"

"Of course I didn't," he says, his voice measured. Suspiciously so. "Who told you that?"

"No one."

"Then why do you think that?"

"It wasn't me. If it's not you, then who did?"

"It was an accident."

"Whose accident?"

"Do I look like I know anything about arson?" he says. "We can't all be you."

I can tell he regrets the comment the exact moment it leaves his mouth. It may not be enough for any sort of charges, but it's enough to make me feel solid in my conviction *not* to continue living with him.

"I didn't mean that," he says. "I *don't* mean that. But you can tell how much stress this has caused us."

"I'm not stupid," I say. "I know your and Lily's relationship wasn't perfect, but that doesn't mean you can just use me as some scapegoat for your failed marriage."

That comment cuts him deep, and it's not just because it's hurtful. Whether it's complete truth or partial truth, I can't tell, but it's enough to stun him into silence.

"I don't know what you think you know," he says, "but you're crazy if you think I'd take such ridiculous lengths to, what, get out of a failing marriage?

"You said it, not me."

His lips tighten and he glares at me in a way that he's never done before. I've never seen such insecurity and hate in his eyes. I can't prove it, but it's the same insecurity I find in some lowly street dealer when you try to accuse him of literally anything.

"So that's why you're leaving?"

"There are a lot of reasons," I say. "But all I'll say right now is that you need to watch your step. If you so much as look at Lily wrong, I'll be there to make sure there's someone to pay for it."

His lips draw together, tight. "You gonna hire your old street thug friends to come and punch holes through my elbows? Is that it?"

"You know what?" I say. "Thank you. You're making this so much easier than I thought it would be. Tell Lily she's a saint for putting up with you for as long as she has."

I continue walking, leaving him to his sad life.

I keep waiting for him to call out. To tell me I'm wrong. To fight for me. To do *anything*. But as I round the corner, another piece of me dies, leaving me that much colder. I'd wanted more than anything in the world to be wrong.

"Is this it?" I send to Estrella.

"Is what it?"

"Are there any other moments you didn't remember? Moments where you didn't start a fire or nearly kill some old friend of mine that'll change how I see things?"

Her pause is pregnant, calculated. *"This is it,"* she says.

"Good," I send to her. I don't think I can take another surprise like this.

"You know," Detective Chu's voice rings out in my ear, "that's not enough evidence to press charges."

"I know," I say. "But it's enough to keep Lily safe. And if it's not...that's what I have you here for, right?"

"We're not bodyguards," Chu says.

"He won't do anything else. Not when he feels like he's being watched. Maybe he'll do the adult thing and just file for divorce." It's the healthiest thing I can hope for.

"I'm sorry," Detective Chu says. "I know they meant a lot to you."

I force a smile, even though he can't see me. "I'm okay," I say. "This is nothing. Just another day in the life of Luna. I'm one hundred percent okay."

THREE

"ACCESS DENIED." The stupid voice rings out in the elevator leading up to Hiro's condo.

"What?" I say. "I got the code right, you dumb bitch." I punch it in again, this time slower, only for the annoying red light to flash in front of my face.

When I try it for a third time, I let out an angry growl and punch the control panel. My fist goes clean through it and into the wall enclosing the elevator.

"Shit," I say. Even with my armor gone, I'd forgotten to "deactivate" my abilities. Now I worry that I've effectively bolted the elevator into the brick outer wall that makes up the shaft. "Shit," I repeat.

"I don't think that helped much," Estrella says, being about as much help as my outburst.

"I don't know what I'm even doing here," I say.

"Where else would we go?" she says. Her voice is soft, sounding just as lonely as I feel.

I let out a derisive laugh, leaning up against the back of the elevator and sliding down to the ground. I'm lucky no one else is around, because I look insane.

"Right," I say. "Where could I go?" I let the thought linger in the air, ignoring the obvious answer.

The only place I could have gone back to was with Damien and Lily, and now with that door shut, I'd hoped I could at least crash in Hiro's old condo. But for whatever reason, that single-story bachelor pad is now off-limits. I look down at my wrist, seeing the emerald green glow as the elevator door shuts.

I wait to hear the grinding of the wall as it tries to go up, but hear and feel nothing. Now's as good a time as any, I decide, before I press a button on the Syncer.

An amorphous gas-looking blob flows out. As the particles twist and turn, I can see the vaguest hints of a pair of eyes, though I can't tell if they're curious, angry, or vacant. Regardless, I can tell it's him. That this lone Spectre Estrella and I agreed to take on is none other than my former mentor.

"Hiro?" I say.

"What?" he responds with a surprising amount of sentience. If I wasn't leaning up against a wall, I would have taken a step back.

"He speaks!" Estrella says.

"Of course I speak," Hiro says, his voice as exhausted as ever. "And I don't appreciate how long it took you to let me out."

"Sorry," I say. I'm not sorry. Him spending an extra few hours in the Syncer is the least of my worries. "I didn't know if I could trust you yet. Spectres have a history of being little shits when they don't have their memories."

"Hey!" Estrella says.

"I'm not sorry."

"Hmph," Hiro says. It's definitely his voice, but his tone, while sentient, is still on the vacant side. Like he feels like he needs to act a certain way, but doesn't know why.

"Any chance you know how to get into your condo?" I say. "Do you even know what a condo is? Do you even know what a code is?"

"It won't work without a DNA scan," he says. The green mist wisps and I can almost visualize him turning to face me. "When you're a wanted man like I am, you learn to take precautions."

"So I can't stay there?"

"Unless you're willing to leap up to the ninth floor, I sincerely doubt it."

While I could do just that, I can't say I'm feeling confident enough about my abilities to try it out.

My eyes are glued to Hiro's ethereal form. It's almost hypnotic how it undulates and turns in on itself as it floats. He's a lot more sentient than Estrella was in his same state. Then again, given how old he was, there's nothing normal about him. "What do you remember?" I say.

"What kind of question is that?" he says. "How would I know what I've forgotten?"

"That's a good point," Estrella says as she emerges from my chest, floating alongside Hiro in her smaller head form.

"Do you...remember what happened in your Mirage?" I say, almost too afraid to ask.

Hiro floats for several long seconds. I almost think he forgot the question when he starts to speak. "I don't know specifically," he says, "but I feel an inclination to express my gratitude. Forgive me, but I don't have the slightest idea of how to do that in this form." This version of Hiro seems a lot more polite than Hiro ever was. I wonder if that'll disappear as time goes on.

"You can just say thank you," Estrella says.

"But for what?" Hiro says.

What do I say? You're welcome for giving you a second chance at life against your will? And with this form of Hiro only carrying partial memories of his life, would he even care?

"You'll find out soon enough," I say.

"What's that mean?" he says.

"Yeah," Estrella says. "Aren't you going to tell him?"

"No. I'll let him remember in his own time." I don't know why, but I feel an odd amount of pressure not to force any memories or obligation. "You hungry?" I say.

"Starving," he responds.

"Hang on," Estrella says. "You need to rest first."

"No time like the present." I stand with a weary groan, feeling a sudden urge to do anything but sit still. Do anything but what I know I need to do.

"Luna?" Estrella's tone is cautious.

"I'm fine. Are you going to help me find another Essence or not?"

I IGNORE Estrella's protests as I dart through the alleys. I run fast, though I'm careful not to run much faster than I normally do—which is harder than you'd think. As it turns out, I can turn my abilities on and off in the real world, but I can't turn them off one by one, with the exception of my armor.

For example, I can't shut off superspeed while turning on my abilities to sense Mirages. So I take it slow. Well, slow-ish. But the last thing I want to do is draw any unwanted attention, or worse, ram my way through a car driving down the road. Oh, God, and what if I ran through a person?

It doesn't take me long to find a Mirage. Its pinprick is almost too easy to find, almost as though it's broadcasting its location.

When I enter, it's easy to see why. I'm confronted with a Spectre the size and shape of a freakin' *kaiju*, and the Mirage itself is some model-sized version of Los Angeles—big enough to feel big, small enough that it doesn't quite feel like a normal-sized city. And the Spectre is hungry. This thing would have been a serious threat to me just twenty-four hours ago.

"Okay, Luna," Estrella says. "Remember, first—"

I don't bother listening to her. Instead, I launch myself at the Spectre, forcing Estrella into her blade form. She transforms just in time for me to cut into the *kaiju* rampaging around mini-L.A. It sits at Level Nine, so I'm still able to cut through it with little issue, but it's not as smooth as I'd expect. I'm not even bothering with a Spectral Sync here. Just not in the mood.

But that's okay. I just muscle my way through as I cut the beast, letting out an aggressive scream as I do, and it feels *good*. The hit takes more physical effort than it should, but given our disparity in levels, it doesn't matter. The Mirage dissipates around me after one violence slice, and I emerge back in the alleyway, with little fanfare as the Spectre's Essence tumbles to the cement floor.

Damn. I'd hoped it would last at least a few hits.

I pick up the Essence, blow off a piece of dirt and hold it out to the green, misty form of Hiro.

"Here," I say. "Eat—"

He doesn't wait for me to finish. His form envelopes my arm, and I can see the Essence disappear from my fingers. After a few seconds, the green mist reels back, twisting and turning in on itself before solidifying into something more gelatinous-looking before turning back into a mist.

I feel the Syncer vibrate on my wrist, but don't bother looking at it. I don't care.

"Well?" I say to Hiro.

His eyes within his misty form turn to me. "Well what?"

I growl and continue walking.

"Where are we going?" Estrella says.

"We're finding another Spectre until he stops being an idiot."

"I think we should take a break."

"No, we need to find another Spectre. Now."

"You're not feeling well."

"Stop telling me how to—"

"You're **NOT FEELING WELL!**" Estrella expands to fill the entire alley, blocking off my exit.

"Get out of my way, Estrella."

"No. You're done. You need to rest. You're going through too much right now. As your sister—"

"This is nothing," I say. "Just another day in my life, okay? You want me to stop? If I stop now, it's over. If I stop, I'm back to ground zero. Again."

"And what are you trying to stop by running around getting yourself killed?"

I don't answer her, because I know there's no good answer. I don't know what I'm doing, but I can't help but be furious at her for standing in my way. "Move," I say.

"Not until you tell me what you're trying to do."

"Get out of my way."

"No."

With a growl, I walk straight *through* her, a disgusting chill running up my spine. But as I walk, the mist around me solidifies, and after a few steps, I realize I'm unable to move altogether.

"Let me go!" I'm not even bothering to keep my voice down, and it cracks. "How are you doing this?"

"I have no idea," she says. "But you need to stop."

"Seriously, let me go. I'll make sure you never have another Essence again, if you don't." It's an empty threat, but it's one I try to deliver as believably as possible, all the while, struggling—fruitlessly—to move through the solidifying mist around me.

"Then how about you just tell me what you're thinking?"

"You wouldn't understand."

"I'm your sister," she says. "I may not have been around for every moment in your life, but don't forget that I was around for most of them, even if you didn't realize it."

For some reason, this is what finally breaks me. Suddenly, I'm fighting Estrella, pulling at the mist not to move forward, but to get down to the ground. To crumple into a pile on the alley floor and just dissolve into it.

"Luna," Estrella says, her voice soft. "It's okay. I'm here for you." Her misty figure now feels less like a restraint and more like an embrace, and I collapse into it, clinging on to her with all my strength.

"I just don't know if I can take it anymore," I say. "First Mom, now Damien. What's so wrong with me that I can't..." I can't finish my sentence, instead erupting into a series of sobs, tears wetting my cheeks. The emotion is so overwhelming I can't even feel embarrassed.

"You still have me," she says. Her voice is soft. Almost angelic. "And we still have Dad."

I try to scoff, but between the tears, sobs and snot, I'm not sure how it comes across. "Please," I say. "He's a mess."

"I know you don't have a lot of good memories with him," she says, "but in a lot of those hard times, when you...checked out...he was there for me. He was there for us."

So much has happened that I'd forgotten one key detail I'd learned over the past several days, and one question I'd had. "Why didn't he tell me about you?"

"He didn't know how aware you were about what was happening and didn't want to scare you."

Again, I try to scoff. I succeed. This one sounds fittingly bitter. "Well, mission accomplished."

"My point is he was there for us. And he's still there for us, if we want him."

I hesitate, almost too worried to continue. "How much do you know about what he's been going through?" I imagine him, laid out on the bed, pants unzipped, a vacant look in his eyes.

"He's suffering as much as you," she says. "Mom left. I don't know if he ever got over losing me. And now, he deals with the fact that you no longer want to be around."

"God forbid I don't want to spend the rest of my life in Skid Row."

"That's not the point," she says. "The point is, he misses you. He loves you. He wants you."

I bite my lip, doubtful. As far as I know, I lost my father to muze years ago. Does he want me more than he wants his next fix?

No. That's not fair. That's not even remotely fair. I know whatever he's going through with muze is separate from whatever is happening between us, but it doesn't feel like it. I still feel angry every time I think about it. And how his dependency seems to drag me back every time.

"I don't know if I can be let down again," I say, my vulnerability almost debilitating.

"But at least this time, we can go through it together."

"You know," a voice calls out from the alley, "the DOSD spends a lot of money trying to keep our abilities under wraps. I know you're going through a lot of things, but running around with two Spectres out may not be the best solution." I turn to see Vero walking down the alley, a hoodie pulled over her blonde hair. If I didn't know her voice right away, I'm not sure I would have recognized her.

I scramble to my feet. It was one thing for Estrella and Hiro—in whatever state he's in—to see this side of me, but it was another for someone else to. I wipe the tears from my face, hoping it just looks like...I dunno, my face is hot or something?

"What, is the government spying on me now?" I say.

Vero rolls her eyes. "You have a netscreen, Luna. They've been spying on you for as long as you could speak. And that's not even mentioning the government-issued Syncer you're wearing."

Right. It's sometimes easy to forget how impossible it is to go off the grid. It baffles me how Hiro was able to avoid capture for all these decades.

"Are you here about the contract?" I say. "Because I still have time. they can't keep pressuring me like—"

"No one knows I'm here," she says, looking around as though trying to assure herself that no one followed her. When her eyes settle back on me, she asks, "Are you okay?"

I avoid wiping my cheeks again in front of her. "What do you want?"

"I wanted to come here to—is that Hiro?" Her eyes settle on the green mist hovering in the air next to me.

"Do we know each other?" Hiro says.

A look of confusion crosses Vero's face. "Not...not really."

"So," I say, "what do you want? I'm in the middle of something."

Vero blinks and takes a step back. "You're right. I'm sorry."

"No, no, no, it's okay," I find myself saying. I'm frantic, almost panicked, though I don't know why. "What'd you want to say?"

"I know I shouldn't be here. I tracked your Syncer—I know that's just weird and creepy."

"It's okay." I know deep down that it really is kind of weird and creepy, but I want to let it pass. "What did you come here to say?"

"Don't take the job," Vero says. Her hands at balled into fists at her sides, her lips tight. I can tell this is the last thing in the world she wants to say. "I can get in a lot of trouble for telling you this, but they don't care about you."

I almost laugh. I'm no idiot. I've lived through enough to know that the government doesn't care about me. But instead, I listen. The last thing I need to do is insult the only friend I have. Oh, no. Is this girl the only one in the world I can consider to be a friend? I file that minor existential crisis for me to dwell on later.

"Yes, I know they need you, and they'll do everything in their power to keep you safe—for now—but as soon as the next opportunity for advancement comes along, they'll sacrifice you or anyone else like you all in the name of progress. I've seen them do it before, and I can't let them do it to anyone else."

I look down at the ground, my stomach plummeting to the floor. I never liked the idea of becoming a government Medium—or *dog*, as Hiro called it—but after everything that's happened, I'd started to warm up to the idea.

It was a promise for a stable job, a stable income, a stable life. A life where I don't have to live hand to mouth, picking up Dad's messes. A life where I can belong.

"So, what happens next, then?" I say. "I say no and the president sends an army of tanks after me?"

She shrugs, hands stuffed in her pockets. "Maybe. Or maybe they're bluffing. You're basically a superhero now. They can't afford to hurt you, because then they'll lose you as an asset. And I don't even know if they can actually hurt you as you are. We've never had something like this happen." Over the course of her comments, her scared shell peels away, and I see a side of her I don't expect—vibrance and excitement. A far cry from her usual odd mix of ditzy and stiff. When she catches my gaze, though, she retreats once again. "I know this is unfair to you. It's your decision."

"Won't this hurt you, too, if I leave? I know your mom has a huge stick up her ass. What if she finds out?"

"I've spent my entire life worrying about what that woman thinks. I'm done."

We stand in awkward silence for several seconds.

"I made this worse, didn't I?" she says. "I don't know what would happen if you said no. Who am I kidding? This is stupid and irresponsible of me. I'm sorr—"

I surprise myself when I lean forward, planting my lips on hers. I expect to meet resistance, or at least surprise. Instead, she steps forward, leaning in. I reach up, pulling her closer and running my hands through the hair. My face flushes and my breath goes heavy. I'm only half-thinking about the fact that we have a pair of Spectres watching us. When we pull free, she rests her forehead against mine. Her cheeks are rosy, as red as mine feel.

"I'm sorry," I say, though I don't stop myself from bringing her into an embrace, resting my cheek against on her shoulder, a lump forming in my swelling throat. A mix of pain and happiness all at once. I don't know what this is, why I did it. I only know that I need to feel close to someone right now—to feel needed.

"It's okay," she says, her voice breathy. She hugs me tighter, and I allow myself to indulge in the feeling for a few seconds before I push her back at arm's length, guilt and distrust smothering my need for human contact.

"Thanks for the warning," I say, shoving my hands in my pockets.

"Do you—"

"Don't," I say, eyes cast toward the ground, my mind a whirlwind. I can't trust my own parents. Why should I be stupid enough to trust her?

After several long seconds, Vero pulls out a Syncer from her hoodie pocket that I recognize as Hiro's. "You'll need this if you don't want the

DOSD breathing down your neck. That is, if you decide to take my advice."

I take the Syncer from her hands, giving a nod of thanks, still avoiding eye contact.

"You still have another thirty-five hours until you have to decide. That gives you plenty of time to do what you have to. Say goodbyes, tie up loose ends."

Another pang of regret. Right. Goodbyes, as in plural. Things most people would have. I'd laugh if it wasn't so pathetic.

I want stand on my toes and pull her down for another kiss, to drown out the emotion and the reality that I'm saying goodbye to one of those people right now, but instead, I turn away.

"Luna," she calls back. "Take care of yourself."

"You, too," I say. Against my better judgment, I mean it. Despite the fact that the next time I see her, she might be trying to kill me again, just as she did the very first time we met.

FOUR

I WALK DOWN the familiar Main Street. It's the same as it ever was. Tents are scattered along the asphalt, voices loud and boisterous. My hands are shoved in my pockets, head down.

No matter what happens, this place will never change. I can leave for another ten years, and something tells me there'll be the same people filing in and out of their homes, the same dealers darkening the same corners (I glance over and catch Gabe's eyes. He acknowledges me with a curt wave), and I'm sure Hank will still be sitting under the marquee for the Main Stay for at least the next decade.

Everything can change all around the world, and everything here will still be the same.

"Where will we go?" Hiro says.

"I don't know," I say. It's impossible to fight the immense guilt that follows me at the very idea of leaving this place behind.

I can feel Hiro rumbling inside my chest as he....groans?

"Hey, hey. Stop whatever you're doing in there," I say with a pound at my chest.

"Sorry," he says. "I'm just...happy."

"Happy?"

"I don't remember everything," he says, "but a part of me opened up when I ate that Essence. I get the distinct feeling I was trapped before. This new feeling of instability. I...I like the idea. It's like I'd been missing it my whole life."

"Speak for yourself," Estrella cuts in. "Luna and I—"

"No," I say. "Maybe he's right." I smile. "Maybe this is all for the best. I've always wanted to leave L.A. Things feel like crap now, but they always turn out for the best, right?"

"What life have you been living?" Estrella says. "I've never heard you sound so positive. Does this have to do with the leftover endorphins from whatever happened back in the alley?"

"Shut up," I say. I try to fight the redness that returns to my cheeks, even though there's no one around to care.

"Luna!" Hank calls out from his spot along the wall under the marquee. Yup, still the same old Hank. "You're back again!"

"Like I never left."

"It's your shortest streak to date. Nine days."

That short, huh? "How's Dad?"

The man shrugs. "Wouldn't know. As far as I know, he hasn't left the building."

Well, that's good news, at least. Or so I hope. Out here, it can go either way. Fifty-fifty, really.

"Tell him I said hi," Hank says.

I wave back at him as I open the door. "You got it."

"Are you ready?" I say as I dodge the trash that litters the lobby. A pang of anxiety rises up—an anxiety I know isn't mine.

"What if he doesn't like me?" Estrella says.

"Hey, I thought you and him were close."

"I mean, we were. But I was in *your* body. Things are different now."

"He'll love you."

I press the button for the elevator.

"But what if he doesn't?"

DING.

"Then he's an idiot. You're the most amazing…Ghost ever. A hell of a lot better than I am. Person. Not Ghost."

That's not enough to assuage her anxiety, and I can almost feel her shivering as the elevator reaches our floor.

I dodge a woman who's passed out on the floor—not dead, I make sure as I pass—and approach the front door. I turn the knob and smile to find it locked.

At least he *seems* like he's taking care of himself.

I scan my netscreen against the lock and for once, the smell of moldy death doesn't pour out from the apartment when I open the door. Don't get me wrong, it doesn't smell very pleasant—no place in this building does —but I at least don't feel like I want to curl up and die.

"Dad?" I don't yell, but try my best to talk over the video feeds.

"Luna?" The man shuffles out from the living room. He's still scrawny, still sickly looking, still on the pathetic side of the spectrum, but he's present. Mentally present. At least for now.

I don't know if I caught him in between doses of muze, but I'm grateful to have done so at the right moment. I look over at the kitchenette. It won't win any awards, but there's nothing on the counter. No moldy food. No rats on the floor. It's like someone lives here.

And all at once, I can feel the weight lifting. It's a burden that had been sitting there my entire life. This idea that he couldn't live without me. That I'd be stuck here forever.

He can, and I'm not.

"Dad?" I say.

"Yes?" he answers. His eyes look back at me, for once, expectantly.

"There's someone I want you to meet."

End of Spectral
Book One

JACE

THANK YOU, PATRONS!

This is my most personal book to date, and I can't thank my Patrons enough who help make it happen ever step of the way.

I hope *Spectral* was worth the wait!

PATRONS

<u>Story Junkie Tier</u>
J Soderberg

<u>Spectre Seeker Tier</u>
Alison Conners

<u>Magite Tier</u>
Bernardo Nuno
Steven Beal
Derek Alan Siddoway

Join us on Patreon and get featured in A.J. Cerna's next book:
Patreon.com/magiabooks

ABOUT A.J. CERNA

A.J. CERNA is an author, film-lover, gamer, and all-around story junkie. Like any healthy kid, he grew up imbibing fantasy novels, anime, manga, and movies, and realized at a young age that writing stories was the best way one could spend their time. Eventually, he found his way into film school, where he got his degree in screenwriting. In his time in Hollywood, he pitched animated series around town and worked in the anime dubbing industry in various capacities. He also ran the film site *LRM Online* as editor-in-chief for several years, which allowed him to write about the stories he loves when he wasn't writing stories himself.

His series consist of *Djinn Tamer* (Arc One finished), *Champions of MythRune* (Finished), *The Mage War Chronicles* (Ongoing), and now, *Spectral* (Ongoing).

When not reading or writing, he can be found hiking, podcasting, gaming, or checking out the latest craft beer breweries.

<u>Books by A.J. Cerna</u>

THE MAGE WAR CHRONICLES
City of Mages (The Mage War Chronicles Book 1)

THE DJINN TAMER SERIES
Djinn Tamer: Starter (Bronze League Book 1)
Djinn Tamer: Rivals (Bronze League Book 2)
Djinn Tamer: Evolution (Bronze League Book 3)

STANDALONES
Champions of MythRune

facebook.com/ajcernawriter

x.com/ajcernawriter

instagram.com/ajcernawriter

tiktok.com/@ajcernawriter

youtube.com/@magiareads

www.ingramcontent.com/pod-product-compliance
Lightning Source LLC
Chambersburg PA
CBHW032101310726
48972CB00001B/49